Harlequin Man of the Month Collection

Passionate, honorable…and a little arrogant—
these men are always sexy and completely
irresistible.

Whether heading an international empire,
saving a family's legacy or leading a kingdom,
our heroes live life with undeniable passion.
And within the pages of this special collection
they meet their match in beautiful, intelligent
and determined women who are up to the
challenge of winning the hearts of these
formidable men!

Wherever you find them—at the office, on an
island or in the bedroom—these heroes are
sure to seduce, because above all else they know
that love is the greatest goal.

If you enjoy these two classic Man of the Month
stories, be sure to check out more books
featuring strong, captivating heroes from the
Harlequin Desire line.

USA TODAY Bestselling Authors

Catherine Mann
and
Olivia Gates

ESCAPING WITH THE BILLIONAIRE

◆ **HARLEQUIN**® MAN OF THE MONTH

Recycling programs
for this product may
not exist in your area.

ISBN-13: 978-0-373-60107-3

Escaping with the Billionaire

Copyright © 2015 by Harlequin Books S.A.

The publisher acknowledges the copyright holders
of the individual works as follows:

The Maverick Prince
Copyright © 2010 by Catherine Mann

Billionaire, M.D.
Copyright © 2010 by Olivia Gates

HARLEQUIN®

www.Harlequin.com

Printed in U.S.A.

CONTENTS

THE MAVERICK PRINCE
Catherine Mann

To my favorite little princesses and princes—
Megan, Frances, James and Zach.
Thank you for inviting Aunt Cathy to your
prince and princess tea parties. The snack cakes
and Sprite were absolutely magical!

Prologue

GlobalIntruder.com
Exclusive: For Immediate Release

Royalty Revealed!

Do you have a prince living next door? Quite possibly!

Courtesy of a positive identification made by one of the GlobalIntruder.com's very own photojournalists, we've successfully landed the scoop of the year. The deposed Medina monarchy has not, as was rumored, set up shop in a highly secured fortress in Argentina. The three Medina heirs—with their billions—have been living under assumed names and rubbing elbows with everyday Americans for decades.

We hear the sexy baby of the family, Antonio,

is already taken in Texas by his waitress girlfriend Shannon Crawford. She'd better watch her back now that word is out about her secret shipping magnate!

Meanwhile, never fear, ladies. There are still two single and studly Medina men left. Our sources reveal that Duarte dwells in his plush resort in Martha's Vineyard. Carlos—a surgeon, no less—resides in Tacoma. Wonder if he makes house calls?

No word yet on their father, King Enrique Medina, former ruler of San Rinaldo, an island off the coast of Spain. But our best reporters are hot on the trail.

For the latest update on how to nab a prince, check back in with the GlobalIntruder.com. And remember, you heard it here first!

Chapter 1

Galveston Bay, Texas

"**K**ing takes the queen." Antonio Medina declared his victory and raked in the chips, having bluffed with a simple high-card hand in Texas Hold'Em.

Ignoring an incoming call on his iPhone, he stacked his winnings. He didn't often have time for poker since his fishing charter company went global, but joining backroom games at his pal Vernon's Galveston Bay Grille had become a more frequent occurrence of late. Since Shannon. His gaze snapped to the long skinny windows on either side of the door leading out to the main dining area where she worked.

No sign of Shannon's slim body, winding her way through the brass, crystal and white linen of the five-star restaurant. Disappointment chewed at him in spite of his win.

A cell phone chime cut the air, then a second right afterward. Not his either time, although the noise still forced his focus back to the private table while two of Vernon Wolfe's cronies pressed the ignore button, cutting the ringing short. Vernon's poker pals were all about forty years senior to Antonio. But the old shrimp-boat captain turned restaurateur had saved Antonio's bacon back when he'd been a teen. So if Vernon beckoned, Antonio did his damnedest to show. The fact that Shannon also worked here provided extra oomph to the request.

Vernon creaked back in the leather chair, also disregarding his cell phone currently crooning "Son of a Sailor" from his belt. "Ballsy move holding with just a king, Tony," he said, his voice perpetually raspy from years of shouting on deck. His face still sported a year-round tan, eyes raccoon ringed from sunglasses. "I thought Glenn had a royal flush with his queen and jack showing."

"I was taught to bluff by the best." Antonio—or Tony Castillo as he was known these days—grinned.

A smile was more disarming than a scowl. He always smiled so nobody knew what he was thinking. Not that even his best grin had gained him forgiveness from Shannon after their fight last weekend.

Resisting the urge to frown, Tony stacked his chips on the scarred wooden table Vernon had pried from his boat before docking himself permanently at the restaurant. "Your pal Glenn needs to bluff better."

Glenn—a coffee addict—chugged his java faster when bluffing. For some reason no one else seemed to notice as the high-priced attorney banged back his third brew laced with Irish whiskey. He then simply shrugged, loosened his silk tie and hooked it on the back of the chair, settling in for the next round.

Vernon swept up the played cards, flipping the king of hearts between his fingers until the cell stopped singing vintage Jimmy Buffett. "Keep winning and they're not going to let me deal you in anymore."

Tony went through the motions of laughing along, but he knew he wasn't going anywhere. This was his world now. He'd built a life of his own and wanted nothing to do with the Medina name. He was Tony Castillo now. His father had honored that. Until recently.

For the past six months, his deposed king of a dad had sent message after message demanding his presence at the secluded island compound off the coast of Florida. Tony had left that gilded prison the second he'd turned eighteen and never looked back. If Enrique was as sick as he claimed, then their problems would have to be sorted out in heaven…or more likely in somewhere hotter even than Texas.

While October meant autumn chills for folks like his two brothers, he preferred the lengthened summers in Galveston Bay. The air conditioner still cranked in the redbrick waterside restaurant in the historic district.

Muffled live music from a flamenco guitarist drifted through the wall along with the drone of dining clientele. Business was booming for Vernon. Tony made sure of that. Vernon had given Antonio a job at eighteen when no one else would trust a kid with sketchy ID. Fourteen years and many millions of dollars later, Tony figured it was only fair some of the proceeds from the shipping business he'd built should buy the aging shrimp-boat captain a retirement plan.

Vernon nudged the deck toward Glenn to cut, then

dealt the next hand. Glenn shoved his buzzing Black-
Berry beside his spiked coffee and thumbed his cards
up for a peek.

Tony reached for his…and stopped…tipping his ear
toward the sound from outside the door. A light laugh
cut through the clanging dishes and fluttering strum of
the Spanish guitar. *Her* laugh. Finally. The simple sound
made him ache after a week without her.

His gaze shot straight to the door again, bracketed
by two windows showcasing the dining area. Shannon stepped in view of the left lengthy pane, pausing to
punch in an order at the servers' station. She squinted behind her cat-eye glasses, the retros giving her a naughty
schoolmarm look that never failed to send his libido
surging.

Light from the globed sconces glinted on her pale
blond hair. She wore her long locks in a messy updo,
as much a part of her work uniform as the knee-length
black skirt and form-fitting tuxedo vest. She looked sexy
as hell—and exhausted.

Damn it all, he would help her without hesitation.
Just last weekend he'd suggested as much when she'd
pulled on her clothes after they'd made love at his Bay
Shore mansion. She'd shut him down faster than the next
heartbeat. In fact, she hadn't spoken to him or returned
his calls since.

Stubborn, sexy woman. It wasn't like he'd offered to
set her up as his mistress, for crying out loud. He was
only trying to help her and her three-year-old son. She
always vowed she would do anything for Kolby.

Mentioning that part hadn't gone well for him, either.

Her lips had pursed tight, but her eyes behind those
sexy black glasses had told him she wanted to throw his

offer back in his face. His ears still rang from the slamming door when she'd walked out. Most women he knew would have jumped at the prospect of money or expensive gifts. Not Shannon. If anything, she seemed put off by his wealth. It had taken him two months to persuade her just to have coffee with him. Then two more months to work his way into bed with her. And after nearly four weeks of mind-bending sex, he was still no closer to understanding her.

Okay, so he'd built a fortune from Galveston Bay being one of the largest importers of seafood. Luck had played a part by landing him here in the first place. He'd simply been looking for a coastal community that reminded him of home.

His real home, off the coast of Spain. Not the island fortress his father had built off the U.S. The one he'd escaped the day he'd turned eighteen and swapped his last name from Medina to Castillo. The new surname had been plucked from one of the many branches twigging off his regal family tree. Tony *Castillo* had vowed never to return, a vow he'd kept.

And he didn't even want to think about how spooked Shannon would be if she knew the well-kept secret of his royal heritage. Not that the secret was his to share.

Vernon tapped the scarred wooden table in front of him. "Your phone's buzzing again. We can hold off on this hand while you take the call."

Tony thumbed the ignore button on his iPhone without looking. He only disregarded the outside world for two people, Shannon and Vernon. "It's about the Salinas Shrimp deal. They need to sweat for another hour before we settle on the bottom line."

Glenn rolled his coffee mug between his palms. "So

when we don't hear back from you, we'll all know you hit the ignore button."

"Never," Tony responded absently, tucking the device back inside his suit coat. More and more he looked forward to Shannon's steady calm at the end of a hectic day.

Vernon's phone chimed again—Good God, what was up with all the interruptions?—this time rumbling with Marvin Gaye's "Let's Get It On."

The grizzled captain slapped down his cards. "That's my wife. Gotta take this one." Bluetooth glowing in his ear, he shot to his feet and tucked into a corner for semi-privacy. "Yeah, sugar?"

Since Vernon had just tied the knot for the first time seven months ago, the guy acted like a twenty-year-old newlywed. Tony walled off flickering thoughts of his own parents' marriage, not too hard since there weren't that many to remember. His mother had died when he was five.

Vernon inhaled sharply. Tony looked up. His old mentor's face paled under a tan so deep it almost seemed tattooed. What the hell?

"Tony." Vernon's voice went beyond raspy, like the guy had swallowed ground glass. "I think you'd better check those missed messages."

"Is something wrong?" he asked, already reaching for his iPhone.

"You'll have to tell us that," Vernon answered without once taking his raccoonlike eyes off Tony. "Actually, you can skip the messages and just head straight for the internet."

"Where?" He tapped through the menu.

"Anywhere." Vernon sank back into his chair like an

anchor thudding to the bottom of the ocean floor. "It's headlining everywhere. You won't miss it."

His iPhone connected to the internet and displayed the top stories—

Royalty Revealed!
Medina Monarchy Exposed!

Blinking fast, he stared in shock at the last thing he expected, but the outcome his father had always feared most. One heading at a time, his family's cover was peeled away until he settled on the last in the list.

Meet the Medina Mistress!

The insane speed of viral news… His gaze shot straight to the windows separating him from the waiters' station, where seconds ago he'd seen Shannon.

Sure enough, she still stood with her back to him. He wouldn't have much time. He had to talk to her before she finished tapping in her order or tabulating a bill.

Tony shot to his feet, his chair scraping loudly in the silence as Vernon's friends all checked their messages. Reaching for the brass handle, he kept his eyes locked on the woman who turned him inside out with one touch of her hand on his bare flesh, the simple brush of her hair across his chest until he forgot about staying on guard. Foreboding crept up his spine. His instincts had served him well over the years—steering him through multi-million-dollar business decisions, even warning him of a frayed shrimp net inching closer to snag his feet.

And before all that? The extra sense had powered his stride as he'd raced through the woods, running from

rebels overthrowing San Rinaldo's government. Rebels
who hadn't thought twice about shooting at kids, even
a five-year-old.

Or murdering their mother.

The Medina cover was about more than privacy. It
was about safety. While his family had relocated to a
U.S. island after the coup, they could never let down
their guard. And damn it all, he'd selfishly put Shannon in the crosshairs simply because he had to have her
in his bed.

Tony clasped her shoulders and turned her around.
Only to stop short.

Her beautiful blue eyes wide with horror said it all.
And if he'd been in doubt? The cell phone clutched in
Shannon's hand told him the rest.

She already knew.

She didn't want to know.

The internet rumor her son's babysitter had read over
the phone had to be a media mistake. As did the five
follow-up articles she'd found in her own ten-second
search with her cell's internet service.

The blogosphere could bloom toxic fiction in minutes,
right? People could say whatever they wanted, make a
fortune off click-throughs and then retract the errone-
ous story the next day. Tony's touch on her shoulders
was so familiar and stirring he simply couldn't be a
stranger. Even now her body warmed at the feel of his
hands until she swayed.

But then hadn't she made the very same mistake with
her dead husband, buying into his facade because she
wanted it to be true?

Damn it, Tony wasn't Nolan. All of this would be explained away and she could go back to her toe-curling affair with Tony. Except they were already in the middle of a fight over trying to give her money—an offer that made her skin crawl. And if he was actually a prince?

She swallowed hysterical laughter. Well, he'd told her that he had money to burn and it could very well be he'd meant that on a scale far grander than she could have ever imagined.

"Breathe," her ex-lover commanded.

"Okay, okay, okay," she chanted on each gasp of air, tapping her glasses more firmly in place in hopes the dots in front of her eyes would fade. "I'm okay."

Now that her vision cleared she had a better view of her place at the center of the restaurant's attention. And when had Tony started edging her toward the door? Impending doom welled inside her as she realized the local media would soon descend.

"Good, steady now, in and out." His voice didn't sound any different.

But it also didn't sound Texan. Or southern. Or even northern for that matter, as if he'd worked to stamp out any sense of regionality from himself. She tried to focus on the timbre that so thoroughly strummed her senses when they made love.

"Tony, please say we're going to laugh over this misunderstanding later."

He didn't answer. His square jaw was set and serious as he looked over her shoulder, scanning. She found no signs of her carefree lover, even though her fingers carried the memory of how his dark hair curled around her fingers. His wealth and power had been undeniable from the start in his clothes and lifestyle, but most of all in his proud carriage. Now she took new note of his aristocratic jaw and cheekbones. Such a damn handsome and charming man. She'd allowed herself to be wowed. Seduced by his smile.

She'd barely come to grips with dating a rich guy, given all the bad baggage that brought up of her dead husband. A crooked sleaze. She'd been dazzled by Nolan's glitzy world, learning too late it was financed by a Ponzi scheme.

The guilt of those destroyed lives squeezed the breath from her lungs all over again. If not for her son, she might very well have curled inside herself and given up after Nolan took his own life. But she would hold strong for Kolby.

"Answer me," she demanded, hoping.

"This isn't the place to talk."

Not reassuring and, oh God, why did Tony still have the power to hurt her? Anger punched through the pain. "How long does it take to say *damned rumor?*"

He slid an arm around her shoulders, tucking her to his side. "Let's find somewhere more private."

"Tell me now." She pulled back from the lure of his familiar scent, minty patchouli and sandalwood, the smell of exotic pleasures.

Tony—Antonio—Prince Medina—whoever the hell he was—ducked his head closer to hers. "Shannon, do you really want to talk here where anyone can listen? The world's going to intrude on our town soon enough."

Tears burned behind her eyes, the room going blurry even with her glasses on. "Okay, we'll find a quiet place to discuss this."

He backed her toward the kitchen. Her legs and his synched up in step, her hips following his instinctively, as if they'd danced together often…and more. Eyes and whispers followed them the entire way. Did everyone already know? Cell phones sang from pockets and vibrated on tabletops as if Galveston quivered on the verge of an earthquake.

No one approached them outright, but fragments drifted from their huddled discussions.

"Could Tony Castillo be—"

"—Medina—"

"—With that waitress—"

The buzz increased like a swarm of locusts closing in on the Texas landscape. On her life.

Tony growled lowly, "There's nowhere here we can speak privately. I need to get you out of Vernon's."

His muscled arm locked her tighter, guiding her through a swishing door, past a string of chefs all immobile and gawking. He shouldered out a side door and she had no choice but to follow.

Outside, the late-day sun kissed his bronzed face, bringing his deeply tanned features into sharper focus. She'd always known there was something strikingly foreign about him. But she'd believed his story of dead parents, bookkeepers who'd emigrated from South America. Her own parents had died in a car accident before she'd graduated from college. She'd thought they'd at least shared similar childhoods.

Now? She was sure of nothing except how her body still betrayed her with the urge to lean into his hard-muscled strength, to escape into the pleasure she knew he could bring.

"I need to let management know I'm leaving. I can't lose this job." Tips were best in the evening and she needed every penny. She couldn't afford the time it would take to get her teaching credentials current again—if she could even find a music-teaching position with cutbacks in the arts.

And there weren't too many people out there in search of private oboe lessons.

"I know the owner, remember?" He unlocked his car, the remote chirp-chirping.

"Of course. What was I thinking? You have connections." She stifled a fresh bout of hysterical laughter.

Would she even be able to work again if the Medina rumor was true? It had been tough enough finding a job when others associated her with her dead husband. Sure, she'd been cleared of any wrongdoing, but many still believed she must have known about Nolan's illegal schemes.

There hadn't even been a trial for her to state her side. Once her husband had made bail, he'd been dead within twenty-four hours.

Tony cursed low and harsh, sailor-style swearing he usually curbed around her and Kolby. She looked around, saw nothing… Then she heard the thundering footsteps a second before the small cluster of people rounded the corner with cameras and microphones.

Swearing again, Tony yanked open the passenger door to his Escalade. He lifted her inside easily, as if she weighed nothing more than the tray of fried gator appetizers she'd carried earlier.

Seconds later he slid behind the wheel and slammed the door a hair's breadth ahead of the reporters. Fists pounded on the tinted windows. Locks auto-clicked. Shannon sagged in the leather seat with relief.

The hefty SUV rocked from the force of the mob. Her heart rate ramped again. If this was the life of the rich and famous, she wanted no part.

Shifting into Reverse then forward, Tony drove, slow but steady. People peeled away. At least one reporter fell on his butt but everyone appeared unharmed.

So much for playing chicken with Tony. She would be wise to remember that.

He guided the Escalade through the historic district a hint over the speed limit, fast enough to put space between them and the media hounds. Panting in the aftermath, she still braced a hand on the dash, her other gripping the leather seat. Yet Tony hadn't even broken a sweat.

His hands stayed steady on the wheel, his expensive watch glinting from the French cuffs of his shirt. Restored brick buildings zipped by her window. A young couple dressed for an evening out stepped off the curb, then back sharply. While the whole idea of being hunted by the paparazzi scared her to her roots, right here in the SUV with Tony, she felt safe.

Safe enough for the anger and betrayal to come bubbling to the surface. She'd been mad at him since their fight last weekend over his continued insistence on giving her money. But those feelings were nothing compared to the rage that coursed through her now. "We're alone. Talk to me."

"It's complicated." He glanced in the rearview mirror. Normal traffic tooled along the narrow street. "What do you want to know?"

She forced herself to say the words that would drive a permanent wedge between her and the one man she'd dared let into her life again.

"Are you a part of that lost royal family, the one everybody thought was hiding in Argentina?"

The Cadillac's finely tuned engine hummed in the

silence. Lights clicked on automatically with the setting sun, the dash glowing.

His knuckles went white on the steering wheel, his jaw flexing before he nodded tightly. "The rumors on the internet are correct."

And she'd thought her heart couldn't break again.

Her pride had been stung over Tony's offer to give her money, but she would have gotten over it. She would have stuck to her guns about paying her own way, of course. But *this?* It was still too huge to wrap her brain around. She'd slept with a prince, let him into her home, her body, and considered letting him into her heart. His deception burned deep.

How could she have missed the truth so completely, buying into his stories about working on a shrimp boat as a teen? She'd assumed his tattoo and the closed over pierced earlobe were parts of an everyman past that seduced her as fully as his caresses.

"Your name isn't even Tony Castillo." Oh God. She pressed the back of her hand against her mouth, suddenly nauseated because she didn't even know the name of the guy she'd been sleeping with.

"Technically, it could be."

Shannon slammed her fists against the leather seat instead of reaching for him as she ached to do. "I'm not interested in technically. Actually, I'm not interested in people who lie to me. Can I even trust that you're really thirty-two years old?"

"It isn't just my decision to share specific details. I have other family members to consider. But if it's any consolation, I really am thirty-two. Are you really twenty-nine?"

"I'm not in a joking mood." Shivering, she thumbed

her bare ring finger where once a three-carat diamond had rested. After Nolan's funeral, she'd taken it off and sold it along with everything else to pay off the mountain of debt. "I should have known you were too good to be true."

"Why do you say that?"

"Who makes millions by thirty-two?"

He cocked an arrogant eyebrow. "Did you just call me a moocher?"

"Well, excuse me if that was rude, but I'm not exactly at my best tonight."

His arms bulged beneath his Italian suit—she'd had to look up the exclusive Garaceni label after she'd seen the coat hanging on his bedpost.

Tony looked even more amazing out of the clothes, his tanned and muscled body eclipsing any high-end wardrobe. And the smiles he brought to her life, his uninhibited laughter were just what she needed most.

How quiet her world had been without him this week. "Sorry to have hurt your feelings, pal. Or should I say, Your Majesty? Since according to some of those stories I'm 'His Majesty's mistress.'"

"Actually, it would be 'Your Highness.'" His signature smile tipped his mouth, but with a bitter edge. "Majesty is for the king."

How could he be so flippant? "Actually, you can take your title and stuff it where the sun—"

"I get the picture." He guided the Escalade over the Galveston Island Causeway, waves moving darkly below. "You'll need time to calm down so we can discuss how to handle this."

"You don't understand. There's no calming down. You lied to me on a fundamental level. Once we made l—" she stumbled over the next word, images of him moving over her, inside her, stealing her words and breath until her stomach churned as fast as the waters below "—after we went to bed together, you should have told me. Unless the sex didn't mean anything special to you. I guess if you had to tell every woman you slept with, there would be no secret."

"Stop!" He sliced the air with his hand. His gleaming Patek Philippe watch contrasted with scarred knuckles, from his sailing days he'd once told her. "That's not true and not the point here. You were safer not knowing."

"Oh, it's for my own good." She wrapped her arms around herself, a shield from the hurt.

"How much do you know about my family's history?"

She bit back the urge to snap at him. Curiosity reined in her temper. "Not much. Just that there was a king of some small country near Spain, I think, before he was overthrown in a coup. His family has been hiding out to avoid the paparazzi hoopla."

"Hoopla? This might suck, but that's the least of my worries. There are people out there who tried to kill my family and succeeded in murdering my mother. There are people who stand to gain a lot in the way of money and power if the Medinas are wiped off the planet."

Her heart ached for all he had lost. Even now, she wanted to press her mouth to his and forget this whole insane mess. To grasp that shimmering connection she'd discovered with him the first time they'd made love in a frenzied tangle at his Galveston Bay mansion.

"Well, believe it, Shannon. There's a big bad world outside your corner of Texas. Right now, some of the worst will start focusing on me, my family and anyone who's close to us. Whether you like it or not, I'll do whatever it takes to keep you and Kolby protected."

Her son's safety? Perspiration froze on her forehead, chilling her deeper. Why hadn't she thought of that? Of course she'd barely wrapped her brain around Tony… Antonio. "Drive faster. Get me home now."

"I completely agree. I've already sent bodyguards ahead of us."

Bodyguards?

"When?" She'd barely been able to think, much less act. What kind of mother was she not to have considered the impact on Kolby? And what kind of man kept bodyguards on speed dial?

"I texted my people while we were leaving through the kitchen."

Of course he had people. The man was not merely the billionaire shipping magnate she'd assumed, he was also the bearer of a surname generations old and a background of privilege she couldn't begin to fathom.

"I was so distracted I didn't even notice," Shannon whispered, sinking into her seat. She wasn't even safe in her own neighborhood anymore.

She couldn't wish this away any longer. "You really are this Medina guy. You're really from some deposed royal family."

His chin tipped with unmistakable regality. "My name is Antonio Medina. I was born in San Rinaldo, third son of King Enrique and Queen Beatriz."

Her heart drumming in her ears, panic squeezed harder at her rib cage. How could she have foreseen this when she met him five months ago at the restaurant, bringing his supper back to the owner's poker game?

Tony had ordered a shrimp po'boy sandwich and a glass of sweet tea.

Poor Boy? How ironic was that?

"This is too weird." And scary.

The whole surreal mess left her too numb to hurt anymore. That would return later, for sure. Her hands shook as she tapped her glasses straight.

She had to stay focused now. "Stuff like this happens in movies or a hundred years ago."

"Or in my life. Now in yours, too."

"Nuh-uh. You and I?" She waggled her hand back and forth between them. "We're history."

He paused at a stop sign, turning to face her fully for the first time since he'd gripped her shoulders at the restaurant. His coal-black eyes heated over her, a bold man of uninhibited emotions. "That fast, you're ready to call an end to what we've shared?"

Her heart picked up speed from just the caress of his eyes, the memory of his hands stroking her. She tried to answer but her mouth had gone dry. He skimmed those scarred knuckles down her arm until his hand rested on hers. Such a simple gesture, nothing overtly erotic, but her whole body hummed with awareness and want.

Right here in the middle of the street, in the middle of an upside down situation, her body betrayed her as surely as he had.

Wrong. Wrong. Wrong. She had to be tough. "I already ended things between us last weekend."

"That was a fight, not a breakup." His big hand splayed over hers, eclipsing her with heat.

"Semantics. Not that it matters." She pulled herself away from him until her spine met the door, not nearly far enough. "I can't be with you anymore."

"That's too damn bad, because we're going to be spending a lot of time together after we pick up your son. There's no way you can stay in your apartment tonight."

"There's no way I can stay with *you*."

"You can't hide from what's been unleashed. Today should tell you that more than anything. It'll find you and your son. I'm sorry for not seeing this coming, but it's here and we have to deal with it."

Fear for her son warred with her anger at Tony. "You had no right," she hissed between clenched teeth, "no right at all to play with our lives this way."

"I agree." He surprised her with that. However, the reprieve was short. "But I'm the only one who can stand between you both and whatever fallout comes from this revelation."

Chapter 2

A bodyguard stood outside the front door of her first-floor apartment. A bodyguard, for heaven's sake, a burly guy in a dark suit who could have passed for a Secret Service employee. She stifled the urge to scream in frustration.

Shannon flung herself out of the Escalade before it came to a complete stop, desperate to see her child, to get inside her tiny apartment in hopes that life would somehow return to normal. Tony couldn't be serious about her packing up to go away with him. He was just using this to try to get back together again.

Although what did a *prince* want with her?

At least there weren't any reporters in the parking lot. The neighbors all seemed to be inside for the evening or out enjoying their own party plans. She'd chosen the large complex for the anonymity it offered. Multiple three-story buildings filled the corner block, making it difficult to tell one apartment from another in the stretches of yellow units with tiny white balconies. At the center of it all, there was a pool and tiny playground, the only luxuries she'd allowed herself. She might not be able to give Kolby a huge yard, but he would have an outdoor place to play.

Now she had to start the search for a haven all over again.

"Here," she said as she thrust her purse toward him, her keys in her hand, "please carry this so I can unlock the door."

He extended his arm, her hobo bag dangling from his big fist. "Uh, sure."

"This is not the time to freak out over holding a woman's purse." She fumbled for the correct key.

"Shannon, I'm here for you. For you and your handbag."

She glanced back sharply. "Don't mock me."

"I thought you enjoyed my sense of humor."

Hadn't she thought just the same thing earlier? How could she say good-bye to Tony—he would never be Antonio to her—forever? Her feet slowed on the walkway between the simple hedges, nowhere near as elaborate as the gardens of her old home with Nolan, but well maintained. The place was clean.

And safe.

Having Tony at her back provided an extra layer of protection, she had to admit. After he'd made his shocking demand that she pack, he'd pulled out his phone and began checking in with his lawyer. From what she could tell hearing one side of the conversation, the news was spreading fast, with no indication of how the Global Intruder's people had cracked his cover. Tony didn't lose his temper or even curse.

But her normally lighthearted lover definitely wasn't smiling.

She ignored the soft note of regret spreading through her for all she would leave behind—this place. *Tony.* He strode alongside her silently, the outside lights casting his shadow over hers intimately, moving, tangling the two together as they walked.

Stopping at her unit three doors down from the corner, Tony exchanged low words with the guard while she slid the key into the lock with shaking hands. She pushed her way inside and ran smack into the babysitter already trying to open up for her. The college senior was majoring in elementary education and lived in the same complex. There might only be seven years between her and the girl in a concert T-shirt, but Shannon couldn't help but feel her own university days spent studying to be a teacher happened eons ago.

Shannon forced herself to stay calm. "Courtney, thanks for calling me. Where's Kolby?"

The sitter studied her with undisguised curiosity— who could blame her?—and pointed down the narrow hall toward the living room. "He's asleep on the couch. I thought it might be better to keep him with me in case any reporters started showing up outside or something." She hitched her bulging backpack onto one shoulder. "I don't think they would stake out his window, but ya never know. Right?"

"Thank you, Courtney. You did exactly the right thing." She angled down the hall to peek in on Kolby.

Her three-year-old son slept curled on the imported leather sofa, one of the few pieces that hadn't been sold to pay off debts. Kolby had poked a hole in the armrest with a fountain pen just before the estate sale. Shannon had strapped duct tape over the tear, grateful for one less piece of furniture to buy to start her new life.

Every penny she earned needed to be tucked away for emergencies. Kolby counted on her, her sweet baby boy in his favorite Thomas the Tank Engine pj's, matching blanket held up to his nose. His blond hair was tousled and spiking, still damp from his bath. She could almost smell the baby-powder sweetness from across the room.

Sagging against the archway with relief, she turned back to Courtney. "I need to pay you."

Shannon took back her hobo bag from Tony and tunneled through frantically, dropping her wallet. Change clanked on the tile floor.

What would a three-year-old think if he saw his mother's face in some news report? Or Tony's, for that matter? The two had only met briefly a few times, but Kolby knew he was Mama's friend. She scooped the coins into a pile, picking at quarters and dimes.

Tony cupped her shoulder. "I've got it. Go ahead and be with your son."

She glanced up sharply, her nerves too raw to take the reminder of how he'd offered her financial help mere moments after sex last weekend. "I can pay my own way."

Holding up his hands, he backed away.

"Fine, Shannon. I'll sit with Kolby." He cautioned her with a look not to mention their plans to pack and leave. *Duh.* Not that she planned to follow all *his* dictates, but the fewer who knew their next move the better for avoiding the press and anyone else who might profit from tracking their moves. Even the best of friends could be bought off.

Speaking of payoffs… "Thank you for calling me so quickly." She peeled off an extra twenty and tried not to wince as she said goodbye to ice cream for the month. She usually traded babysitting with another flat-broke single mom in the building when needed for work and dates. Courtney was only her backup, which she couldn't—and didn't—use often. "I appreciate your help."

Shaking her head, Courtney took the money and passed back the extra twenty. "You don't need to give me all that, Mrs. Crawford. I was only doing my job. And I'm not gonna talk to the reporters. I'm not the kind of person who would sell your story or something."

"Really," Shannon urged as she folded the cash back into her hand, "I want you to have it."

Tony filled the archway. "The guard outside will walk you home, just to make sure no one bothers you."

"Thanks, Mr. Castillo. Um, I mean…" Courtney stuffed the folded bills into her back pocket, the college coed eyeing him up and down with a new awareness. "Mr. Medina… Sir? I don't what to call you."

"Castillo is fine."

"Right, uh, bye." Her face flushed, she spun on her glitter flip-flops and took off.

Shannon pushed the door closed, sliding the bolt and chain. Locking her inside with Tony in a totally quiet apartment. She slumped back and stared down the hallway, the ten feet shrinking even more with the bulk of his shoulders spanning the arch. Light from the cheap brown lamp glinted off the curl in his black hair.

No wonder Courtney had been flustered. He wasn't

just a prince, but a fine-looking, one-hundred-percent *man*. The kind with strong hands that could finesse their way over a woman's body with a sweet tenderness that threatened to buckle her knees from just remembering. Had it only been a week since they'd made love in his mammoth jetted tub? God knows she ached as if she'd been without him for months.

Even acknowledging it was wrong with her mind, her body still wanted him.

Tony wanted her.
In his arms.
In his bed.
And most of all, he wanted her back in his SUV, heading away from here. He needed to use any methods of persuasion possible and convince her to come to his house. Even if the press located his home address, they wouldn't get past the gates and security. So how to convince Shannon? He stared down the short tiled hallway at her.

Awareness flared in her eyes. The same slam of attraction he felt now and the first time he'd seen her five months ago when he'd stopped by after a call to play cards. Vernon had mentioned hiring a new waitress but Tony hadn't thought much of it—until he met her.

When Tony asked about her, the old guy said he didn't know much about Shannon other than her crook of a husband had committed suicide rather than face a jury. Shannon and her boy had been left behind, flat broke. She'd worked at a small diner for a year and a half before that and Vernon had hired her on a hunch. Vernon and his softie heart.

Tony stared at her now every bit as intently as he had

that first time she'd brought him his order. Something about her blue-gray eyes reminded him of the ocean sky just before a storm. Tumultuous. Interesting.

A challenge. He'd been without a challenge for too long. Building a business from nothing had kept him charged up for years. What next?

Then he'd seen her.

He'd spent his life smiling his way through problems and deals, and for the first time he'd found someone who saw past his bull. Was it the puzzle that tugged him? If so, he wasn't any closer to solving the mystery of Shannon. Every day she confused him more, which made him want her more.

Pushing away from the door, she strode toward him, efficiently, no hip swish, just even, efficient steps. Then she walked out of her shoes, swiping one foot behind her to kick them to rest against the wall. No shoes in the house. She'd told him that the two times he'd been allowed over her threshold for no more than fifteen minutes. Any liaisons between them had been at his bayside mansion or a suite near the restaurant. He didn't really expect anything to happen here with her son around, even asleep.

And given the look on her face, she was more likely to pitch him out. Better to circumvent the boot.

"I'll stay with your son while you pack." He removed his shoes and stepped deeper into her place, not fancy, the sparse generic sort of a furnished space in browns and tan—except for the expensive burgundy leather sofa with a duct-taped *X* on the armrest.

Her lips thinned. "About packing, we need to discuss that further."

"What's to talk about?" He accepted their relationship was still on hold, but the current problems with his identity needed to be addressed. "Your porch will be full by morning."

"I'll check into a hotel."

With the twenty dollars and fifty-two cents she had left in her wallet? He prayed she wasn't foolish enough to use a credit card. Might as well phone in her location to the news stations.

"We can talk about where you'll stay *after* you pack."

"You sound like a broken record, Tony."

"*You*'re calling *me* stubborn?"

Their standoff continued, neither of them touching, but he was all too aware of her scrubbed fresh scent. Shannon, the whole place, carried an air of some kind of floral cleaner. The aroma somehow calmed and stirred at the same time, calling to mind holding her after a mind-bending night of sex. She never stayed over until morning, but for an hour or so after, she would doze against his chest. He would breathe in the scent of her and him and *them* blended together.

His nose flared.

Her pupils widened.

She stumbled back, her chest rising faster. "I do need to change my clothes. Are you sure you'll be all right with Kolby?"

It was no secret the couple of times he'd met the boy, Kolby hadn't warmed up to him. Nothing seemed to work, not ice cream or magic coin tricks. Tony figured maybe the boy was still missing his father.

That jerk had left Shannon bankrupt and vulnerable. "I can handle it. Take all the time you need."

"Thank you. I'm only going to change clothes, though.

No packing yet. We'll have to talk more first, Tony—um, Antonio."

"I prefer to be called *Tony*." He liked the sound of it on her tongue.

"Okay…Tony." She spun on her heel and headed toward her bedroom.

Her steps still efficient, albeit faster, were just speedy enough to bring a slight swing to her slim hips in the pencil-straight skirt. Thoughts of peeling it down and off her beautiful body would have to wait until she had the whole Antonio/Tony issue sorted out.

If only she could accept that he'd called himself Tony Castillo almost longer than he'd remembered being Antonio Medina.

He even had the paperwork to back up the Castillo name. Creating another persona hadn't been that difficult, especially once he'd saved enough to start his first business. From then on, all transactions were shuttled through the company. Umbrella corporations. Living in plain sight. His plan had worked fine until someone, somehow had pierced the new identities he and his brothers had built. In fact, he needed to call his brothers, whom he spoke to at most a couple of times a year. But they might have insights.

They needed a plan.

He reached inside his jacket for his iPhone and ducked into the dining area where he could see the child but wouldn't wake him. He thumbed the seven key on his speed dial…and Carlos's voice mail picked up. Tony disconnected without leaving a message and pressed the eight key.

"Speak to me, my brother." Duarte Medina's voice

came through the phone. They didn't talk often, but these weren't normal circumstances.

"I assume you know." He toyed with one of Shannon's hair bands on the table.

"Impossible to miss."

"Where's Carlos? He's not picking up." Tony fell back into their clipped shorthand. They'd only had each other growing up and now circumstances insisted they stay apart. Did his brothers have that same feeling, like they'd lost a limb?

"His secretary said he got paged for an emergency surgery. He'll be at least another couple of hours. Apparently Carlos found out as he was scrubbing in, but you know our brother." Duarte, the middle son, tended to play messenger with their father. The three brothers spoke and met when they could, but there were so many crap memories from their childhood, those reunions became further apart.

Tony scooped up the brown band, a lone long strand of her blond hair catching the light. "When a patient calls…"

"Right."

It could well be hours before they heard from Carlos, given the sort of painstaking reconstructive surgeries he performed on children. "Any idea how this exploded?"

His brother hissed a long angry curse. "The Global Intruder got a side-view picture of me while I was visiting our sister."

Their half sister Eloisa, their father's daughter from an affair shortly after they had escaped to the States. Enrique had still been torn up with grief from losing his wife…not to mention the guilt. But apparently not so torn up and remorseful he couldn't hop into bed with someone else. The woman had gone on to marry another man who'd raised her daughter as his own.

Tony had only met his half sister once as a teen, a few years before he'd left the island compound. She'd only been seven at the time. Now she'd married into a high-profile family jam-packed with political influence and a fat portfolio. Could she be at fault for bringing the media down on their heads for some free PR for her new in-laws? Duarte seemed to think she wanted anonymity as much as the rest of them. But could he have misjudged her?

"Why were you visiting Eloisa?" Tony tucked the band into his pocket.

"Family business. It doesn't matter now. Her in-laws were there. Eloisa's sister-in-law—a senator's wife—slipped on the dock. I kept her from falling into the water. Some damn female reporter in a tree with a tele-photo lens caught the mishap. Which shouldn't have mattered, since Senator Landis and his wife were the focus of the picture. I still don't know how the photog-rapher pegged me from a side view, but there it is. And I'm sorry for bringing this crap down on you."

Duarte hadn't done anything wrong. They couldn't live in a bubble. In the back of Tony's mind, he'd always known it was just a matter of time until the cover story blew up in their faces. He'd managed to live away from the island anonymously for fourteen years, his two older brothers even longer.

But there was always the hope that maybe he could stay a step ahead. Be his own man. Succeed on his own merits. "We've all been caught in a picture on occasion. We're not vampires. It's just insane that she was able to make the connection. Perfect storm of bad luck."

"What are your plans for dealing with this perfect storm?"

"Lock down tight while I regroup. Let me know when you hear from Carlos."

Ending the call, Tony strode back into the living room, checked on Kolby—still snoozing hard—and dropped to the end of the sofa to read messages, his in-box already full again. By the time Tony scrolled through emails that told him nothing new, he logged on to the internet for a deeper peek. And winced. Rumors were rampant.

That his father had died of malaria years ago—false.

Supposition that Carlos had plastic surgery—again, false.

Speculation that Duarte had joined a Tibetan monastery—definitely false.

And then there were the stories about him and Shannon, which actually happened to be true. The whole "Monarch's Mistress" was really growing roots out there in cyberspace. Guilt kicked him in the gut that Shannon would suffer this kind of garbage because of him. The media feeding frenzy would only grow, and before long they would stir up all the crap about her thief of a dead husband. He tucked away his phone in disgust.

"That bad?" Shannon asked from the archway.

She'd changed into jeans and a simple blue tank top. Her silky blond hair glided loosely down her shoulders, straight except for a slight crimped ring where she'd bound it up on her head for work. She didn't look much older than the babysitter, except in her weary—wary—eyes.

Leaning back, he extended his legs, leather creaking as he stayed on the sofa so as not to spook her. "The internet is exploding. My lawyers and my brothers' lawyers are all looking into it. Hopefully we'll have the leak plugged soon and start some damage control. But we can't stuff the genie back into the bottle."

"I'm not going away with you." She perched a fist on one shapely hip.

"This isn't going to die down." He kept his voice even and low, reasonable. The stakes were too important for all of them. "The reporters will swarm you by morning, if not sooner. Your babysitter will almost inevitably cave in to one of those gossip-rag offers. Your friends will sell photos of the two of us together. There's a chance people could use Kolby to get to me."

"Then we're through, you and I." She reached for her sleeping son on the sofa, smoothing his hair before sliding a hand under his shoulders as if to scoop him up.

Tony touched her arm lightly, stopping her. "Hold on before you settle him into his room." As far as Tony was concerned, they would be back in his Escalade in less than ten minutes. "Do you honestly think anyone's going to believe the breakup is for real? The timing will seem too convenient."

She sagged onto the arm of the sofa, right over the silver *X*. "We ended things last weekend."

Like hell. "Tell that to the papers and see if they believe you. The truth doesn't matter to these people. They probably printed photos of an alien baby last week. Pleading a breakup isn't going to buy you any kind of freedom from their interest."

"I know I need to move away from Galveston." She glanced around her sparsely decorated apartment, two pictures of Kolby the only personal items. "I've accepted that."

There wouldn't be much packing to do.

"They'll find you."

She studied him through narrowed eyes. "How do I know you're not just using this as an excuse to get back together?"

Was he? An hour ago, he would have done anything to get into her bed again. While the attraction hadn't diminished, since his cover was blown, he had other concerns that overshadowed everything else. He needed to determine the best way to inoculate her from the toxic fallout that came from associating with Medinas. One thing for certain, he couldn't risk her striking out on her own.

"You made it clear where we stand last weekend. I get that. You want nothing to do with me or my money." He didn't move closer, wasn't going to crowd her. The draw between them filled the space separating them just fine on its own. "We had sex together. Damn good sex. But that's over now. Neither one of us ever asked for or expected more."

Her gaze locked with his, the room silent but for their breathing and the light snore of the sleeping child. Kolby. Another reminder of why they needed to stay in control.

In fact, holding back made the edge sharper. He skimmed his knuckles along her collarbone, barely touching. A week ago, that pale skin had worn the rasp of his beard. She didn't move closer, but she didn't back away, either.

Shannon blinked first, her long lashes sweeping closed while she swallowed hard. "What am I supposed to do?"

More than anything he wanted to gather her up and tell her everything would be okay. He wouldn't allow anything less. But he also wouldn't make shallow promises.

Twenty-seven years ago, when they'd been leaving San Rinaldo on a moonless night, his father had assured them everything would be fine. They would be reunited soon.

His father had been so very wrong.

Tony focused on what he could assure. "A lot has happened in a few hours. We need to take a step back for damage assessment tonight at my home, where there are security gates, alarms, guards watching and surveillance cameras."

"And after tonight?"

"We'll let the press think we are a couple, still deep in that affair." He indulged himself in one lengthy, heated eye-stroke of her slim, supple body. "Then we'll stage a more public breakup later, on our terms, when we've prepared a backup plan."

She exhaled a shaky breath. "That makes sense."

"Meanwhile, my number-one priority is shielding you and Kolby." He sifted through options, eliminating one idea after another until he was left with only a single alternative.

Her hand fell to rest on her sleeping son's head. "How do you intend to do that?"

"By taking you to the safest place I know." A place he'd vowed never to return. "Tomorrow, we're going to visit my father."

Chapter 3

"Visit your father?" Shannon asked in total shock. Had Tony lost his mind? "The King of San Rinaldo? You've got to be kidding."

"I'm completely serious." He stared back at her from the far end of the leather sofa, her sleeping son between them.

Resisting Tony had been tough enough this past week just knowing he was in the same town. How much more difficult would it be with him in the same house for one night much less days on end? God, she wanted to run. She bit the inside of her lip to keep from blurting out something she would regret later. Sorting through her options could take more time than they appeared to have.

Kolby wriggled restlessly, hugging his comfort blanket tighter. Needing a moment to collect her thoughts and her resolve, she scooped up her son.

"Tony, we'll have to put this discussion on hold." She cradled her child closer and angled down the hall, ever aware of a certain looming prince at her back. "Keep the lights off, please."

Shadows playing tag on the ceiling, she lowered Kolby into the red caboose bed they'd picked out together when she moved into the apartment. She'd been trying so hard to make up for all her son had lost. As if there was some way to compensate for the loss of his father, the loss of security. Shannon pressed a kiss to his forehead, inhaling his precious baby-shampoo smell.

When she turned back, she found Tony waiting in the doorway, determination stamped on his square jaw. Well, she could be mighty resolute too, especially when it came to her son. Shannon closed the curtains before she left the room and stepped into the narrow hall.

She shut the door quietly behind her. "You have to know your suggestion is outrageous."

"The whole situation is outrageous, which calls for extraordinary measures."

"Hiding out with a king? That's definitely what I would call extraordinary." She pulled off her glasses and pinched the bridge of her nose.

Before Nolan's death she'd worn contacts, but couldn't afford the extra expense now. How much longer until she would grow accustomed to glasses again?

She stared at Tony, his face clear up close, everything in the distance blurred. "Do you honestly think I would want to expose myself, not to mention Kolby, to more scrutiny by going to your father's? Why not just hide out at your place as we originally discussed?"

God, had she just agreed to stay with him indefinitely?

"My house is secure, up to a point. People will figure out where I live and they'll deduce that you're with me. There's only one place I can think of where no one can get to us."

Frustration buzzed in her brain. "Seems like their telephoto lenses reach everywhere."

"The press still hasn't located my father's home after years of trying."

But she thought… "Doesn't he live in Argentina?"

He studied her silently, the wheels almost visibly turning in his broad forehead. Finally, he shook his head quickly.

"No. We only stopped off there to reorganize after escaping San Rinaldo." He adjusted his watch, the only nervous habit she'd ever observed in him. "My father did set up a compound there and paid a small, trusted group of individuals to make it look inhabited. Most of them also escaped San Rinaldo with us. People assumed we were there with them."

What extreme lengths and expense their father had gone to. But then wasn't she willing to do anything to protect Kolby? She felt a surprise connection to the old king she'd never met. "Why are you telling me this much if it's such a closely guarded secret?"

He cupped her shoulder, his touch heavy and familiar, *stirring.* "Because it's that important I persuade you."

Resisting the urge to lean into him was tougher with each stroke of his thumb against the sensitive curve of her neck. "Where *does* he live then?"

"I can't tell you that much," he said, still touching and, God, it made her mad that she didn't pull away.

"Yet you expect me to just pack up my child and follow you there." She gripped his wrist and moved away from his seductive touch.

"I detect a note of skepticism in your voice." He shoved his hands in his pockets.

"A note? Try a whole freaking symphony, Tony." The sense of betrayal swelled inside her again, larger and larger until it pushed bitter words out. "Why should I trust you? Especially now?"

"Because you don't have anyone else or they would have already been helping you."

The reality deflated her. She only had a set of in-laws who didn't want anything to do with her or Kolby since they blamed her for their son's downfall. She was truly alone.

"How long would we be there?"

"Just until my attorneys can arrange for a restraining order against certain media personnel. I realize that restraining orders don't always work, but having one will give us a stronger legal case if we need it. It's one thing to stalk, but it's another to stalk and violate a restraining order. And I'll want to make sure you have top-of-the-line security installed at your new home. That should take about a week, two at the most."

Shannon fidgeted with her glasses. "How would we get there?"

"By plane." He thumbed the face of his watch clean again.

That meant it must be far away. "Forget it. You are not going to isolate me that way, cut me off from the world. It's the equivalent of kidnapping me and my son."

"Not if you agree to go along." He edged closer, the stretch of his hard muscled shoulders blocking out the light filtering from the living area. "People in the military get on planes all the time without knowing their destination."

She tipped her chin upward, their faces inches apart. Close enough to feel his heat. Close enough to kiss.

Too close for her own good. "Last time I checked, I wasn't wearing a uniform." Her voice cracked ever so slightly. "I didn't sign on for this."

"I know, Shanny...." He stroked a lock of her hair intimately. "I *am* sorry for all this is putting you through, and I will do my best to make the next week as easy for you as possible."

The sincerity of his apology soothed the ragged edges of her nerves. It had been a long week without him. She'd been surprised by how much she had missed his spontaneous dates and late-night calls. His bold kisses and intimate caresses. She couldn't lie to herself about how much he affected her on both an emotional and physical level. Otherwise this mess with his revealed past wouldn't hurt her so deeply.

Her hand clenched around her glasses. He gently slid them from her hand and hooked them on the front of her shirt. The familiarity of the gesture kicked her heart rate up a notch.

Swaying toward him, she flattened her hands to his chest, not sure if she wanted to push him away or pull him nearer. Thick longing filled the sliver of space between them. An answering awareness widened his pupils, pushing and thinning the dark brown of his eyes.

He lowered his head closer, closer still until his mouth hovered over hers. Heated breaths washed over her, stirring even hotter memories and warm languid longing. She'd thought the pain of Nolan's deceit had left her numb for life...until she saw Tony.

"Mama?"

The sound of her son calling out from his room jolted her back to reality. And not only her. Tony's face went from seductive to intent in a heartbeat. He pulled the door open just as Kolby ran through and into his mother's arms.

"Mama, Mama, Mama…" He buried his face in her neck. "Monster in my window!"

Tony shot through the door and toward the window in the child's room, focused, driven and mentally kicking himself for letting himself be distracted.

He barked over his shoulder, "Stay in the hall while I take a look."

It could be nothing, but he'd been taught at a young age the importance of never letting down his guard. Adrenaline firing, he jerked the window open and scanned the tiny patch of yard.

Nothing. Just a Big Wheel lying on its side and a swing dangling lazily from a lone tree.

Maybe it was only a nightmare. This whole blast from the past had him seeing bogeymen from his own childhood, too. Tony pushed the window down again and pulled the curtains together.

Shannon stood in the door, her son tucked against her. "I could have sworn I closed the curtains."

Kolby peeked up. "I opened 'em when I heard-ed the noise."

And maybe this kid's nightmare was every bit as real as his own had been. On the off chance the boy was right, he had to check. "I'm going outside. The guard will stay here with you."

She cupped the back of her child's head. "I already

warned the guard. I wasn't leaving you to take care of the 'monster' by yourself."

Dread kinked cold and tight in his gut. What if something had happened to her when she had stepped outside to speak to the guard? He held in the angry words, not wanting to upset her son.

But he became more determined by the second to persuade her and the child to leave Galveston with him. "Let's hope it was nothing but a tree branch. Right, kiddo?"

Tony started toward the door just as his iPhone rang. He glanced at the ID and saw the guard's number. He thumbed the speaker phone button. "Yes?"

"Got him," the guard said. "A teenager from the next complex over was trying to snap some pictures on his cell phone. I've already called the police."

A sigh shuddered through Shannon, and she hugged her son closer, and God, how Tony wanted to comfort her.

However, the business of taking care of her safety came first. "Keep me posted if there are any red flags when they interview the trespasser. Good work. Thanks."

He tucked his phone back into his jacket, his heart almost hammering out of his chest at the close call. This could have been worse. He knew too well from past experience how bad it could have been.

And apparently so did Shannon. Her wide blue eyes blinked erratically as she looked from corner to corner, searching shadows.

To hell with giving her distance. He wrapped an arm around her shoulders until she leaned on him ever so slightly. The soft press of her against him felt damn right in a day gone wrong.

Then she squeezed her eyes closed and straightened. "Okay, you win."

"Win what?"

"We'll go to your home tonight."

A hollow victory, since fear rather than desire motivated her, but he wasn't going to argue. "And tomorrow?"

"We'll discuss that in morning. Right now, just take us to your house."

Tony's Galveston house could only be called a mansion.

The imposing size of the three-story structure washed over Shannon every time they drove through the scrolled iron gates. How Kolby could sleep through all of this boggled her mind, but when they'd convinced him the "monster" was gone—thanks to the guard—Kolby had been all yawns again. Once strapped into the car seat in the back of Tony's Escalade, her son had been out like a light in five minutes.

If only her own worries could be as easily shaken off. She had to think logically, but fears for Kolby nagged her. Nolan had stolen so much more than money. He'd robbed her of the ability to feel safe, just before he took the coward's way out.

Two acres of manicured lawn stretched ahead of her in the moonlight. The estate was intimidating during the day, and all the more ominously gothic at night with shadowy edges encroaching. It was one thing to visit the place for a date.

It was another to take shelter here, to pack suitcases and accept his help.

She'd lived in a large house with Nolan, four thousand square feet, but she could have fit two of those homes inside Tony's place. In the courtyard, a concrete horse fountain was illuminated, glowing in front of the burgundy stucco house with brown trim so dark it was almost black. His home showcased the Spanish architecture prevalent in Texas. Knowing his true heritage now, she could see why he would have been drawn to this area.

Silently he guided the SUV into the garage, finally safe and secure from the outside world. For how long?

He unstrapped Kolby from the seat and she didn't argue. Her son was still sleeping anyway. The way Tony's big hands managed the small buckles and shuffled the sleeping child onto his shoulder with such competence touched her heart as firmly as any hothouse full of roses.

Trailing him with a backpack of toy trains and trucks, she dimly registered the house that had grown familiar after their dates to restaurants, movies and the most amazing concerts. Her soul, so starved for music, gobbled up every note.

Her first dinner at his home had been a five-course catered meal with a violinist. She could almost hear the echoing strains bouncing lightly off the high-beamed ceiling, down to the marble floor, swirling along the inlay pattern to twine around her.

Binding her closer to him. They hadn't had sex that night, but she'd known then it was inevitable.

That first time, Tony had been thoughtful enough to send out to a different restaurant than his favored Vernon's, guessing accurately that when a person worked eight hours a day in one eating establishment, the food there lost its allure.

He'd opted for Italian cuisine. The meal and music and elegance had been so far removed from paper plate dinners of nuggets and fries. While she adored her son and treasured every second with him, she couldn't help but be wooed by grown-up time to herself.

Limited time as she'd never spent the night here. Until now.

She followed Tony up the circular staircase, hand on the crafted iron banister. The sight of her son sleeping so limp and relaxed against Tony brought a lump to her throat again.

The tenderness she felt seeing him hold her child reminded her how special this new man in her life was. She'd chosen him so carefully after Nolan had died, seeing Tony's innate strength and honor. Was she really ready to throw that away?

He stopped at the first bedroom, a suite decorated in hunter green with vintage maps framed on the walls. Striding through the sitting area to the next door, he flipped back the brocade spread and set her son in the middle of the high bed.

Quietly, she put a chair on either side as a makeshift bed rail, then tucked the covers over his shoulders. She kissed his little forehead and inhaled his baby-fresh scent. Her child.

The enormity of how their lives had changed tonight swelled inside her, pushing stinging tears to the surface. Tony's hand fell to rest on her shoulder and she leaned back....

Holy crap.

She jolted away. How easily she fell into old habits around him. "I didn't mean..."

"I know." His hand fell away and tucked into his

pocket. "I'll carry up your bags in a minute. I gave the house staff the night off."

She followed him, just to keep their conversation soft, not because she wasn't ready to say good-night. "I thought you trusted them."

"I do. To a point. It's also easier for security to protect the house with fewer people inside." He gestured into the sitting area. "I heard what you said about feeling cut off from the world going to my father's and I understand."

His empathy slipped past her defenses when they were already on shaky ground being here in his house again. Remembering all the times they'd made love under this very roof, she could almost smell the bath salts from last weekend. And with him being so understanding on top of everything else…

He'd lied. She needed to remember that.

"I realize I have to do what's right for Kolby." She sagged onto the striped sofa, her legs folding from an emotional and exhausting night. "It scares the hell out of me how close a random teenager already got to my child, and we're only a couple of hours into this mess. It makes me ill to think about what someone with resources could do."

"My brothers and I have attorneys. They'll look into pressing charges against the teen." He sat beside her with a casual familiarity of lovers.

Remember the fight. Not the bath salts. She inched toward the armrest. "Let me know what the attorneys' fees are, please."

"They're on retainer. Those lawyers also help us communicate with each other. My attorney will know we're going to see my father if you're worried about making sure someone is aware of your plans."

Someone under his employ, all of this bought with Tony's money that she'd rejected a few short days ago. And she couldn't think of any other way. "You trust this man, your lawyer?"

"I have to." The surety in his voice left little room for doubt. "There are some transactions that can't be avoided no matter how much we want to sever ties with the past."

A darker note in his voice niggled at her. "Are you talking about yourself now?"

He shrugged, broad shoulders rippling the fabric of his fine suit.

Nuh-uh. She wasn't giving up that easily. She'd trusted so much of her life to this man, only to find he'd misled her.

Now she needed something tangible, something honest from him to hold on to. Something to let her know if that honor and strength she'd perceived in him was real. "You said you didn't want to break off our relationship. If that's true, this would be a really good time to open up a little."

Angling toward her, Tony's knee pressed against hers, his eyes heating to molten dark. "Are you saying we're good again?"

"I'm saying…" She cleared her throat that had suddenly gone cottony dry. "Maybe I could see my way clear to forgiving you if I knew more about you."

He straightened, his eyes sharp. "What do you want to know?"

"Why Galveston?"

"Do you surf?"

What the hell? She watched the walls come up in his eyes. She could almost feel him distancing himself from her. "Tony, I'm not sure how sharing a *Surf's Up* moment is going to make things all better here."

"But have you ever been surfing?" He gestured, his hands riding imaginary waves. "The Atlantic doesn't offer as wild a ride as the Pacific, but it gets the job done, especially in Spain. Something to do with the atmospheric pressure coming down from the UK. I still remember the swells tubing." He curled his fingers around into the cresting circle of a wave.

"You're a *surfer?*" She tried to merge the image of the sleek business shark with the vision of him carefree on a board. And instead an image emerged of his abandon when making love. Her breasts tingled and tightened, awash in the sensation of sea spray and Tony all over her skin.

"I've always been fascinated with waves."

"Even when you were in San Rinaldo." The picture of him began to make more sense. "It's an island country, right?"

She'd always thought the nautical art on his walls was tied into his shipping empire. Now she realized the affinity for such pieces came from living on an island. So much about him made sense.

His surfing hand soared to rest on the gold-flecked globe beside the sofa. Was it her imagination or was the gloss dimmer over the coast of Spain? As if he'd rubbed his finger along that area more often, taking away the sheen over time.

He spun the globe. "I thought you didn't know much about the Medinas."

"I researched you on Google on my phone while we were driving over." Concrete info had been sparse compared to all the crazy gossip floating about, but there were some basics. Three sons. A monarch father. A mother who'd been killed as they were escaping. Her heart squeezed thinking of him losing a parent so young, not much older than Kolby.

She pulled a faltering smile. "There weren't any surfer pictures among the few images that popped up."

Only a couple of grainy formal family portraits of three young boys with their parents, everyone happy. Some earlier photos of King Enrique looking infinitely regal.

"We scrubbed most pictures after we escaped and regrouped." His lighthearted smile contrasted with the darker hue deepening his eyes. "The internet wasn't active in those days."

The extent of his rebuilding shook her to her shoes. She'd thought she had it rough leaving Louisiana after her husband's arrest and death. How tragic to have your past wiped away. The enormity of what had happened to his family, of how he'd lived since then, threatened to overwhelm her.

How could she not ache over all he'd been through? "I saw that your mother died when I read up on your past. I'm so sorry."

He waved away her sympathy. "When we got to… where my father lives now, things were isolated. But at least we still had the ocean. Out on the waves, I could forget about everything else."

Plowing a hand through his hair, he stared just past her, obviously locked in some deep memories. She sensed she was close, so close to the something she needed to reassure her that placing herself and her son in his care would be wise, even if there weren't gossip seekers sifting through her trash.

She rested her hand on his arm. "What are you thinking?"

"I thought you might like to learn next spring. Unless you're already a pro."

"Not hardly." Spring was a long way off, a huge commitment she wasn't anywhere near ready to make to anyone. The thought of climbing on a wave made her stomach knot almost as much as being together that long. "Thanks for the offer, but I'll pass."

"Scared?" He skimmed his knuckles over her collarbone, and just that fast the sea-spray feel tingled through her again.

"Hell, yes. Scared of getting hurt."

His hand stilled just above her thumping heart. Want crackled in the air. Hers? Or his? She wasn't sure. Probably equal measures from both of them. That had never been in question. And too easily he could draw her in again. Learning more about him wasn't wise after all, not tonight.

She pulled away, her arms jerky, her whole body out of whack. She needed Tony's lightness now. Forget about serious peeks into each other's vulnerable pasts. "No surfing for me. Ever try taking care of a toddler with a broken leg?"

"When did you break your leg?" His eyes narrowed. "Did he hurt you? Your husband?"

How had Tony made that leap so quickly?

"Nolan was a crook and a jerk, but he never raised a hand to me." She shivered, not liking the new direction their conversation had taken at all. This was supposed to teach her more about him. Not the other way around. "Do we have to drag more baggage into this?"

"If it's true."

"I told you. He didn't abuse me." Not physically. "Having a criminal for a husband is no picnic. Knowing I missed the signs… Wondering if I let myself be blind to it because I enjoyed the lifestyle… I don't even know where to start in answering those questions for myself."

She slumped, suddenly exhausted, any residual adrenaline fizzling out. Her head fell back.

"Knowing you as I do, I find it difficult to believe you would ever choose the easy path." Tony thumbed just below her eyes where undoubtedly dark circles were all but tattooed on her face. "It's been a long day. You should get some rest. If you want, I'll tuck you in," he said with a playful wink.

She found the old Tony much easier to deal with than the new. "You're teasing, of course."

"Maybe…" And just that fast the light in his eyes flamed hotter, intense. "Shanny, I would hold you all night if you would let me. I would make sure no one dared threaten you or your son again."

And she wanted to let him do just that. But she'd allowed herself to depend on a man before… "If you hold me, we both know I won't get any rest, and while I'll have pleasure tonight, I'll be sorry tomorrow. Don't you think we have enough wrong between us right now without adding another regret to the mix?"

"Okay…." Tony gave her shoulder a final squeeze and stood. "I'll back off."

Shannon pushed to her feet alongside him, her hands fisted at her sides to keep from reaching for him. "I'm still mad over being kept in the dark, but I appreciate all the damage control."

"I owe you that much and more." He kissed her lightly on the lips without touching her anywhere else, lingering long enough to remind her of the reasons they clicked. Her breath hitched and it was all she could do not to haul him in closer for a firmer, deeper connection.

Pulling back, he started toward the door.

"Tony?" Was that husky voice really hers?

He glanced over his shoulder. So easily she could take the physical comfort waiting only a few feet away in his arms. But she had to keep her head clear. She had to hold strong to carve out an independent life for her and her son and that meant drawing clear boundaries.

"Just because I might be able to forgive you doesn't mean you're welcome in my bed again."

Chapter 4

She wasn't in her own bed.

Shannon wrestled with the tenacious grip of her shadowy nightmare, tough as hell to do when she couldn't figure out where she was. The ticking grandfather clock, the feel of the silky blanket around her, none of it was familiar. And then a hint of sandalwood scent teased her nose a second before...

"Hey." Tony's voice rumbled through the dark. "It's okay. I'm here."

Her heart jumped. She bolted upright, the cashmere afghan twisting around her legs and waist. Blinking fast, she struggled to orient herself to the surroundings so different from her apartment, but the world blurred in front of her from the dark and her own crummy eyesight. Shannon pressed her hands to the cushiony softness of a sofa and everything came rushing back. She was at Tony's, in the sitting room outside where Kolby slept.

"It's okay," Tony continued to chant, squeezing her shoulder in his broad hand as he crouched beside the couch.

Swinging her feet to the ground, she gathered the haunting remnants of her nightmare. Shadows smoked through her mind, blending into a darker mass of memories from the night Nolan died, except Tony's face superimposed itself over that of her dead husband.

Nausea burned her throat. She swallowed back the bite of bile and the horror of her dream. "Sorry, if I woke you." Oh, God, her son. "Is Kolby all right?"

"Sleeping soundly."

"Thank goodness. I wouldn't want to frighten him." She took in Tony's mussed hair and hastily hauled on jeans. The top button was open and his chest was bare. Gulp. "I'm sorry for disturbing you."

"I wasn't asleep." He passed her glasses to her.

As she slid them on, his tattoo came into focus, a nautical compass on his arm. Looking closer she realized his hair was wet. She didn't want to think about him in the shower, a tiled spa cubicle they'd shared more than once. "It's been a tough night all around."

"Want to talk about what woke you up?"

"Not really." Not ever. To anyone. "I think my fear for Kolby ran wild in my sleep. Dreams are supposed to help work out problems, but sometimes, it seems they only make everything scarier."

"Ah, damn, Shanny, I'm sorry for this whole mess." He sat on the sofa and slid an arm around her shoulders.

She stiffened, then decided to hell with it all and leaned back against the hard wall of chest. With the nightmare so fresh in her mind, she couldn't scavenge the will to pull away. His arms banded around her in an instant and her head tucked under his chin. Somehow it was easier to accept this comfort when she didn't have to look in his eyes. She'd been alone with her bad dreams for so long. Was it wrong to take just a second's comfort from his arms roped so thick with muscles nothing could break through to her? She would be strong again in a minute.

The grandfather clock ticked away minutes as she stared at his hands linked over her stomach—at the lighter band of skin where his watch usually rested. "Thanks for coming in to check on us, especially so late."

"It can be disconcerting waking in an unfamiliar place alone." His voice vibrated against her back, only her thin nightshirt between them and his bare chest.

Another whiff of his freshly showered scent teased her nose with memories of steam-slicked bodies.

"I've been here at least a dozen times, but never in this room. It's a big house." They'd met five months ago, started dating two months later…had starting sleeping together four weeks ago. "Strange to think we've shared the shower, but I still haven't seen all of your home."

"We tended to get distracted once our feet hit the steps," he said drily.

True enough. They'd stayed downstairs on early dinner dates here, but once they'd ventured upstairs…they'd always headed straight for his suite.

"That first time together—" Shannon remembered was after an opera when her senses had been on overload and her hormones on hyperdrive from holding back "—I was scared to death."

The admission tumbled out before she could think,

but somehow it seemed easier to share such vulnerabilities in the dark.

His muscles flexed against her, the bristle of hair on his arms teasing goose bumps along her skin. "The last thing I ever want to do is frighten you."

"It wasn't your fault. That night was a big leap of faith for me." The need to make him understand pushed past walls she'd built around herself. "Being with you then, it was my first time since Nolan."

He went completely still, not even breathing for four ticks of the clock before she felt his neck move with a swallow against her temple. "No one?"

"No one." Not only had Tony been her sole lover since Nolan, he'd been her second lover ever.

Her track record for picking men with secrets sucked.

His gusty sigh ruffled her hair. "I wish you would have told me."

"What would that have changed?"

"I would have been more…careful."

The frenzy of their first time stormed her mind with a barrage of images…their clothes fluttering to carpet the stairs on their way up. By the top of the steps they were naked, moonlight bathing his olive skin and casting shadows along the cut of muscles. Kissing against the wall soon had her legs wrapped around his waist and he was inside her. That one thrust had unfurled the tension into shimmering sensations and before the orgasm finished tingling all the way to the roots of her hair, he'd carried her to his room, her legs still around him. Again, she'd found release in bed with him, then a languid, leisurely completion while showering together.

Just remembering, an ache started low, throbbing between her legs. "You were great that night, and you know it." She swatted his hand lightly. "Now wipe the arrogant grin off your face."

"You can't see me." His voice sounded somber enough.

"Am I right, though?"

"Look at me and see."

She turned around and dared to peer up at him for the first time since he'd settled on the couch behind her. Her intense memories of that evening found an echo in his serious eyes far more moving than any smile.

Right now, it was hard to remember they weren't a couple anymore. "Telling you then would have made the event too serious."

Too important.

His offer to "help" her financially still loomed unresolved between them, stinging her even more than last weekend after the enormous secret he'd kept from her. Why couldn't they be two ordinary people who met at the park outside her apartment complex? What would it have been like to get to know Tony on neutral, normal ground? Would she have been able to see past the pain of her marriage?

She would never know.

"Shannon." His voice came out hoarse and hungry. "Are you okay to go back to sleep now? Because I need to leave."

His words splashed a chill over her heated thoughts. "Of course, you must have a lot to take care of with your family."

"You misunderstand. I *need* to leave, because you're killing me here with how much I've hurt you. And as if that wasn't enough to bring me to my knees, every time you move your head, the feel of your hair against my chest just about sends me over the edge." His eyes burned with a coal-hot determination. "I'll be damned before I do anything to break your trust again."

Before she could unscramble her thoughts, he slid his arms from her and ducked out the door as silently as he'd arrived. Colder than ever without the heat of Tony all around her, she hugged the blanket closer.

No worries about any more nightmares, because she was more than certain she wouldn't be able to go back to sleep.

By morning, Tony hadn't bothered turning down the covers on his bed. After leaving Shannon's room, he'd spent most of the night conferring with his lawyer and a security firm. Working himself into the ground to distract himself from how much he hurt from wanting her.

With a little luck and maneuvering, he could extend his week with her into two weeks. But bottom line, he *would* ensure her safety.

At five, he'd caught a catnap on the library sofa, jolting awake when Vernon called him from the front gate. He'd buzzed the retired sea captain through and rounded up breakfast.

His old friend deserved some answers.

Choosing a less formal dining area outside, he sat at the oval table on the veranda shaded by a lemon tree, Vernon beside him with a plate full of churros. Tony thumbed the edge of the hand-painted stoneware plate—a set he'd picked up from a local craftsman to support the dying art of the region.

Today of all days, he didn't want to think overlong on why he still ate his same childhood breakfast—deep-fried strips of potato dough. His mother had always poured a thick rich espresso for herself and mugs of hot chocolate for her three sons, an informal ritual in their centuries-old castle that he now knew was anything but ordinary.

Vernon eyed him over the rim of his coffee cup. "So it's all true, what they're saying in the papers and on the internet?"

Absurd headlines scrolled through his memory, alongside reports that had been right on the money. "My brother's not a Tibetan monk, but the general gist of that first report from the Global Intruder is correct."

"You're a prince." He scrubbed a hand over his dropped jaw. "Well, hot damn. Always knew there was something special about you, boy."

He preferred to think anything "special" about him came from hard work rather than a genetic lottery win. "I hope you understand it wasn't my place to share the details with you."

"You have brothers and a father." He stirred a hefty dollop of milk into his coffee, clinking the spoon against the edges of the stoneware mug. "I get that you need to consider their privacy, as well."

"Thanks, I appreciate that."

He wished Shannon could see as much. He'd hoped bringing her here would remind her of all that had been good between them. Instead those memories had only come back to bite him on the ass when she'd told him that he was her first since her husband died. The revelation still sucker punched the air from his gut.

Where did they go from there? Hell if he knew, but at least he had more time to find out. Soon enough he would have her in his private jet that waited fueled and ready a mile away.

The older man set down his mug. "I respect that you gotta be your own man."

"Thank you again." He'd expected Vernon to be angry over the secrecy, had even been concerned over losing his friendship.

Vernon's respect meant a lot to him, as well as his advice. From day one when Tony had turned in his sparse job application, Vernon had treated him like a son, showing him the ropes. They had a lot of history. And just like fourteen years ago, he offered unconditional acceptance now.

His mentor leaned forward on one elbow. "What does your family have to say about all of this?"

"I've only spoken with my middle brother." He pinched off a piece of a churro drizzled with warm honey. Popping it into his mouth, he chewed and tried not think of how much of his past stayed imprinted on him.

"According to the papers, that would be Duarte. Right?" When Tony nodded, Vernon continued, "Any idea how the story broke after so many years?"

And wasn't that the million-dollar question? He, his brothers and their lawyers were no closer to the answer on that one today than they'd been last night. "Duarte doesn't have any answers yet, other than some photojournalist caught him in a snapshot and managed to track down details. Which is damn strange. None of us look the same since we left San Rinaldo as kids."

"And there are no other pictures of you in the interim?"

"Only a few stray shots after I became Tony. Carlos's face has shown up in a couple of professional magazines." But the image was so posed and sterile, Tony wasn't sure he would recognize his own sibling on the street. For the best.

His father always insisted photos would provide dangerous links, as if he'd been preparing them from the beginning to split up. Or preparing them for his death.

Not the normal way for a kid to live, but they weren't a regular family. He'd grown accustomed to it eventually…until it almost seemed normal. Until he was faced with a regular person's life, like Shannon's treasured photos of her son.

He broke off another inch of a churro. His hand slowed halfway to his mouth as he got that feeling of "being watched." He checked right fast—

Kolby stood in the open doorway, blanket trailing from his fist.

Uh, okay. So now what? He'd only met the child a few times before last night and none had gone particularly well. Tony had chalked it up to Kolby being shy around strangers or clingy. Judging by the thrust of his little jaw and frown now, there was no mistaking it. The boy didn't like him.

That needed to change. "Hey, kiddo. Where's your mom?"

Kolby didn't budge. "Still sleepin'."

Breaking the ice, Vernon tugged out a chair. "Wanna have a seat and join us?"

Never taking his eyes off Tony, Kolby padded across the tile patio and scrambled up to sit on his knees. Silently, he simply blinked and stared with wide blue-gray eyes just like Shannon's, his blond hair spiking every which way.

Vernon wiped his mouth, tossed his linen napkin on

the plate and stood. "Thanks for the chow. I need to check on business. No need to see me out."

As his old friend deserted ship, unease crawled around inside Tony's gut. His experience with children was nonexistent, even when he'd been a kid himself. He and his brothers had been tutored on the island. They'd been each other's only playmates.

The island fortress had been staffed with security guards, not the mall cop sort, but more like a small deployed military unit. Cleaning staff, tutors, the chef and groundskeepers were all from San Rinaldo, older supporters of his father who'd lost their families in the coup. They shared a firm bond of loyalty, and a deep-seated need for a safe haven.

Working on the shrimp boat had felt like a vacation, with the wide open spaces and no boundaries. Most of all he enjoyed the people who didn't wear the imprint of painful loss in their eyes.

But still, there weren't any three-year-olds on the shrimp boat.

What did kids need? "Are you hungry?"

"Some of that." Kolby pointed to Tony's plate of churros. "With peanut bubber."

Grateful for action instead of awkward silence, he shoved to his feet. "Peanut butter it is then. Follow me."

Once he figured out where to look. He'd quit cooking for himself about ten years ago and the few years he had, he wasn't whipping up kiddie cuisine.

About seven minutes later he unearthed a jar from the cavernous pantry and smeared a messy trail down a churro before chunking the spoon in the sink.

Kolby pointed to the lid on the granite countertop. "We don't waste."

"Right." Tony twisted the lid on tight. Thinking of Shannon pinching pennies on peanut butter, for crying out loud, he wanted to buy them a lifetime supply.

As he started to pass the plate to Kolby, a stray thought broadsided him. Hell. Was the kid allergic to peanuts? He hadn't even thought to ask. Kolby reached. Tony swallowed another curse.

"Let's wait for your mom."

"Wait for me why?" Her softly melodic voice drifted over his shoulder from across the kitchen.

He glanced back and his heart kicked against his ribs. They'd slept together over the past month but never actually *slept*. And never through the night.

Damn, she made jeans look good, the washed pale fabric clinging to her long legs. Her hair flowed over her shoulders and down her back, still damp from a shower. He remembered well the silky glide of it through his fingers…and so not something he should be thinking about with her son watching.

Tony held up the plate of churros. "Can he eat peanut butter?"

"He's never tried it that way before, but I'm sure he'll like it." She slipped the dish from his grip. "Although, I'm not so certain that breakable stoneware is the best choice for a three-year-old."

"Hey, kiddo, is the plate all right with you?"

"'S okay." Kolby inched toward his mother and wrapped an arm around her leg. "Like trains better. And milk."

"The milk I can handle." He yanked open the door on the stainless-steel refrigerator and reached for the jug. "I'll make sure you have the best train plates next time."

"Wait!" Shannon stopped him, digging into an oversized bag on her shoulder and pulling out a cup with a vented lid. "Here's his sippy cup. It's not Waterford, but it works better."

Smoothly, she filled it halfway and scooped up the plate. Kolby held on to his mother all the way back to the patio.

For the first time he wondered why he hadn't spent more time with the boy. Shannon hadn't offered and he hadn't pushed. She sat and pulled Kolby onto her lap, plate in front just out of his reach. The whole family breakfast scenario wrapped around him, threatening his focus. He skimmed a finger along his shirt collar— Hell. He stopped short, realizing he wasn't wearing a tie.

She pinched off a bite and passed it to her son. "I had a lot of time to think last night."

So she hadn't slept any better than he had. "What did you think about after I left?"

Her eyes shot up to his, pink flushing her face. "Going to see your father, of course."

"Of course." He nodded, smiling.

"Of course," Kolby echoed.

As the boy licked the peanut butter off the churro, she traced the intricate pattern painted along the edge of the plate, frowning. "I would like to tell Vernon and your lawyer about our plans for the week and then I'll come with you."

He'd won. She would be safe, and he would have more time to sway her. Except it really chapped his hide that she trusted him so little she felt the need to log her travel itinerary. "Not meaning to shoot myself in the foot here, but why Vernon instead of my lawyer? Vernon is my friend. I financed his business."

"You own the restaurant?" Her slim fingers gravitated back to the china. "*You* are responsible for my paychecks? I thought the Grille belonged to Vernon."

"You didn't know?" Probably a good thing or he might well have never talked her into that first date. "Vernon was a friend when I needed one. I'm glad I could return the favor. He's more than delivered on the investment."

"He gave you a job when your past must have seemed spotty," she said intuitively.

"How did you figure that out?"

"He did the same for me when I needed a chance." A bittersweet smile flickered across her face much like how the sunlight filtered through the lemon tree to play in her hair. "That's the reason I trust him."

"You've worked hard for every penny you make there."

"I know, but I appreciate that he was fair. No handouts, and yet he never took advantage of how much I needed that job. He's a good man. Now back to our travel plans." She rested her chin on her son's head. "Just to be sure, I'll also be informing my in-laws—Kolby's grandparents."

His brows slammed upward. She rarely mentioned them, only that they'd cut her out of their lives after their son died. The fact that she would keep such cold fish informed about their grandson spoke of an innate sense of fair play he wasn't sure he would have given in her position.

"Apparently you trust just about everyone more than me."

She dabbed at the corners of her mouth, drawing his attention to the plump curve of her bottom lip. "Apparently so."

Not a ringing endorsement of her faith in him, but he would take the victory and focus forward. Because before sundown, he would return to his father's island home off the coast of Florida.

She was actually in a private plane over...
Somewhere.

Since the window shades were closed, she had no idea whether they were close to land or water. So where were they? Once airborne, she'd felt the plane turn, but quickly lost any sense of whether they were going north or south, east or west. Although north was unlikely given he'd told her to pack for warm weather.

How far had they traveled? Tough to tell since she'd napped and she had no idea how fast this aircraft could travel. She'd been swept away into a world beyond anything she'd experienced, from the discreet impeccable service to the sleeping quarters already made up for her and Kolby on arrival. Questions about her food preferences had resulted in a five-star meal.

Shannon pressed a hand to her jittery stomach. God, she hoped she'd made the right decision. At least her son seemed oblivious to all the turmoil around them.

The cabin steward guided Kolby toward the galley kitchen with the promise of a snack and a video. As they walked toward the back, he dragged his tiny fingers along the white leather seats. At least his hands were clean.

But she would have to make a point of keeping sharp objects out of Kolby's reach. She shuddered at the image of a silver taped *X* on the luxury upholstery.

Her eyes shifted to the man filling the deep seat across from her couch. Wearing gray pants and a white shirt with the sleeves rolled up, he focused intently on the laptop screen in front of him, seemingly oblivious to anyone around him.

She hated the claustrophobic feeling of needing his help, not to mention all the money hiding out entailed. Dependence made her vulnerable, something she'd sworn would never happen again. Yet here she was, entrusting her whole life to a man, a man who'd lied to her.

However, with her child's well-being at stake, she couldn't afford to say no.

More information would help settle the apprehension plucking at her nerves like heart strings. Any information, since apparently everything she knew about him outside of the bedroom was false. She hadn't even known he owned the restaurant where she worked.

Ugh.

Of course it seemed silly to worry about being branded as the type who sleeps with the boss. Having an affair with a drop-dead sexy prince trumped any other gossip. "How long has it been since you saw your father?"

Tony looked up from his laptop slowly. "I left the island when I was eighteen."

"Island?" Her hand grazed the covered window as she envisioned water below. "I thought you left San Rinaldo as a young boy."

"We did." He closed the computer and pivoted the chair toward her, stretching his legs until his feet stopped intimately close to hers. "I was five at the time. We relocated to another island about a month after we escaped."

She scrunched her toes in her gym shoes. Her scuffed canvas was worlds away from his polished loafers and a private plane. And regardless of how hot he looked, she wouldn't be seduced by the trappings of his wealth.

Forcing her mind back on his words rather than his body, she drew her legs away from him. Was the island on the east coast or west coast? Provided Enrique Medina's compound was even near the U.S. "Your father chose an island so you and your brothers would feel at home in your new place?"

He looked at her over the white tulips centered on the cherry coffee table. "My father chose an island because it was easier to secure."

Gulp. "Oh. Right."

That took the temperature down more than a few degrees. She picked at the piping on the sofa.

Music drifted from the back of the plane, the sound of a new cartoon starting. She glanced down the walkway. Kolby was buckled into a seat, munching on some kind of crackers while watching the movie, mesmerized. Most likely by the whopping big flat screen.

Back to her questions. "How much of you is real and what's a part of the new identity?"

"My age and birthday are real." He tucked the laptop into an oversized briefcase monogrammed with the Castillo Shipping Corporation logo. "Even my name is technically correct, as I told you before. Castillo comes from my mother's family tree. I took it as my own when I turned eighteen."

Resting her elbow on the back of the sofa, she propped her head in her palm, trying her darnedest to act as casual as he appeared. "What does your father think of all you've accomplished since leaving?"

"I wouldn't know." He reclined, folding his hands

over his stomach, drawing her eyes and memories to his rock-hard abs.

Her toes curled again until they cracked inside her canvas sneakers. "What does he think of us coming now?"

"You'll have to ask him." His jaw flexed.

"Did you even tell him about the extra guests?" She resisted the urge to smooth the strain away from the bunched tendons in his neck. How odd to think of comforting him when she still had so many reservations about the trip herself.

"I told his lawyer to inform him. His staff will make preparations. Kolby will have whatever he needs."

Who was this coolly factual man a hand stretch away? She almost wondered if she'd imagined carefree Tony... except he'd told her that he liked to surf. She clung to that everyday image and dug deeper.

"Sounds like you and your father aren't close. Or is that just the way royalty communicates?" If so, how sad was that?

He didn't answer, the drone of the engines mingling with the cartoon and the rush of recycled air through the vents. While she wanted her son to grow up independent with a life of his own, she also planned to forge a bond closer than cold communications exchanged between lawyers and assistants.

"Tony?"

His eyes shifted to the shuttered window beside her head. "I didn't want to live on a secluded island any longer. So I left. He disagreed. We haven't resolved the issue."

Such simple words for so deep a breach where attorneys handled *all* communiqués between them. The lack of communication went beyond distant to estrangement. This wasn't a family just fractured by location. Something far deeper was wrong.

Tucking back into his line of sight, she pressed ahead. This man had already left such a deep imprint on her life, she knew she wouldn't forget him. "What have your lawyers told your father about Kolby and me? What did they tell your dad about our relationship?"

"Relationship?" He pinned her with his dark eyes, the intensity of his look—of him—reaching past the tulips as tangibly as if he'd taken that broad hand and caressed her. He was such a big man with the gentlest of touches.

And he was thorough. God, how he was thorough.

Her heart pounded in her ear like a tympani solo, hollow and so loud it drowned out the engines.

"Tony?" she asked. She *wanted*.

"I let him know that we're a couple. And that you're a widow with a son."

It was one thing to carry on a secret affair with him. Another to openly acknowledge to people—to family— that they were a couple.

She pressed hard against her collarbone, her pulse pushing a syncopated beat against her fingertips. "Why not tell your father the truth? That we broke up but the press won't believe it."

"Who says it's not the truth? We slept together just a week ago. Seems like less than that to me, because I swear I can still catch a whiff of your scent on my skin." He leaned closer and thumbed her wrist.

Her fingers curled as the heat of his touch spread farther. "But about last weekend—"

"Shanny." He tapped her lips once, then traced her rounded sigh. "We may have argued, but when I'm in the room with you, my hand still gravitates to your back by instinct."

Her heart drummed faster until she couldn't have responded even if she tried. But she wasn't trying, too caught up in the sound of him, the desire in his every word.

"The pull between us is that strong, Shannon, whether I'm deep inside you or just listening to you across a room." A half smile kicked a dimple into one cheek. "Why do you think I call you late at night?"

She glanced quickly at the video area checking to make sure her son and the steward where still engrossed in Disney, then she whispered, "Because you'd finished work?"

"You know better. Just the sound of you on the other end of the line sends me rock—"

"Stop, please." She pressed her fingers to his mouth. "You're only hurting us both."

Nipping her fingers lightly first, he linked his hand with hers. "We have problems, without a doubt, and you have reason to be mad. But the drive to be together hasn't eased one bit. Can you deny it? Because if you can, then that is it. I'll keep my distance."

Opening her mouth, she formed the words that would slice that last tie to the relationship they'd forged over the past few months. She fully intended to tell him they were through.... But nothing came out. Not one word.

Slowly, he pulled back. "We're almost there."

Almost where? Back together? Her mind scrambled to keep up with him, damn tough when he kept jumbling her brain. She was a flipping magna cum laude graduate. She resented feeling like a bimbo at the mercy of her libido. But how her libido sang arias around this man…

He shoved to his feet and walked away. Just like that, he cut their conversation short as if they both hadn't been sinking deep into a sensual awareness that had brought them both such intense pleasure in the past. She tracked the lines of his broad shoulders, down to his trim waist and taut butt showcased so perfectly in tailored pants.

Her fingers dug deep into the sofa with restraint. He stopped by Kolby and slid up the window covering.

"Take a look, kiddo, we're almost there." Tony pointed at the clear glass toward the pristine sky.

Ah. *There.* As in they'd arrived there, at his father's island. She'd been so caught up in the sensual draw of undiluted Tony that she'd temporarily forgotten about flying away to a mystery location.

Scrambling down the sofa, she straightened her glasses and stared out the window, hungry for a peek at their future—temporary—home. And yes, curious as hell about the place where Tony had grown up. Sure enough, an island stretched in the distance, nestled in miles and miles of sparkling ocean. Palm trees spiked from the lush landscape. A dozen or so small outbuildings dotted a semicircle around a larger structure.

The white mansion faced the ocean in a *U* shape, constructed around a large courtyard with a pool. She barely registered Kolby's "oohs" and "aahs" since she was pretty much overwhelmed by the sight herself.

Details were spotty but she would get an up-close view soon enough of the place Tony had called home for most of his youth. Even from a distance she couldn't miss the grand scale of the sprawling estate, the unmistakable sort that housed royalty.

The plane banked, lining up with a thin islet alongside the larger island. A single strip of concrete marked the private runway. As they neared, a ferryboat came into focus. To ride from the airport to the main island? They sure were serious about security.

The intercom system crackled a second before the steward announced, "We're about to begin our descent to our destination. Please return to your seats and secure your lap belts. Thank you, and we hope you had a pleasant flight."

Tony pulled away from the window and smiled at her again. Except now, the grin didn't reach his eyes. Her stomach fluttered, but this time with apprehension rather than arousal.

Would the island hold the answers she needed to put Tony in her past? Or would it only break her heart all over again?

Chapter 5

Daylight was fading fast and a silence fourteen years old between him and his father was about to be broken.

Feet braced on the ferry deck, Tony stared out over the rail at the island where he'd spent the bulk of his childhood and teenage years. He hated not being in command of the boat almost as much as he hated returning to this place. Only concern for Shannon and her son could have drawn him back where the memories grew and spread as tenaciously as algae webbing around coral.

Just ahead, a black skimmer glided across the water, dipping its bill into the surface. With each lap of the waves against the hull, Tony closed off insidious emotions before they could take root inside him and focused on the shore.

An osprey circled over its nest. Palm trees lined the beach with only a small white stucco building and a two-lane road. Until you looked closer and saw the guard tower.

When he'd come to this island off the coast of St. Augustine at five, there were times he'd believed they were home…that his father had moved them to another part of San Rinaldo. In the darkest nights, he'd woken in a cold sweat, certain the soldiers in camouflage were going to cut through the bars on his windows and take him. Other nights he imagined they'd already taken him and the bars locked him in prison.

On the worst of nights, he'd thought his mother was still alive, only to see her die all over again.

Shannon's hand slid over his elbow, her touch tentative, her eyes wary. "How long did I sleep on the plane?"

"A while." He smiled to reassure her, but the feeling didn't come from his gut. Damn, but he wished the past week had never happened. He would pull her soft body against him and forget about everything else.

Wind streaked her hair across her face. "Oh, right. If you tell me, I might get a sense of how far away we are from Galveston. I might guess where we are. Being cut off from the world is still freaking me out just a little."

"I understand, and I'll to do my best to set things right as soon as possible." He wanted nothing more than to get off this island and return to the life he'd built, the life he chose. The only thing that made coming back here palatable was having Shannon by his side. And that rocked the deck under his feet, realizing she held so much influence over his life.

"Although, I have to admit," she conceded as she tucked her son closer, "this place is so much more than I expected."

Her gaze seemed to track the herons picking their

way along the shore, sea oats bowing at every gust. Her grayish-blue eyes glinted with the first hints of excitement. She must not have noticed the security cameras tucked in trees and the guard on the dock, a gun strapped within easy reach.

Tony gripped the rail tighter. "There's no way to prepare a person."

Kolby squealed, pitching forward in his mother's arms.

"Whoa…" Tony snagged the kid by the back of his striped overalls. "Steady there."

A hand pressed to her chest, Shannon struggled for breath. "Thank God you moved so fast. I can't believe I looked away. There's just so much to see, so many distractions."

The little guy scowled at Tony. "Down."

"Buddy," Tony stated as he shook his head, "sometime you're going to have to like me."

"Name's not buddy," Kolby insisted, bottom lip out.

"You're right. I'm just trying to make friends here." Because he intended to use this time to persuade Shannon breaking up had been a crappy idea. He wondered how much the child understood. Since he didn't know how else to approach him, he opted for straight up honesty. "I like your mom, so it's important that you like me."

Shannon's gasp teased his ear like a fresh trickle of wind off the water. As much as he wanted to turn toward her, he kept his attention on the boy.

Kolby clenched Tony's shirt. "Does you like *me?*"

"Uh, sure." The question caught him off guard. He hadn't thought about it other than knowing it was important to win the son over for Shannon's sake. "What do you like?"

"Not you." He popped his bottom lip back in. "Down, pwease."

Shannon caught her son as he leaned toward her. Confusion puckering her brow, her eyes held Tony's for a second before she pointed over the side. "Is that what you wanted to see, sweetie?"

A dolphin zipped alongside the ferry. The fin sliced through the water, then submerged again.

Clapping his tiny hands, Kolby chanted, "Yes, yes, yes."

Again, Shannon saw beauty. He saw something entirely different. The dolphins provided port security. His father had gotten the idea from his own military service, cutting-edge stuff back then. The island was a minikingdom and money wasn't an object. Except this kingdom had substantially fewer subjects.

Tony wondered again if the secluded surroundings growing up could have played into his lousy track record with relationships as an adult. There hadn't been any teenage dating rituals for practice. And after he left, he'd been careful with relationships, never letting anything get too complicated. Work and a full social life kept him happy.

But the child in front of him made things problematic in a way he hadn't foreseen.

For years he'd been pissed off at his father for the way they'd had to live. And here he was doing the same to Kolby. The kid was entertained for the moment, but that would end fast for sure.

Protectiveness for both the mother and son seared his veins. He wouldn't let anything from the Medina past mark their future. Even if that meant he had to re-claim the very identity he'd worked his entire adult-hood to shed.

The ferry slid against the dock. They'd arrived at the island.

And Prince Antonio Medina was back.

What was it like for Tony to come back after so long away? And it wasn't some happy homecoming, given the estrangement and distance in this family that com-municated through lawyers.

Shannon wanted to reach across the limousine to him, but Tony had emotionally checked out the moment the ferry docked. Of course he'd been Mr. Manners while leaving the ferry and stepping into the Mercedes limo.

Watch your step... Need help? However, the smiles grew darker by the minute.

Maybe it was her own gloomy thoughts tainting her perceptions. At least Kolby seemed unaffected by their moods, keeping his nose pressed to the window the whole winding way to the pristine mansion.

Who wouldn't stare at the trees and the wildlife and finally, the palatial residence? White stucco with a clay tiled roof, arches and opulence ten times over, the place was the size of some hotels or convention centers. Ex-cept no hotel she'd stayed in sported guards armed with machine guns.

What should have made her feel safer only served to remind her money and power didn't come without burdens. To think, Tony had grown up with little or no exposure to the real world. It was a miracle he'd turned out normal.

If you could call a billionaire prince with a penchant for surfing "normal."

The limousine slowed, easing past a towering marble fountain with a "welcome" pineapple on top—and wasn't that ironic in light of all those guards? Once the vehicle stopped, more uniformed security appeared from out of nowhere to open the limo. Some kind of servant— a butler perhaps—stood at the top of the stairs. While Tony had insisted he wanted nothing to do with his birthplace, he seemed completely at ease in this surreal world. For the first time, the truth really sunk in.

The stunningly handsome—stoically silent—man walking beside her had royal blood singing through his veins.

"Tony?" She touched his elbow.

"After you," he said, simply gesturing ahead to the double doors sweeping open.

Scooping Kolby onto her hip, she took comfort in his sturdy little body and forged ahead. Inside. *Whoa.*

The cavernous circular hall sported gold-gilded archways leading to open rooms. Two staircases stretched up either side, meeting in the middle. And, uh, stop the world, was that a Picasso on the wall?

Her canvas sneakers squeaked against marble floors as more arches ushered her deeper into the mansion. And while she vowed money didn't matter, she still wished she'd packed different shoes. Shannon straightened the straps on Kolby's favorite striped overalls, the ones he swore choo-choo drivers wore. She'd been so frazzled when she'd tossed clothes into a couple of overnight bags, picking things that would make him happy.

Just ahead, French doors opened on to a veranda that overlooked the ocean. Tony turned at the last minute, guiding her toward what appeared to be a library. Books filled three walls, interspersed with windows and a sliding brass ladder. Mosaic tiles swirled outward on the floor, the ceiling filled with frescos of globes and conquistadors. The smell of fresh citrus hung in the air, and not just because of the open windows. A tall potted orange tree nestled in one corner beneath a wide skylight.

An older man slept in a wingback by the dormant fireplace. Two large brown dogs—some kind of Ridgeback breed, perhaps?—lounged to his left and right.

Tony's father. A no-kidding king.

Either age or illness had taken a toll, dimming the family resemblance. But in spite of his nap, he wasn't going gently into that good night. No slippers and robe for this meeting. He wore a simple black suit with an ascot rather than a tie, his silver hair slicked back. Frailty and his pasty pallor made her want to comfort him.

Then his eyes snapped open. The sharp gleam in his coal dark eyes stopped her short.

Holy Sean Connery, the guy might be old but he hadn't lost his edge.

"Welcome home, *hijo prodigo.*" *Prodigal son.*

Enrique Medina spoke in English but his accent was still unmistakably Spanish. And perhaps a bit thick with emotion? Or was that just wishful thinking on her part for Tony's sake?

"Hello, Papa." Tony palmed her back between her shoulder blades. "This is Shannon and her son Kolby."

The aging monarch nodded in her direction. "Welcome, to you and to your son."

"Thank you for your hospitality and your help, sir." She didn't dare wade into the whole *Your Highness* versus *Your Majesty* waters. Simplicity seemed safest.

Toying with a pocket watch in his hand, Enrique continued, "If not for my family, you would not need my assistance."

Tony's fingers twitched against her back. "Hopefully we won't have to impose upon you for long. Shannon and her son only need a place to lay low until this blows over."

"It won't blow over," Enrique said simply.

Ouch. She winced.

Tony didn't. "Poor choice of words. Until things calm down."

"Of course." He nodded regally before shifting his attention her way. "I am glad to have you here, my dear. You brought Tony home, so you have already won favor with me." He smiled and for the first time, she saw the family resemblance clearly.

Kolby wriggled, peeking up from her neck. "Whatsa matter with you?"

"Shhh…Kolby." She pressed a quick silencing kiss to his forehead. "That's a rude question."

"It's an honest question. I do not mind the boy." The king shifted his attention to her son. "I have been ill. My legs are not strong enough to walk."

"I'm sorry." Kolby eyed the wheelchair folded up and tucked discreetly alongside the fireplace. "You musta been bery sick."

"Thank you. I have good doctors."

"You got germs?"

A smile tugged at the stern face. "No, child. You and your mother cannot catch my germs."

"That's good." He stuffed his tiny fists into his pockets. "Don't like washin' my hands."

Enrique laughed low before his hand fell to rest on one dog's head. "Do you like animals?"

"Yep." Kolby squirmed downward until Shannon had no choice but to release him before he pitched out of her arms. "Want a dog."

Such a simple, painfully normal wish and she couldn't afford to supply it. From the pet deposit required at her apartment complex to the vet bills… It was out of her budget. Guilt tweaked again over all she couldn't give her child.

Yet hadn't Tony been denied so much even with such wealth? He'd lost his home, his mother and gained a gilded prison. Whispers of sympathy for a motherless boy growing up isolated from the world softened her heart when she most needed to hold strong.

Enrique motioned Kolby closer. "You may pet my dog. Come closer and I will introduce you to Benito and Diablo. They are very well trained and will not hurt you."

Kolby didn't even hesitate. Any reservations her son felt about Tony certainly didn't extend to King Enrique—or his dogs. Diablo sniffed the tiny, extended hand.

A cleared throat startled Shannon from her thoughts. She glanced over her shoulder and found a young woman waiting in the archway. In her late twenties, wearing a Chanel suit, she obviously wasn't the housekeeper.

But she was stunning with her black hair sleeked back in a simple clasp. She wore strappy heels instead of sneakers. God, it felt silly to be envious of someone she didn't know, and honestly, she only coveted the pretty red shoes.

"Alys," the older man commanded, "enter. Come meet

my son and his guests. This is my assistant, Alys Reyes de la Cortez. She will show you to your quarters."

Shannon resisted the urge to jump to conclusions. It wasn't any of her business who Enrique Medina chose for his staff and she shouldn't judge a person by their appearance. The woman was probably a rocket scientist, and Shannon wouldn't trade one single sticky hug from her son for all the high-end clothes on the planet.

Not that she was jealous of the gorgeous female with immaculate clothes, who fit perfectly into Tony's world. After all, he hadn't spared more than a passing glance at the woman.

Still, she wished she'd packed a pair of pumps.

An hour later, Shannon closed her empty suitcases and rocked back on her bare heels in the doorway of her new quarters.

A suite?

More like a luxury condominium within the mansion. She sunk her toes into the Persian rug until her chipped pink polish disappeared in the apricot-and-gray pattern. She and Kolby had separate bedrooms off a sitting area with an eating space stocked more fully than most kitchens. The balcony was as large as some yards.

Had the fresh-cut flowers been placed in here just for her? She dipped her face into the crystal vase of lisianthus with blooms that resembled blue roses and softened the gray tones in the decor.

After Alys had walked them up the lengthy stairs to their suite, Kolby had run from room to room for fifteen minutes before winding down and falling asleep in an exhausted heap under the covers. He hadn't even noticed the toy box at the end of his sleigh bed yet, he'd been so curious about their new digs. Tony had given them space while she unpacked, leaving for his quarters with a simple goodbye and another of those smiles that didn't reach his eyes.

The quiet echoed around her, leaving her hyperaware of other sounds…a ticking grandfather clock in the hall…the crashing ocean outside… Trailing her fingers along the camelback sofa, she looked through the double doors, moonlight casting shadows along her balcony. Her feet drew her closer until the shadows took shape into the broad shoulders of a man leaning on the railing.

Tony? He felt like a safe haven in an upside-down day. But how had he gotten there without her noticing his arrival?

Their balconies must connect, which meant someone had planned for them to have access to each other's rooms. Had he been waiting for her? Anticipation hummed through her at the notion of having him all to herself.

Shannon unlocked and pushed open the doors to the patio filled with topiaries, ferns and flowering cacti. A swift ocean breeze rolled over her, lifting her hair and fluttering her shirt along her skin in whispery caresses. God, she was tired and emotional and so not in the right frame of mind to be anywhere near Tony. She should go to bed instead of staring at his sinfully sexy body just calling to her to rest her cheek on his back and wrap her arms around his waist. Her fingers fanned against her legs as she remembered the feel of him, so much more intense with his sandalwood scent riding the wind.

Need pooled warm and languid and low, diluting her already fading resistance.

His shoulders bunched under his starched white shirt

a second before he glanced over his shoulder, his eyes haunted. Then they cleared. "Is Kolby asleep?"

"Yes, and thank you for all the preparations. The toys, the food…the flowers."

"All a part of the Medina welcome package."

"Perhaps." But she'd noticed a few too many of their favorites for the choices to have been coincidental. She moved forward hesitantly, the tiles cool against the bottoms of her feet. "This is all…something else."

"Leaving San Rinaldo, we had to downsize." He gave her another of those dry smiles.

More sympathy slid over her frustration at his secrets. "Thank you for bringing us here. I know it wasn't easy for you."

"I'm the reason you have to hide out in the first place until we line up protection for you. Seems only fair I should do everything in my power to make this right."

Her husband had never tried to fix any of his mistakes, hadn't even apologized after his arrest in the face of irrefutable evidence. She couldn't help but appreciate the way Tony took responsibility. And he cared enough to smooth the way for her.

"What about you?" She joined him at the swirled iron railing. "You wouldn't have come here if it weren't for me. What do you hope to accomplish for yourself?"

"Don't worry about me." He leaned back on his elbows, white shirt stretching open at the collar to reveal the strong column of his neck. "I always look out for myself."

"Then what are you gaining?"

"More time with you, at least until the restraining order is in place." The heat of his eyes broadcast his intent just before he reached for her. "I've always been clear about how much I want to be with you, even on that first date when you wouldn't kiss me good-night."

"Is that why you chased me? Because I said no?"

"But you didn't keep saying no and still, here I am turned on as hell by the sound of your voice." He plucked her glasses off, set them aside and cradled her face in his palms. "The feel of your skin."

While he owned an empire with corporate offices that took up a bayside block, his skin still carried the calluses of the dockworker and sailor he'd been during his early adulthood. He was a man who certainly knew how to work with his hands. The rasp as he lightly caressed her cheekbones reminded her of the sweet abrasion when he explored farther.

He combed through along her scalp, strands slithering across his fingers. "The feel of your hair."

A moan slipped past her lips along with his name, "Tony…"

"Antonio," he reminded her. "I want to hear you say my name, know who's here with you."

And in this moment, in his eyes, he was that foreign prince, less accessible than her Tony, but no less exciting and infinitely as irresistible, so she whispered, "Antonio."

His touch was gentle, his mouth firm against hers. She parted her lips under his and invited in the familiar sweep, taste and pure sensation. Clutching his elbows, she swayed, her breasts tingling, pulling tight. Before she could think or stop herself, she brushed slightly from side to side, increasing the sweet pleasure of his hard chest teasing her. His hard thigh between her legs.

She stepped backward.

And tugged him with her.

Toward the open French doors leading into her bedroom, her body overriding her brain as it always seemed to do around Tony. She squeezed her legs together tighter against the firm pressure of his muscled thigh, so close, too close. She wanted, *needed* to feel him move inside her first.

Sinking her fingernails deeper, she ached to ask him to stay with her, to help her forget the worries waiting at home. "Antonio—"

"I know." He eased his mouth from hers, his chin scraping along her jaw as he nuzzled her hair and inhaled. "We need to stop."

Stop? She almost shrieked in frustration. "But I thought... I mean, you're here and usually when we let things go this far, we finish."

"You're ready to resume our affair?"

Affair. Not just one night, one satisfaction, but a relationship with implications and complications. Her brain raced to catch up after being put on idle while her body took over. God, what had she almost done? A few kisses along with a well-placed thigh, and she was ready to throw herself back in his bed.

Planting her hands on his chest, she stepped away. "I can't deny that I miss you and I want you, but I have no desire to be labeled a Medina mistress."

His eyebrows shot up toward his hairline. "Are you saying you want to get married?"

Chapter 6

"Married?" Shannon choked on the word, her eyes so wide with shock Tony was almost insulted. "No! No, definitely not."

Her instant and emphatic denial left zero room for doubt. She wasn't expecting a proposal. Good thing, since that hadn't crossed his mind. Until now.

Was he willing to go that far to protect her?

She turned away fast, her hands raised as she raced back into the sitting area. "Tony—Antonio—I can't talk to you, look at you, risk kissing you again. I need to go to bed. To sleep. Alone."

"Then what do you want from me?"

"To end this craziness. To stop thinking about you all the time."

All the time?

He homed in on her words, an obvious slip on her

part because while she'd been receptive and enthusiastic in bed, she'd given him precious little encouragement once they had their clothes back on again. Their fight over his simple offer of money still stung. Why did she have to reject his attempt to help?

She paced, restlessly lining up her shoes beside the sofa, scooping Kolby's tiny train from a table, lingering to rearrange the blue flowers. "You've said you feel the same. Who the hell wants to be consumed by this kind of ache all the time? It's damned inconvenient, especially when it can't lead anywhere. It's not like you were looking for marriage."

"That wasn't my intention when we started seeing each other." Yet somehow the thought had popped into his head out there on the patio. Sure, it had shocked the crap out of him at first. Still left him reeling. Although not so much that he was willing to reject the idea outright. "But since you've brought it up—"

Her hands shot up in front of her, between them. "Uh-uh, no sirree. You were the one to mention the *M* word."

"Fine, then. The marriage issue is out there, on the table for discussion. Let's talk it through."

She stopped cold. "This isn't some kind of business merger. We're talking about our lives here, and not just ours. I don't have the luxury of making another mistake. I already screwed up once before, big-time. My son's well-being depends on my decisions."

"And I'm a bad choice because?"

"Do not play with my feelings. Damn it, Tony." She jabbed him in the chest with one finger. "You know I'm attracted to you. If you keep this up, I'll probably cave and we'll have sex. We probably would have on the plane if the steward and my son hadn't been around. But

I would have been sorry the minute the orgasm chilled and is that really how you want it to be between us? To have me waking up regretting it every time?"

With images of the two of them joining the mile-high club fast-tracking from his brain to his groin, he seriously considered saying to hell with regrets. Let this insanity between them play out, wherever it took them.

Her bed was only a few steps away, offering a clear and tempting place to sink inside her. He would sweep away her clothes and the covers— His gaze hooked on the afghan draped along the end corner of the mattress.

Damn. Who had put that there? Could his father be deliberately jabbing him with reminders of their life as a family in hopes of drawing him back into the fold? Of course Enrique would, manipulative old cuss that he was.

That familiar silver blanket sucker punched him back to reality. He would recognize the one-of-a-kind afghan anywhere. His mother had knitted it for him just before she'd been killed, and he'd kept it with him like a shield during the whole hellish escape from San Rinaldo. Good God, he shouldn't have had to ask her why he was a bad choice. He knew the reason well.

Tony stumbled back, away from the memories and away from this woman who saw too much with her perceptive gray-blue eyes.

"You're right, Shannon. We're both too exhausted to make any more decisions today. Sleep well." His voice as raw as his memory-riddled gut, he left.

Dazed, Shannon stood in the middle of the sitting room wondering what the hell had just happened.

One second she'd been ready to climb back into Tony's arms and bed, the next they'd been talking about marriage. And didn't that still stun her numb with thoughts of how horribly things had ended with Nolan?

But only seconds after bringing up the marriage issue, Tony had emotionally checked out on her again. At least he'd prevented them from making a mistake. It was a mistake, right?

Eyeing her big—empty—four-poster bed, she suddenly wasn't one bit sleepy. Tony overwhelmed her as much as the wealth. She walked into her bedroom, studying the Picasso over her headboard, this one from the artist's rose period, a harlequin clown in oranges and pinks. She'd counted three works already by this artist alone, including some leggy elephant painting in Kolby's room.

She'd hidden the crayons and markers.

Laughing at the absurdity of it all, she fingered a folded cashmere afghan draped over the corner of the mattress. So whispery soft and strangely worn in the middle of this immaculately opulent decor. The pewter-colored yarn complemented the apricot and gray tones well enough, but she wondered where it had come from. She tugged it from the bed and shook it out.

The blanket rippled in front of her, a little larger than a lap quilt, not quite long enough for a single bed. Turning in a circle she wrapped the filmy cover around her and padded back out to the balcony. She hugged the cashmere wrap tighter and curled up in a padded lounger, letting the ocean wind soothe her face still warm from Tony's touch.

Was it her imagination or could she smell hints of him even on the blanket? Or was he that firmly in her senses as well as her thoughts? What was it about Tony that reached to her in ways Nolan never had? She'd responded to her husband's touch, found completion, content with her life right up to the point of betrayal.

But Tony... Shannon hugged the blanket tighter. She hadn't been hinting at marriage, damn it. Just the thought of giving over her life so completely again scared her to her toes.

So where did that leave her? Seriously considering becoming exactly what the media labeled her—a monarch's mistress.

Tony heard...the silence.

Finally, Shannon had settled for the night. Thank God. Much longer and his willpower would have given out. He would have gone back into her room and picked up where they'd left off before he'd caught sight of the damn blanket.

This place screwed with his head, so much so he'd actually brought up marriage, for crying out loud. It was like there were rogue waves from his past curling up everywhere and knocking him off balance. The sooner he could take care of business with his father the sooner he could return to Galveston with Shannon, back to familiar ground where he stood a better chance at reconciling with her.

Staying out of her bed for now was definitely the wiser choice. He walked down the corridor, away from her and that blanket full of memories. He needed his focus sharp for the upcoming meeting with his father. This time, he would face the old man alone.

Charging down the hall, he barely registered the familiar antique wooden benches tucked here, a strategic table and guard posted there. Odd how quickly he slid right back into the surroundings even after so long away. And even stranger that his father hadn't changed a thing.

The day had been one helluva ride, and it wasn't over yet. Enrique had been with his nurse for the past hour, but should be ready to receive him now.

Tony rounded the corner and nodded to the sentinel outside the open door to Enrique's personal quarters. The space was made for a man, no feminine touches to soften the room full of browns and tans, leather and wood. Enrique saved his Salvador Dali collection for himself, a trio of the surrealist's "soft watches" melting over landscapes.

The old guy had become more obsessed with history after his had been stolen from him.

Enrique waited in his wheelchair, wearing a heavy blue robe and years of worries.

"Sit," his father ordered, pointing to his old favored chair.

When Tony didn't jump at his command, Enrique sighed heavily and muttered under his breath in Spanish. "Have a seat," he continued in his native tongue. "We need to talk, *mi hijo.*"

They did, and Tony had to admit he was curious—concerned—about his father's health. Knowing might not have brought him home sooner, but now that he was here, he couldn't ignore the gaunt angles and sallow pallor. "How sick are you really?" Tony continued in Spanish, having spoken both languages equally once they'd left San Rinaldo. "No sugar coating it. I deserve the truth."

"And you would have heard it earlier if you had returned when I first requested."

His father had never *requested* anything in his life.

The stubborn old cuss had been willing to die alone rather than actually admit how ill he was.

Of course Antonio had been just as stubborn about ignoring the demands to show his face on the island. "I am here now."

"You and your brothers have stirred up trouble." A great big *I told you so* was packed into that statement.

"Do you have insights as to how this leaked? How did that reporter identify Duarte?" His middle brother wasn't exactly a social guy.

"Nobody knows, but my people are still looking into it. I thought you would be the one to expose us," his father said wryly. "You always were the impetuous one. Yet you've behaved decisively and wisely. You have protected those close to you. Well done."

"I am past needing your approval, but I thank you for your help."

"Fair enough, and I'm well aware that you would not have accepted that help if Shannon Crawford was not involved. I would be glad to see one of my sons settled and married before I die."

His gut pitched much like a boat tossed by a wave. "Your illness is that bad?" An uneasy silence settled, his father's rattling breaths growing louder and louder. "Should I call a nurse?"

Or his assistant? He wasn't sure what Alys Reyes de la Cortez was doing here, but she was definitely different from the older staff of San Rinaldo natives Enrique normally hired.

"I may be old and sick, but I don't need to be tucked into bed like a child." His chin tipped.

"I'm not here to fight with you."

"Of course not. You're here for my help."

And he had the feeling his father wasn't going to let him forget it. They'd never gotten along well and apparently that hadn't changed. He started to rise. "If that's all then, I will turn in."

"Wait." His father polished his eighteen-karat gold pocket watch with his thumb. "My assistance comes at a price."

Shocked at the calculating tone, Tony sank back into his chair. "You can't be serious."

"I am. Completely."

He should have suspected and prepared himself. "What do you want?"

"I want you to stay for the month while you wait for the new safety measures to be implemented."

"Here? That's all?" He made it sound offhand but already he could feel the claustrophobia wrap around his throat and tighten. The Dali art mocked him with just how slippery time could be, a life that ended in a flash or a moment that extended forever.

"Is it so strange I want to see what kind of man you have matured into?"

Given Enrique had expected Tony to break their cover, he must not have had high expectations for his youngest son. And that pissed him off. "If I don't agree? You'll do what? Feed Shannon and her son to the lions?"

"Her son can stay. I would never sacrifice a child's safety. The mother will have to go."

He couldn't be serious. Tony studied his father for some sign Enrique was bluffing…but the old guy didn't have a "tell." And his father hadn't hesitated to trust his own wife's safety to others. What would stop him from sending Shannon off with a guard and a good-luck wish?

"She would never leave without her child." Like his mother. Tony restrained a wince.

"That is not my problem. Are you truly that unwilling to spend a month here?"

"What if the restraining order comes through sooner?"

"I would ask you to stay as a thanks for my assistance. I have risked a lot for you in granting her access to the island."

True enough, or so it would feel to Enrique with his near agoraphobic need to stay isolated from the world.

"And there are no other conditions?"

A salt-and-pepper eyebrow arched. "Do you want a contract?"

"Do you? If Shannon decides to leave by the weekend, I could simply go, too. What's the worst you can do? Cut me out of the will?" He hadn't taken a penny of his father's money.

"You always were the most amusing of my sons. I have missed that."

"I'm not laughing."

His father's smile faded and he tucked the watch into a pocket, chain jingling to a rest. "Your word is sufficient. You may not want any part of me and my little world here, but you are a Medina. You are my son. Your honor is not in question."

"Fair enough. If you're willing to accept my word, then a month it is." Now that the decision was made, he wondered why his father had chosen that length of time. "What's your prognosis?"

"My liver is failing," Enrique said simply without any hint of self-pity. "Because of the living conditions when I was on the run, I caught hepatitis. It has taken a toll over the years."

Thinking back, Tony tried to remember if his father had been sick when they'd reunited in South America before relocating to the island…but he only recalled his father being coolly determined. "I didn't know. I'm sorry."

"You were a child. You did not need to be informed of everything."

He hadn't been told much of *anything* in those days, but even if he had, he wasn't sure he would have heard. His grief for his mother had been deep and dark. That, he remembered well. "How much longer do you have?"

"I am not going to kick off in the next thirty days."

"That isn't what I meant."

"I know." His father smiled, creases digging deep. "I have a sense of humor, too."

What had his father been like before this place? Before the coup? Tony would never know because time was melting away like images in the Dali paintings on the wall.

While he had some memories of his mother from that time, he had almost none of his father until Enrique had met up with them in South America. The strongest memory he had of Enrique in San Rinaldo? When his father gathered his family to discuss the evacuation plan. Enrique had pressed his pocket watch into Tony's hands and promised to reclaim it. But even at five, Tony had known his father was saying goodbye for what could have been the last time. Now, Enrique wanted him back to say goodbye for the last time again.

How damned ironic. He'd brought Shannon to this place because she needed him. And now he could only think of how much he needed to be with her.

Chapter 7

Where was Tony?

The next day after lunch, Shannon stood alone on her balcony overlooking the ocean. Seagulls swooped on the horizon while long-legged blue herons stalked prey on the rocks. Kolby was napping. A pot of steeped herbal tea waited on a tiny table along with dried fruits and nuts.

How strange to have such complete panoramic peace during such a tumultuous time. The balcony offered an unending view of the sea, unlike the other side with barrier islands. The temperature felt much the same as in Galveston, humid and in the seventies.

She should make the most of the quiet to regain her footing. Instead, she kept looking at the door leading into Tony's suite and wondering why she hadn't seen him yet.

Her morning had been hectic and more than a little

overwhelming learning her way around the mansion with Alys. As much as she needed to resist Tony, she'd missed having his big comforting presence at her side while she explored the never-ending rooms packed nonchalantly with priceless art and antiques.

And they'd only toured half of the home and grounds.

Afterward, Alys had introduced two women on hand for sitter and nanny duties. Shannon had been taken aback by the notion of turning her son over to total strangers, although she had to confess, the guard assigned to shadow Kolby reassured her. She'd been shown letters of recommendation and résumés for each individual. Still, Shannon had spent the rest of the morning getting to know each person in case she needed to call on their help.

Interestingly, none of the king's employees gave away the island's location despite subtle questions about traveling back to their homes. Everyone on Enrique's payroll seemed to understand the importance of discretion, as well as seeing to her every need. Including delivering a closet full of clothes that just happened to fit. Not that she'd caved to temptation yet and tried any of it on. A gust rolling off the ocean teased the well-washed cotton of her sundress around her legs as she stood on the balcony.

The click of double doors opening one suite down snapped her from her reverie. She didn't even need to look over her shoulder to verify who'd stepped outside. She knew the sound of his footsteps, recognized the scent of him on the breeze.

"Hello, Tony."

His Italian loafers stopped alongside her feet in simple pink-and-brown striped flip-flops. *Hers.* Not ones from the new stash.

Leaning into her line of sight, he rested his elbows on the iron rail. "Sorry not to have checked in on you sooner. My father and I spent the morning troubleshooting on a conference call with my brothers and our attorneys."

Of course. That made sense. "Any news?"

"More of the same. Hopefully we can start damage control with some valid info leaked to the press to turn the tide. There's just so much out there." He shook his head sharply then forced a smile. "Enough of that. I missed you at lunch."

"Kolby and I ate in our suite." The scent of Tony's sandalwood aftershave had her curling her toes. "His table manners aren't up to royal standards."

"You don't have to hide in your rooms. There's no court or ceremony here." Still, he wore khakis and a monogrammed blue button-down rolled up at the sleeves rather than the jeans and shorts most everyday folks would wear on a beach vacation.

And he looked mighty fine in every starched inch of fabric.

"Formality or not, there are priceless antiques and art all easily within a child's reach." She trailed her fingers along the iron balustrade. "This place is a lot to absorb. We need time. Although I hope life returns to normal sooner rather than later."

Could she simply pick up where she'd left off? Things hadn't been so great then, given her nearly bankrupt account and her fight with Tony over more than money, over her very independence. Yet hadn't she been considering resuming the affair just last night?

Sometimes it was tough to tell if her hormones or her heart had control these days.

He extended his hand. "You're right. Let's slow things down. Would you like to go for a walk?"

"But Kolby might wake up and ask for m—"

"One of the nannies can watch over him and call us the second his eyes open. Come on. I'll update you on the wackiest of the internet buzz." A half grin tipped one side of his tanned face. "Apparently one source thinks the Medinas have a space station and I've taken you to the mother ship."

Laughter bubbled, surprising her, and she just let it roll free with the wind tearing in from the shore. God, how she needed it after the stressful past couple of days—a stressful week for that matter, since she had broken off her relationship with Tony. "Lead the way, my alien lover."

His smile widened, reaching his eyes for the first time since their ferry had pulled up to the island. The power outshone the world around her until she barely noticed the opulent surroundings on their way through the mansion to the beach.

The October sun high in the sky was blinding and warm, hotter than when she'd been on the balcony, inching up toward eighty degrees perhaps. Her mind started churning with possible locations. Could they be in Mexico or South America? Or were they still in the States? California or—

"We're off the coast of Florida."

Glancing up sharply, she swallowed hard, not realizing until that moment how deeply the secrecy had weighed on her. "Thank you."

He waved aside her gratitude. "You would have figured it out on your own in a couple of days."

Maybe, but given the secrecy of Enrique's employees, she wasn't as certain. "So, what about more of those wacky internet rumors?"

"Do you really want to discuss that?"

"I guess not." She slid off her flip-flops and curled her toes in the warm sand. "Thank you for all the clothes for me and for Kolby, the toys, too. We'll enjoy them while we're here. But you know we can't keep them."

"Don't be a buzz kill." He tapped her nose just below the bridge of her glasses. "My father's staff ordered everything. I had nothing to do with it. If it'll make you happy, we'll donate the lot to Goodwill after you leave."

"How did he get everything here so fast?" She strode into the tide, her shoes dangling from her fingers.

"Does it matter?" He slid off his shoes and socks and joined her, just into the water's reach.

With the more casual and familiar Tony returning, some of the tension left her shoulders. "I guess not. The toys are awesome, of course, but Kolby enjoys the dogs most. They seem incredibly well trained."

"They are. My father will have his trainers working with the dogs to bond with your son so they will protect him as well if need be while you are here."

She shivered in spite of the bold beams of sunshine overhead. "Can't a dog just be a pet?"

"Things aren't that simple for us." He looked away, down the coast at an osprey spreading its wings and diving downward.

How many times had he watched the birds as a child and wanted to fly away, too? She understood well the need to escape a golden cage. "I'm sorry."

"Don't be." He rejected her sympathy outright.

Pride iced his clipped words, and she searched for a safer subject.

Her eyes settled on the rippling crests of foam frosting the gray-blue shore. "Is this where you used to surf?"

"Actually, the cove is pretty calm." He pointed ahead to an outcropping packed with palm trees. "The best spot is about a mile and a half down. Or at least it was. Who knows after so many years?"

"You really had free rein to run around the island." She stepped onto a sandbar that fingered out into the water. As a mother, she had a tough time picturing her child exploring this junglelike beach at will.

"Once I was a teenager, pretty much. After I was through with schooling for the day, of course." A green turtle popped his head from the water, legs poking from the shell as he swam out and slapped up the beach. "Although sometimes we even had class out here."

"A field trip to the beach? What fun teachers you had."

"Tutors."

"Of course." The stark difference in their upbringings wrapped around her like seaweed lapping at her ankles. She tried to shake free of the clammy negativity. "Surfing was your P.E.?"

"Technically, we had what you would call phys ed, but it was more of a health class with martial arts training."

During her couple of years teaching high-school band and chorus before she'd met Nolan, some of her students went to karate lessons. But they'd gone to a gym full of other students, rather than attending in seclusion with only two brothers for company. "It's so surreal to think you never went to prom, or had an after-school job or played on a basketball team."

"We had games here…but you're right in that there was no stadium of classmates and parents. No cheer-leaders." He winked and smiled, but she sensed he was using levity as a diversion.

How often had he done that in the past and she'd missed out hearing his real thoughts or feelings because she wanted things to be uncomplicated?

Shannon squeezed his bulging forearm. "You would have been a good football player with your size."

"Soccer." His bicep twitched under her touch. "I'm from Europe, remember?"

"Of course." Unlikely she would ever forget his roots now that she knew. And she wanted to learn more about this strong-jawed man who thought to order a minia-ture motorized Jeep for her son—and then give credit to his father.

She tucked her hand into the crook of his arm as she swished through the ebbs and flow of the tidewaters. "So you still think of yourself as being from Europe? Even though you were only five when you came to the U.S.?"

His eyebrows pinched together. "I never really thought of this as the U.S. even though I know how close we are."

"I can understand that. Everything here is such a mix of cultures." While the staff spoke English to her, she'd heard Spanish spoken by some. Books and magazines and even instructions on labels were a mix of English, Spanish and some French. "You mentioned thinking this was still San Rinaldo when you got here."

"Only at first. My father told us otherwise."

What difficult conversations those must have been

between father and sons. So much to learn and adjust to so young. "We've both lost a lot, you and I. I wonder if I sensed that on some level, if that's what drew us to each other."

He slid an arm around her shoulders and pulled her closer while they kicked through the surf. "Don't kid yourself. I was attracted to how hot you looked walking away in that slim black skirt. And then when you glanced over your shoulder with those prim glasses and do-me eyes." He whistled long and low. "I was toast from the get-go."

Trying not to smile, her skin heating all the same, she elbowed him lightly. "Cro-Magnon."

"Hey, I'm a red-blooded male and you're sexy." He traced the cat-eye edge of her glasses. "You're also entirely too serious at the moment. Life will kick us in the ass all on its own soon enough. We're going to just enjoy the moment, remember? No more buzz kills."

"You're right." Who knew how much longer she would have with Tony before this mess blew up in her face? "Let's go back to talking about surfing and high-school dances. You so would have been the bad boy."

"And I'll bet you were a good girl. Did you wear those studious glasses even then?"

"Since I was in the eighth grade." She'd hated how her nose would sweat in the heat when she'd marched during football games. "I was a dedicated musician with no time for boys."

"And now?"

"I want to enjoy this beautiful ocean and a day with absolutely nothing to do." She bolted ahead, kicking through the tide, not sure how to balance her impulsive need for Tony with her practical side that demanded she stay on guard.

Footsteps splashed behind her a second before Tony scooped her up. And she let him.

The warm heat of his shoulder under her cheek, the steady pump of his heart against her side had her curling her arms around his neck. "You're getting us all wet."

His eyes fell to her shirt. His heart thumped faster. "Are you having fun?"

"Yes, I am." She toyed with the springy curls at the nape of his neck. "You always make sure of that, whether it's an opera or a walk by the beach."

"You deserve to have more fun in your life." He held her against his chest with a familiarity she couldn't deny. "I would make things easier for you. You know that."

"And you know where I stand on that subject." She cupped his face, his stubble so dark and thick that he wore a perpetual five o'clock shadow. "This—your protection, the trip, the clothes and toys—it's already much more than I'm comfortable taking."

She needed to be clear on that before she even considered letting him closer again.

He eased her to her feet with a lingering glide of her body down his. "We should go back."

The desire in his eyes glinted unmistakably in the afternoon sun. Yet, he pulled away.

Her lips hungered and her breasts ached—and *he* was walking away again, in spite of all he'd said about how much he wanted her. This man confused the hell out of her.

Five days later, Shannon lounged on the downstairs lanai and watched her son drive along the beach in his miniature Jeep, dogs romping alongside. This was the first time she'd been left to her own devices in days. She'd never been romanced so thoroughly in her life. True to his word, over the past week Tony had been at his most charming.

Could her time here already be almost over?

Sipping freshly squeezed lemonade—although the drink tasted far too amazing for such a simple name—she savored the tart taste. Of course everything seemed sharper, crisper as tension seeped from her bones. The concerns of the world felt forever away while the sun warmed her skin and the waves provided a soothing sound track to her days.

And she had Tony to thank for it all. She'd never known there were so many entertainment options on an island. Of course Enrique Medina had spared no expense in building his compound.

A movie screening room with all the latest films piped in for private viewing.

Three different dining rooms for everything from family style to white-tie.

Rec room, gym, indoor and outdoor swimming pools.

She could still hear Kolby's squeal of delight over the stable of horses and ponies.

Throughout it all, Tony had been at her side with tantalizing brushes of his strong body against hers. All the while his rich chocolate-brown eyes reminded Shannon that the next move was up to her. Not that they stood a chance at finding privacy today. The grounds buzzed with activity, and today, no sign of Tony.

Behind her, the doors snicked open. Tony? Her heart stuttered a quick syncopation as she glanced back.

Alys walked toward her, high heels clicking on the

tiled veranda as she angled past two guards comparing notes on their twin BlackBerry phones. Shannon forced herself to keep the smile in place. It would be rude to frown in disappointment, especially after how helpful the woman had been.

Too bad the disappointment wasn't as easy to hide from herself. No doubt about it, Tony was working his way back into her life.

The king's assistant stopped at the fully stocked outdoor bar and poured a glass of lemonade from the crystal pitcher.

Shannon thumbed the condensation on the cold glass. "Is there something you need?"

"Antonio wanted me to find you, and I have." She tapped her silver BlackBerry attached to the waistband of her linen skirt. Ever crisp with her power suit and French manicure. As usual the elegant woman didn't have a wrinkle in sight, much less wince over working in heels all day. "He'll be out shortly. He's finishing up a meeting with his father."

"I should get Kolby." She swung her feet to the side. How silly to be glad she'd caved and used some of the new clothes. She had worn everything she brought with her twice and while the laundry service easily kept up with her limited wardrobe, she'd begun to feel a little ungrateful to not wear at least a few of the things that someone had gone to a lot of trouble to provide. Shannon smoothed the de la Renta scoop-necked dress, the fabric so decadently soft it caressed her skin with every move.

"No need to stop the boy's fun just yet. Antonio is on his way." Alys perched on the edge of the lounger, glass on her knee.

Shannon rubbed the hem of her dress between two

fingers much like Kolby with his blanket when he needed soothing. "I hear you're the one who ordered all the new clothes. Thank you."

Alys saw to everything else in this smoothly run place. "No need for thanks. It's my job."

"You have excellent taste." She tugged the hem back over her knees.

"I saw your photo online and chose things that would flatter your frame and coloring. It's fun to shop on someone else's dime."

More than a dime had gone into this wardrobe. Her closet sported new additions each morning. Everything from casual jeans and designer blouses to silky dresses and heels to wear for dinner. An assortment of bathing suits to choose from....

And the lingerie. A decadent shiver slid down her spine at the feel of the fine silks and satins against her skin. Although it made her uncomfortable to think of this woman choosing everything.

Alys turned her glass around and around on her knee. "The expense you worry about is nothing to them. They can afford the finest. It would bother them to see you struggling. Now you fit in and that gives the king less to worry about."

God forbid her tennis shoes should make the king uncomfortable. But saying as much would make her sound ungrateful, so she toyed with her glasses, pulling them off and cleaning them with her napkin even though they were already crystal clear. The dynamics of this place went beyond any household she'd ever seen. Alys seemed more comfortable here than Tony.

Shannon slid her glasses back on. "If you don't mind

my asking, how long have you been working for the king?"

"Only three months."

How long did she intend to stay? The island was luxurious, but in more of a vacation kind of way. It was so cut off from the world, time seemed to stand still. What kind of life could the woman build in this place?

Abruptly, Alys leaped to her feet. "Here is Antonio now."

He charged confidently through the door, eyes locked on Shannon. "Thank you for finding her, Alys."

The assistant backed away. "Of course." Alys stepped out of hearing range, giving them some privacy.

Forking a hand through his hair—messing up the precise combing from his conference with his father—Tony wore a suit without a tie. The jacket perhaps a nod toward meeting with his father? His smile was carefree, but his shoulders bore the extra tension she'd come to realize accompanied time he had spent with the king.

"How did your meeting go?"

"Don't want to talk about that." Tony plucked a lily from the vase on the bar, snapped the stem off and tucked the bloom behind her ear. "Would much rather enjoy the view. The flower is almost as gorgeous as you are."

The lush perfume filled each breath. "All the fresh flowers are positively decadent."

"I wish I could take credit, but there's a hothouse with a supply that's virtually unlimited."

Yet another amenity she wouldn't have guessed, although it certainly explained all the fresh-cut flowers. "Still," she repeated as she touched the lily tucked in her hair, "I appreciate the gesture."

"I would make love to you on a bed of flowers if you let me." He thumbed her earlobe lightly before skimming his knuckles along her collarbone.

How easy it would be to give over to the delicious seduction of his words and his world. Except she'd allowed herself to fall into that trap before.

And of course there was that little technicality that *he* had been the one holding back all week. "What about thorns?"

He laughed, his hand falling away from her skin and palming her back. "Come on, my practical love. We're going out."

Love? She swallowed to dampen her suddenly cottony mouth. "To lunch?"

"To the airstrip."

Her stomach lurched. This slice of time away was over already? "We're leaving?"

"Not that lucky, I'm afraid. Your apartment is still staked out with the press and curious royalty groupie types. You may want to consider a gated community on top of the added security measures. I know the cost freaks you out, but give my lawyer another couple of days to work on those restraining orders and we can take it from there. As for where we're going today, we're greeting guests and I'd like you to come along."

They weren't leaving. Relief sang through her so intensely it gave her pause.

Tony cocked his head to the side. "Would you like to come with me?"

"Uh, yes, I think so." She struggled to gather her scrambled thoughts and composure. "I just need to settle Kolby."

Alys cleared her throat a few feet away. "I've already

notified Miss Delgado, the younger nanny. She's ordering a picnic lunch and bringing sand toys. Then of course she will watch over him during his naptime if needed. I assume that's acceptable to you?"

Her son would enjoy that more than a car ride and waiting around for the flight. She was growing quite spoiled having afternoons completely free while Kolby napped safely under a nanny's watchful care. "Of course. That sounds perfect."

Shannon smiled her thanks and reached out to touch the woman's arm. Except Alys wasn't looking at her. The king's assistant had her eyes firmly planted elsewhere.

On Tony.

Shock nailed her feet to the tiles. Then a fierce jealousy vibrated through her, a feeling that was most definitely ugly and not her style. She'd thought herself above such a primitive emotion, not to mention Tony hadn't given the woman any encouragement.

Still, Shannon fought the urge to link her arm with his in a great big "mine" statement. In that unguarded moment, Alys revealed clearly what she hoped to gain from living here.

Alys wanted a Medina man.

Chapter 8

Tony guided the Porsche Cayenne four-wheel drive along the island road toward the airstrip, glad Shannon was with him to ease the edge on the upcoming meeting. Although having her with him brought a special torment all its own.

The past week working his way back into her good graces had been a painful pleasure, sharpening the razor edge on his need to have her in his bed again. Spending time with her had only shown him more reasons to want her. She mesmerized him with the simplest things.

When she sat on the pool edge and kicked her feet through the water, he thought of those long legs wrapped around him.

Seeing her sip a glass of lemonade made him ache to taste the tart fruit on her lips.

The way she cleaned her glasses with a gust of breath

fogging the frames made him think of her panting in his ear as he brought her to completion.

Romancing his way back into her good graces was easier said than done. And the goal of it all made each day on this island easier to bear.

And after they returned to Galveston? He would face that then. Right now, he had more of his father's past to deal with.

"Tony?" Bracing her hand against the dash as the rutted road challenged even the quality shock absorbers, she looked so right sitting in the seat next to him. "You still haven't told me who we're picking up. Your brothers, perhaps?"

Steering the SUV under the arch of palm trees lining both sides of the road, he searched for the right words to prepare Shannon for something he'd never shared with a soul. "You're on the right track." His hands gripped the steering wheel tighter. "My sister. Half sister, actually. Eloisa."

"A sister? I didn't know...."

"Neither does the press." His half sister had stayed under the radar, growing up with her mother and stepfather in Pensacola, Florida. Only recently had Eloisa reestablished contact with their father. "She's coming here to regroup, troubleshoot. Prepare. Now that the Medina secret is out, her story will also be revealed soon enough."

"May I ask what that story might be?"

"Of course." He focused on the two-lane road, a convenient excuse to make sure she didn't see any anger pushing past his boundaries. "My father had a relationship with her mother after arriving in the U.S., which resulted in Eloisa. She's in her midtwenties now."

Shannon's eyes went wide behind her glasses.

"Yeah, I know." Turning, he drove from the jungle road onto a waterside route leading to the ferry station. "That's a tight timeline between when we left San Rinaldo and the hookup." Tight timeline in regard to his mother's death.

"That must have been confusing for you. Kolby barely remembers his father and it's been tough for him to accept you. And we haven't had to deal with adding another child to the mix."

A child? With Shannon? An image of a dark-haired baby—his baby—in her arms blindsided him, derailing his thoughts away from his father in a flash. His foot slid off the accelerator. Shaking free of the image was easier said than done as it grew roots in his mind—Kolby stepping into the picture until a family portrait took shape.

God, just last week he'd been thinking how he knew nothing about kids. She was the one hinting at marriage, not him. Although she said the opposite until he didn't know what was up.

Things with Shannon weren't as simple as he'd planned at the outset. "My father's affair was his own business."

"Okay, then." She pulled her glasses off and fogged them with her breath. She dried them with the hem of her dress. "Do you and your sister get along?"

He hauled his eyes from Shannon's glasses before he swerved off onto the beach. Or pulled onto the nearest side road and to hell with making it to the airstrip on time.

"I've only met her once before." When Tony was a teenager. His father had gone all out on that lone visit with his seven-year-old daughter. Tony didn't resent Eloisa. It wasn't her fault, after all. In fact, he grew even more pissed off at his father. Enrique had responsibilities to his daughter. If he wanted to stay out of her life, then fine. Do so. But half measures were bull.

Yet wasn't that what he'd been offering Shannon? Half measures?

Self-realization sucked. "She's come here on her own since then. She and Duarte have even met up a few times, which in a roundabout way brought on the media mess."

"How so?" She slid her glasses back in place.

"Our sister married into a high-profile family. Eloisa's husband is the son of an ambassador and brother to a senator. He's a Landis."

She sat up straighter at the mention of America's political royalty. Talk about irony.

Tony slowed for a fuel truck to pass. "The Landis name naturally comes with media attention." He accelerated into the parking lot alongside the ferry station, the boat already close to shore. An airplane was parked on the distant airstrip. "Her husband—Jonah—likes to keep a low profile, but that's just not possible."

"What happened?"

"Duarte was delivering one of our father's messages, which put him on a collision course with a press camera. We're still trying to figure out how the Global Intruder made the connection. Although, it's a moot point now. Every stray photo of all of us has been unearthed, every detail of our pasts."

"Of my past?" Her face drained of color.

"I'm afraid so."

All the more reason for her to stay on the island. Her husband's illegal dealings, even his suicide, had hit the headlines again this morning, thanks to muckrakers looking for more scandal connected to the Medina story. He would only be able to shield Shannon from that for so long. She had a right to know.

"I've grown complacent this week." She pressed a hand to her stomach. "My poor in-laws."

The SUV idled in the parking spot, the ferry already preparing to dock. He didn't have much time left alone with her.

Tony skimmed back her silky blond hair. "I'm sorry all this has come up again. And I hate it that I can't do more to fix things for you."

Turning toward his touch, she rested her face in his hand. "You've helped this week."

He wanted to kiss her, burned to recline the seats and explore the hint of cleavage in her scoop-necked dress. And damned if that wasn't exactly what he planned to do.

Slanting his mouth over her, he caught her gasp and took full advantage of her parted lips with a determined sweep of his tongue. Need for her pumped through his veins, fast-tracked blood from his head to his groin until he could only feel, smell, taste undiluted *Shannon*. Her gasp quickly turned to a sigh as she melted against him, the curves of her breasts pressed to his chest, her fingernails digging deeply into his forearms as she urged him closer.

He was more than happy to accommodate.

It had been so long, too long since they'd had sex before their argument over his damned money. Nearly fourteen days that seemed like fourteen years since he'd had his hands on her this way, fully and unrestrained, tunneling under her clothes, reacquainting himself with the perfection of her soft skin and perfect curves. She fit against him with a rightness he knew extended even further with their clothes off. A hitch in her throat, the flush rising on the exposed curve of her breasts keyed him in to her rising need, as if he couldn't already tell by the way she nearly crawled across the seat to get closer.

Shannon wanted sex with him every bit as much as he wanted her. But that required privacy, not a parking lot in clear view of the approaching ferry.

Holding back now was the right move, even if it was killing him.

"Come on. Time to meet my sister." He slid out of her arms and the SUV and around to her door before she could shuffle her purse from her lap to her shoulder.

He opened the door and she smiled her thanks without speaking, yet another thing he appreciated about her. She sensed when he didn't want to talk anymore. He'd shared things with women over the years, but until her, he'd never found one with whom he could share silence.

The lapping waves, the squawk of gulls, the endless stretch of water centered him, steadying his steps and reminding him how to keep his balance in a rocky world.

Resting his head on Shannon's back, he waited while the ferry finished docking. His sister and her husband stood at the railing. Eloisa's husband hooked an arm around her shoulders, the couple talking intently.

Eloisa might not be a carbon copy of their father, but she carried an air of something unmistakably Medina about her. His father had once said she looked like their grandmother. Tony wouldn't know, since he couldn't remember his grandparents who'd all died before he was born.

The loudspeaker blared with the boat captain announcing their arrival. Disembarking, the couple stayed close together, his brother-in-law broadcasting a protective air. Jonah was the unconventional Landis, according to the papers. If so, they should get along just fine.

The couple stepped from the boat to the dock, and up close Eloisa didn't appear nearly as calm as from a distance. Lines of strain showed in her eyes.

"Welcome," Tony said. "Eloisa, Jonah, this is Shannon Crawford, and I'm—"

"Antonio, I know." His sister spoke softly, reserved. "I recognize you both from the papers."

He'd met Eloisa once as a child when she'd visited the island. She'd come back recently, but he'd been long gone by then.

They were strangers and relatives. Awkward, to say the least.

Jonah Landis stepped up. "Glad you could accommodate our request for a visit so quickly."

"Damage control is important."

Eloisa simply took his hand, searching his face. "How's our father?"

"Not well." Had Shannon just stepped closer to him? Tony kept his eyes forward, knowing in his gut he would see sympathy in her eyes. "He says his doctors are doing all they can."

Blinking back tears, Eloisa stood straighter with a willowy strength. "I barely know him, but I can't envision a world without him in it. Sounds crazy, I'm sure."

He understood too well. Making peace was hard as hell, yet somehow she seemed to have managed.

Jonah clapped him on the back. "Well, my new bro, I need to grab Eloisa's bags and meet you at the car."

A Landis who carried his own luggage? Tony liked the unpretentious guy already.

And wasn't that one of the things he liked most about Shannon? Her down-to-earth ways in spite of her wealthy lifestyle with her husband. She seemed completely unimpressed with the Medina money, much less his defunct title.

For the first time he considered she might be right. She may be better off without the strain of his messed-up family.

Which made him a selfish bastard for pursuing her. But he couldn't seem to pull back now when his world had been rocked on its foundation. The sailor in him recognized the only port in the storm, and right now, only a de la Renta dress separated him from what he wanted—needed—more than anything.

However, he needed to choose his time and place carefully with the private island growing more crowded by the minute.

The next afternoon, Shannon sat beside Tony in the Porsche four-wheel drive on the way to the beach. He'd left her a note to put on her bathing suit and meet him during Kolby's naptime. She'd been taken aback at the leap of excitement in her stomach over spending time alone with him.

The beach road took them all the way to the edge of the shoreline. He shifted the car in Park, his legs flexing in black board shorts as he left the car silently. He'd been quiet for the whole drive, and she didn't feel the need to fill the moment with aimless babbling. Being together and quiet had an appeal all its own.

Tugging on the edge of the white cover-up, she eyed the secluded stretch of beach. Could this be the end of the "romancing" and the shift back to intimacy? Her stomach fluttered faster.

She stepped from the car before he could open her door. Wind ruffled his hair and whipped his shorts, low slung on his hips. She knew his body well but still the muscled hardness hitched her breath in her throat. Bronzed and toned—smart, rich and royal to boot. Life had handed him an amazing hand, and yet he still chose to work insane hours. In fact, she'd spent more time with him this past week than during the months they'd dated in Galveston.

And everything she learned confused her more than solving questions.

She jammed her hands in the pockets of her cover-up. "Are you going to tell me why we're here?"

"Over there." He pointed to a cluster of palm trees with surfboards propped and waiting.

"You're kidding, right? Tony, I don't surf, and the water must be cold."

"You'll warm up. The waves aren't high enough today for surfing. But there're still some things even a beginner can do." He peeled off his T-shirt and she realized she was staring, damn it. "You won't break anything. Trust me."

He extended a hand.

Trust? Easier said than done. She eyed the boards and looked back at him. They were on the island, she reminded herself, removed from real life. And bottom line, while she wasn't sure she trusted him with her heart, she totally trusted him with her body. He wouldn't let anything happen to her.

Decision made, she whipped her cover-up over her head, revealing her crocheted swimsuit. His eyes flamed over her before he took her cover-up and tossed it in the SUV along with his T-shirt. He closed his hands around hers in a warm steady grip and started toward the boards.

She eyed the pair propped against trees—obviously set up in advance for their outing. One shiny and new, bright white with tropical flowers around the edges. The other was simpler, just yellow, faded from time and use. She looked at the water again, starting to have second—

"Hey." He squeezed her hand. "We're just going to paddle out. Nothing too adventurous today, but I think you're going to find even slow and steady has some unexpected thrills."

And didn't that send her heart double timing?

Thank goodness he moved quickly. Mere minutes later she was on her stomach, on the board, paddling away from shore to…nowhere. Nothing but aqua-blue waters blending into a paler sky. Mild waves rolled beneath her but somehow never lifted her high enough to be scary, more of a gentle rocking. The chilly water turned to a neutral sluice over her body, soothing her into becoming one with the ocean.

One stroke at a time she let go of goals and racing to the finish line. Her life had been on fast-paced frenetic since Nolan died. Now, for the first time in longer than she could remember, she was able to unwind, almost hypnotized by the dip, dip, dip of her hands and Tony's into the water.

Tension she hadn't even realized kinked her muscles began to ease. Somehow, Tony must have known. She turned her head to thank him and found him staring back at her.

She threaded her fingers through the water, sun baking her back. "It's so quiet out here."

"I thought you would appreciate the time away."

"You were right." She slowed her paddling and just floated. "You've given over a lot of your time to make sure Kolby and I stayed entertained. Don't you need to get back to work?"

"I work from the island using my computer and telecoms." His hair, even darker when wet, was slicked back from his face, his damp skin glinting in the sun. "More and more of business is being conducted that way."

"Do you ever sleep?"

"Not so much lately, but that has nothing to do with work." He held her with his eyes locked on her face, no suggestive body sweep, just intense, undiluted Tony.

And she couldn't help but wonder why he went to so much trouble when they weren't sleeping together anymore. If his conscience bothered him, he could have assigned guards to watch over her and she wouldn't have argued for Kolby's sake. Yet here he was. With her.

"What do you see in me?" She rested her cheek on her folded hands. "I'm not fishing for compliments, honest to God, it's just we seem so wrong for each other on so many levels. Is it just the challenge, like building your business?"

"Shanny, you take *challenge* to a whole 'nother level."

She flicked water in his face. "I'm being serious here. No joking around, please."

"Seriously?" He stared out at the horizon for a second as if gathering his thoughts. "Since you brought up the business analogy, let's run with that. At work you would be someone I want on my team. Your tenacity, your refusal to give up—even your frustrating rejection of my help—impress the hell out of me. You're an amazing woman, so much so that sometimes I can't even look away."

He made her feel strong and special with a few words. After feeling guilty for so long, of wondering if she could hold it all together for Kolby, she welcomed the reassurance coursing through her veins as surely as the current underneath her.

Tony slid from his board and ducked under. She watched through the clear surface as he freed the ankle leash attaching him to his board.

Resurfacing beside her, he stroked the line of her back. "Sit up for a minute."

"What?" She'd barely heard him, too focused on the feel of his hand low on her waist.

"Sit up on the board and swing your legs over the side." He held the edge. "I won't let you fall."

"But your board's drifting." She watched the faded yellow inch away.

"I'll get it later. Come on." He palmed her back, helping her balance as finally, she wriggled her way upright.

She bobbled. Stifled a squeal. Then realized what was the worst that could happen? She would be in the water. Big deal. And suddenly the surfboard steadied a little, still rocking but not out of control. The waters lapped around her legs, cool, exciting.

"I did it." She laughed, sending her voice out into that endlessness.

"Perfect. Now hold still," he said and somehow slid effortlessly behind her.

Her balance went haywire again for a second, the horizon tilting until she was sure they would both topple over.

"Relax," he said against her ear. "Out here, it's not about fighting, it's the one place you can totally let go."

The one place *he* could let go? And suddenly she realized this was about more than getting her to relax. He was sharing something about himself with her. Even a man as driven and successful as himself needed a break from the demands of everyday life. Perhaps because of moments like these he kept it all together rather than letting the tension tighten until it snapped.

She fit herself against him, his legs behind hers as they drifted. Her muscles slowly melted until she leaned into him. The waves curled underneath, his chest wet and bristly against her skin. A new tension coiled inside her, deep in her belly. Her swimsuit suddenly felt too tight against her breasts that swelled and yearned for the brush of the air and Tony's mouth.

His palms rested on her thighs. His thumbs circled a light massage, close, so close. Water ebbed and flowed over her heated core, waves sweeping tantalizing caresses on her aching flesh. Her head sagged onto his shoulder.

With each undulation of the board, he rocked against her, stirring, growing harder until he pressed fully erect along her spine. Every roll of the board rubbing their bodies against each other had to be as torturous for him as it was for her. His hands moved higher on her legs, nearer to what she needed. Silently. Just as in tune with each other as when they'd been paddling out.

She worried at first that someone might see, but with their backs to the shore and water…she could lose herself in the moment. Already his breaths grew heavier against her ear, nearly as fast as her own.

They could both let go and find completion right here

without ever moving. Simply feeling his arousal against her stirred Shannon to a bittersweet edge. And good God, that scared the hell out of her.

The wind chilled, and she recognized the sting of fear all too well. She'd thought she could ride the wave, so to speak, and just have an affair with Tony.

But this utter abandon, the loss of control, the way they were together, it was anything but simple, something she wasn't sure she was ready to risk.

Scavenging every bit of her quickly dwindling willpower, she grabbed his wrists, moved his hands away…

And dived off the side of the board.

Chapter 9

Tony propped his surfboard against a tree and turned to take Shannon's. The wariness in her eyes frustrated the hell out of him. He could have sworn she was just as into the moment out there as he was—an amazing moment that had been seconds away from getting even better.

And then she'd vaulted off the board and into the water.

Staying well clear of him, she'd said she was ready to return to shore. She hadn't spoken another word since. Had he blown a whole week's worth of working past her boundaries only to wreck it in one afternoon? Problem was, he still didn't know what had set her off.

She stroked a smudge of sand from his faded yellow board. "Is it all right to leave them here so far from where we started?"

They'd drifted at least a mile from the SUV. "I'll buy new ones. I'm a filthy rich prince, remember?"

Yeah, sexual frustration was making him a little cranky, and he suspected no amount of walking would take the edge off. Worse yet, she didn't even rise to the bait of his crabby words full of reminders of why they'd broken up in the first place.

Fine. Who the hell knew what she needed?

He started west and she glided alongside him. The wind picked up, rustling the trees and sweeping a layer of sand around his ankles.

Shannon gasped.

"What?" Tony looked fast. "Did you step on something? Are you getting chilly?"

Shaking her head, she pointed toward the trees, branches and leaves sweeping apart to reveal the small stone chapel. "Why didn't I notice that when we drove here?"

"We approached the beach from a different angle."

"It's gorgeous." Her eyes were wide and curious.

"No need to look so surprised. I told you that we lived here 24/7. My father outfitted the island with everything we would need, from a small medical clinic to that church." He took in the white stone church, mission bell over the front doors. It wasn't large, but big enough to accommodate everyone here. His older brother had told him once it was the only thing on the island built to resemble a part of their old life.

"Were you an altar server?"

Her voice pulled him back to the present.

"With a short-lived tenure." He glanced down at her, so damn glad she was talking to him again. "I couldn't sit still and the priest frowned on an altar server bringing a bag of books and Legos to keep himself entertained during the service."

"Legos?" She started walking again. "Really?"

"Every Sunday as I sat out in the congregation. I would have brought more, but the nanny confiscated my squirt gun."

"Don't be giving Kolby any ideas." She elbowed him lightly, then as if realizing what she'd done, picked up her pace.

Hell no, he wasn't losing ground that fast. "The nanny didn't find my knife, though."

Her mouth dropped open. "You brought a knife to church?"

"I carved my initials under the pew. Wanna go see if they're still there?"

She eyed the church, then shook her head. "What's all this about today? The surfing and then stories about Legos?"

Why? He hadn't stopped to consider the reasons, just acting on instinct to keep up with the crazy, out-of-control relationship with Shannon. But he didn't do things without a reason.

His gut had pointed him in this direction because... "So that you remember there's a man in here." He thumped his chest. "As well as a filthy rich prince."

But no matter what he said or how far he got from this place, the Medina heritage coursed through his veins. Regardless of how many times he changed his name or started over, he was still Antonio Medina. And Shannon had made it clear time and time again, she didn't want that kind of life. Finally, he heard her.

Several hours later, Shannon shoved her head deeper into the industrial-sized refrigerator in search of a midnight snack. A glass of warm milk just wasn't going to cut it.

Eyeing the plate of *trufas con cognac* and small cups of *crema catalana,* she debated whether to go for the brandy truffles or cold custard with caramel on top.... She picked one of each and dropped into a seat at the steel table.

Silence bounced and echoed in the cavernous kitchen. She was sleepy and cranky and edgy. And it was all Tony's fault for tormenting her with charming stories and sexy encounters on the water—then shutting her out. She nipped an edge of the liqueur-flavored chocolate. Amazing. Sighing, she sagged back in the chair.

Since returning from their surfing outing, he'd kept his distance. She'd thought they were getting closer on a deeper level when he'd shared about his sister and even the Lego, then, wham. He'd turned into the perfect— distant—host at the stilted family dinner.

Not that she'd been able to eat a bite.

Now, she was hungry, in spite of the fact she'd finished off the truffle. She spooned a scoop of custard into her mouth, although she suspected no amount of gourmet pastries would satisfy the craving gnawing her inside.

When she'd started dating Tony, she'd taken a careful, calculated risk because her hormones had been hollering for him and she'd been a long, long time without sex. Okay, so her hormones hadn't been shouting for just any man. Only Tony. A problem that didn't seem to have abated in the least.

"Ah, hell." Tony's low curse startled her upright in her seat.

Filling the archway, he studied her cautiously. He wore jeans and an open button-down that appeared hastily tossed on. He fastened two buttons in the middle, slowly shielding the cut of his six-pack abs.

Cool custard melted in her mouth, her senses singing. But her heart was aching and confused. She toyed with the neck of her robe nervously. The blue peignoir set covered her from neck to toes, but the loose-fitting chiffon and lace brushed sensual decadence against her skin. The froufrou little kitten heels to match had seemed over-the-top in her room, but now felt sexy and fun.

Her hands shook. She pressed them against the steel-topped table. "Don't mind me. I'm just indulging in a midnight feeding frenzy. I highly recommend the custard cups in the back right corner of the refrigerator."

He hesitated in the archway as if making up his mind, then walked deeper into the kitchen, passing her without touching. "I was thinking in terms of something more substantial, like a sandwich."

"Are princes allowed to make their own snacks?"

"Who's going to tell me no?" He kicked the fridge closed, his hands full of deli meat, cheese and lettuce, a jar of spread tucked under his elbow.

"Good point." She swirled another spoonful. "I hope the cook doesn't mind I've been foraging around. I actually used the stove, too, when I cooked a late-night snack for Kolby. He woke up hungry."

Tony glanced over from his sandwich prep. "Is he okay?"

"Just a little homesick." Her eyes took in the sight of the Tony she remembered, a man who wore jeans low-slung on his hips. And rumpled hair…she enjoyed the disobedient swirls in his hair most.

"I'm sorry for that." His shoulders tensed under the loose chambray.

"Don't get me wrong, I appreciate how everyone has gone out of their way for him. The gourmet kid cuisine makes meals an adventure. I wish I had thought to tell him rolled tortillas are snakes and caterpillars." Pasta was called worms or a nest. "I'm even becoming addicted to Nutella crepes. But sometimes, a kid just needs the familiar feel of home."

"I understand." His sandwich piled high on a plate, he took a seat—across from her rather than beside as he would have in the past.

"Of course you do." She clenched her hands together to keep from reaching out to him. "Well, I'll have to make sure the cook knows I tried to put everything back where I found it."

"He's more likely to be upset that you called him a cook rather than a chef."

"Ah, a chef. Right. All those nuances between your world and mine." How surreal to be having a conversation with a prince over a totally plebian hoagie.

Tony swiped at his mouth with a linen napkin and draped it over his knee again. "You ran in a pretty high-finance world with your husband."

Her husband's dirty money.

She shoved away the custard bowl. Thoughts of the media regurgitating that mess for public consumption made her nauseated. She wasn't close to her in-laws, but they would suffer hearing their precious son's reputation smeared again.

And God help them all if her own secrets were somehow discovered.

Best to lie low and keep to herself. Although she was finding it increasingly difficult to imagine how she would restart her life. Even if she was able to renew her teaching credentials, who was going to want to hire the infamous Medina Mistress who'd once been married to a crook? When this mess was over, she would have to dig deep to figure out how to recreate a life for herself and Kolby.

Could Tony be having second thoughts about their relationship? His strict code of honor would dictate he take care of her until the media storm passed, but she didn't want to be his duty.

They'd dated. They'd had sex. But she only just realized how much of their relationship had been superficial as they both dodged discussing deeper, darker parts of their past.

Still, she wasn't ready to plunge into the murkiest of waters that made up her life with Nolan. She wasn't even sure right now if Tony would want to hear.

But regardless of how things turned out between them, she needed him to understand the real her. "I didn't grow up with all those trappings of Nolan's world. My dad was a high-school science teacher and a coach. My mom was the elementary-school secretary. We had enough money, but we were by no means wealthy." She hesitated, realizing… "You probably already know all of that."

"Why would you think so?" he asked, although he hadn't denied what she said.

"If you've had to be so worried about security and your identity, it makes sense you or your lawyer or some security team you've hired would vet people in your life."

"That would be the wise thing to do."

"And you're a smart man."

"I haven't always acted wisely around you."

"You've been a perfect gentleman this week and you know it," she said, as close as she could come to hinting that she ached for his touch, his mouth on her body, the familiar rise of pleasure and release he could bring.

Tony shrugged and tore into his sandwich again, a grandfather clock tolling once in the background.

"Kolby thinks we're on vacation."

"Good." He finished chewing, tendons in his strong neck flexing. "That's how he should remember this time in his life."

"It's unreal how you and your father have shielded him from the tension in your relationship."

"Obviously not well enough to fool you." His boldly handsome face gave nothing away.

"I know some about your history, and it's tough to miss how little the two of you talk. Your father's an interesting man." She'd enjoyed after-dinner discussions with Enrique and Eloisa about current events and the latest book they'd read.

The old king may have isolated himself from the world, but he'd certainly stayed abreast with the latest news. The discussions had been enlightening on a number of levels, such as how the old king wasn't as clipped and curt with his daughter as he was with Tony.

Tony stared at the last half of his snack, tucking a straggly piece of lettuce back inside. "What did you make for Kolby?"

His question surprised her, but if it kept him talking...

"French toast. It's one of his favorite comfort foods. He likes for me to cut the toast into slices so he can dip it into the syrup. Independence means a lot, even to a three-year-old." It meant a lot to adults. She reached for her bowl to scrape the final taste of custard and licked the spoon clean. The caramel taste exploded into her starving senses like music in her mouth.

Pupils widening with awareness until they nearly pushed away his brown irises, Tony stared back at her across the table, intense, aroused. Her body recognized the signs in him well even if he didn't move so much as an inch closer.

She set the spoon down, the tiny clink echoing in the empty kitchen. "Tony, why are you still awake?"

"I'm a night owl. Some might call me an insomniac."

"An insomniac? I didn't know that." She laughed darkly. "Although how could I since we've never spent an entire night together? Have you had the problem long?"

"I've always been this way." He turned the plate around on the table. "My mother tried everything from warm milk to a 'magic' blanket before just letting me stay up. She used to cook for me too, late at night."

"Your mother, the queen, cooked?" She inched to the edge of her chair, leaning on her elbows, hoping to hold his attention and keep him talking.

"She may have been royalty even before she married my father, but there are plenty in Europe with blue blood and little money." Shadows chased each other across his eyes. "My mother grew up learning the basics of managing her own house. She insisted we boys have run of the kitchen. There were so many everyday places that were off-limits to us for safety reasons, she wanted us to have the normalcy of popping in and out of the kitchen for snacks."

Like any other child. A child who happened to live in a sixteenth-century castle. She liked his mother, a woman she would never meet but felt so very close to at the moment. "What did she cook for you?"

"A Cyclops."

"Excuse me?"

"It's a fried egg with a buttered piece of bread on top." He swirled his hand over his plate as if he could spin an image into reality. "The bread has a hole pinched out of the middle so the egg yolk peeks out like a—"

"Like a Cyclops. I see. My mom called it a Popeye." And with the memory of a simple egg dish, she felt the connection to Tony spin and gain strength again.

He glanced up, a half smile kicking into his one cheek. "Cyclops appealed to the bloodthirsty little boy in me. Just like Kolby and the caterpillar and snake pasta."

To hell with distance and waiting for him to reach out, she covered his hand with hers. "Your mother sounds wonderful."

He nodded briefly. "I believe she was."

"Believe?"

"I have very few memories of her before she…died." He turned his hand over and stroked hers with his thumb. "The beach. A blanket. Food."

"Scents do tend to anchor our memories more firmly."

More shadows drifted through his eyes, darker this time, like storm clouds. *Died* seemed such a benign word to describe the assassination of a young mother, killed because she'd married a king. A vein pulsed visibly in Tony's temple, faster by the second. He'd dealt with such devastating circumstances in life honorably, while her husband had turned to stealing and finally, to taking the ultimate coward's way out.

She held herself very still, unthreatening. Her heart ached for him on a whole new and intense level. "What do you remember about when she died? About leaving San Rinaldo?"

"Not much really." He stayed focused on their connected hands, tracing the veins on her wrist with exaggerated concentration. "I was only five."

So he'd told her before. But she wasn't buying his nonchalance. "Traumatic events seem to stick more firmly in our memory. I recall a car accident when I couldn't have been more than two." She wouldn't back down now, not when she was so close to understanding the man behind the smiles and bold gestures. "I still remember the bright red of the Volkswagen bug."

"You probably saw pictures of the car later," he said dismissively, then looked up sharply, aggressively full of bravado. The storm clouds churned faster with each throb of the vein on his temple. He stroked up her arm with unmistakable sensual intent. "How much longer are you going to wait before you ask me to kiss you again? Because right now, I'm so on fire for you, I want to test out the sturdiness of that table."

"Tony, can you even hear yourself?" she asked, frustrated and even a bit insulted by the way he was jerking her around. "One minute you're Prince Romance and Restraint, the next you're ignoring me over dinner. Then you're spilling your guts. Now, you proposition me— and not too suavely, I might add. Quite frankly, you're giving me emotional whiplash."

His arms twitched, thick roped muscles bulging against his sleeves with restrained power. "Make no mistake, I have wanted you every second of every day. It's all I can do not to haul you against me right now and to hell with the dozens of people that might walk in. But today on the water and tonight here, I'm just not sure this crazy life of mine is good enough for you."

Her body burned in response to his words even as her mind blared a warning. Tony had felt the increasing connection too, and it scared him. So he'd tried to run her off with the crude offer of sex on the table.

Well too damn bad for him, she wasn't backing down. She'd wanted this, *him,* for too long to turn away.

Chapter 10

He'd wanted Shannon back in his bed, but somewhere between making a sandwich and talking about eggs, she'd peeled away walls, exposing thoughts and memories that were better forgotten. They distracted. Hurt. Served no damn purpose.

Anger grated his raw insides. "So? What'll it be? Sex here or in your room?"

She didn't flinch and she didn't leave. Her soft hand stayed on top of his as she looked at him with sad eyes behind her glasses. "Is that what this week has been about?"

He let his gaze linger on the vee of her frothy nightgown set. Lace along the neckline traced into the curve of her breasts the way his hands ached to explore. "I've been clear from the start about what I want."

"Are you so sure about that?"

"What the hell is that supposed to mean?" he snapped.

Sliding from her chair, she circled the table toward him, her heels clicking against the tile. She stopped beside him, the hem of her nightgown set swirling against his leg. "Don't confuse me with your mother."

"Good God, there's not a chance of that." He toppled her into his lap and lowered his head, determined to prove it to her.

"Wait." She stopped him with a hand flattened to his chest just above the two closed buttons. Her palm cooled his overheated skin, calming and stirring, but then she'd always been a mix of contradictions. "You suffered a horrible trauma as a child. No one should lose a parent, especially in such an awful way. I wish you could have been spared that."

"I wish my *mother* had been spared." His hands clenched in her robe, his fists against her back.

"And I can't help but wonder if you helping me—a mother with a young child—is a way to put her ghost to rest. Putting your own ghosts to rest in the process."

Given the crap that had shaken down in his past, he'd done a fine job turning his life around. Frustration poured acid on his burning gut. "You've spent a lot of time thinking about this."

"What you told me this afternoon and tonight brought things into focus."

"Well, thanks for the psychoanalysis." His words came out harsh, but right now he needed her to walk away. "I would offer to pay you for the services, but I wouldn't want to start another fight."

"Sounds to me like you're spoiling for one now." Her eyes softened with more of that concern that grated along his insides. "I'm sorry if I overstepped and hit a nerve."

A nerve? She'd performed a root canal on his emotions. His brain echoed with the retort of gunfire stuttering, aimed at him, his brothers. His mother. He searched for what to say to shut down this conversation, but he wasn't sure of anything other than his need for a serious, body-draining jog on the beach. Problem was? The beach circled right back around to this place.

Easing from his lap, she stood and he tamped down the swift kick of disappointment. Except she didn't leave. She extended her hand and linked her fingers with his.

Just a simple connection, but since he was raw to the core, her touch fired deep.

"Shannon," he said between teeth clenched tight with restraint, "I'm about a second from snapping here. So unless you want me buried heart deep inside you in the next two minutes, you need to go back to your room."

Her hold stayed firm, cool and steady.

"Shannon, damn it all, you don't know what you're doing. You don't want any part of the mood I'm in." Her probing may have brought on the mood, but he wouldn't let it contaminate her.

Angling down with slow precision, she pressed her lips to his. Not moving. Only their mouths and hands linked.

He wanted—needed—to move her away gently. But his fingers curled around the softness of her arm.

"Shanny," he whispered against her mouth, "tell me to leave."

"Not a chance. I only have one question."

"Go ahead." He braced himself for another emotional root canal.

She brought his hand to her chest, pressing his palm against her breast. "Do you have a condom?"

Relief splashed over him like a tidal wave. "Hell, yes, I have one, two in fact, in my wallet. Because even when we're not talking, I know the way we are together could combust at any second. And I will always, always make sure you're protected and safe."

Standing, he scooped her into his arms. Purring her approval, she hooked her hands behind his neck and tipped her face for a full kiss. The soft cushion of her breasts against his chest sent his libido into overdrive. He throbbed against the sweet curve of her hip. At the sweep of tongue, the taste of caramel and *her,* he fought the urge to follow through on the impulse to have her here, now, on the table.

He sketched his mouth along her jaw, down to her collarbone, the scent of her lavender body wash reminding him of shared showers at his place. "We need to go upstairs."

"The pantry is closer." She nipped his bottom lip. "And empty. We can lock the door. I need you now."

"Are you su—?"

"Don't even say it." She dipped her hands into the neckline of his loose shirt, her fingernails sinking insistently deep. "I want you. No waiting."

Her words closed down arguments and rational thought. He made a sure-footed beeline across the tiled floor toward the pantry. Shannon nuzzled his neck, kissed along his jaw, all the while murmuring disjointed words of need that stoked him higher—made his feet move faster. As he walked, her silky blond hair and whispery robe trailed, her sexy little heels dangling from her toes.

Dipping at the door, he flipped the handle and shouldered inside the pantry, a food storage area the size of a small bedroom. The scent of hanging dried herbs coated the air, the smell earthy. He slid her glasses from her face and set them aside on a shelf next to rows of bottled water.

As the door eased closed, the space darkened and his other senses increased. She reached for the light switch and he clasped her wrist, stopping her.

"I don't need light to see you. Your beautiful body is fired into my memory." His fingers crawled up her leg, bunching the frothy gown along her soft thigh, farther still to just under the curve of her buttocks. "Just the feel of you is about more than my willpower can take."

"I don't want your willpower. I'm fed up with your restraint. Give me the uninhibited old Tony back." Her husky voice filled the room with unmistakable desire.

Pressing her hips closer, he tasted down her neck, charting his way to her breasts. An easy swipe cleared the fabric from her shoulders and he found a taut nipple. Damn straight he didn't need light. He knew her body, knew just how to lave and tease the taut peak until she tore at his shirt with frantic hands.

His buttons popped and cool air blanketed his back, warm Shannon writhing against his front. Hooking a finger along the rim of her bikini panties, he stroked her silky smooth stomach. Tugging lightly, he started the scrap of fabric downward until she shimmied them the rest of the way off.

Stepping closer, the silky gown bunched between them, she flattened her hand to the fly of his jeans. He went harder against the pleasure of her touch. Shannon. Just Shannon.

She unzipped his pants and freed his arousal. Clasping him in her fist, she stroked once, and again, her thumb working over his head with each glide. His eyes slammed shut.

Her other hand slipped into his back pocket and pulled out his wallet. A light crackle sounded as she tore into the packet. Her deft fingers rolled the sheath down the length of him with torturous precision.

"Now," she demanded softly against his neck. "Here. On the stepstool or against the door, I don't care as long as you're inside me."

Gnawing need chewed through the last of his restraint. She wanted this. He craved her. No more waiting. Tony backed her against the solid panel of the door, her fingernails digging into his shoulders, his back, lower as she tucked her hand inside his jeans and boxers.

Arching, urging, she hooked her leg around his, opening for him. Her shoe clattered to the floor but she didn't seem to notice or care. He nudged at her core, so damp and ready for him. He throbbed—and thrust.

Velvet heat clamped around him, drew him deeper, sent sparks shooting behind his eyelids. In the darkened room, the pure essence of Shannon went beyond anything he'd experienced. And the importance of that expanded inside him, threatening to drive him to his knees.

So he focused on her, searching with his hands and mouth, moving inside and stroking outside to make sure she was every bit as encompassed by the mind-numbing ecstasy. She rocked faster against him. Her sighs came quicker, her moans of pleasure higher and louder until he captured the sound, kissing her and thrusting with his tongue and body. He explored the soft inside of her mouth, savoring the soft clamp of her gripping him with spasms he knew signaled her approaching orgasm.

Teeth gritted, he held back his own finish. Her face

pressed to his neck. Her chants of *yes, yes, yes* synced with his pulse and pounding. Still, he held back, determined to take her there once more. She bowed away from the door, into him, again and again until her teeth sunk into his shoulder on a stifled cry of pleasure.

The scent of her, of slick sex and *them* mixed with the already earthy air.

Finally—*finally*—he could let go. The wave of pleasure pulsing through him built higher, roaring louder in his ears. He'd been too long without her. The wave crested. Release crashed over him. Rippling through him. Shifting the ground under his feet until his forehead thumped against the door.

Hauling her against his chest, heart still galloping, as they both came back down to earth in the pantry.

The pantry, for God's sake?

His chances of staying away from Shannon again were slim. That path didn't work for either of them. But if they were going to be together, he would make sure their next encounter was total fantasy material.

Sun glinting along the crystal-clear pool, Shannon tugged Kolby's T-shirt over his head and slid his feet into tiny Italian leather sandals. She'd spent the morning splashing with her son and Tony's sister, and she wasn't close to working off pent-up energy. Even the soothing ripple of the heated waters down the fountain rock wall hadn't stilled the jangling inside her.

After making love in the pantry, she and Tony had locked themselves in her room where he'd made intense and thorough love to her. Her skin remembered the rasp of his beard against her breasts, her stomach, the insides of her thighs. How could she still crave even more from him? She should be in search of a good nap rather than wondering when she could get Tony alone again.

Of course she would have to find him first.

He'd left via her balcony just as the morning sun peeked over the horizon. Now that big orange glow was directly overhead and no word from him. She deflated her son's water wings. The hissing air and the maternal ritual reminded her of Tony's revelations just before they'd ended up in the closet.

Could he be avoiding her to dodge talking further? He'd made no secret of using sex to skirt the painful topic. She couldn't even blame him when she'd been guilty of the same during their affair. What did this do to their deadline to return home?

Kolby yanked the hem of her cover-up. "Want another movie."

"We'll see, sweetie." Kolby was entranced by the large home theater, but then what child wouldn't be?

Tony's half sister shaded her eyes in the lounger next to them, an open paperback in her other hand. "I can take him in if you want to stay outside. Truly, I don't mind." She toyed with her silver shell necklace, straightening the conch charm.

"But you're reading. And aren't you leaving this afternoon? I don't want to keep you from your packing."

"Do you honestly think any guest of Enrique Medina is bothered by packing their own suitcases? Get real." She snorted lightly. "I have plenty of time. Besides, I've been wanting to check out the new Disney movie for my library's collection."

She'd learned Eloisa was a librarian, which explained the satchel of books she'd brought along. Her husband was an architect who specialized in restoring historic landmarks. They were an unpretentious couple caught up in a maelstrom. "What if the screening room doesn't have the movie you w—" She stopped short. "Of course they have whatever you're looking for on file."

"A bit intimidating, isn't it?" Eloisa pulled on her wraparound cover-up, tugging her silver necklace out so the conch charm was visible. "I didn't grow up with all of this and I suspect you didn't, either."

Shannon rubbed her arms, shivering in spite of the eighty-degree day. "How do you keep from letting it overwhelm you?"

"I wish I could offer you reassurance or answers, but honestly I'm still figuring out how to deal with all of this myself. I had only begun to get to know my birth father a few months ago." She looked back at the mission-style mansion, her eyebrows pinching together. "Now the whole royal angle has gone public. They haven't figured out about me. Yet. That's why we're here this week, to talk with Enrique and his attorneys, to set up some preemptive strikes."

"I'm sorry."

Thank God Eloisa had the support of her husband. And Tony had been there for her. Who was there for him? Even his brothers hadn't shown up beyond sterile conference calls.

"You have nothing to apologize for, Shannon. I'm only saying it's okay to feel overwhelmed. Cut yourself some slack and do what you can to stay level. Let me watch a movie with your son while you swim or enjoy a bubble bath or take a nap. It's okay."

Indecision warred inside her. These past couple of weeks she'd had more help with Kolby than since he was born. Guilt tweaked her maternal instincts.

"Please, Mama?" Kolby sidled closer to Eloisa. "I like Leesa."

Ah, and just like that, her maternal guilt worried in another direction, making her fret that she hadn't given her son enough play dates or socialization. Funny how a mother worried no matter what.

Shannon nodded to Tony's sister. "If you're absolutely sure."

"He's a cutie, and I'm guessing he will be asleep before the halfway point. Enjoy the pool a while longer. It'll be good practice for me to spend time with him." She smiled whimsically as she ruffled his damp hair. "Jonah and I are hoping to have a few of our own someday."

"Thank you. I accept gratefully." Shannon remembered well what it felt like to be young and in love and hopeful for the future. She couldn't bring herself to regret Nolan since he'd given her Kolby. "I hope we'll have the chance to speak again before you leave this afternoon?"

"Don't worry." Eloisa winked. "I imagine we'll see each other again."

With a smile, Shannon hugged her little boy close, inhaling his baby-fresh scent with a hint of chlorine.

He squirmed, his cheeks puffed with a wide smile. "Wanna go."

She pressed a quick kiss to his forehead. "Be good for Mrs. Landis."

Eloisa took his hand. "We'll be fine."

Kolby waved over his shoulder without a backward glance.

Too restless for a bath or nap, she eyed the pool and whipped off her cover-up. Laps sounded like the wisest option. Diving in, she stared through the chlorinated depths until her eyes burned, forcing her to squeeze them shut. She lost herself in the rhythm of slicing her arms through the heated water, no responsibilities, no outside world. Just the *thump, thump, thump* of her heart mingling with the roar of the water passing over her ears.

Five laps later, she flipped underwater and resurfaced face up for a backstroke. She opened her eyes and, oh my, the view had changed. Tony stood by the waterfall in black board shorts.

Whoa. Her stomach lurched into a swan dive. Tony's bronzed chest sprinkled with hair brought memories of their night together, senses on overload from the darkened herb-scented pantry, later in the brightly lighted luxury of her bedroom. Who would have thought dried oregano and rosemary could be aphrodisiacs?

His eyes hooked on her crocheted two piece with thorough and unmistakable admiration. He knew every inch of her body and made his appreciation clear whether she wore high-end garb or her simple black waitress uniform, wilted from a full shift. God, how he was working his way into her heart as well as her life.

She swam toward the edge with wide lazy strokes. "Is Kolby okay?"

"Enjoying the movie and popcorn." He knelt by the edge, his elbow on one knee drawing her eye to the nautical compass tattooed on his bicep. "Although with the way his head is drooping, chances are he'll be asleep anytime now."

"Thank you for checking on him." She resisted the urge to ask Tony what *he'd* been doing since he left her early this morning.

"Not a problem." His fingers played through the water in front of her without touching but so close the swirls caressed her breasts. "I said I intended to romance you and I got sidetracked. I apologize for that. The woman I'm with should be treated like a princess."

His *princess?* Shock loosened her hold on the edge of the pool. Tony caught her arm quickly and eased her from the water to sit next to him. His gaze swept her from soaking wet hair to dripping toes. Appreciation smoked, darkening his eyes to molten heat she recognized well.

He tipped her chin with a knuckle scarred from handling sailing lines. "Are you ready to be royally romanced?"

Chapter 11

A five-minute walk later, Tony flattened his palm to Shannon's back and guided her down the stone path leading from the mansion to the greenhouse. Her skin, warmed from the sun, heated through her thin cover-up. Soon, he hoped to see and feel every inch of her without barriers.

He'd spent the morning arranging a romantic backdrop for their next encounter. Finding privacy was easier said than done on this island, but he was persistent and creative. Anticipation ramped inside him.

He was going to make things right with her. She deserved to be treated like a princess, and he had the resources to follow through. His mind leaped ahead to all the ways he could romance her back on the mainland now that he understood her better—once he fulfilled the remaining weeks he'd promised his father.

A kink started in his neck.

Squeezing his hand lightly, she followed him along the rocky path, the mansion smaller on the horizon. Few trees stood between them and the glass building ahead. Early on, Enrique had cleared away foliage for security purposes.

"Where are we going?"

"You'll see soon."

Farther from shore, a sprawling oak had been saved. The mammoth trunk declared it well over a hundred years old. As a kid, he'd begged to keep this one for climbing. His father had gruffly agreed. The memory kicked over him, itchy and ill timed.

He brushed aside a branch, releasing a flock of butterflies soaring toward the conservatory, complete with two wings branching off the main structure. "This is the greenhouse I told you about. It also has a café-style room."

Enrique had done his damnedest to give his sons a "normal" childhood, as much as he could while never letting them off the island. Tony had undergone some serious culture shock after he'd left. At least working on a shrimper had given him time to absorb the mainland in small bites. Back then, he'd even opted to rent a sailboat for a home rather than an apartment.

As they walked past a glass gazebo, Shannon tipped her face to his. Sunlight streaked through the trees, bathing her face. "Is that why the movie room has more of a theater feel?"

Nodding, he continued, "There's a deli at the ferry station and an ice cream parlor at the creamery. I thought we could take Kolby there."

He hoped she heard his intent to try with her son as well, to give this relationship a real chance at working.

"Kolby likes strawberry flavored best," she said simply.

"I'll remember that," he assured her. And he meant it. "We also have a small dental clinic. And of course there's the chapel."

"They've thought of everything." Her mouth oohed over a birdbath with doves drinking along the edge.

"My father always said a monarch's job was to see to the needs of his people. This island became his mini-kingdom. Because of the isolation, he needed to make accommodations, try to create a sense of normalcy." Clouds whispered overhead and Tony guided her faster through the garden. "He's started a new round of renovations. A number of his staff members have died of old age. That presents a new set of challenges as he replaces them with employees who aren't on the run, people who have options."

"Like Alys."

"Exactly," he said, just as the skies opened up with an afternoon shower. "Now, may I take you to lunch? I know this great little out-of-the-way place with kick-ass fresh flowers."

"Lead on." Shannon tugged up the hood on her cover-up and raced alongside him.

As the rain pelted faster, he charged up the stone steps leading to the conservatory entrance. Tony threw open the double doors, startling a sparrow into flight around the high glass ceiling in the otherwise deserted building. A quick glance around assured him that yes, everything was exactly as he'd ordered.

* * *

"Ohmigod, Tony!" Shannon gasped, taking in the floral feast for her eyes as well as her nose. "This is breathtaking."

Flipping the hood from her head, she plunged deeper into the spacious greenhouse where a riot of scents and colors waited. Classical music piped lowly from hidden speakers. Ferns dangled overhead. Unlike crowded nurseries she'd visited in the past, this space sprawled more like an indoor floral park.

An Italian marble fountain trickled below a skylight, water spilling softly from a carved snake's mouth as it curled around some reclining Roman.god. Wrought-iron screens sported hydrangeas and morning glories twining throughout, benches in front for reading or meditation. Potted palms and cacti added height to the interior landscape. Tiered racks of florist's buckets with cut flowers stretched along a far wall. She spun under the skylight, immersing herself in the thick perfume, sunbeams and Debussy's *Nocturnes*.

While she could understand Tony's point about not wanting to be isolated here indefinitely, she appreciated the allure of the magical retreat Enrique had created. Even the rain *tap, tap, tapping* overhead offered nature's lyrical accent to the soft music.

Slowing her spin, she found Tony staring at her with undeniable arousal. Tony, and only Tony because the space appeared otherwise deserted. Her skin prickled with awareness at the muscular display of him in nothing but board shorts and deck shoes.

"Are we alone?" she asked.

"Completely," he answered, gesturing toward a little round table set for two, with wine and finger foods.

"Help yourself. There are stuffed mussels, fried squid, vegetable skewers, cold olives and cheese."

She strode past him, without touching but so close a magnetic field seemed to activate, urging her to seal her body to his.

"It's been so wonderful here indulging in grown-up food after so many meals of chicken nuggets and pizza." She broke off a corner of ripe white cheese and popped it in her mouth.

"Then you're going to love the beverage selection." Tony scooped up a bottle from the middle of the table. "Red wine from Basque country or sherry from southern Spain?"

"Red, please. But can we wait a moment on the food? I want to see everything here first."

"I was hoping you would say that." He passed her a crystal glass, half full.

She sipped, staring at him over the rim. "Perfect."

"And there's still more." His fingers linked with hers, he led her past an iron screen to a secluded corner.

Vines grew tangled and dense over the windows, the sun through the glass roof muted by rivulets of rain. A chaise longue was tucked in a corner. Flower petals speckled the furniture and floor. Everything was so perfect, so beautiful, it brought tears to her eyes. God, it still scared her how much she wanted to trust her feelings, trust the signals coming from Tony.

To hide her eyes until she could regain control, she rushed to the crystal vase of mixed flowers on the end table and buried her face in the bouquet. "What a unique blend of fragrances."

"It's a specially ordered arrangement. Each flower was selected for you because of its meaning."

Touched by the detailed thought he'd put into the encounter, she pivoted to face him. "You told me once you wanted to wrap me in flowers."

"That's the idea here." His arms banded around her waist. "And I was careful to make sure there will be no thorns. Only pleasure."

If only life could be that simple. With their time here running out, she couldn't resist.

"You're sure we won't be interrupted?" She set her wineglass on the end table and linked her fingers behind his neck. "No surveillance cameras or telephoto lenses?"

"Completely certain. There are security cameras outside, but none inside. I've given the staff the afternoon off and our guards are not Peeping Toms. We are totally and completely alone." He anchored her against him, the rigid length of his arousal pressing into her stomach with a hefty promise.

"You prepared for this." And she wanted this, wanted him. But… "I'm not sure I like being so predictable."

"You are anything but predictable. I've never met a more confusing person in my life." He tugged a damp lock of her hair. "Any more questions?"

She inhaled deeply, letting the scents fill her with courage. "Who can take off faster the other person's clothes?"

"Now there's a challenge I can't resist." He bunched her cover-up in his hands and peeled the soft cotton over her head.

Shaking her hair free, she leaned into him just as he slanted his mouth over hers. His fingers made fast work of the ties to her bathing suit top. The crocheted triangles fell away, baring her to the steamy greenhouse air.

She nipped his ear where a single dot-shaped scar

stayed from a healed-over piercing. A teenage rebellion, he'd told her once. She could envision him on a Spanish galleon, a swarthy and buffed pirate king.

For a moment, for *this* moment, she let herself indulge in foolish fantasies, no fears. She would allow the experience to sweep her away as smoothly as she brushed off his board shorts. She pushed aside the sterner responsible voice inside her that insisted she remember past mistakes and tread cautiously.

"It's been too damn long." He thumbed off her swimsuit bottom.

"Uh, hello?" She kicked the last fabric barrier away and prayed other barriers could be as easily discarded. "It's been less than eight hours since you left my room."

"Too long."

She played her fingers along the cut of his sculpted chest, down the flat plane of his washboard stomach. Pressing her lips to his shoulder, she kissed her way toward his arm until she grazed the different texture of his tattooed flesh—inked with a black nautical compass. "I've always wanted to ask why you chose this particular tattoo."

His muscles bunched and twitched. "It symbolizes being able to find my way home."

"There's still so much I don't know about you." Concerns trickled through her like the rain trying to find its way inside.

"Hey, we're here to escape. All that can wait." He slipped her glasses from her face and placed them on the end table.

Parting through the floral arrangement to the middle, he slipped out an orchid and pinched off the flower. He trailed the bloom along her nose, her cheekbones and jaw in a silky scented swirl. "For magnificence."

Her knees went wobbly and she sat on the edge of the chaise, tapestry fabric rough on the backs on her thighs, rose-petal smooth. He tucked the orchid behind her ear, easing her back until she reclined.

Returning to the vase, he tugged free a long stalk with indigo buds and explored the length of her arm, then one finger at a time. Then over her stomach to her other hand and back up again in a shivery path that left her breathless.

"Blue salvia," he said, "because I think of you night and day."

His words stirred her as much as the glide of the flower over her shoulder. Then he placed it on the tiny pillow under her head.

A pearly calla lily chosen next, he traced her collarbone before lightly dipping between her breasts.

"Shannon," he declared hoarsely, "I chose this lily because you are a majestic beauty."

Detouring, he sketched the underside of her breast and looped round again and again, each circle smaller until he teased the dusky tip. Her body pulled tight and tingly. Her back arched into the sweet sensation and he transferred his attention to her other breast, repeating the delicious pattern.

Reaching for him, she clutched his shoulders, aching to urge him closer. "Tony…"

Gently, he clasped her wrists and tucked them at her sides. "No touching or I'll stop."

"Really?"

"Probably not, because I can't resist you." He left the

lily in her open palm. "But how about you play along anyway? I guarantee you'll like the results."

Dark eyes glinting with an inner light, Tony eased free… "A coral rose for passion."

His words raspy, his face intense, he skimmed the bud across her stomach, lower. Lower still. Her head fell back, her eyes closed as she wondered just how far he would dare go.

The silky teasing continued from her hip inward, daring more and even more. A husky moan escaped between her clenched lips.

Still, he continued until the rose caressed…oh my. Her knee draped to the side giving him, giving the flower, fuller access as he teased her. Gooseflesh sprinkled her skin. Her body focused on the feelings and perfumes stoking desire higher.

A warm breath steamed over her stomach with only a second's warning before his mouth replaced the flower. Her fingers twitched into a fist, crushing the lily and releasing a fresh burst of perfume. A flick of his tongue, alternated with gentle suckles, caressed and coaxed her toward completion.

Her head thrashed as she chased her release. He took her to the brink, then retreated, drawing out the pleasure until the pressure inside her swelled and throbbed…

And bloomed.

A cry of pleasure burst free and she didn't bother holding it back. She rode the sensation, gasping in floral-tinged breaths.

His bold hands stroked upward as he slid over her, blanketing her with his hard, honed body. She hooked a languid leg over his hip. Her arm draped his shoulders as she drew him toward her, encouraging him to press inside.

The smell of crushed flowers clung to his skin as she kissed her way along his chest, back up his neck. He filled her, stretched her, moved inside her. She was surprised to feel desire rising again to a fevered pitch. Writhing, she lost herself in the barrage of sensations. The bristle of his chest hair against her breasts. The silky softness of flower petals against her back.

And the scents—she gasped in the perfect blend of musk and sex and earthy greenhouse. She raked his back, broad and strong and yet so surprisingly gentle, too.

He was working his way not only into her body but into her heart. When had she ever stood a chance at resisting him? As much as she tried to tell herself it was only physical, only an affair, she knew this man had come to mean so much more to her. He reached her in ways no one ever had before.

She grappled at the hard planes of his back, completion so close all over again.

"Let go and I'll catch you," he vowed against her ear and she believed him.

For the first time in so long, she totally trusted.

The magnitude exploded inside her, blasting through barriers. Pleasure filled every niche. Muscles knotted in Tony's back as he tensed over her and growled his own hoarse completion against her ear.

Staring up at the rain-splattered skylight, tears burning her eyes again, she held Tony close. She felt utterly bare and unable to hide any longer. She'd trusted him with her body.

Now the time had come to trust him with her secrets.

Chapter 12

Tony watched Shannon on his iPhone as she talked to Kolby. She'd assured him that she wanted to stay longer in their greenhouse getaway, once she checked on her son.

Raindrops pattered slowly on the skylight, the afternoon shower coming to an end. Sunshine refracted off the moisture, casting prisms throughout the indoor garden.

He had Shannon back in his bed and in his life and he intended to do anything it took to keep her there. The chemistry between them, the connection—it was one of a kind. The way she'd calmly handled his bizarre family setup, keeping her down-to-earth ways in the face of so much wealth... Finally, he'd found a woman he could trust, a woman he could spend his life with. Coming back to the island had been a good thing after all, since it had made him realize how unaffected she was by the trappings. In a compass, she would be the magnet, a grounding center.

And he owed her so much better than he'd delivered thus far. He'd wrecked Shannon's life. It was up to him to fix it. Here, alone with her in the bright light of day, he couldn't avoid the truth.

They would get married.

The decision settled inside him with a clean fit, so much so he wondered why he hadn't decided so resolutely before now. His feelings for her ran deep. He knew she cared for him, too. And marrying each other would solve her problems.

They were making progress. He could tell she'd been swayed by the flowers, the ambience.

A plan formed in his mind. Later tonight he would take her to the chapel, lit with candles, and he would propose, while the lovemaking they'd shared here was still fresh in her memory.

Now he just had to figure out the best way to persuade her to say yes.

Thumbing the off button, she disconnected her call. "The nanny says Kolby has only just woken up and she's feeding him a snack." She passed his phone to him and curled against his side on the chaise. "Thanks for not teasing me about being overprotective. I can't help but worry when I'm not with him."

"I would too, if he was mine," he said. Then her surprised expression prompted him to continue, "Why do you look shocked?"

"No offense meant." She smoothed a hand along his chest. "It's just obvious you and he haven't connected."

Something he would need to rectify in order to be a

part of Shannon's life. "I will never let you or him down the way his father did."

She winced and he could feel her drawing back into herself. He wanted all barriers gone between them as fully as they'd tossed aside their clothes.

"Hey, Shannon, stay with me here." He cupped her bare hip. "I asked you before if your husband hit you and you said no. Did you lie about that?"

Sitting up abruptly, she gathered her swimsuit off the floor.

"Let's get dressed and then we can talk." She yanked on the suit bottom briskly.

Waiting, he slid on his board shorts. She tied the bikini strings behind her neck with exaggerated effort, all the while staring at the floor. A curtain of tousled blond locks covered her face. Just when he'd begun to give up on getting an answer, she straightened, shaking her hair back over her shoulders.

"I was telling the truth when I said Nolan never laid a hand on me. But there are things I need to explain in order for you to understand why it's so difficult for me to accept help." Determination creased her face. "Nolan was always a driven man. His perfectionism made him successful in business. And I'd been brought up to believe marriage is forever. How could I leave a man because he didn't like the way I hung clothes in the closet?"

He forced his hands to stay loose on his knees, keeping his body language as unthreatening as possible when he already sensed he would want to beat the hell out of Nolan Crawford by the end of this conversation—if he wasn't already dead.

Plucking a flower petal from her hair, she rubbed the coral-colored patch between two fingers. "Do you know how many people laughed at me because I was upset that he didn't want me to work? He said he wanted us to have more time together. Somehow any plans I made with others were disrupted. After a while I lost contact with my friends."

The picture of isolation came together in his head with startling clarity. He understood the claustrophobic feeling of being cut off from the rest of the world. Although he couldn't help but think his father's need to protect his children differed from an obsessive—abusive—husband dominating his wife. Rage simmered, ready to boil.

She scooped her cover-up from the floor and clutched it to her stomach. "Then I got pregnant. Splitting up became more complicated."

Hating like hell the helpless feeling, he passed her glasses back to her. It was damn little, but all he could see her accepting from him right now.

With a wobbly smile, she slid them on her face and seemed to take strength from them. "When Kolby was about thirteen months old, he spiked a scary high fever while I was alone with him. Nolan had always gone with us to pediatric checkups. At the ER, I was a mess trying to give the insurance information. I had no idea what to tell them, because Nolan had insisted I not 'worry' about such things as medical finances. That day triggered something in me. I needed to take care of my son."

He took her too-cold hand and rubbed it between his.

"Looking back now I see the signs were there. Nolan's computer and cell phone were password protected. He considered it an invasion of privacy if I asked who he was speaking to. I thought he was cheating. I never considered..."

He squeezed her hand in silent encouragement.

"So I decided to learn more about the finances, because if I needed to leave him, I had to make sure my son's future was protected and not spirited away to some Cayman account." She fidgeted, her fingers landing on the blue salvia—*I think of you often* took on a darker meaning. "I was lucky enough to figure out his computer password."

"*You* discovered the Ponzi scheme?" Good God, what kind of strength would it take to turn in her own husband?

"It was the hardest thing I've ever done, but I handed over the evidence to the police. He'd stolen so much from so many people, I couldn't stay silent. His parents posted bail, and I wasn't given warning." She spun the stem between her thumb and forefinger. "When he walked back into the house, he had a gun."

Shock nailed him harder than a sail boom to the gut.

"My God, Shannon. I knew he'd committed suicide but I had no idea you were there. I'm so damn sorry."

"That's not all, though. For once the media didn't uncover everything." She drew herself up straight. "Nolan said he was going to kill me, then Kolby and then himself."

Her words iced the perspiration on his brow. This was so much worse than he'd foreseen. He cupped an arm around her shoulders and pulled her close. She trembled and kept twirling the flower, but she didn't stop speaking.

"His parents pulled up in the driveway." A shuddering sigh racked her body, her profile pained. "He realized he wouldn't have time to carry out his original plan. Thank

God he locked himself in his office before he pulled the trigger and killed himself."

"Shannon." Horror threatened to steal his breath, but for her, he would hold steady. "I don't even know what to say to fix the hell you were put through."

"I didn't tell his parents what he'd planned. They'd lost their son and he'd been labeled a criminal." She held up the blue salvia. "I couldn't see causing them more grief when they thought of him."

Her eyes were filled with tears and regret. Tony kissed her forehead, then pulled her against his chest. "You were generous to the memory of a man who didn't deserve it."

"I didn't do it for him. No matter what, he's the father of my child." She pressed her cheek harder against him and hugged him tightly. "Kolby will have to live with the knowledge that his dad was a crook, but I'll be damned before I'll let my son know his own father tried to kill him."

"You've fought hard for your son." He stroked her back. "You're a good mother and a strong woman."

She reminded him of a distant memory, of his own mother wrapping him in a silver blanket as they left San Rinaldo and telling him the shield would keep him safe. She'd been right. If only he could have protected her, as well.

Easing away, Shannon scrubbed her damp cheeks. "Thank God for Vernon. I'd sold off everything to pay Nolan's debts, even my piano and my oboe. The first waitressing job I landed in Louisiana didn't cover expenses. We were running out of options when Vernon hired me. Everyone else treated me like a pariah. Even Nolan's parents didn't want anything to do with either of us. So many people insisted I must have known what he was doing. That I must have tucked away money for myself. The gossip and the rumors were hell."

Realization, understanding spewed inside him like the abrupt shower of the sprinklers misting over the potted plants. He'd finally found a woman he could trust enough to propose marriage.

Only to find a husband was likely the last thing she ever wanted again.

Three hours later, Shannon sat on the floor in her suite with Kolby, rolling wooden trains along a ridged track. An ocean breeze spiraled through the open balcony door. She craved the peace of that boundless horizon. Never again would she allow herself to be hedged in as she'd been in her marriage.

After she'd finished dredging up her past, she'd needed to see her son. Tony had been understanding, although she could sense he wanted to talk longer. Once she'd returned to her suite, she'd showered and changed—and had been with her son ever since.

The past twenty-four hours had been emotionally charged on so many levels. Tony had been supportive and understanding, while giving her space. He'd also been a tender—thorough—lover.

Could she risk giving their relationship another try once they returned to the mainland? Was it possible for her to be a part of a normal couple?

A tug on her shirt yanked her attention back to the moment. Kolby looked up at her with wide blue eyes. "I'm hungry."

"Of course, sweetie. We'll go down to the kitchen and see what we can find." Hopefully the cook—the *chef*—

wouldn't object since he must be right in the middle of supper prep. "We just need to clean up the toys first."

As she reached for the train set's storage bin, she heard a throat clear behind her and jerked around to find her on-again lover standing in the balcony doorway.

Her stomach fluttered with awareness, and she pressed her sweaty palms to her jeans. "How long have you been there?"

"Not long." Tony had showered and changed as well, wearing khakis and a button-down. "I can make his snack."

Whoa, Tony was seeking time with her son? That signaled a definite shift in their relationship. Although she'd seen him make his own breakfast in the past, she couldn't miss the significance of this moment and his efforts to try.

Turning him away would mean taking a step back. "Are you sure?"

Because God knows, she still had a boatload of fears.

"Positive," he said, his voice as steady as the man.

"Okay then." She pressed a hand over her stomach full of butterflies. "I'll just clean up here—"

"We've got it, don't we, pal?"

Kolby eyed him warily but he didn't turn away, probably because Tony kept his distance. He wasn't pushing. Maybe they'd both learned a lot these past couple of weeks.

"Okay, then." She stood, looking around the room, unsure what to do next. "I'll just, uh…"

Tony touched her hand lightly. "You mentioned selling your piano and I couldn't miss the regret in your voice. There's a Steinway Grand in the east wing. Alys or one of the guards can show you where if you would like to play."

Would she? Her fingers twitched. She'd closed off so much of her old life, including the good parts. Her music had been a beautiful bright spot in those solitary years of her life with Nolan. How kind of Tony to see beyond the surface of the harrowing final moments that had tainted her whole marriage. In the same way he'd chosen flowers based on facets of her personality, he'd detected the creativity she'd all but forgotten, honoring it in a small, simple offer.

Nodding her head was tougher than she thought. Her body went a little jerky before she could manage a response. "I would like that. Thank you for thinking of it and for spending time with Kolby."

He was a man who saw beyond her material needs… a man to treasure.

Her throat clogging with emotion, she backed from the room, watching the tableau of Tony with her son. Antonio Medina, a prince and billionaire, knelt on the floor with Kolby, cleaning up a wooden train set.

Tony chunked the caboose in the bin. "Has your mom ever cooked you a Cyclops?"

"What's a cycle-ops?" His face was intent with interest.

"The sooner we clean up the trains, the sooner I can show you."

She pressed a hand to her swelling heart. Tony was handling Kolby with ease. Her son would be fine.

After getting directions from Alys, Shannon found the east wing and finally the music room. What a simple way to describe such an awe-inspiring space. More of a circular ballroom, wooden floors stretched across, with a coffered ceiling that added texture as well as sound control. Crystal chandeliers and sconces glittered in the late-afternoon sun.

And the instruments… Her feet drew her deeper into the room, closer to the gold-gilded harp and a Steinway grand piano. She stroked the ivory keys reverently, then zipped through a scale. Pure magic.

She perched on the bench, her hands poised. Unease skittered up her spine like a double-timed scale, a sense of being watched. Pivoting around, she searched the expansive room….

Seated in a tapestry wingback, Enrique Medina stared back at her from beside a stained-glass window. Even with his ill health, the deposed monarch radiated power and charisma. His dogs asleep on either side, he wore a simple dark suit with an ascot, perfectly creased although loose fitting. He'd lost even more weight since her arrival.

Enrique thumbed a gold pocket watch absently. "Do not mind me."

Had Tony sent her to this room on purpose, knowing his father would be here? She didn't think so, given the stilted relationship between the two men. "I don't want to disturb you."

"Not at all. We have not had a chance to speak alone, you and I," he said with a hint of an accent.

The musicality was pleasing to the ear. Every now and then, a lilt in certain words reminded her of how Tony spoke, small habits that she hadn't discerned as being raised with a foreign language. But she could hear the similarity more clearly when listening to his father.

While she'd seen the king daily during her two weeks on the island, those encounters had been mostly during meals. He'd spent the majority of his time with his daughter. But since Eloisa and her husband had left this afternoon, Enrique must be at loose ends. Shannon envied them that connection, and missed her own parents all the more. How much different her life might have been if they hadn't died. Her mother had shared a love of music.

She stroked the keyboard longingly. "Who plays the piano?"

"My sons took lessons as a part of the curriculum outlined by their tutors."

"Of course, I should have realized," she said. "Tony can play?"

Laughter rattled around inside his chest. "That would be a stretch. My youngest son can read music, but he did not enjoy sitting still. Antonio rushed through lessons so he could go outside."

"I can picture that."

"You know him well then." His sharp brown eyes took in everything. "Now my middle boy, Duarte, is more disciplined, quite the martial arts expert. But with music?" Enrique waved dismissively. "He performs like a robot."

Her curiosity tweaked for more details on Tony's family. Over the past couple of weeks, their relationship had deepened, and she needed more insights to still the fears churning her gut. "And your oldest son, Carlos? How did he fare with the piano lessons?"

A dark shadow crossed Enrique's face before he schooled his regal features again. "He had a gift. He's a surgeon now, using that touch in other ways."

"I can see how the two careers could tap into the same

skill," she said, brushing her fingers over the gleaming keys.

Perhaps she could try again to find a career that tapped into her love of music. What a gift it would be to bring joy deeper into her life again.

Enrique tucked one hand into his pocket. "Do you have feelings for my son?"

His blunt question blindsided her, but she should have realized this cunning man never chatted just for conversation's sake. "That is a personal question."

"And I may not have time to wait around for you to feel comfortable answering."

"You're playing the death card? That's a bit cold, don't you think, sir?"

He laughed, hard and full-out like Tony did—or like he used to. "You have a spine. Good. You are a fine match for my stubborn youngest."

Her irritation over his probing questions eased. What parent didn't want to see their children settled and happy? "I appreciate your opening your home to me and my son and giving us a chance to get to know you."

"Diplomatically said, my dear. You are wise to proceed thoughtfully. Regrets are a terrible thing," he said somberly. "I should have sent my family out of San Rinaldo sooner. I waited too long and Beatriz paid the price."

The darker turn of the conversation stilled her. She'd wanted more insights into Tony's life, yet this was going so much deeper than she had anticipated.

Enrique continued, "It was such chaos that day when the coup began. We had planned for my family to take one escape route and I would use another." His jaw flexed sharply in his gaunt face. "I made it out, and the rebels found my family. Carlos was injured trying to save his mother."

The picture of violence and terror he painted sounded like something from a movie, so unreal, yet they'd lived it. "Tony and your other sons witnessed the attack on their mother?"

"Antonio had nightmares for a year, and then he became obsessed with the beach and surfing. From that day on, he lived to leave the island."

She'd known the bare bones details of their escape. But the horror they'd lived through, the massive losses rolled over her with a new vividness. Tony's need to help her had more to do with caring than control. He didn't want to isolate her or smother her by managing everything the way her husband had. Tony tried to help her because he'd failed to save someone else he cared about.

Somehow, knowing this made it easier for her to open her heart. To take a chance beyond their weeks here.

Without question, he would have to understand her need for independence, but she also had to appreciate how he'd been hurt, how those hurts had shaped him. And as Antonio Medina and Tony Castillo merged in her mind, she couldn't ignore the truth any longer.

She loved him.

Approaching footsteps startled her, drawing her focus from the past and toward the arched entry. Tony stepped into view just when her defenses were at their lowest. No doubt her heart was in her eyes. She started toward him, only to realize *his* eyes held no tender feelings.

The harsh angles of his face blared a forewarning before he announced, "There's been a security breach."

Chapter 13

Shock jolted through Shannon, followed closely by fear. "A security breach? Where's Kolby?"

She shot to her feet and ran across the music room to Tony. The ailing king reached for his cane, his dogs waking instantly, beating her there by a footstep. Enrique steadied himself with a hand against the wall, but he was up and moving. "What happened?"

"Kolby is fine. No one has been hurt, but we have taken another hit in the media."

Enrique asked, "Have they located the island?"

"No," Tony said as Alys slid into view behind him. "It happened at the airport when Eloisa and Jonah's flight landed in South Carolina. The press was waiting, along with crowds of everyday people wanting a picture to sell for an easy buck."

Shannon's stomach lurched at another assault in the

news. "Could the frenzy have to do with the Landis family connections?"

"No," Tony said curtly. "The questions were all about their vacation with Eloisa's father the king."

Alys angled past Tony with a wheelchair. "Your Majesty, I'll take you to your office so you can speak to security directly."

The king dropped into the wheelchair heavily. "Thank you, Alys." His dogs loped into place alongside him. "I am ready."

Nerves jangled, Shannon started to follow, but Tony extended a hand to stop her.

"We need to talk."

His chilly voice stilled her feet faster than any arm across the entranceway. Had he been holding back because of concerns for his father's health? "What's wrong? What haven't you told me?"

She stepped closer for comfort. He crossed his arms over his chest.

"The leak came from this house. There was a call placed from here this afternoon—at just the right time— to an unlisted cell number."

"Here? But your father's security has been top notch." No wonder he was so concerned.

Tony unclipped his iPhone from his waistband. "We have security footage of the call being made."

Thumbing the controls, he filled the screen with a still image of a woman on the phone, a woman in a white swimsuit cover-up, hood pulled over her head.

A cover-up just like hers? "I don't understand. You think this is *me?* Why would I tip off the media?"

His mouth stayed tight-lipped and closed, and his eyes... Oh God, she recognized well that condemning look from the days following Nolan's arrest and then his death.

Steady. Steady. She reminded herself Tony wasn't Nolan or the other people who'd betrayed her, and he had good reasons to be wary. She drew in a shuddering breath.

"I understand that Enrique brought you up to be unusually cautious about the people in your life. And he had cause after what happened to your mother." Thoughts of Tony as a small child watching his mother's murder brushed sympathy over her own hurt. "But you have to see there's nothing about me that would hint at this kind of behavior."

"I know you would do anything to secure your son's future. Whoever sold this information received a hefty payoff." He stared back at her with cold eyes and unswerving surety.

In a sense he was right. She would do anything for Kolby. But again, Tony had made a mistake. He'd offered her money before, assuming that would equate security to her. She had deeper values she wanted to relay to her son, like the importance of earning a living honorably. Tony had needed to prove that himself in leaving the island. Why was it so difficult to understand she felt the same way?

Her sympathy for him could only stretch so far.

"You actually believe I betrayed you? That I placed everyone here at risk for a few dollars?" Anger frothed higher and higher inside her. "I never wanted any of this. My son and I can get by just fine without you and your movie theater." She swatted his arm. "Answer me, damn you."

"I don't know what to think." He pinched the bridge

of his nose. "Tell me it was an accident. You called a friend just to shoot the breeze because you were homesick and that friend sold you out."

Except as she'd already told him and he must remember, she didn't have friends, not anymore. Apparently she didn't even have Tony. "I'm not going to defend myself to you. Either you trust me or you don't."

He gripped her shoulders, his touch careful, his eyes more tumultuous. "I want a future with you. God, Shannon, I was going to ask you to marry me later tonight. I planned to take you back to the chapel, go inside this time and propose."

Her heart squeezed tight at the image he painted. If this security nightmare hadn't occurred, she would have been swept off her feet. She would have been celebrating her engagement with him tonight, because by God, she would have said yes. Now, that wasn't possible.

"You honestly thought we could get married when you have so little faith in me?" The betrayal burned deep. And hadn't she sworn she'd never again put herself in a position to feel that sting from someone she cared about? "You should have included some azaleas in the bouquet you chose for us. I hear they mean fragile passion."

She shrugged free of his too tempting touch. The hole inside her widened, ached.

"Damn it all, Shannon, we're talking." He started toward her.

"Stop." She held up a hand. "Don't come near me. Not now. Not ever."

"Where are you going?" He kept his distance this time. "I need to know you're safe."

"Has the new security system been installed at my apartment?"

His mouth tight, he nodded. "But we're still working on the restraining orders. Given the renewed frenzy because of Eloisa's identity—"

"The new locks and alarms will do for now."

"Damn it, Shannon—"

"I have to find Alys so she can make the arrangements." She held her chin high. Pride and her child were all she had left now that her heart was shattered to pieces. "Kolby and I are returning to Texas."

"Where are Shannon and her son?"

His father's question hammered Tony's already pounding head. In his father's study, he poured himself three fingers of cognac, bypassing the Basque wine and the memories it evoked. Shannon wrapped around him, the scent of lilies in her hair. "You know full well where she is. Nothing slips past you here."

They'd spent the past two hours assessing the repercussions of the leak. The media feeding frenzy had been rekindled with fresh fuel about Eloisa's connection to the family. Inevitable, yet still frustrating. It gnawed at his gut to think Shannon had something to do with this, although he reassured himself it must have been an accident.

And if she'd simply slipped up and made a mistake, he could forgive her. She hadn't lived the Medina way since the cradle. Remembering all the intricacies involved in maintaining such a high level of security was difficult. If she would just admit what happened, they could move on.

His father rolled back from the computer desk, his large dogs tracking his every move from in front of the fireplace. "Apparently I do not know everything happening under my roof, because somebody placed a call putting Eloisa's flight at risk. I trusted someone I shouldn't have."

"You trusted me and my judgment." He scratched his tightening rib cage.

His father snorted with impatience. "Do not be an impulsive jackass. Think with your brain and not your heart."

"Like you've always done?" Tony snapped, his patience for his father's cryptic games growing short. "No thank you."

Once he finished his one-month obligation, he wouldn't set foot on this godforsaken island again. If memories of his life here before were unhappy, now they were gut-wrenching. His father should come to the mainland anyway for medical treatment. Even Enrique's deep coffers couldn't outfit the island with unlimited hospital options.

Enrique poured himself a drink and downed it swiftly. "I let my heart guide me when I left San Rinaldo. I was so terrified something would happen to my wife and sons that I did not think through our escape plan properly."

Invincible Enrique was admitting a mistake? Tony let that settle inside him for a second before speaking.

"You set yourself up as a diversion. Sounds pretty selfless to me." He'd never doubted his father's bravery or cool head.

"I did not think it through." He refilled his glass and stared into the amber liquid, signs of regret etched deep in his forehead. Illness had never made the king appear weak, but at this moment, the ghosts of an old past showed a vulnerability Tony had never seen before. "If

I had, I would have taken into account the way Carlos would react if things went to hell. I arrogantly considered my plan foolproof. Again, I thought with my emotions and those assassins knew exactly how to target my weakness."

Tony set aside his glass without touching a drop. Empathy for his father seared him more fully than alcohol. Understanding how it felt to have his feelings ripped up through his throat because of a woman gave him insights to his father he'd never expected. "You did your best at the time."

Could he say the same when it came to Shannon?

"I tried to make that right with this island. I did everything in my power to create a safe haven for my sons."

"But we all three left the protection of this place."

"That doesn't matter to me. My only goal was keeping you safe until adulthood. By the time you departed, you took with you the skills to protect yourself, to make your way in the world. That never would have been possible if you'd grown up with obligations to a kingdom. For that, I'm proud."

Enrique's simply spoken words enveloped him. Even though his father wasn't telling him anything he didn't already know, something different took root in him. An understanding. Just as his mother had made the silver security blanket as a "shield," to make him feel protected, his father had been doing the same. His methods may not have been perfect, but their situation had been far from normal. They'd all been scrambling to patch together their lives.

Some of his understanding must have shown on his face, because his father smiled approvingly.

"Now, son, think about Shannon logically rather than acting like a lovesick boy."

Lovesick boy? Now that stung more than a little. And the reason? Because it was true. He did love her, and that had clouded his thinking.

He loved her. And he'd let his gut drive his conclusions rather than logic. He forced his slugging heart to slow and collected what he knew about Shannon. "She's a naturally cautious woman who wouldn't do anything to place her son at risk. If she had a call to make, she would check with you or I to make sure the call was safe. She wouldn't have relied on anyone else's word when it comes to Kolby."

"What conclusion does that lead you to?"

"We never saw the caller's face. I made an assumption based on a female in a bathing suit cover-up. The caller must have been someone with detailed knowledge of our security systems in order to keep her face shielded. A woman of similar build. A person with something to gain and little loyalty to the Medinas…" His brain settled on… "Alys?"

"I would bet money on it." The thunderous anger Enrique now revealed didn't bode well for the assistant who'd used her family connections to take advantage of an ailing king with an aging staff. "She was even the one to order Shannon's clothes. It would be easy to make sure she had the right garb…."

Shannon had done nothing wrong.

"God, I wonder if Alys could have even been responsible for tipping off the Global Intruder about that photo of Duarte when it first ran, before he was identified." The magnitude of how badly he'd screwed up threatened to kick his knees out from under him. He braced a hand on his father's shoulder, touching his dad for the first time in fourteen years. "Where the hell is Alys?"

Enrique swallowed hard. He clapped his hand over Tony's for a charged second before clearing his throat.

"Leave Alys to me." His royal roots showed through again as he assumed command. "Don't you have a more pressing engagement?"

Tony checked his watch. He had five minutes until the ferry pulled away for the airstrip. No doubt his father would secure the proof of Alys's deception soon, but Shannon needed—hell, she deserved—to know that he'd trusted in her innocence without evidence.

He had a narrow, five-minute window to prove just how much he loved and trusted her.

The ferry horn wailed, signaling they were disconnecting from the dock. The crew was stationed at their posts, lost in the ritual of work.

Kolby on her hip, Shannon looked at the exotic island for the last time. This was hard, so much harder than she'd expected. How would she ever survive going back to Galveston where even more memories of Tony waited? She couldn't. She would have to start over somewhere new and totally different.

Except there was no place she could run now that would be free of Medina reminders. The grocery store aisles would sport gossip rags. Channel surfing could prove hazardous. And she didn't even want to think of how often she would be confronted with Tony's face peering back at her from an internet headline, reminding her of how little faith he'd had in her. As much as she wanted to say to hell with it all and accept whatever he offered, she wouldn't settle for half measures ever again.

Tears blurred the exotic shoreline, sea oats dotting the last bit of sand as they pulled away. She squeezed her eyes closed, tears cool on her heated cheeks.

"Mommy?" Kolby patted her face.

She scavenged a wobbly smile and focused on his precious face. "I'm okay, sweetie. Everything's going to be fine. Let's look for a dolphin."

"Nu-uh," he said. "Why's Tony running? Can he come wif us, pretty pwease?"

What? She followed the path of her son's pointing finger....

Tony sprinted down the dock, his mouth moving but his words swallowed up by the roar of the engines and churning water behind the ferry. Her heart pumped in time with his long-legged strides. She almost didn't dare hope, but then Tony had always delivered the unexpected.

Lowering Kolby to the deck with one arm, she leaned over the rail, straining to hear what he said. Still, the wind whipped his words as the ferry inched away. Disappointment pinched as she realized she would have to wait for the ferry to travel back again to speak to him. So silly to be impatient, but her heart had broken a lifetime's worth in one day.

Just as she'd resigned herself to waiting, Tony didn't stop running. Oh my God, he couldn't actually be planning to—

Jump.

Her heart lodged in her throat for an expanded second as he was airborne. Then he landed on deck with the surefooted ease of an experienced boater. Tony strode toward her with even, determined steps, the crew parting to make way.

He extended his hand, his fist closed around a clump of sea oats, still dripping from where he'd yanked them up. "You'll have to use your imagination here because I didn't have much time." He passed her one stalk. "Imagine this is a purple hyacinth, the 'forgive me' flower. I hope you will accept it, along with my apology."

"Go ahead. I'm listening." Although she didn't take his pretend hyacinth. He had a bit more talking to do after what he'd put her through.

Kolby patted his leg for attention. Winking down at the boy, Tony passed him one of the sea oats, which her son promptly waved like a flag. With Kolby settled, Tony shifted his attention back to Shannon.

"I've been an idiot," he said. Sea spray dampened his hair, increasing the rebellious curls. "I should have known you wouldn't do anything to put Kolby or my family at risk. And if you'd done so inadvertently, you would have been upfront about it." He told her all the things she'd hoped to hear earlier.

While she appreciated the romanticism of his gesture, a part of her still ached that he'd needed proof. Trust was such a fragile thing, but crucial in any relationship.

"What brought about this sudden insight to my character? Did you find some new surveillance tape that proves my innocence?"

"I spoke to my father. He challenged me, made me think with my head instead of my scared-as-hell heart. And thank God he did, because once I looked deeper I realized Alys must have made the call. I can't help but wonder if she's the one who made the initial leak to the press. We don't have proof yet, but we'll find it."

Alys? Shannon mulled over that possibility, remembering the way the assistant had stared at Tony with such hunger. She'd sensed the woman wanted to be a Medina. Perhaps Alys had also wanted all the public princess perks to go with it rather than a life spent in hiding.

Tony extended his hand with the sea oats again, tickling them across Kolby's chin lightly before locking eyes with Shannon. "But none of that matters if you don't trust me."

Touching the cottony white tops of the sea oats, she weighed her words carefully. This moment could define the rest of her life. "I realize the way you've grown up has left marks on you...what happened with your mother...living in seclusion here. But I can't always worry when that's going to make you push me away again just because you're afraid I'll betray you."

Her fingers closed around his. "I've had so many people turn away from me. I can't—I won't—spend my life proving myself to you."

"And I don't expect you to." He clasped both hands around hers, his skin callused and tough, a little rough around the edges like her impetuous lover. "You're absolutely right. I was wrong. What I feel for you, it's scary stuff. But the thought of losing you is a helluva lot scarier than any alternative."

"What exactly are you saying?" She needed him to spell it out, every word, every promise.

"My life is complicated and comes with a lot more cons than pros. There's nothing to stop Alys from spilling everything she knows, and if so, it's really going to hit the fan. A life with me won't be easy. To the world, I am a Medina. And I hope you will consent to be a Medina, too."

He knelt in front of her with those sea oats—officially now her favorite plant.

"Shannon, will you be my bride? Let me be your husband and a father to Kolby." He paused to ruffle the boy's hair, eliciting a giant smile from her son. "As well as any other children we may have together. I can't promise I won't be a jackass again. I can almost guarantee that I will. But I vow to stick with it, stick with us, because you mean too much to me for me to ever mess this up again."

Sinking to her knees, she fell into his arms, her son enclosed in the circle. "Yes, I'll marry you and build a family and future with you. Tony Castillo, Antonio Medina, and any other name you go by, I love you, too. You've stolen my heart for life."

"Thank God." He gathered her closer, his arms trembling just a hint.

She lost track of how long they knelt that way until Kolby squirmed between them, and she heard the crew applauding and cheering. Together, she and Tony stood as the ferry captain shouted orders to turn the boat around.

Standing at the deck with Tony, she stared at the approaching island, a place she knew they would visit over the years. She clasped his arm, her cheek against his compass tattoo. Tony rested his chin on her head.

His breath caressed her hair. "The legend about the compass is true. I've found my way home."

Surprised, she glanced up at him. "Back to the island?"

Shaking his head, he tucked a knuckle under her chin and brushed a kiss across her mouth. "Ah, Shanny, *you* are my home."

* * * * *

BILLIONAIRE, M.D.
Olivia Gates

To Natashya and Shane.

This one is definitely for you both.

Chapter 1

She opened her eyes to another world.

A world filled with grainy grayness, like a TV channel with no transmission. But she didn't care.

This world had an angel watching over her.

And not just any angel. An archangel. If archangels were the personification of beauty and power, were hewn out of living rock and bronze and unadulterated maleness.

His image floated in the jumble of light and shadow, making her wonder if this was a dream. Or a hallucination. Or worse.

Probably worse. In spite of the angel's presence. Or because of it. Angels didn't watch over anyone who wasn't in some serious trouble, did they?

Would be a shame if he turned out to be the angel of death. Why make him so breathtaking if he was just a life-force extractor? He was way overqualified. Such overkill was uncalled for, if you asked her. Or maybe his extreme attractiveness was designed to make his targets willing to go where he led?

She'd be more than willing. *If* she could move.

She couldn't. Gravity overwhelmed her, squashed her back onto something that suddenly felt like a bed of thorns. Every cell in her body started to squirm, every nerve firing impulses. But the cells had no connection to each other and the nerves were unable to muster one spark of voluntary movement. Distress bombarded her, noise rose in her ears, pounding, nauseating her....

His face came closer, stilled the vertigo, swept over the cacophony, stifling it.

Her turmoil subsided. She didn't have to fight the pull of gravity, didn't have to fear the paralysis.

He was here. And he'd take care of everything.

She had no idea how she knew that. But she knew it. She knew *him*.

Not that she had any idea who he was.

But everything inside her told her that she was safe, that everything would be okay. Because he was here.

Now if only she could get any part of her to work.

She shouldn't feel so inert upon waking up. But was she waking up? Or was she dreaming? That would explain the detachment between brain and body. That would explain *him*. He was too much to be real.

But she knew he was real. She just knew she wasn't imaginative enough to have made him up.

She knew something else, too. This man was important. In general. And to her, he was more than important. Vital.

"Cybele?"

Was that his voice? That dark, fathomless caress?

It so suited the sheer magnificence of his face....

"Can you hear me?"

Boy, could she. She more than heard him. His voice spread across her skin, her pores soaking it up as if they were starved for nourishment. It permeated her with its richness, its every inflection sparking an inert nerve, restarting a vital process, reviving her.

"Cybele, if you can hear me, if you're awake this time, *por favor,* answer me."

Por favor? Spanish? Figured. So that's where the tinge of an accent came from—English intertwining with the sensuous music of the Latin tongue. She wanted to answer him. She wanted him to keep talking. Each syllable out of those works of art he had for lips, crooned in that intoxicating voice, was lulling her back to oblivion, this time a blissful one.

His face filled her field of vision. She could see every shard of gold among the emerald, moss and caramel that swirled into a luminous color she was certain she'd never seen except in his eyes.

She wanted to stab her fingers into the lushness of his raven mane, cup that leonine head, bring him even closer so she could pore over every strand's hue and radiance. She wanted to trace each groove and slash and plane that painted his face in complexity, wanted to touch each radiation of character.

This was a face mapped with anxiety and responsibility and distinction. She wanted to absorb the first, ease the second and marvel at the third. She wanted those lips against her own, mastering, filling her with the tongue that wrapped around those words and created such magic with them.

She knew she shouldn't be feeling anything like that now, that her body wasn't up to her desires. Her *body* knew that, but didn't acknowledge its incapacitation. It just needed him, close, all that maleness and bulk and power, all that tenderness and protection.

She craved this man. She'd always craved him.

"Cybele, *por Dios*, say something."

It was the raggedness, tearing at the power of his voice, that stirred her out of her hypnosis, forced her vocal cords to tauten, propelled air out of her lungs through them to produce the sound he demanded so anxiously.

"I c-can hear you...."

That came out an almost soundless rasp. From the way he tilted his ear toward her mouth, it was clear he wasn't sure whether she *had* produced sound or if he'd imagined it, whether it had been words or just a groan.

She tried again. "I'm a-awake...I think...I hope, a-and I h-hope you're r-real...."

She couldn't say anything more. Fire lanced in her throat, sealing it with a molten agony. She tried to cough up what felt like red-hot steel splinters before they burned through her larynx. Her sand-filled eyes gushed tears, ameliorating their burning dryness.

"Cybele!"

And he was all around her. He raised her, cradled her in the curve of a barricade of heat and support, seeping warmth into her frozen, quivering bones. She sank in his power, surrendered in relief as he cupped her head.

"Don't try to talk anymore. You were intubated for long hours during your surgery and your larynx must be sore."

Something cool touched her lips, then something

warm and spicily fragrant lapped at their parched seam. Not his lips or his tongue. A glass and a liquid. She instinctively parted her lips and the contents rushed in a gentle flow, filling her mouth.

When she didn't swallow, he angled her head more securely. "It's a brew of anise and sage. It will soothe your throat."

He'd anticipated her discomfort, had been ready with a remedy. But why was he explaining? She would swallow anything he gave her. If she could without feeling as if nails were being driven into her throat. But he wanted her to. She had to do what he wanted.

She squeezed her eyes against the pain, swallowed. The liquid slid through the rawness, its peppery tinge bringing more tears to her eyes. That lasted only seconds. The soreness subsided under the balmy taste and temperature.

She moaned with relief, feeling rejuvenated with every encouraging sweep of tenderness that his thumb brushed over her cheek as she finished the rest of the glass's contents.

"Better now?"

The solicitude in his voice, in his eyes, thundered through her. She shuddered under the impact of her gratitude, her need to hide inside him, dissolve in his care. She tried to answer him, but this time it was emotion that clogged her throat.

But she *had* to express her thankfulness.

His face was so close, clenched with concern, more magnificent in proximity, a study of perfection in slashes of strength and carvings of character. But haggardness had sunk redness into his eyes, iron into his jaw, and the unkemptness of a few days' growth of rough silk over that jaw and above those lips caused her heart to twist. The need to absorb his discomforts and worries as he had hers mushroomed inside her.

She turned her face, buried her lips into his hewn cheek. The bristle of his beard, the texture of his skin, the taste and scent of him tingled on her flesh, soaked into her senses. A gust of freshness and virility coursed through her, filled her lungs. His breath, rushing out on a ragged exhalation.

She opened her lips for more just as he jerked around to face her. It brought his lips brushing hers. And she knew.

This was the one thing she'd needed. This intimacy. With him.

Something she'd always had before and had missed? Something she'd had before and had lost? Something she'd never had and had long craved?

It didn't matter. She had it now.

She glided her lips against his, the flood of sensuality and sweetness of her flesh sweeping against his sizzling through her.

Then her lips were cold and bereft, the enclosure of muscle and maleness around her gone.

She slumped against what she now realized was a bed.

Where had he gone? Had it all been a hallucination? A side effect of emerging from a coma?

Her eyes teared up again with the loss. She turned her swimming head, searching for him, terrified she'd find only emptiness.

Far from emptiness, she registered her surroundings for the first time, the most luxurious and spacious hospital suite she'd ever seen. But if he wasn't there…

Her darting gaze and hurtling thoughts came to an abrupt halt.

He *was* there. Standing where he'd been when she'd first opened her eyes. But his image was distorted this time, turning him from an angel into a wrathful, inapproachable god who glowered down at her with disapproval.

She blinked once, then again, her heart shedding its sluggish rhythm for frantic pounding.

It was no use. His face remained cast in coldness. Instead of the angel she'd thought would do anything to protect her, this was the face of a man who'd stand aside and brood down at her as she drowned.

She stared up at him, something that felt as familiar as a second skin settling about her. Despondence.

It had been an illusion. Whatever she'd thought she'd seen on his face, whatever she'd felt flooding her in waves, had been her disorientation inventing what she wanted to see, to feel.

"It's clear you can move your head. Can you move everything else? Are you in any pain? Blink if it's too uncomfortable to talk. Once for yes, twice for no."

Tears surged into her eyes again. She blinked erratically. A low rumble unfurled from his depths. Must be frustration with her inability to follow such a simple direction.

But she couldn't help it. She now recognized his questions for what they were. Those asked of anyone whose consciousness had been compromised, as she was now certain hers had been. Ascertaining level of awareness, then sensory and motor functions, then pain level and site. But there was no personal worry behind the questions anymore, just clinical detachment.

She could barely breathe with missing his tenderness and anxiety for her well-being. Even if she'd imagined them.

"Cybele! Keep your eyes open, stay with me."

The urgency in his voice snapped through her, made her struggle to obey him. "I c-can't...."

He seemed to grow bigger, his hewn face etched with fierceness, frustration rippling off him. Then he exhaled. "Then just answer my questions, and I'll leave you to rest."

"I f-feel numb but..." She concentrated, sent signals to her toes. They wiggled. That meant everything in between them and her brain was in working order. "Seems...motor functions are...intact. Pain—not certain. I feel sore...like I've been flattened under a—a brick wall. B-but i-it's not pain indicating damage..."

Just as the last word was out, all aches seemed to seep from every inch of her body to coalesce in one area. Her left arm.

In seconds she shot beyond the threshold of containable pain into brain-shredding agony.

It spilled from her lips on a butchered keen. "M-my arm..."

She could swear he didn't move. But she found him beside her again, as if by magic, and cool relief splashed over the hot skewers of pain, putting them out.

She whimpered, realized what he'd done. She had an intravenous line in her right arm. He'd injected a drug—a narcotic analgesic from the instantaneous action—into the saline, flicked the drip to maximum.

"Are you still in pain?" She shook her head. He exhaled heavily. "That's good enough for now. I'll come back later...." He started to move away.

"No." Her good hand shot out without conscious volition, fueled by the dread that he'd disappear and she'd never see him again. This felt instinctive, engrained, the desperation that she could lose him. Or was it the resignation that he was already lost to her?

Her hand tightened around his, as if stronger contact would let her read his mind, reanimate hers, remind her what he'd been to her.

He relinquished her gaze, his incandescent one sweeping downward to where her hand was gripping his. "Your reflexes, motor power and coordination seem to be back to normal. All very good signs you're recovering better than my expectations."

From the way he said that, she guessed his expectations had ranged from pessimistic to dismal. "That… should be…a relief."

"Should be? You're not glad you're okay?"

"I am. I guess. Seems…I'm not…all there yet." The one thing that made her feel anything definite was him. And he could have been a mile away with the distance he'd placed between them. "So…what happened…to me?"

The hand beneath hers lurched. "You don't remember?"

"It's all a…a blank."

His own gaze went blank for an endless moment. Then it gradually focused on her face, until she felt it was penetrating her, like an X-ray that would let him scan her, decipher her condition.

"You're probably suffering from post-traumatic amnesia. It's common to forget the traumatic episode."

Spoken like a doctor. Everything he'd said and done so far had pointed to him being one.

Was that all he was to her? Her doctor? Was that how he knew her? He'd been her doctor before the "traumatic episode" and she'd had a crush on him? Or had he just read the vital statistics on her admission papers? Had she formed dependence on and fascination for him when she'd been drifting in and out of consciousness as he'd managed her condition? Had she kissed a man who was here only in his professional capacity? A man who could be in a relationship, maybe married with children?

The pain of her suppositions grew unbearable. And she just had to know. "Wh-who are you?"

The hand beneath hers went still. All of him seemed to become rock, as if her question had a Medusa effect.

When he finally spoke, his voice had dipped an octave lower, a bass, slowed-down rasp, "You don't know me?"

"Sh-should I?" She squeezed her eyes shut as soon as the words were out. She'd just kissed him. And she was telling him that she had no idea who he was. "I know I should...b-but I can't r-remember."

Another protracted moment. Then he muttered, "You've forgotten me?"

She gaped up at him, shook her head, as if the movement would slot some comprehension into her mind. "Uh...I may have forgotten...how to speak, too. I had this...distinct belief language skills...are the last to go... e-even in total...memory loss. I thought...saying I can't remember you...was the same as saying...I forgot who y-you are."

His gaze lengthened until she thought he wouldn't speak again. Ever. Then he let out a lung-deflating exhalation, raked his fingers through his gleaming wealth of hair. "I'm the one who's finding it hard to articulate.

Your language skills are in perfect condition. In fact, I've never heard you speak that much in one breath."

"M-many fractured…breaths…you mean."

He nodded, noting her difficulty, then shook his head, in wonder it seemed. "One word to one short sentence at a time was your norm."

"So you…*do* know me. E-extensively, it seems."

The wings of his thick eyebrows drew closer together. "I wouldn't label my knowledge of you extensive."

"I'd label it…en-encyclopedic."

Another interminable silence. Then another darkest-bass murmur poured from him, thrumming every neuron in her hypersensitive nervous system. "It seems your memory deficit is the only thing that's extensive here, Cybele."

She knew she should be alarmed at this verdict. She wasn't.

She sighed. "I love…the way…you say…my name."

And if she'd thought he'd frozen before, it was nothing compared to the stillness that snared him now. It was as if time and space had hit a pause button and caught him in their stasis field.

Then, in such a controlled move, as if he were afraid she was made of soap bubbles and she'd burst if he as much as rattled the air around her, he sat down beside her on her pristine white bed.

His weight dipped the mattress, rolling her slightly toward him. The side of her thigh touched his through the thickness of his denim pants, through her own layers of covering. Something slid through the mass of aches that constituted her body, originating from somewhere deep within her, uncoiling through her gut to pool into her loins.

She was barely functioning, and he could wrench that kind of response from her every depleted cell? What would he do to her if she were in top condition? What *had* he done? Because she was certain this response to him wasn't new.

"You really don't remember who I am at all."

"You really...are finding it hard...to get my words, aren't you?" Her lips tugged. She was sure there was no humor in this situation, that when it all sank in she'd be horrified about her memory loss and what it might signify of neurological damage.

But for now, she just found it so endearing that this man, who she didn't need memory to know was a powerhouse, was so shaken by the realization.

It also said he cared what happened to her, right? She could enjoy that belief now, even if it proved to be a delusion later.

She sighed again. "I thought it was clear...what I meant. At least it sounded...clear to me. But what would I know? When I called your...knowledge of me...encyclopedic, I should have added...compared to mine. I haven't only...forgotten who you are, I have no idea... who *I* am."

Chapter 2

Rodrigo adjusted the drip, looking anywhere but at Cybele.

Cybele. His forbidden fruit. His ultimate temptation.

The woman whose very existence had been like corrosive acid coursing through his arteries. The woman the memory of whom he would have given anything to wake up free of one day.

And it was she who'd woken up free of the memory of him.

It had been two days since she'd dropped this bomb on him.

He was still reverberating with the shock.

She'd told him she didn't remember the existence that was the bane of his. She'd forgotten the very identity that had been behind the destruction of one life. And the poisoning of his own.

And he shouldn't care. Shouldn't *have* cared. Not beyond the care he offered his other patients. By all testi-
monies, he went above and beyond the demands of duty
and the dictates of compassion for each one. He shouldn't
have neglected everyone and everything to remain by
her side, to do everything for her when he could have
delegated her care to the highly qualified professionals
he'd painstakingly picked and trained, those he paid far
more than money to keep doing the stellar job they did.

He hadn't. During the three interminable days after
her surgery until she woke up, whenever he'd told himself to tend to his other duties, he couldn't. She'd been
in danger, and it had been beyond him to leave her.

Her inert form, her closed eyes, had been what had
ruled him. The drive to get her to move, to open her
eyes and look at him with those endless inky skies that
had been as inescapable as a black hole since they'd first
had him in their focus, had been what motivated him.

Periodically she had opened them, but there had
been no sight or comprehension in them, no trace of
the woman who'd invaded and occupied his thoughts
ever since he'd laid eyes on her.

Yet he'd prayed that, if she never came back, her body
would keep on functioning, that she'd keep opening her
eyes, even if it was just a mechanical movement with no
sentience behind it.

Two days ago, she'd opened those eyes and the blankness had been replaced by the fog of confusion. His
heart had nearly torn a hole in her ribs when coherence
had dawned in her gaze. Then she'd looked at him and
there had been more.

He should have known then that she was suffering
from something he hadn't factored in. Finding her dis-

tance and disdain replaced by warmth that had escalated to heat should have given him his first clue. Having her nuzzle him like a feline delighted at finding her owner, then that kiss that had rocked him to his foundations, should have clenched the diagnosis.

The Cybele Wilkinson he knew—his nemesis— would never have looked at or touched him that way if she were in her right mind. If she knew who he was.

It had still taken her saying that she wasn't and didn't to explain it all. And he'd thought *that* had explained it all.

But it was even worse. She didn't remember herself.

There was still something far worse. The temptation not to fill in the spaces that had consumed her memories, left her mind a blank slate. A slate that could be inscribed with anything that didn't mean they had to stay enemies.

But they had to. Now more than ever.

"I see you're still not talking to me."

Her voice, no longer raspy, but a smooth, rich, molten caress sweeping him from the inside out, forced him to turn his eyes to her against his will. "I've talked to you every time I came in."

"Yeah, two sentences every two hours for the past two days." She huffed something that bordered on amusement. "Feels like part of your medication regimen. Though the sparseness really contrasts with the intensiveness of your periodic checkups."

He could have relegated *those*, which hadn't needed to be so frequent, or so thorough, to nurses under his residents' supervision. But he hadn't let anyone come near her.

He turned his eyes away again, pretended to study

her chart. "I've been giving you time to rest, for your throat to heal and for you to process the discovery of your amnesia."

She fidgeted, dragging his gaze back to her. "My throat has been perfectly fine since yesterday. It's a miracle what some soothing foods and drinks and talking to oneself can do. And I haven't given my amnesia any thought. I know I should be alarmed, but I'm not. Maybe it's a side effect of the trauma, and it will crash on me later as I get better. *Or*…I'm subconsciously relieved not to remember."

His voice sounded alien as he pushed an answer past the brutal temptation, the guilt, the rage, at her, at himself, at the whole damned universe. "Why wouldn't you want to remember?"

Her lips crooked. "If I knew, it wouldn't be a subconscious wish, would it? Am I still making sense only in my own ears?"

He tore his gaze away from her lips, focused on her eyes, cleared thorns from his throat. "No. I am not having an easy time processing the fact that you have total memory loss."

"And without memories, my imagination is having a field day thinking of outlandish explanations for why I'm not in a hurry to have my memories back. At least they seem outlandish. They might turn out to be the truth."

"And what are those theories?"

"That I was a notorious criminal or a spy, someone with a dark and dangerous past and who's in desperate need of a second chance, a clean slate. And now that it's been given to me, I'd rather not remember the past—my own identity most of all."

She struggled to sit up, groaning at the aches he knew her body had amassed. He tried to stop himself.

He failed. He lunged to help her, tried not to feel the supple heat of her flesh fill his hands as he pulled her up, adjusted her bed to a gentle slope. He struggled to ignore the gratitude filling her eyes, the softness of trust and willingness exhibited by every inch of her flesh. He roared inwardly at his senses as the feel and scent of her turned his insides to molten lava, his loins to rock. He gritted his teeth, made sure her intravenous line and the other leads monitoring her vital signs were secure.

Her hands joined his in checking her line and leads, an unconscious action born of engrained knowledge and ongoing application. He stepped away as if from a fiery pit.

She looked up at him, those royal-blue eyes filling with a combo of confusion and hurt at his recoil. He took one more step back before he succumbed to the need to erase that crestfallen expression.

She lowered her eyes. "So—you're a doctor. A surgeon?"

He was, for once, grateful for her questions. "Neurosurgeon."

She raised her eyes again. "And from the medical terms filling my mind and the knowledge of what the machines here are and what the values they're displaying mean—I'm some kind of medical professional, too?"

"You were a senior trauma/reconstructive surgery resident."

"Hmm, that blows my criminal or spy theories out of the water. But maybe I was in another form of trouble before I ended up here? A ruinous malpractice suit?

Some catastrophic mistake that killed someone? Was I about to have my medical license revoked?"

"I never suspected you had this fertile an imagination."

"Just trying to figure out why I'm almost relieved I don't remember a thing. Was I perhaps running away to start again where no one knows me? Came here and… hey, where *is* here?"

He almost kept expecting her to say *gotcha*. But the notion of Cybele playing a trick on him was more inconceivable than her total memory loss. "This is my private medical center. It's on the outskirts of Barcelona."

"We're in Spain?" Her eyes widened. His heart kicked. Even with her lids still swollen and her face bruised and pallid, she was the most beautiful thing he'd ever seen. "Okay, scratch that question. As far as my general knowledge can tell—and I feel it remains unaffected—there is no Barcelona anywhere else."

"Not that I know of, no."

"So—I sound American."

"You are American."

"And you're Spanish?"

"Maybe to the world, which considers all of Spain one community and everyone who hails from there as Spanish. But I am Catalan. And though in Catalonia we have the same king, and a constitution that declares 'the indissoluble unity of the Spanish nation,' we were the first to be recognized as a *Nacionalidad* and a *Comunidad Autónoma* or a distinct historical nationality and an autonomous community, along with the Basque Country and Galicia. There are now seventeen such communities that make up Spain, with our rights to self-government recognized by the constitution."

"Fascinating. Sort of a federation, like the United States."

"There are similarities, but it's a different system. The regional governments are responsible for education, health, social services, culture, urban and rural development and, in some places, policing. But contrary to the States, Spain is described as a decentralized country, with central government spending estimated at less than twenty percent." And he was damned if he knew why he was telling her all that, now of all times.

She chewed her lower lip that was once again the color of deep pink rose petals. His lips tingled with the memory of those lips, plucking at them, bathing them with intoxicating heat and moistness. "I knew some of that, but not as clearly as you've put it."

He exhaled his aggravation at the disintegration of his sense and self-control. "Pardon the lesson. My fascination with the differences between the two systems comes from having both citizenships."

"So you acquired the American citizenship?"

"Actually, I was born in the States, and acquired my Spanish citizenship after I earned my medical degree. Long story."

"But you have an accent."

He blinked his surprise at the implication of her words, something he'd never suspected. "I spent my first eight years in an exclusively Spanish-speaking community in the States and learned English only from then on. But I was under the impression I'd totally lost the accent."

"Oh, no, you haven't. And I hope you never lose it. It's *gorgeous*."

Everything inside him surged. This was something

else he'd never considered. What she'd do to him if, instead of hostility, admiration and invitation spread on her face, invaded her body, if instead of bristling at the sight of him, she looked at him as if she'd like nothing more than to feast on him. As she was now.

What was going on here? How had memory loss changed her character and attitude so diametrically? Did that point to more neurological damage than he'd feared? Or was this what she was really like, what her reaction to him would have been if not for the events that had messed up their whole situation?

"So…what's your name? What's mine, too, apart from Cybele?"

"You're Cybele Wilkinson. I'm Rodrigo."

"Just…Rodrigo?"

She used to call him Dr. Valderrama, and in situations requiring informality she'd avoided calling him anything at all. But now she pressed back into her pillows, let his name melt on her tongue as if it were the darkest, richest chocolate. He felt her contented purr cascade down his body, caress his aching hardness….

This was unbelievable. That she could do this to him *now*. Or at all. It was worse than unbelievable. It was unacceptable.

He shredded his response. "Rodrigo Edmundo Arrellano i Bazán Valderrama i de Urquiza."

Her eyes widened a fraction more with each surname. Then a huff that bordered on a giggle escaped her. "I did ask."

His lips twisted. "That's an excerpt of my names, actually. I can rattle off over forty more surnames."

She giggled for real this time. "That's a family tree going back to the Spanish Inquisition."

"The Catalan, and the Spanish in general, take family trees very seriously. Because both maternal and paternal ancestors are mentioned, each name makes such a list. The Catalan also put *i* or *and* between surnames."

"And do I have more than the measly Wilkinson?"

"All I know is that your father's name was Cedric."

"Was? H-he's dead?"

"Since you were six or seven, I believe."

She seemed to have trouble swallowing again. He had to fist his hands against the need to rush to her side again.

His heart still hammered in protest against his restraint when she finally whispered, "Do I have a mother? A family?"

"Your mother remarried and you have four half siblings. Three brothers and one sister. They all live in New York City."

"D-do they know what happened to me?"

"I did inform them. Yesterday." He hadn't even thought of doing so until his head nurse had stressed the necessity of alerting her next of kin. For the seventh time. He hadn't even registered the six previous times she had mentioned it.

He waited for her next logical question. If they were on their way here to claim responsibility for her.

His gut tightened. Even with all he had against her, not the least of which was the reaction she wrenched from him, he hated to have to answer that question. To do so, he'd have to tell her that her family's response to her danger had been so offhand, he'd ended the phone call with her mother on a barked, "Don't bother explaining your situation to me, Mrs. Doherty. I'm sure you'd be of more use at your husband's business dinner than you would be at Cybele's bedside."

But her next question did not follow a logical progression. Just as this whole conversation, which she'd steered, hadn't. "So...what happened to me?"

And this was a question he wanted to avoid as fiercely.

No way to do that now that she'd asked so directly. He exhaled. "You were in a plane crash."

A gasp tore out of her. "I just knew I was in an accident, that I wasn't attacked or anything, but I thought it was an MVA or something. But...a plane crash?" She seemed to struggle with air that had gone thick, lodging in her lungs. He rocked on his heels with the effort not to rush to her with an oxygen mask and soothing hands. "Were there many injured o-or worse?"

Dios. She really remembered nothing. And he was the one who had to tell her. Everything. "It was a small plane. Seated four. There were only...two onboard this time."

"Me and the pilot? I might not remember anything, but I just know I can't fly a plane, small or otherwise."

This was getting worse and worse. He didn't want to answer her. He didn't want to relive the three days before she'd woken up, that had gouged their scars in his psyche and soul.

He could pretend he had a surgery, escape her interrogation.

He couldn't. Escape. Stop himself from answering her. "He was flying the plane, yes."

"Is—is he okay, too?"

Rodrigo gritted his teeth against the blast of pain that detonated behind his sternum. "He's dead."

"Oh, God...." Her tears brimmed again and he

couldn't help himself anymore. He closed the distance he'd put between them, stilled the tremors of her hand with both of his. "D-did he die on impact?"

He debated telling her that he had. He could see survivor's guilt mushrooming in her eyes. What purpose did it serve to tell her the truth but make her more miserable?

But then he always told his patients the truth. Sooner or later that always proved the best course of action.

He inhaled. "He died on the table after a six-hour surgery."

During those hours, he'd wrestled with death, gaining an inch to lose two to its macabre pull, knowing that it would win the tug-of-war. But what had wrecked his sanity had been knowing that while he fought this losing battle, Cybele had been lying in his ER tended to by others.

Guilt had eaten through him. Triage had dictated he take care of her first, the one likely to survive. But he couldn't have let Mel go without a fight. It had been an impossible choice. Emotionally, professionally, morally. He'd gone mad thinking she'd die or suffer irreversible damage because he'd made the wrong one.

Then he'd lost the fight for Mel's life among colleagues' proclamations that it had been a miracle he'd even kept him alive for hours when everyone had given up on him at the accident scene.

He'd rushed to her, knowing that while he'd exercised the ultimate futility on Mel, her condition had worsened. Terror of losing her, too, had been the one thing giving him continued access to what everyone extolled as his vast medical knowledge and surgical expertise.

"Tell me, please. The details of his injuries."

He didn't want to tell her how terrible it had all been.

But he had to. He inhaled a stream of what felt like aerosolized acid, then told her.

Her tears flowed steadily over a face gone numb with horror throughout his chilling report.

She finally whispered, "How did the accident happen?"

He needed this conversation to be over. He gritted his teeth. "That is one thing only you can know for sure. And it'll probably be the last memory to return. The crash site and plane were analyzed for possible whys and hows. The plane shows no signs of malfunction and there were no distress transmissions prior to the crash."

"So the pilot just lost control of the plane?"

"It would appear so."

She digested this for a moment. "What about my injuries?"

"You should only concern yourself now with recuperating."

"But I need to know a history of my injuries, their progression and management, to chart my recuperation."

He grudgingly conceded her logic. "On site, you were unconscious. You had a severely bleeding scalp wound and bruising all over your body. But your severest injury was comminuted fractures of your left ulna and radius."

She winced as she looked down on her splinted arm. "What was my Glasgow Coma Scale scoring?"

"Eleven. Best eye response was three, with your eyes opening only in response to speech. Best verbal response was four, with your speech ranging from random words to confused responses. Best motor function was four with flexion withdrawal response to pain. By the time I operated on you, your GCS had plunged to five."

"Ouch. I was heading for decorticate coma. Did I have intracranial hemorrhage?"

He gave a difficult nod. "It must have been a slow leak. Your initial CTs and MRIs revealed nothing but slight brain edema, accounting for your depressed consciousness. But during the other surgery, I was informed of your deteriorating neurological status, and new tests showed a steadily accumulating subdural hematoma."

"You didn't shave my hair evacuating it."

"No need. I operated via a new minimally invasive technique I've developed."

She gaped at him. "You've developed a new surgical technique? Excuse me while my mind, tattered as it is, barrels in awe."

He grunted something dismissive. She eyed him with a wonder that seemed only to rise at his discomfort. Just as he almost growled *stop it*, she raised one beautifully dense and dark eyebrow at him. "I trust I wasn't the guinea pig for said technique?"

Cybele gazed up at Rodrigo, a smile hovering on her lips.

His own lips tightened. "You're fine, aren't you?"

"If you consider having to get my life story from you as *fine*."

The spectacular wings of his eyebrows snapped together. That wasn't annoyance or affront. That was mortification. Pain, even.

Words couldn't spill fast enough from her battered brain to her lips. "God, that was such a lame joke. Just shows I'm in no condition to know how or when to make one. I owe you my life."

"You owe me nothing. I was doing my job. And I

didn't even do it well. I'm responsible for your current condition. It's my failure to manage you first that led to the deepening of the insult to your brai—"

"The pilot's worst injuries were neurological." She cut him short. It physically hurt to see the self-blame eating at him.

"Yes, but that had nothing to do with my decision—"

"And I bet you're the best neurosurgeon on the continent."

"I don't know about that, but being the most qualified one on hand didn't mea—"

"It *did* mean you had to take care of him yourself. And my initial condition misled you into believing my case wasn't urgent. You did the right thing. You fought for this man as he deserved to be fought for. And then you fought for me. And you saved me. And then, I'm certain my condition is temporary."

"We have no way of knowing that. Having total memory loss with the retention of all faculties of language and logic and knowledge and no problem in accumulating new memories is a very atypical form of amnesia. It might never resolve fully."

"Would that be a bad thing, in your opinion? If the idea of regaining my memories is almost…distressing, maybe my life was so bad, I'm better off not remembering it?"

He seemed at a loss for words. Then he finally found some. "I am not in a position to know the answer to that. But I am in a position to know that memory loss is a neurological deficit, and it's my calling to fix those. I can't under any circumstances wish that this wouldn't resolve. Now, if you'll excuse me, I need to tend to my other patients. I'll be back every three hours to check on you."

With a curt nod, he turned and left her, exiting the huge, opulent suite in strides loaded with tense grace.

She wanted to run after him, beg him to come back.

What could possibly explain all this turmoil and her severe attraction to him? Had they been lovers, married even, and they'd separated, or maybe divorced...?

She suddenly lurched as if from the blow of an ax as a memory lodged in her brain. No...a knowledge.

She *was* married.

And it was certainly not to Rodrigo.

Chapter 3

Rodrigo did come back in three hours. And stayed for three minutes. Long enough to check on her and adjust her medical management. Then he repeated that pattern for the next three days. She even felt him come in during her fitful sleep.

She hadn't had the chance to tell him what she'd remembered.

No. She hadn't *wanted* to tell him. Discovering she was married, even if she didn't know to whom, wasn't on her list of things to share with him of all people.

And he probably already knew.

She *could* have told him that she'd also remembered who she was. But then, she hadn't remembered much beyond the basics he'd told her.

This boded well for her memory deficit, if it was receding so early.

She didn't want it to recede, wanted to cling to the blankness with all her strength.

But it was no use. A few hours ago, a name had trickled into the parting darkness of her mind. Mel Braddock.

She was certain that was her husband's name. But she couldn't put a face to the name. The only memory she could attach to said name was a profession. General surgeon.

Beyond that, she remembered nothing of the marriage. She knew only that something dark pressed down on her every time the knowledge of it whispered in her mind.

She couldn't possibly feel this way if they'd been on good terms. And if he wasn't here, days after his wife had been involved in a serious accident, were they separated, getting divorced even? She was certain she was still married. Technically, at least. But the marriage was over. That would explain her overriding emotions for Rodrigo, that she innately knew it was okay to feel them.

On the strike of three hours, Rodrigo returned. And she'd progressed from not wanting to bring up any of it to wanting to scream it all at the top of her lungs.

He made no eye contact with her as he strode in flanked by two doctors and a nurse. He never came unescorted anymore. It was as if he didn't want to be alone with her again.

He checked her chart, informed his companions of his adjustment of her medications as if she wasn't in the room much less a medical professional who could understand everything they were saying. Frustration frothed inside her. Then it boiled over.

"I remembered a few things."

Rodrigo went still at her outburst. The other people

in the room fidgeted, eyed her uncomfortably before turning uncertain gazes to their boss. Still without looking at her, he hung her chart back at the foot of the bed, murmured something clearly meant for the others' ears alone. They rushed out in a line.

The door had closed behind the last departing figure for over two minutes before he turned his eyes toward her.

She shuddered with the force of his elemental impact. *Oh, please. Let me have the right to feel this way about him.*

The intensity of his being buzzed in her bones—of his focus, of his…wariness?

Was he anxious to know what she remembered? Worried about it? Because he suspected what it was—the husband she remembered only in name? He'd told her of her long-dead father, her existing family, but not about that husband. Would he have told her if she hadn't remembered?

But there was something more in his vibe. Something she'd felt before. After she'd kissed him. Disapproval? Antipathy?

Had they been on bad terms before the accident? How could they have been, if she felt this vast attraction to him, untainted by any negativity? Had the falling out been her fault? Was he bitter? Was he now taking care of her to honor his calling, his duty, giving her extra special care for old times' sake, yet unable to resume their intimacy? *Had* they been intimate? Was he her lover?

No. He wasn't.

She might not remember much about herself, but the thought of being in a relationship, no matter how unhealthy, and seeking involvement with another felt abhorrent to her, no matter how inexorable the temptation. And then, there was him. He radiated nobility. She just knew Rodrigo Valderrama would never poach on another man's grounds, never cross the lines of honor, no matter how much he wanted her or how dishonorable the other man was.

But there was one paramount proof that told her they'd never been intimate. Her body. It burned for him but knew it had never had him. It would have borne his mark on its every cell if it had.

So what did it all mean? He had to tell her, before something beside memories short-circuited inside her brain.

He finally spoke. "What did you remember?"

"Who I am. That I'm married." He showed no outward reaction. So he *had* known. "Why didn't you tell me?"

"You didn't ask."

"I asked about family."

"I thought you were asking about flesh-and-blood relatives."

"You're being evasive."

"Am I?" He held her gaze, making her feel he was giving her a psyche and soul scan. Maybe trying to steer her thoughts, too. "So you remember everything?"

She exhaled. "I said I remembered 'a few things.' Seems I'm a stickler for saying exactly what I mean."

"You said you remembered who you were, and your marriage. That's just about everything, isn't it?"

"Not when I remember only the basics about myself, the name you told me, that I went to Harvard Medical School, that I worked at St. Giles Hospital and that I'm twenty-nine. I know far less than the basics about my marriage. I remembered only that I have a husband, and his name and profession."

"That's all?"

"The rest is speculation."

"What kind of speculation?"

"About the absence of both my family and husband more than a week after I've been involved in a major accident. I can only come up with very unfavorable explanations."

"What would those be?"

"That I'm a monster of such megaproportions that no one felt the need to rush to my bedside." Something flared in his eyes, that harshness. So she was right? He thought so, too? Her heart compressed as she waited for him to confirm or negate her suspicions. When he didn't, she dejectedly had to consider his silence as corroboration, condemnation. She still looked for a way out for herself, for her family. "Unless it is beyond them financially to make the trip here?"

"As far as I know, finances are no issue to your family."

"So you told them I was at death's door, and no one bothered to come."

"I told them no such thing. You weren't at death's door."

"It *could* have gone either way for a while."

Silence. Heavy. Oppressive. Then he simply said, "Yes."

"So I'm on the worst terms with them."

It seemed he'd let this go uncommented on, too. Then he gave a noncommittal shrug. "I don't know about the worst terms. But it's my understanding you're not close."

"Not even with my mother?"

"Especially with your mother."

"Great. See? I was right when I thought I was better off not remembering. Not knowing."

"It isn't as bad as you're painting it. By the time I called your family, you were stable, and there really was nothing for any of them to do but wait like the rest of us. Your mother did call twice for updates, and I told her you were doing very well. Physically. Psychologically, I suggested it might not be a good thing in this early phase for you to be jogged by their presence or contact, any more than you already are."

He was making excuses for her family, her mother. If they'd cared, they wouldn't have been satisfied with long-distance assurances. Or maybe he had discouraged them from coming, so he wouldn't introduce an unpredictable emotional element into her neurological recovery?

The truth was, she didn't care right now how things really stood with her family. What she was barely able to breathe from needing to know was her status with her husband.

"And that's my not-so-bad situation with my family. But from my husband's pointed absence, I can only assume the worst. That maybe we're separated or getting divorced."

She wanted him to say, *Yes, you are.*

Please, say it.

His jaw muscles bunched, his gaze chilled. When he finally spoke it felt like an arctic wind blasting her, freezing her insides with this antipathy that kept spiking out of nowhere.

"Far from being separated, you and your husband have been planning a second honeymoon."

Cybele doubted the plane crashing into the ground had a harder impact than Rodrigo's revelation.

Her mind emptied. Her heart spilled all of its beats at once.

For a long, horrified moment she stared at him, speech skills and thought processes gone, only blind instincts left. They all screamed *run, hide, deny.*

She'd been so certain…so…certain…

"A second honeymoon?" She heard her voice croaking. "Does that mean we…we've been married long?"

He waited an eternity before answering. At least it felt that way. By the time he did, she felt she'd aged ten years. "You were married six months ago."

"Six *months?* And already planning a second honeymoon?"

"Maybe I should have said honeymoon, period. Circumstances stopped you from having one when you first got married."

"And yet my adoring husband isn't here. Our plans probably were an attempt to salvage a marriage that was malfunctioning beyond repair, and we shouldn't have bothered going through the motions…."

She stopped, drenched in mortification. She instinctively knew she wasn't one to spew vindictiveness like that. Her words had been acidic enough to eat through the gleaming marble floor.

Their corrosiveness had evidently splashed Rodrigo. From the way his face slammed shut, he clearly disapproved of her sentiments and the way she'd expressed them. Of her.

"I don't know much about your relationship. But his reason for not being at your bedside *is* uncontestable. He's dead."

She lurched as if he'd backhanded her.

"He was flying the plane," she choked.

"You remember?"

"No. Oh, God." A geyser of nausea shot from her depths. She pitched to the side of the bed. Somehow she found Rodrigo around her, holding her head and a pan. She retched emptily, shook like a bell that had been struck by a giant mallet.

And it wasn't from a blow of grief. It was from one of horror, at the anger and relief that were her instinctive reactions.

What kind of monster was she to feel like that about somebody's death, let alone that of her husband? Even if she'd fiercely wanted out of the relationship. Was it because of what she felt for Rodrigo? She'd wished her husband dead to be with him?

No. *No.* She just knew it hadn't been like that. It had to have been something else. Could her husband have been abusing her? Was she the kind of woman who would have suffered humiliation and damage, too terrified to block the blows or run away?

She consulted her nature, what transcended memory, what couldn't be lost or forgotten, what was inborn and unchangeable.

It said, no way. If that man had abused her, emotionally or physically, she would have carved his brains out with forceps and sued him into his next few reincarnations.

So what did this mess mean?

"Are you okay?"

She shuddered miserably. "If feeling mad when I should be sad is okay. There must be more wrong with me than I realized."

After the surprise her words induced, contemplation settled on his face. "Anger *is* a normal reaction in your situation."

"What?" He knew why it was okay to feel so mad at a dead man?

"It's a common reaction for bereaved people to feel anger at their loved ones who die and leave them behind. It's worse when someone dies in an accident that that someone had a hand in or caused. The first reaction after shock and disbelief is rage, and it's all initially directed toward the victim. That also explains your earlier attack of bitterness. Your subconscious must have known that he was the one flying the plane. It might have recorded all the reports that flew around you at the crash site."

"You're saying I speak Spanish?"

He frowned. "Not to my knowledge. But maybe you approximated enough medical terminology to realize the extent of his injuries…."

"Ya lo sé hablar español."

She didn't know which of them was more flabbergasted.

The Spanish words had flowed from a corner in her mind to her tongue without conscious volition. And she certainly knew what they meant. *I know how to speak Spanish.*

"I…had no idea you spoke Spanish."

"Neither did I, obviously. But I get the feeling that the knowledge is partial…fresh."

"Fresh? How so?"

"It's just a feeling, since I remember no facts. It's like I've only started learning it recently."

He fixed her with a gaze that seeped into her skin,

mingled into the rapids of her blood. Her temperature inched higher.

Was he thinking what she was thinking? That she'd started learning Spanish because of him? To understand his mother tongue, understand *him* better, to get closer to him?

At last he said, "Whatever the case may be, you evidently know enough Spanish to validate my theory."

He was assigning her reactions a perfectly human and natural source. Wonder what he'd say if she set him straight?

She bet he'd think her a monster. And she wouldn't blame him. She was beginning to think it herself.

Next second she was no longer thinking it. She knew it.

The memory that perforated her brain like a bullet was a visual. An image that corkscrewed into her marrow. The image of Mel, the husband she remembered with nothing but anger, whose death aroused only a mixture of resentment and liberation.

In a wheelchair.

Other facts dominoed like collapsing pillars, crushing everything beneath their impact. Not memories, just knowledge.

Mel had been paralyzed from the waist down. In a car accident. *During* their relationship. She didn't know if it had been before or after they'd gotten married. She didn't think it mattered.

She'd been right when she'd hypothesized why no one had rushed to her bedside. She was heartless.

What else could explain harboring such harshness toward someone who'd been so afflicted? The man she'd promised to love in sickness and in health? The one she'd basically felt "good riddance" toward when death *did* them part?

In the next moment, the air was sucked out of her lungs from a bigger blow.

"Cybele? *¿Te duele?*"

Her ears reverberated with the concern in Rodrigo's voice, her vision rippled over the anxiety warping his face.

No. She wasn't okay.

She was a monster. She was amnesic.

And she was pregnant.

Chapter 4

Excruciating minutes of dry retching later, Cybele lay surrounded by Rodrigo, alternating between episodes of inertness and bone-rattling shudders.

He soothed her with the steady pressure of his containment, wiping her eyelids and lips in fragrant coolness, his stroking persistent, hypnotic. His stability finally earthed her misery.

He tilted the face she felt had swollen to twice its original size to his. "You remembered something else?"

"A few things," she hiccuped, struggled to sit up. The temptation to lie in his arms was overwhelming. The urge only submerged her under another breaker of guilt and confusion.

He helped her sit up, then severed all contact, no doubt not wanting to continue it a second beyond necessary.

Needing to put more distance between them, she swung her numb legs to the floor, slipped into the downy slippers that were among the dozens of things he'd supplied for her comfort, things that felt tailored to her size and needs and desires.

She wobbled with her IV drip pole to the panoramic window overlooking the most amazing verdant hills she'd ever seen. Yet she saw nothing but Rodrigo's face, seared into her retinas, along with the vague but nausea-inducing images of Mel in his wheelchair, his rugged good looks pinched and pale, his eyes accusing.

She swung around, almost keeled over. She gasped, saw Rodrigo's body bunch like a panther about to uncoil in a flying leap. He was across the room, but he'd catch her if she collapsed.

She wouldn't. Her skin was crackling where he'd touched her. She couldn't get enough of his touch but couldn't let him touch her again. She held out a detaining hand, steadied herself.

He still rose but kept his distance, his eyes catching the afternoon sun, which poured in ropes of warm gold through the wall-to-wall glass. Their amalgamated color glowed as he brooded across the space at her, his eyebrows lowered, his gaze immobilizing.

She hugged her tender left shoulder, her wretchedness thickening, hardening, settling into concrete deadness. "The things I just remembered…I wouldn't call them real memories. At least, not when I compare them to the memories I've been accumulating since I regained consciousness. I remember those in Technicolor, frame by frame, each accompanied by sounds and scents and sensations. But the things I just recalled came in colorless, soundless and shapeless, like skeletons of data and knowledge. Like headings without articles. If that makes any sense."

He lowered his eyes to his feet, before raising them again, the surgeon in him assessing. "It makes plenty of sense. I've dealt with a lot of post-traumatic amnesia cases, studied endless records, and no one described returning memories with more economy and efficiency than you just did. But it's still early. Those skeletal memories will be fleshed out eventually…."

"I don't want them fleshed out. I want them to stop coming, I want what came back to disappear." She squeezed her shoulder, inducing more pain, to counteract the skewer turning in her gut. "They'll keep exploding in my mind until they blow it apart."

"What did you remember this time?"

Her shoulders sagged. "That Mel was a paraplegic."

He didn't nod or blink or breathe. He just held her gaze. It was the most profound and austere acknowledgment.

And she moaned the rest. "And I'm pregnant."

He blinked, slowly, the motion steeped in significance. He knew. And it wasn't a happy knowledge. Why?

One explanation was that she'd been leaving Mel, but he'd become paralyzed and she'd discovered her pregnancy and it had shattered their plans. Was that the origin of the antipathy she had felt radiating from him from time to time? Was he angry at her for leading him on then telling him that she couldn't leave her husband now that he was disabled and she was expecting his child?

She wouldn't know unless he told her. It didn't seem he was volunteering any information.

She exhaled. "Judging from my concave abdomen, I'm in the first trimester."

"Yes." Then as if against his better judgment, he added, "You're three weeks pregnant."

"Three *weeks*…? How on earth do you know that? Even if you had a pregnancy test done among others before my surgery, you can't pinpoint the stage of my pregnancy that accurate—" Her words dissipated under another gust of realization. "I'm pregnant through IVF. That's how you know how far along I am."

"Actually, you had artificial insemination. Twenty days ago."

"Don't tell me. You know the exact hour I had it, too."

"It was performed at 1:00 p.m."

She gaped at him, finding nothing to explain that too-specific knowledge. And the whole scenario of her pregnancy.

If it had been unplanned and she'd discovered it after she'd decided to leave Mel, that would still make her a cold-blooded two-timer. But it hadn't been unplanned. Pregnancies didn't come more planned than *that*. Evidently, she'd *wanted* to have a baby with Mel. So much that she'd made one through a procedure, when he could no longer make one with her the normal way. The intimate way.

So their marriage *had* been healthy. Until then. Which gave credence to Rodrigo's claim that they'd been planning a honeymoon. Maybe to celebrate her pregnancy.

So how come her first reaction to his death was bitter relief, and to her pregnancy such searing dismay?

What kind of twisted psyche did she have?

There was only one way to know. Rodrigo. He kept filling in the nothingness that had consumed most of what seemed to have been a maze of a life. But he was doing so reluctantly, cautiously, probably being of the school that thought providing another person's memories would make reclaiming hers more difficult, or would taint or distort them as they returned.

She didn't care. Nothing could be more tainted or distorted than her own interpretations. Whatever he told her would provide context, put it all in a better light. Make her someone she could live with. She had to pressure him into telling her what he knew....

Her streaking thoughts shrieked to a halt.

She couldn't *believe* she hadn't wondered. About *how* he knew what he knew. She'd let his care sweep her up, found his knowledge of her an anchoring comfort she hadn't thought to question.

She blurted out the questions under pressure. "Just how do you know all this? How do you know me? And Mel?"

The answer detonated in her mind.

It was that look in his eyes. Barely curbed fierceness leashed behind the steel control of the surgeon and the suave refinement of the man. She remembered *that* look. *Really* remembered it. Not after she'd kissed him. Long before that. In that life she didn't remember.

In that life, Rodrigo had despised her.

And it hadn't been because she'd led him on, then wouldn't leave Mel. It was worse. Far worse.

He'd been Mel's best friend.

The implications of this knowledge were horrifying.

However things had been before, or worse, *after* Mel had been disabled, if she'd exhibited her attraction to Rodrigo, then he had good reason to detest her. The best.

"You remembered."

She raised hesitant eyes at his rasp. "Sort of."

"Sort of? Now that's eloquent. More skeletal head-lines?"

There was that barely contained fury again. She blinked back distress. "I remember that you were his closest friend, and that's how you know so much about us, down to the hour we had a procedure to conceive a baby. Sorry I can't do better." And she was damned if she'd ask him what the situation between *them* had been. She dreaded he'd verify her speculations. "I'm sure the rest will come back. In a flood or bit by bit. No need to hang around here waiting for either event. I want to be discharged."

He looked at her as if she'd sprouted two more sets of eyes. "Get back in bed, now, Cybele. Your lucidity is disintegrating with every moment on your feet, every word out of your mouth."

"Don't give me the patronizing medical tone, Dr. Valderrama. I'm a license-holding insider, if you re-member."

"You mean if *you* remember, don't you?"

"I remember enough. I can recuperate outside this hospital."

"You can only under meticulous medical supervi-sion."

"I can provide that for myself."

"You mean you don't 'remember' the age-proven adage that doctors make the worst patients?"

"It has nothing to do with remembering it, just not subscribing to it. I can take care of myself."

"No, you can't. But I will discharge you. Into my custody. I will take you to my estate to continue your recuperation."

His declaration took the remaining air from her lungs.

His custody. His estate. She almost swayed under the impact of the images that crowded her mind, of what both would be like, the temptation to jump into his arms and say *Yes, please*.

She had to say no. Get away from him. And fast. "Listen, I was in a terrible accident, but I got off pretty lightly. I would have died if you and your ultra-efficient medical machine hadn't intervened, but you did, and you fixed me. I'm fine."

"You're so far from fine, you could be in another galaxy."

It was just *wrong*. That he'd have a sense of humor, too. That it would surface now. And would pluck at her own humor strings.

She sighed at her untimely, inappropriate reaction. "Don't exaggerate. All I have wrong with me is a few missing memories."

"A few? Shall we make a list of what you do remember, those headlines with the vanished articles, and another of the volumes you've had erased and might never be able to retrieve, then revisit your definition of 'a few'?"

"Cute." And he was. In an unbearably virile and overruling way. "But at the rate I'm retrieving headlines, I'll soon have enough to fill said volumes."

"Even if you do, that isn't your only problem. You had a severe concussion with brain edema and subdural hematoma. I operated on you for ten hours. Half of those were with orthopedic and vascular surgeons as we put your arm back together. Ramón said it was the most intricate open reduction and internal fixation of his career, while Bianca and I had a hell of a time repairing your blood vessels and nerves. Afterward, you were comatose for three days and woke up with a total memory deficit. Right now your neurological status is suspect, your arm is useless, you have bruises and contusions from head to toe and you're in your first trimester. Your body will need double the time and effort to heal during this most physiologically demanding time. It amazes me you're talking, and that much, moving at all and not lying in bed disoriented and sobbing for more painkillers."

"Thanks for the rundown of my condition, but seems I'm more amazing than you think. I'm pretty lucid and I can talk as endlessly as *you* evidently can. And the pain is nowhere as bad as before."

"You're pumped full of painkillers."

"No, I'm not. I stopped the drip."

"What?" He strode toward her in steps loaded with rising tension. He inspected her drip, scowled down on her. "When?"

"The moment you walked out after your last inspection."

"That means you have no more painkillers in your system."

"I don't need any. The pain in my arm is tolerable now. I think it was coming out of the anesthesia of unconsciousness that made it intolerable by comparison."

He shook his head. "I think we also need to examine your definition of 'pretty lucid.' You're not making sense to me. Why feel pain at all, when you can have it dealt with?"

"Some discomfort keeps me sharp, rebooting my system instead of lying in drug-induced comfort, which might mask some deterioration in progress. What about *that* doesn't make sense to you?"

He scowled. "I *was* wondering what kept you up and running."

"Now you know. *And* I vividly recall my medical training. I may be amnesic but I'm not reckless. I'll take every precaution, do things by the post-operative, post-trauma book…."

"I'm keeping you by my side until I'm satisfied that you're back to your old capable-of-taking-on-the-world self."

That silenced whatever argument she would have fired back.

She'd had the conviction that he didn't think much of her.

So he believed she was strong, but despised her because she'd come on stronger to him? Could she have done something so out-of-character? She abhorred infidelity, found no excuse for it. At least the woman who'd awakened from the coma did not.

Then he surprised her more. "I'm not talking about how you were when you were with Mel, but before that."

She didn't think to ask how he knew what she'd been like before Mel. She was busy dealing with the suspicion that he was right, that her relationship with Mel *had* derailed her.

More broad lines resurfaced. How she'd wanted to be nothing like her mother, who'd left a thriving career to serve the whims of Cybele's stepfather, how she'd thought she'd never marry, would have a child on her own when her career had become unshakable.

Though she didn't have a time line, she sensed that until months ago, she'd held the same convictions.

So how had she found herself married, at such a crucial time as her senior residency year, and pregnant, too?

Had she loved Mel so much that she'd been so blinded? Had she had setbacks in her job in consequence, known things would keep going downhill and that was why she remembered him with all this resentment? Was that why she'd found an excuse to let her feelings for Rodrigo blossom?

Not that there could be an excuse for that.

But strangely, she wasn't sorry she was pregnant. In fact, that was what ameliorated this mess, the one thing she was looking forward to. That…and, to her mortification, being with Rodrigo.

Which was exactly why she couldn't accept his carte blanche proposal.

"Thank you for the kind offer, Rodrigo—"

He cut her off. "It's neither kind nor an offer. It's imperative and it's a decision."

Now *that* was a premium slice of unadulterated autocracy.

She sent up a fervent thank-you for the boost to her seconds-ago-nonexistent resistance. "Imperative or imperious? Decision or dictate?"

"Great language recall and usage. And take your pick."

"I think it's clear I already did. And whatever you choose to call your *offer*, I can't accept it."

"You mean you won't."

"Fine. If you insist on dissecting my refusal. I won't."

"It seems you *have* forgotten all about me, Cybele. If you remembered even the most basic things, you'd know that when I make a decision, saying no to me is not an option."

Cybele stared at him. Life was grossly, horribly unfair. How did one being end up endowed with all that?

And she'd thought he had it all before she'd seen him crook his lips in that I-click-my-fingers-and-all-sentient-beings-obey quasi smile.

Now there was one thought left in her mind. An urge. To get as far away from him as possible. Against all logic. And desire.

Her lips twisted, too. "I didn't get that memo. Or I 'forgot' I did. So *I* can say no to you. Consider it a one-off anomaly."

That tigerlike smirk deepened. "You can say what you want. I'm your surgeon and what *I* say goes."

The way he'd said *your surgeon*. Everything clamored inside her, wishing he was her anything-and-everything, for real.

She shook her head to disperse the idiotic yearnings. "I'll sign any waiver you need me to. I'm taking full responsibility."

"I'm the one taking full responsibility for you. If you do remember being a surgeon, you know that my being yours makes me second only to God in this situation. You have no say in God's will, do you?"

"You're taking the God complex too literally, aren't you?"

"My status in your case is an uncontestable fact. You're in my care and will remain there until I'm satisfied you no longer need it. The one choice I leave up to you is whether I follow you up in my home as my guest, or in my hospital as my patient."

Cybele looked away from his hypnotic gaze, his logic. But there was no escaping either. It *had* been desperation, wanting to get away from him. She *wasn't* in a condition to be without medical supervision. And who best to follow her up but her own surgeon? The surgeon who happened to be the best there was?

She knew he was. He was beyond the best. A genius. With billions and named-after-him revolutionary procedures and equipment to prove it.

But even had she been fit, she wouldn't have wanted to be discharged. For where could she go but home? A home she recalled with nothing but dreariness?

And she didn't want to be with anyone else. Certainly not with her mother and family. She remembered them as if they were someone else's unwanted acquaintances. Disappointing and distant. Their own actions reinforced that impression. The sum total of their concern over her accident and Mel's death had been a couple of phone calls. When told she was fine, didn't need anything, it seemed they'd considered it an excuse to stop worrying—if they *had* been worried—dismiss her and return to their real interests. She didn't remember specifics from her life with them, but this felt like the final straw in a string of lifelong letdowns.

She turned her face to him. He was watching her as if he'd been manipulating her thoughts, steering her toward the decision he wanted her to make. She wouldn't put mental powers beyond him. What was one more covert power among the glaringly obvious ones?

She nodded her capitulation.

He tilted his awesome head at her. "You concede your need for my supervision?" He wanted a concession in words? Good luck with that. She nodded again. "And which will it be? Guest or patient?"

He wanted her to pick, now? She'd hoped to let things float for a couple of days, until she factored in the implications of being either, the best course of action....

Just great. A scrambled memory surely hadn't touched her self-deception ability. Seemed she had that in spades.

She knew what the best course of action was. She *should* say patient. Should stay in the hospital where the insanities he provoked in her would be curbed, where she wouldn't be able to act on them. She *would* say patient.

Then she opened her mouth. "As if you don't already know."

She barely held back a curse, almost took the sullen words back.

She didn't. She was mesmerized by his watchfulness, by seeing it evaporate in a flare of...something. Triumph?

She had no idea. It was exhausting enough trying to read her own thoughts and reactions. She wasn't up to fathoming his. She only hoped he'd say something superior and smirking. It might trip a fuse that would make her retreat from the abyss of stupidity and self-destructiveness, do what sense and survival were yelling for her to do. Remain here, remain a patient to him, nothing more.

"It'll be an honor to have you as my guest, Cybele." Distress brimmed as the intensity in his eyes drained, leaving them as gentle as his voice. It was almost spilling over when that arrogance she'd prayed for coated his face. "It's a good thing you didn't say 'patient,' though. I would have overruled you again."

She bristled. "Now look here—"

He smoothly cut across her offense. "I would have, because I built this center to be a teaching hospital, and if you stay, there is no way I can fairly stop the doctors and students from having constant access to you, to study your intriguing neurological condition."

Seemed not only did no one say no to him, no one ever won an argument with him, either. He'd given her the one reason that would send her rocketing out of this hospital like a cartoon character with a thick trail of white exhaust clouds in her wake.

No way would she be poked and prodded by med students and doctors-in-training. In the life that felt like a half-remembered documentary of someone else's, she'd been both, then the boss of a bunch of the latter. She knew how nothing—starting with patients' comfort, privacy, even basic human rights—stood in the way of acquiring their coveted-above-all experience.

She sighed. "You always get what you want, don't you?"

"No. Not always."

The tormented look that seized his face arrested her in midbreath. Was this about…her? Was *she* something he wanted and couldn't get?

No. She just knew what she felt for him had always been only on her side. On his, there'd been nothing inappropriate. He'd never given her reason to believe the feelings were mutual.

This…despondency was probably about failing to save Mel. That had to be the one thing he'd wanted most. And he hadn't gotten it.

She swallowed the ground glass that seemed to fill her throat. "I—I think I'll take a nap now."

He inhaled, nodded. "Yes, you do that."

He started to turn away, stopped, his eyes focusing far in the distance. He seemed to be thinking terrible things.

A heart-thudding moment later, without looking back again, he muttered, "Mel's funeral is this afternoon." She gasped. She'd somehow never thought of that part. He looked back at her then, face gripped with urgency, eyes storming with entreaty. "You should know."

She gave a difficult nod. "Thanks for telling me."

"Don't thank me. I'm not sure I should have."

"Why? You don't think I can handle it?"

"You seem to be handling everything so well, I'm wondering if this isn't the calm before the storm."

"You think I'll collapse into a jibbering mess somewhere down the road?"

"You've been through so much. I wouldn't be surprised."

"I can't predict the future. But I'm as stable as can be now. I—I want to go. I have to."

"You don't have to do anything, Cybele. Mel wouldn't have wanted you to go through the added trauma."

So Mel had cared for her? Wanted the best for her?

She inhaled, shook her head. "I'm coming. You're not going to play the not-neurologically-stable-enough card, are you?"

His eyes almost drilled a crater of conflicted emotions between her own. "You should be okay. If you do everything I say."

"And what is that?"

"Rest now. Attend the funeral in a wheelchair. And leave when I say. No arguments."

She hadn't the energy to do more than close her eyelids in consent. He hesitated, then walked back to her, took her elbow, guided her back to the bed. She sagged down on it.

He, too, dropped down, to his haunches. Heartbeats shook her frame as he took one numb foot after the other, slid off slippers that felt as if they were made of hot iron. He rose, touched her shoulder, didn't need to apply force. She collapsed like water in a fountain with its pressure lost. He scooped up her legs, swung them over the bed, swept the cotton cover over her, stood back and murmured, "Rest."

Without another look, he turned and crossed the room as if he'd been hit with a fast-forward button.

The moment the door clicked shut, shudders overtook her.

Rest? He really thought she could? After what he'd just done? Before she had to attend her dead husband's funeral?

She ached. For him, because of him, because she breathed, with guilt, with lack of guilt.

She could only hope that the funeral, the closure ritual, might open up the locked, pitch-black cells in her mind.

Maybe then she'd get answers. And absolution.

Chapter 5

She didn't rest.

Four hours of tossing in bed later, at the entry of a genial brunette bearing a black skirt suit and its accessories, Cybele staggered up feeling worse than when she'd woken from her coma.

She winced a smile of thanks at the woman and insisted she didn't need help dressing. Her fiberglass arm cast was quite light and she could move her shoulder and elbow joints well enough to get into the front-fastening jacket and blouse.

After the woman left, she stood staring at the clothes Rodrigo had provided for her. To attend the funeral of the husband she didn't remember. Didn't want to remember.

She didn't need help dressing. She needed help de-stressing.

No chance of that. Only thing to do was dress the

part, walk in and out of this. Or rather, get wheeled in and out.

In minutes she was staring at her reflection in the full-wall mirror in the state-of-the-art, white and gray bathroom.

Black wool suit, white silk blouse, two-inch black leather shoes. All designer items. All made as if for her.

A knock on the door ripped her out of morbid musings over the origin of such accuracy in judging her size.

She wanted to dart to the door, snatch it open and yell, *Let's get it over with.*

She walked slowly instead, opened the door like an automaton. Rodrigo was there. With a wheelchair. She sat down without a word.

In silence, he wheeled her through his space-age center to a gigantic elevator that could accommodate ten gurneys and their attending personnel. This was obviously a place equipped and staffed to deal with mass casualty situations. She stared ahead as they reached the vast entrance, feeling every eye on her, the woman their collective boss was tending to personally.

Once outside the controlled climate of the center, she shivered as the late February coolness settled on her face and legs. He stopped before a gleaming black Mercedes 600, slipped the warmth of the cashmere coat she realized had been draped over his arm all along around her shoulders as he handed her into the back of the car.

In moments he'd slid in beside her on the cream leather couch, signaled the chauffeur and the sleek beast of a vehicle shot forward soundlessly, the racing-by vistas of the Spanish countryside the only proof that it was streaking through the nearly empty streets.

None of the beauty zooming by made it past the surface of her awareness. All deeper levels converged on him. On the turmoil in the rigidity of his profile, the coiled tension of his body.

And she couldn't bear it anymore. "I'm...so sorry."

He turned to her. "What are you talking about?"

The harshness that flickered in his eyes, around his lips made her hesitate. It didn't stop her. "I'm talking about Mel." His eyes seemed to lash out an emerald flare. She almost backed down, singed and silenced. She forged on. "About your loss." His jaw muscles convulsed then his face turned to rock, as if he'd sucked in all emotion, buried it where it would never resurface for anyone to see. "I don't remember him or our relationship, but you don't have that mercy. You've lost your best friend. He died on your table, as you struggled to save him...."

"As I *failed* to save him, you mean."

His hiss hit her like the swipe of a sword across the neck.

She nearly suffocated on his anguish. Only the need to drain it made her choke out, "You didn't fail. There was nothing you could have done." His eyes flared again, zapping her with the force of his frustration. "Don't bother contradicting me or looking for ways to shoulder a nonexistent blame. Everyone knew he was beyond help."

"And that's supposed to make me feel better? What if I don't want to feel better?"

"Unfounded guilt never did anyone any good. Certainly not the ones we feel guilty over."

"How logical you can be, when logic serves no purpose."

"I thought you advocated logic as what serves every purpose."

"Not in this instance. And what I feel certainly isn't hurting me any. I'm as fit as an ox."

"So you're dismissing emotional and psychological pain as irrelevant? I know that as surgeons we're mainly concerned with physical disorders, things we can fix with our scalpels, but—"

"But nothing. I'm whole and hearty. Mel is dead."

"Through no fault of yours!" She couldn't bear to see him bludgeoning himself with pain and guilt that way. "That's the only point I'm making, the only one to *be* made here. I know it doesn't make his loss any less traumatic or profound. And I am deeply sorry for—everyone. You, Mel, his parents, our baby."

"But not yourself?"

"No."

The brittle syllable hung between them, loaded with too much for mere words to express, and the better for it, she thought.

Twenty minutes of silence later her heart hiccupped in her chest. They were entering a private airport.

With every yard deeper into the lush, grassy expanses, tentacles of panic slid around her throat, slithered into her mind until the car came to a halt a few dozen feet from the stairs of a gleaming silver Boeing 737.

She blindly reached out to steady herself with the one thing that was unshakeable in her world. Rodrigo.

His arm came around her at the same moment she sought his support, memories billowing inside her head like the sooty smoke of an oil-spill fire. "This is where we boarded the plane."

He stared down at her for a suspended moment before closing his eyes. "*Dios, lo siento,* Cybele—I'm so sorry. I didn't factor in what it would do to you, being here, where your ordeal began."

She snatched air into her constricted lungs, shook her head. "It's probably the right thing to do, bringing me here. Maybe it'll get the rest of my memories to explode back at once. I'd welcome that over the periodic detonations."

"I can't take credit for attempting shock therapy. We're here for Mel's funeral." She gaped at him. He elaborated. "It's not a traditional funeral. I had Mel's parents flown over from the States so they can take his body home."

She struggled to take it all in. Mel's body. Here. In that hearse over there. His parents. She didn't remember them. At all. They must be in the Boeing. Which had to be Rodrigo's. They'd come down, and she'd see them. And instead of a stricken widow they could comfort and draw solace from, they'd find a numb stranger unable to share their grief.

"Rodrigo…" The plea to take her back now, that she'd been wrong, couldn't handle this, congealed in her throat.

He'd turned his head away. A man and a woman in their early sixties had appeared at the jet's open door.

He reached for his door handle, turned to her. "Stay here."

Mortification filled her. She was such a wimp. He'd felt her reluctance to face her in-laws, was sparing her.

She couldn't let him. She owed them better than that. She'd owe any grieving parents anything she could do to lessen their loss. "No, I'm coming with you. And no wheelchair, please. I don't want them to think I'm worse than I am." He pursed his lips, then nodded, exited the car. In seconds he was on her side, handing her out. She crushed his formal suit's lapel. "What are their names?"

His eyes widened, as if shocked all over again at the total gaps in her memory. "Agnes and Steven Braddock."

The names rang distant bells. She hadn't known them long, or well. She was sure of that.

The pair descended as she and Rodrigo headed on an intercept course. Their faces became clearer with every step, setting off more memories. Of how Mel had looked in detail. And in color.

Her father-in-law had the same rangy physique and wealth of hair, only it was gray where Mel's had been shades of bronze. Mel had had the startlingly turquoise eyes of her mother-in-law.

She stopped when they were a few steps way. Rodrigo didn't.

He kept going, opened his arms, and the man and woman rushed right into them. The three of them merged into an embrace that squeezed her heart dry of its last cell of blood.

Everything hurt. Burned. She felt like strips were being torn out of her flesh. Acid filled her eyes, burned her cheeks.

The way he held them, the way they sought his comfort and consolation as if it was their very next breath, the way they all clung together... The way he looked, wide open and giving everything inside him for the couple to take their fill of, to draw strength from...

Just when she would have cried out *Enough—please*, the trio dissolved their merger of solace, turned, focused on her. Then Agnes closed the steps between them.

She tugged Cybele into a trembling hug, careful not to brush against her cast. "I can't tell you how worried we were for you. It's a prayer answered to see you so well." So well? She'd looked like a convincing post-mortem rehearsal last time she'd consulted a mirror. But then, compared to Mel, she was looking great. "It's why we were so late coming here. Rodrigo couldn't deal with this, with anything, until you were out of danger."

"He shouldn't have. I can't imagine how you felt, having to put th-this off."

Agnes shook her head, the sadness in her eyes deepening. "Mel was already beyond our reach, and coming sooner would have served no purpose. You were the one who needed Rodrigo's full attention so he could pull you through."

"He did. And while everyone says he's phenomenal with all his patients, I'm sure he's gone above and beyond even by his standards. I'm as sure it's because I was Mel's wife. It's clear what a close friend of the whole family he is."

The woman looked at her as if she'd said Rodrigo was in reality a reptile. "But Rodrigo isn't just a friend of the family. He's our son. He's Mel's brother."

Cybele felt she'd stared at Agnes for ages, feeling her words reverberating in her mind in shock waves.

Rodrigo. Wasn't Mel's best friend. Was his brother. *How?*

"You didn't know?" Agnes stopped, tutted to herself. "What am I asking. Rodrigo told us of your memory loss. You've forgotten."

She hadn't. She was positive. This was a brand-new revelation.

Questions heaved and pitched in her mind, splashed

against the confines of her skull until she felt they'd shatter it.

Before she could relieve the pressure, launch the first few dozen, Rodrigo and Steven closed in on them. Rodrigo stood back as Steven mirrored his wife's actions and sentiments.

"We've kept Cybele on her feet long enough," Rodrigo addressed the couple who claimed to be his parents. "Why don't you go back to the car with her, Agnes, while Steven and I arrange everything."

Agnes? Steven? He didn't call them mother and father?

She would have asked to be involved if she wasn't burning for the chance to be alone with Agnes, to get to the bottom of this.

As soon as they settled into the car, Cybele turned to Agnes. And all the questions jammed in her mind.

What would she ask? How? This woman was here to claim her son's body. What would she think, feel, if said son's widow showed no interest in talking about him and was instead panting to know all about the man who'd turned out to be his brother?

She sat there, feeling at a deeper loss than she had since she'd woken up in this new life. Rodrigo's chauffeur offered them refreshments. She parroted what Agnes settled on, mechanically sipped her mint tea every time Agnes did hers.

Suddenly Agnes started to talk, the sorrow that coated her face mingling with other things. Love. Pride.

"Rodrigo was six, living in an exclusively Hispanic community in Southern California, when his mother died in a factory accident and he was taken into the system. Two years later, when Mel was six, we decided that he needed a sibling, one we'd realized we'd never be able to give him."

So that was it. Rodrigo was adopted.

Agnes went on. "We took Mel with us while we searched, since our one criteria for the child we'd adopt was that he get along with Mel. But Mel antagonized every child we thought was suited to our situation, got them to turn nasty. Then Rodrigo was suggested to us. We were told he was everything Mel wasn't—responsible, resourceful, respectful, with a steady temperament and a brilliant mind. But we'd been told so many good things about other children and we'd given up hope that any child would pass the test of interaction with Mel. Then Rodrigo walked in.

"After he introduced himself in the little English he knew, enquired politely why we were looking for another child, he asked to be left alone with Mel. Unknown to both boys, we were taken to where children's meetings with prospective parents were monitored. Mel was at his nastiest, calling Rodrigo names, making fun of his accent, insulting his parentage and situation. We were mortified that he even knew those…words, and would use them so viciously. Steven thought he felt threatened by Rodrigo, as he had by any child we sought. I told him whatever the reason, I couldn't let Mel abuse the poor boy, that we'd been wrong and Mel didn't need a sibling but firmer treatment until he outgrew his sullenness and nastiness. He hushed me, asked me to watch. And I watched.

"Rodrigo had so far shown no reaction. By then, other boys had lashed out, verbally and physically, at Mel's bullying. But Rodrigo sat there, watching him in what appeared to be deep contemplation. Then he stood up and calmly motioned him closer. Mel rained more abuse on him, but when he still didn't get the usual reaction, he seemed to be intrigued. I was certain Rodrigo would deck him and sneer *gotcha* or something. I bet Mel thought the same.

"We all held our breath as Rodrigo put a hand in his pocket. My mind streaked with worst-case scenarios. Steven surged up, too. But the director of the boys' home detained us. Then Rodrigo took out a butterfly. It was made of cardboard and elastic and metal springs and beautifully hand-painted. He wound it up and let it fly. And suddenly Mel was a child again, giggling and jumping after the butterfly as if it were real.

"We knew then that Rodrigo had won him over, that our search for a new son was over. I was shaking as we walked in to ask Rodrigo if he'd like to come live with us. He was stunned. He said no one wanted older children. We assured him that we did want him, but that he could try us out first. He insisted it was he who would prove himself to us. He turned and shook Mel's hand, told him he'd made other toys and promised to teach him how to make his own."

The images Agnes had weaved were overwhelming. The vision of Rodrigo as a child was painfully vivid. Self-possessed in the face of humiliation and adversity, stoic in a world where he had no one, determined as he proved himself worthy of respect.

"And did he teach him?" she asked.

Agnes sighed. "He tried. But Mel was short-fused, impatient, never staying with anything long enough for it to bear fruit. Rodrigo never stopped trying to involve him, get him to experience the pleasures of achievement.

We loved him with all our hearts from the first day, but loved him more for how hard he tried."

"So your plan that a sibling would help Mel didn't work?"

"Oh, no, it did. Rodrigo did absorb a great deal of Mel's angst and instability. He became the older brother Mel emulated in everything. It was how Mel ended up in medicine."

"Then he must have grown out of his impatience. It takes a lot of perseverance to become a doctor."

"You really don't remember a thing about him, do you?" Now what did that mean? Before she pressed for an elaboration, Agnes sighed again. "Mel was brilliant, could do anything if only he set his mind to it. But only Rodrigo knew how to motivate him, to keep him in line. And when Rodrigo turned eighteen, he moved out."

"Why? Wasn't he happy with you?"

"He assured us that his need for independence had nothing to do with not loving us or not wanting to be with us. He confessed that he'd always felt the need to find his roots."

"And you feared he was only placating you?"

Agnes's soft features, which showed a once-great beauty lined by a life of emotional upheavals, spasmed with recalled anxiety. "We tried to help as he searched for his biological family, but his methods were far more effective, his instincts of where to look far sharper. He found his maternal relatives three years later and his grandparents were beside themselves with joy. Their whole extended family welcomed him with open arms."

Cybele couldn't think how anyone wouldn't. "Did he learn the identity of his father?"

"His grandparents didn't know. They had had a huge

quarrel with his mother when she got pregnant and she wouldn't reveal the father's identity. She left home, saying she'd never return to their narrow-minded world. Once they had calmed down, they searched for her everywhere, kept hoping she'd come home. But they never heard from her again. They were devastated to learn their daughter was long dead, but ecstatic that Rodrigo had found them."

"And he changed his name from yours to theirs then?"

"He never took our name, just kept the name his mother had used. There were too many obstacles to our adopting him, and when he realized our struggles, he asked us to stop trying, said he knew we considered him our son and we didn't need to prove it to him. He was content to be our foster son to the world. He was eleven at the time. When he found his family, he still insisted *we* were his real family, since it was choice and love that bound us and not blood. He didn't legally take their names until he made sure we knew that it just suited his identity more to have his Catalan names."

"And you still thought he'd walk out of your life."

Agnes exhaled her agreement. "It was the worst day of my life when he told us that he was moving to Spain as soon as his medical training was over. I thought my worst fears of losing him had come true."

It struck Cybele as weird that Agnes didn't consider the day Mel had died the worst day of her life. But she was too intent on the story for the thought to take hold. "But you didn't lose him."

"I shouldn't have worried. Not with Rodrigo. I should have known he'd never abandon us, or even neglect us. He never stopped paying us the closest attention, was a constant presence in our lives—more so even than Mel, who lived under the same roof. Mel always had a problem expressing his emotions, and showed them with material, not moral, things. That's probably why he… he…" She stopped, looked away.

"He what?" Cybele tried not to sound rabid with curiosity. They were getting to some real explanation here. She knew it.

She almost shrieked with frustration when Agnes ignored her question, returned to her original topic. "Rodrigo continued to rise to greater successes but made sure we were there to share the joy of every step with him. Even when he moved here, he never let us or Mel feel that he was far away. He was constantly after us to move here, too, to start projects we've long dreamed of, offered us everything we'd need to establish them. But Mel said Spain was okay for vacations but he was a New Yorker and could never live anywhere else. Though it was a difficult decision, we decided to stay in the States with him. We thought he was the one who…needed our presence more. But we do spend chunks of every winter with Rodrigo, and he comes to the States as frequently as possible."

And she'd met him during those frequent trips. Over and over. She just knew it. But she was just as sure, no matter how spotty her memory was, that *this* story hadn't been volunteered by anyone before. She was certain she hadn't been told Rodrigo was Mel's foster brother. Not by Mel, not by Rodrigo.

Why had neither man owned up to this fact?

Agnes touched her good hand. "I'm so sorry, my dear. I shouldn't have gone on and on down memory lane."

And the weirdest thing was, Agnes's musings hadn't been about the son she'd lost, but the son she'd acquired thirty years ago. "I'm glad you did. I need to know anything that will help me remember."

"And did you? Remember anything?"

It wasn't a simple question to ascertain her neurological state. Agnes wanted to know something. Something to do with what she'd started to say about Mel then dropped, as if ashamed, as if too distressed to broach it.

"Sporadic things," Cybele said cautiously, wondering how to lead back to the thread of conversation she just knew would explain why she'd felt this way about Mel, and about Rodrigo.

Agnes turned away from her. "They're back."

Cybele jerked, followed Agnes's gaze, frustration backing up in her throat. Then she saw Rodrigo prowling in those powerful, control-laden strides and the sight of him drowned out everything else.

Suddenly a collage of images became superimposed over his. Of her and Mel going out with Rodrigo and a different sexpot each time, women who'd fawned over him and whom he'd treated with scathing disinterest, playing true to his reputation as a ruthless playboy.

Something else dislodged in her mind, felt as if an image had moved from the obscurity of her peripheral vision into the clarity of her focus. How Mel had become exasperating around Rodrigo.

If these were true memories, they contradicted everything Agnes had said, everything she'd sensed about Rodrigo. They showed him as the one who was erratic and inconstant, who'd had a disruptive, not a stabilizing, effect on Mel. Could she have overlooked all that, and her revulsion toward promiscuous men, under the spell of his charisma? Or could that have been his attraction? The challenge of his unavailability? The ambition of being the one to tame the big bad wolf? Could she have been that perverse and stupid…?

"Are you ready, Agnes?"

Cybele lurched at the sound of Rodrigo's fathomless baritone.

Stomach churning with the sickening conjectures, she dazedly watched him hand Agnes out of the car. Then he bent to her.

"Stay here." She opened her mouth. A gentle hand beneath her jaw closed it for her. "No arguments, remember?"

"I want to do what you're all going to do," she mumbled.

"You've had enough. I shouldn't have let you come at all."

"I'm fine. Please."

That fierceness welled in his eyes again. Then he gave a curt nod, helped her out of the car.

She didn't only want to be there for these people to whom she felt such a powerful connection. She also hoped she'd get more answers from Agnes before she and Steven flew back home.

Cybele watched Rodrigo stride with Steven to the hearse, where another four men waited. One was Ramón Velázquez, her orthopedic surgeon and Rodrigo's best friend—for real—and partner.

Rodrigo and Ramón shared a solemn nod then opened the hearse's back door and slid the coffin out. Steven and the three other men joined in carrying it to the cargo bay of the Boeing.

Cybele stood transfixed beside Agnes, watching the grim procession, her eyes flitting between Rodrigo's face and Steven's. The same expression gripped both. It was the same one on Agnes's face. Something seemed… off about that expression.

Conjectures ping-ponged inside her head as everything seemed to fast-forward until the ritual was over, and Steven walked back with Rodrigo to join Agnes in hugging Cybele farewell. Then the Braddocks boarded the Boeing and Rodrigo led Cybele back to the Mercedes.

The car had just swung out of the airfield when she heard the roar of the jet's takeoff. She twisted around to watch it sail overhead before it hurtled away, its noise receding, its size diminishing.

And it came to her, why she knew that off expression. It was the exhausted resignation exhibited by families of patients who died after long, agonizing terminal illnesses. It didn't add up when Mel's death had been swift and shocking.

Something else became glaringly obvious. She turned to Rodrigo. He was looking outside his window.

She hated to intrude on the sanctity of his heartache. But she had to make sense of it all. "Rodrigo, I'm sorry, but—"

He rounded on her, his eyes simmering in the rays penetrating the mirrored window. "Don't say you're sorry again, Cybele."

"I'm sor—" She swallowed the apology he seemed unable to hear from her. "I was going to apologize for interrupting your thoughts. But I need to ask. *They* didn't ask. About my pregnancy."

He seemed taken aback. Then his face slammed shut. "Mel didn't tell them."

This was one answer she hadn't considered. Yet another twist. "Why? I can understand not telling them of our intention to have a baby this way, in case it didn't work. But after it did, why didn't he run to them with the news?"

His shrug was eloquent with his inability to guess Mel's motivations. With his intention to drop the subject.

She couldn't accommodate him. "Why didn't *you* tell them?"

"Because it's up to you whether or not to tell them."

"They're my baby's grandparents. Of course I want to tell them. If I'd realized they didn't know, I would have. It would have given them solace, knowing that a part of their son remains."

His jaw worked for a moment. Then he exhaled. "I'm glad you *didn't* bring it up. You're not in any shape to deal with the emotional fallout of a disclosure of this caliber. And instead of providing the solace you think it would have, at this stage, the news would have probably only aggravated their repressed grief."

But it *hadn't* been repressed grief she'd sensed from them.

Then again, what did she know? Her perceptions might be as scrambled as her memories. "You're probably right." *As usual,* she added inwardly. "I'll tell them when I'm back to normal and I'm certain the pregnancy is stable."

He lowered his eyes, his voice, and simply said, "Yes."

Feeling drained on all counts, she gazed up at him— the mystery that kept unraveling only to become more tangled. The anchor of this shifting, treacherous new existence of hers.

And she implored, "Can we go home now, please?"

Chapter 6

He took her home. His home.

They'd driven back from the airport to Barcelona city center. From there it had taken over an hour to reach his estate.

By the time they approached it at sunset, she felt saturated with the sheer beauty of the Catalan countryside.

Then they passed through the electronic, twenty-foot wrought-iron gates, wound through the driveway, and with each yard deeper into his domain, she realized. There was no such thing as a limit to the capacity to appreciate beauty, to be stunned by it.

She turned her eyes to him. He'd been silent save for necessary words. She'd kept silent, too, struggling with the contradictions of what her heart told her and what her memories insisted on, with wanting to ask him to dispel her doubts.

But the more she remembered everything he'd said and done, everything everyone had said about him in the past days, the more only one conclusion made sense. Her memories had to be false.

He turned to her. After a long moment, he said, deep, quiet, "Welcome to Villa Candelaria, Cybele."

She swallowed past the emotions, yet her "Thank you" came out a tremulous gasp. She tried again. "When did you buy this place?"

"Actually, I built it. I named it after my mother."

The lump grew as images took shape and form. Of him as an orphan who'd never forgotten his mother until he one day was affluent enough to build such a place and name it after her, so her memory would continue somewhere outside of his mind and…

Okay, she'd start weeping any second now. Better steer this away from personal stuff. "This place looks… massive. Not just the building, but the land, too."

"It's thirty thousand square feet over twenty acres with a mile-long waterfront. Before you think I'm crazy to build all this for myself, I built it hoping it would become the home of many families, affording each privacy and land for whatever projects and pursuits they wished for. Not that it worked out that way."

The darkness that stained his face and voice seared her. He'd wished to surround himself with family. And he'd been thwarted at every turn, it seemed. Was he suffering from the loneliness and isolation she felt were such an integral part of her own psyche?

"I picked this land completely by chance. I was driving once, aimlessly, when I saw that crest of a hill overlooking this sea channel." She looked where he was pointing. "The vision slammed into my mind fully formed. A villa built into those rock formations as if it was a part of them."

She reversed the process, imagining those elements without the magnificent villa they now hugged as if it *were* an intrinsic part of their structure. "I always thought of the Mediterranean as all sandy beaches."

"Not this area of the northern Iberian coastline. Rugged rock is indigenous here."

The car drew to a smooth halt in front of thirty-foot-wide stone steps among landscaped, terraced plateaus that surrounded the villa from all sides.

In seconds Rodrigo was handing her out and insisting she sit in the wheelchair she hadn't used much today. She acquiesced, wondered as he wheeled her up the gentle slope beside the steps if it had always been there, for older family members' convenience, or if it had been installed to accommodate Mel's condition.

Turning away from futile musings, she surrendered to the splendor all around her as they reached a gigantic patio that surrounded the villa. On one side it overlooked the magnificent property that was part vineyards and orchards and part landscaped gardens, with the valley and mountains in the distance, and on the other side, the breathtaking sea and shoreline.

The patio led to the highest area overlooking the sea, a massive terrace garden that was illuminated by golden lights planted everywhere like luminescent flowers.

He took her inside and she got rapid impressions of the interior as he swept her to the quarters he'd designated for her.

She felt everything had been chosen with an eye for uniqueness and comfort, simplicity and grandeur, blending sweeping lines and spaces with bold wall colors, honey-colored ceilings and furniture that complemented both. French doors and colonial pillars merged seamlessly with the natural beauty of hardwood floors accentuated by marble and granite. She knew she could spend weeks poring over every detail, but in its whole, she felt this was a place this formidable man had wanted his family to love, to feel at home in from the moment they set foot in it. She knew *she* did. And she hadn't technically set foot in it yet.

Then she did. He opened a door, wheeled her in then helped her out of the chair. She stood as he wheeled the chair to one side, walked out to haul in two huge suitcases that had evidently been transported right behind them.

He placed one on the floor and the other on a luggage stand at the far side of the room, which opened into a full-fledged dressing room.

She stood mesmerized as he walked back to her.

He was overwhelming. A few levels beyond that.

He stopped before her, took her hand. She felt as though it burst in flames. "I promise you a detailed tour of the place. Later. In stages. Now you have to rest. Doctor's orders."

With that he gave her hand a gentle press, turned and left.

The moment the door clicked closed behind him, she staggered to lean on it, exhaled a choppy breath.

Doctor's orders. *Her* doctor...

She bit her lip. Hours ago, she'd consigned her husband's body to his parents. And all she could think of was Rodrigo. There wasn't even a twinge of guilt toward Mel. There *was* sadness, but it was the sadness she knew she'd feel for any human being's disability and death. For his loved ones' mourning. Nothing more.

What was wrong with her? What had been wrong with her and Mel? Or was there more wrong with her mind than she believed?

Her lungs deflated on a dejected exhalation.

All she could do now was never let any of those who'd loved and lost Mel know how unaffected by his loss she was. What did it matter what she felt in the secrecy of her heart and mind if she never let the knowledge out to hurt others? She couldn't change the way she felt, should stop feeling bad about it. It served no purpose, did no one any good.

With that rationalization reached, she felt as if a ten-pound rock had been lifted off her heart. Air flowed into her lungs all of a sudden, just as the lovely surroundings registered in her appreciation centers.

The room—if a thirty-something-by forty-something-foot space with a twelve-foot ceiling could be called that—was a manifestation of the ultimate in personal space.

With walls painted sea blue and green, furniture of dark mahogany and ivory ceilings and accents, it was soothingly lit by golden lamps of the side and standing variety. French doors were draped in gauzy powder-blue curtains that undulated in the twilight sea breeze, wafting scents of salt and freshness with each billow. She sighed away her draining tension and pushed from the wood-paneled door.

She crossed the gleaming hardwood floor to the suitcases. They were more evidence of Rodrigo's all-inclusive care. She was certain she'd never owned anything so exquisite. She wondered what he'd filled them with.

If the outfit she had on was any indication, no doubt an array of haute couture and designer items, molding to her exact shape and appealing to her specific tastes.

She tried to move the one on the floor, just to set it on its wheels. Frantic pounding boomed in her head.

Man—what *had* he gotten her to wear? Steel armor in every shade? And he'd made the cases look weightless when he'd hauled them both in, simultaneously. She tugged again.

"¡Parada!"

She swung around at the booming order, the pounding in her head crashing down her spine to settle behind her ribs.

A robust, unmistakably Spanish woman in her late thirties was plowing her way across the room, alarm and displeasure furrowing the openness of her olive-skinned beauty.

"Rodrigo warned me that you'd give me a hard time."

Cybele blinked at the woman as she slapped her hand away from the suitcase's handle and hauled it onto the king-sized, draped-in-ivory-silk bed. She, too, made it look so light. Those Spaniards—uh, Catalans—must have something potent in their water.

The woman rounded on her, vitality and ire radiating from every line. Even her shoulder-length, glossy dark brown hair seemed pissed off. "He told me that you'd be a troublesome charge, and from the way you were trying to bust your surgery scar open, he was right. As he always is."

So it wasn't only she who thought he was always practically infallible. Her lips tugged as she tried to placate the force of nature before her. "I don't have a surgery scar to bust, thanks to Rodrigo's revolutionary minimally invasive approach."

"You have things in there—" the woman stabbed a finger in the air pointing at Cybele's head "—you can bust, no? What you busted before, necessitating such an approach."

From the throb of pain that was only now abating, she had to concede that. She'd probably raised her intracranial pressure tenfold trying to drag that behemoth of a bag. As she shrugged, she remembered Rodrigo telling her something.

She'd been too busy watching his lips wrap around each syllable to translate the words into an actual meaning. She now replayed them, made sense of them.

Rodrigo had said Consuelo, his cousin who lived here with her husband and three children and managed the place for him, would be with her shortly to see to her every need and to the correct and timely discharge of his instructions. She'd only nodded then, lost in his eyes. She now realized what he'd meant.

He didn't trust her to follow his instructions, was assigning a deputy to enforce their execution. And he certainly knew how to pick his wardens.

She stuck out her hand with a smile tugging at her lips. "You must be Consuelo. Rodrigo told me to expect you."

Consuelo took her hand, only to drag her forward and kiss her full on both cheeks.

Cybele didn't know what stunned her more, the affectionate salute, or Consuelo resuming her disapproval afterward.

Consuelo folded her arms over an ample bosom artfully contained and displayed by her floral dress with the lime background. "Seems Rodrigo didn't *really* tell you what to expect. So let *me* make it clear. I received you battered and bruised. I'm handing you back in tip-top shape. *I* won't put up with you not following Rodrigo's orders. I'm not soft and lenient like him."

"Soft and lenient?" Cybele squeaked her incredulity. Then she coughed it out on a laugh. "I wasn't aware there were two Rodrigos. I met the intractable and inexorable one."

Consuelo tutted. "If you think Rodrigo intractable and inexorable, wait till you've been around me twenty-four hours."

"Oh, the first twenty-four seconds were a sufficient demo."

Consuelo gave her an assessing look, shrewdness simmering in her dark chocolate eyes. "I know your type. A woman who wants to do everything for herself, says she can handle it when she can't, keeps going when she shouldn't, caring nothing about what it costs her, and it's all because she dreads being an imposition, because she hates accepting help even when she dearly needs it."

"Whoa. Spoken like an expert."

"*¡Maldita sea, es cierto!*—that's right. It takes one mule-headed, aggravatingly independent woman to know another."

Another laugh overpowered Cybele. "Busted."

"*Sí,* you are. And I'm reporting your reckless behavior to Rodrigo. He'll probably have you chained to my wrist by your good arm until he gives you a clean bill of health."

"Not that I wouldn't be honored to have you as my… uh, keeper, but can I bribe you into keeping silent?"

"You can. And you know how."

"I don't try to lift rock-filled suitcases again?"

"And do everything I say. *When* I say it."

"Uh…on second thought, I'll take my chances with Rodrigo."

"Ha. Try another one. Now hop to it. Rodrigo told me what kind of day—what kind of *week* you've had. You're doing absolutely nothing but sleeping and resting for the next one. And eating. You look like you're about to vanish."

Cybele laughed as she whimsically peered down at her much lesser endowments. She could see how they were next to insubstantial by the superlush Consuelo's standards.

This woman would be good for her. As she was sure Rodrigo had known she would be. Every word out of her mouth tickled funny bones Cybele hadn't known existed.

Consuelo hooked her arm through Cybele's good one, walked her to bed then headed alone to the en suite bathroom. She talked all the time while she ran a bubble bath, emptied the suitcases, sorted everything in the dressing room, and laid out what Cybele would wear to bed. Cybele loved listening to her husky, vibrant voice delivering perfect English dipped in the molasses of her all-out Catalan accent. By the time she led Cybele to the all-marble-and-gold-fixtures, salonlike bathroom, she'd told her her life story. At least, everything that had happened since she and her husband had become Rodrigo's house- and groundskeepers.

Cybele insisted she could take it from there. Consuelo insisted on leaving the door open. Cybele insisted she'd call out to prove she was still awake. Consuelo threatened to barge in after a minute's silence. Cybele countered she could sing to prove her wakefulness then everyone within hearing distance would suffer the consequences of Consuelo's overprotection.

Guffawing and belting out a string of amused Catalan, Consuelo finally exited the bathroom.

Grinning, Cybele undressed. The grin dissolved as she stared at herself in the mirror above the double sinks' marble platform.

She had a feeling there'd once been more of her. Had she lost weight? A lot of it? Recently? Because she'd been unhappy? If she had been, why had she planned a pregnancy and a second honeymoon with Mel? What did Rodrigo think of the way she looked? Not now, since she looked like crap, but before? Was she his type? Did he have a type? Did he have a woman now? More than one…?

Oh, God…she couldn't finish a thought without it settling back on him, could she?

She clamped down on the spasm that twisted through her at the idea, the images of him with a woman…any other woman.

How insane was it to be jealous, when up to eight days ago she'd been married to his brother?

She exhaled a shuddering breath and stepped into the warm, jasmine-and-lilac-scented water. She moaned as she submerged her whole body, felt as if every deep-seated ache surged to her surface, bled through her pores to mingle with the bubbles and fluid silk that enveloped her.

She raised her eyes, realized the widescreen window was right across from her, showcasing a masterpiece of heavenly proportions. Magnificent cloud formations in every gradation of silver morphing across a darkening royal blue sky and an incandescent half moon.

Rodrigo's face superimposed itself on the splendor, his voice over the lapping of water around her, the swishing of blood in her ears. She shut her eyes, tried to sever the spell.

"Enough."

Consuelo's yelled *"¿Qué?"* jerked Cybele's eyes open. Mortification threatened to boil her bathwater.

God—she'd cried that out loud.

She called out the first thing that came to her, to explain away her outburst. "Uh…I said I'm coming out. I've had enough."

And she had. In so many ways. But there was one more thing that she prayed she would soon have enough of. Rodrigo.

Any bets she never would?

It was good to face her weakness. Without self-deception, she'd be careful to plan her actions and control her responses, accept and expect no more than the medical supervision she was here for during her stay. Until it came to an end.

As it inevitably would.

Rodrigo stood outside Cybele's quarters, all his senses converged on every sound, every movement transmitted from within.

He'd tried to walk away. He couldn't. He'd leaned on her door, feeling her through it, tried to contain the urge to walk back in, remain close, see and hear and feel for himself that she was alive and aware.

The days during which she'd lain inert had gouged a fault line in his psyche. The past days since she'd come back, he hadn't been able to contemplate putting more than a few minutes' distance between them. It had been all he could do not to camp out in her room as he had during her coma. He had constantly curbed himself so he wouldn't suffocate her with worry, counted down every second of the three hours he'd imposed on himself between visits.

After he'd controlled the urge, he'd summoned Consuelo, had dragged himself away. Then he'd heard Consuelo's shout.

He hadn't barged into the room only because he'd frozen with horror for the seconds it took him to realize Consuelo had exclaimed *Stop,* and Consuelo's gregarious tones and Cybele's gentler, melodic ones had carried through the door, explaining the whole situation.

Now he heard Cybele's raised voice as she chattered with Consuelo from the bathroom. In a few minutes, Consuelo would make sure Cybele was tucked in bed and would walk out. He had to be gone before that. Just not yet.

He knew he was being obsessive, ridiculous, but he couldn't help it. The scare was too fresh, the trauma too deep.

He hadn't been there for Mel, and he'd died.

He had to be there for Cybele.

But to be there for her, he had to get ahold of himself. And to do that, he had to put today behind him.

It had felt like spiraling down through hell. Taking her to that airfield, realizing too late what he'd done, seeing his foster parents after months of barely speaking to them, only to give them the proof of his biggest failure. Mel's body.

The one thing mitigating this disaster was Cybele's memory loss. It *was* merciful. For her. For him, too. He didn't know if he could have handled her grief, too, had she remembered Mel.

But—was it better to have reprieve now, than to have it all come back with a vengeance later? Wouldn't it have been better if her grief coincided with his? Would he be able to bear it, to be of any help if she fell apart when he'd begun healing?

But then he had to factor in the changes in her.

The woman who'd woken up from the coma was not the Cybele Wilkinson he'd known the past year. Or the one Mel had said had become so volatile, she'd accused him of wanting her around only as the convenient help rolled into one with a medical supervisor—and who'd demanded a baby as proof that he valued her as his wife.

Rodrigo had at first found that impossible to believe. She'd never struck him as insecure or clingy. Just the opposite. But then her actions had proved Mel right.

So which persona was really her? The stable, guile-less woman she'd been the past five days? The irritable introvert she'd been before Mel's accident? Or the neurotic wreck who'd made untenable emotional demands of him when he'd been wrecked himself?

And if this new persona was a by-product of the accident, of her injuries, once she healed, once she regained all her memories, would she revert? Would the woman who was bantering so naturally with Consuelo, who'd consoled him and wrestled verbally with him and made him forget everything but her, disappear?

He forced himself away from the door. Consuelo was asking what Cybele would like for breakfast. In a moment she'd walk out.

He strode away, speculations swarming inside his head.

He was staring at the haggard stranger in mourning clothes in his bathroom mirror when he realized something.

It made no difference. Whatever the answers were, no matter what she was, or what would happen from now on, it didn't matter.

She was in his life now. To stay.

Chapter 7

"You don't have post-traumatic amnesia."

Cybele's eyes rounded at Rodrigo's proclamation.

Her incredulity at his statement was only rivaled by the one she still couldn't get over; that he'd transferred a miniature hospital to his estate so he could test and chart her progress daily.

Apart from wards and ORs, he had about everything else on site. A whole imaging facility with X-ray, MRI, CT machines and even a PET scan machine, which seemed like overkill just to follow up her arm's and head's healing progress. A comprehensive lab for every known test to check up on her overall condition and that of her pregnancy. Then there were the dozen neurological tests he subjected her to daily, plus the physiotherapy sessions for her fingers.

They'd just ended such a session and were heading

out to the barbecue house at the seafront terrace garden to have lunch, after which he'd said they'd explore more of the estate.

He was walking beside her, his brows drawn together, his eyes plastered to the latest batch of results from another dozen tests. So what did he mean, she didn't have…?

Terrible suspicion mushroomed, clouding the perfection of the day.

Could he think she'd capitalized on a transient memory loss and had been stringing him along for the past four weeks? Or worse, that she'd never had memory loss, that she was cunning enough, with a convoluted enough agenda, to have faked it from the start?

And she blurted it out, "You think I'm pretending?"

"What?" He raised his eyes sluggishly, stared ahead into nothingness as if the meaning of her words was oozing through his mind, searching for comprehension. Then it hit him. Hard. His head jerked toward her, his frown spectacular. *"No."*

She waited for him to elaborate. He didn't, buried his head back into the tests.

So she prodded. "So what do you mean I don't have PTA? I woke up post-trauma with amnesia. Granted, it's not a classic case, but what else could it be?"

Instead of answering, he held the door of the terrace pergola open for her. She stepped out into the late March midday, barely stopped herself from moaning as the sweet saltiness of the sea breeze splashed her face, weaved insistent fingers through her hair.

He looked down at her as they walked, as if he hadn't heard her question. She shivered, not from the delicious coolness of the wind, but from the caress of his gaze, which followed the wind's every movement over her face and through her hair.

At least, that was how it felt to her. It was probably all in her mind, and he was lost in thought and not seeing her at all.

He suddenly turned his eyes again to the tests, validating her interpretation. "Let's review your condition, shall we? You started out having total retrograde amnesia, with all the memories formed before the accident lost. Then you started retrieving 'islands of memory,' when you recalled those 'skeletal' events. But you didn't suffer from any degree of anterograde amnesia, since you had no problems creating new memories after the injury. Taking all that into account, and that it has been over four weeks and the 'islands' have not coalesced into a uniform landmass…"

"As uniform as could be, you mean," she interrupted. "Even so-called healthy people don't remember everything in their lives—most things not in reliable detail and some things not at all."

"Granted. But PTA that lasts that long indicates severe brain injury, and it's clear from your clinical condition and all of your tests that you are not suffering from any cognitive, sensory, motor or coordination deficits. An isolated PTA of this magnitude is unheard of. That is why I'm leaning toward diagnosing you with a hybrid case of amnesia. The trauma might have triggered it, but the major part of your memory deficit is psychogenic, not organic."

She chewed her lip thoughtfully. "So we're back to what I said minutes after I regained consciousness. I *wanted* to forget."

"Yes. You diagnosed yourself fresh out of a coma."

"It wasn't really a diagnosis. I was trying to figure out why I had no other symptoms. When I didn't find an explanation, I thought either my medical knowledge had taken a hit, or that neurology was never my strong point in my parallel existence. I thought you would know that cases like mine exist. But they don't. Turns out I don't really have amnesia, I'm just hysterical."

His gaze whipped to hers, fierce, indignant. "Psychogenic amnesia is no less real than organic. It's a self-preservation mechanism. I also wouldn't label the psychogenic ingredient of your memory loss as hysterical, but rather functional or dissociative. In fact, I don't support the hysterical nomenclature and what it's come to be associated with—willful and weak-willed frenzy."

Hot sweetness unfurled inside her. He was defending her to herself. Pleasure surged to her lips, making them tingle. "So you think I have a repressed-memory type functional amnesia."

He nodded, ultraserious. "Yes. Here, take a look at this. This is your last MRI." She looked. "It's called functional imaging. After structural imaging revealed no physical changes in your brain, I looked at the function. You see this?" She did. "This abnormal brain activity in the limbic system led to your inability to recall stressful and traumatic events. The memories are stored in your long-term memory, but access to them has been impaired through a mixture of trauma and psychological defense mechanisms. The abnormal activity explains your partial memory recovery. But now that I'm certain there's nothing to worry about organically, I'm relaxed about when total recovery occurs."

"*If* it ever does." If he was right, and she couldn't

think how he wasn't, she might be better off if it never did.

Psychogenic amnesia sufferers included soldiers and childhood abuse, rape, domestic violence, natural disaster and terrorist attack victims. Sufferers of severe enough psychological stress, internal conflict or intolerable life situations. And if her mind had latched on to the injury as a trigger to purge her memories of Mel and her life with him, she'd probably suffered all three.

But that still didn't explain her pregnancy or the honeymoon they were heading to when they'd had the accident.

Rodrigo stemmed the tide of confusion that always overcame her when she came up against those points.

"Anyway," he said. "While explanations have been proposed to explain psychogenic amnesia, none of them have been verified as the mechanism that fits all types. I prefer to set aside the Freudian, personal semantic belief systems and betrayal trauma theories to explain the condition. I lean toward the theory that explains the biochemical imbalance that triggers it."

"That's why you're a neurosurgeon and not a neurologist or psychiatrist. Where others are content to deal with insults to the psyche, you dig down to the building blocks of the nervous system, cell by cell, neurotransmitter by neurotransmitter."

"I admit, I like to track any sign or symptom, physical or psychological, back to its causative mechanism, to find the *'exactly* how' after others explain the 'why.'"

"And that's why you're a researcher and inventor."

He focused on her eyes for a second before he turned his own back to the tests, his skin's golden-bronze color deepening.

He was embarrassed!

She'd noticed on many occasions that, although he was certain of his abilities, he wasn't full of himself and didn't expect or abide adulation, despite having every reason to feel superior and to demand and expect being treated as such.

But this—to actually blush at her admiration! Oh, Lord, but he was delicious, scrumptious. Edible. And adorable.

And he ignored her praise pointedly. "So—I favor the theory that postulates that normal autobiographical memory processing is blocked by altered release of stress hormones in the brain during chronic stress conditions. With the regions of expanded limbic system in the right hemisphere more vulnerable to stress and trauma, affecting the body's opioids, hormones and neurotransmitters, increased levels of glucocorticoid and mineralocorticoid receptor density affect the anterior temporal, orbitofrontal cortex, hippocampal and amygdalar regions."

She couldn't help it. Her lips spread so wide they hurt. "I bet you're having a ball talking to a doctor/patient. Imagine all the translation into layman's terms you'd have to do if you wanted to say *that* to someone who didn't get the lingo."

He blinked, surprise tingeing his incredible eyes. Then that incendiary smile of his flowed over his face, crooked his divine-work-of-art lips. "It has been a very freeing experience, spoiling even, not to keep looking for ways to explain what I'm doing or what's happening and fearing I won't be clear enough or that you'll misinterpret it no matter what I say and develop false expectations, positive or negative." He shook his head in self-deprecation, switching back to solemn in a blink.

"But that was far too involved, anyway. My point is, you might have appeared or thought you were coping with your situation before the accident, but according to your current condition, you weren't."

She pursed her lips in an effort to stop herself from grinning uncontrollably and giving in to the urge to lunge at him, tickle him out of his seriousness. "So you're saying I was headed for psychogenic amnesia, anyway?"

"No, I'm saying the unimaginable stress of experiencing a plane crash, plus the temporary brain insult you suffered, disrupted the balance that would have kept your memory intact in the face of whatever psychological pressure you were suffering."

She raised an eyebrow, mock-indignant. "You're trying very hard to find neurologically feasible explanations backed by complex theories and medical expressions to dress up the fact that you've diagnosed me as a basket case, aren't you?"

"No! I certainly haven't. You're in no way…" He stopped abruptly when she couldn't hold back anymore, let the smile split her face. Incredulity spread over his face. "You're playing me!"

She burst out laughing. "Yep. For quite some time now. But you were so involved in your explanations, so careful not to give me any reason to feel silly or undeserving of concern or follow-up since my condition is 'only in my mind,' you didn't notice."

One formidable eyebrow rose, a calculating gleam entering his eyes, an unbearably sexy curl twisting his lips. "Hmm, seems I have underestimated the stage of your progress."

"Been telling you so for—"

"Quite some time now. Yes, I get it. But now that I'm certain your brain is in fine working order, nuts-and-bolts-wise, being the guy who cares about nothing but the hardware, I think I can safely stop treating you like you're made of fresh paint."

A laugh cracked out of her at his metaphor. He kept surprising her. She'd be thinking he was this ultra-cerebral, all-work genius of a man, then out of the blue, he'd let this side of him show. The most witty and wickedly fun person she'd ever known. And she did know that for a fact. She remembered all of her life before Mel now.

She pretended to wipe imaginary sweat off her brow. "Phew, I thought I'd never get you to stop."

"Don't be so happy. Until minutes ago, I would have let you trampoline-jump all over me. Now I think you don't warrant the walking-on-eggshells preferential treatment anymore. You deserve some punishment for making fun of my efforts to appear all-knowing."

"Making fun of them, or debunking them?"

"Payback is getting steeper by the word."

She made a cartoonish face. "What can you do to a poor patient who has expanded limbic system issues and increased levels of glucocorticoid and mineralocorticoid receptor density messing with her anterior temporal, or-bitofrontal cortex, hippocampal and amygdalar regions?"

"That's it. I'm exacting retribution."

"What will you do? Make me go to my room?"

"I'll make you eat what I cook. And that's for starters. I'll devise something heinous while phase one is underway."

"You mean *more* heinous than your cooking?"

He rumbled something from his gut, devilry igniting in his eyes. She giggled and rushed ahead, felt like she was flying there, borne on the giddy pleasure of his pursuing chuckles.

When she reached the steps, his voice boomed behind her, concern gripping its rich power. "Slow down."

She did, waited for him to catch up with her in those strides that ate up ten of her running steps in five.

She grinned up into his no-longer-carefree, admonishing eyes. "I thought I wasn't getting the fresh-paint treatment any longer."

"You've hereby moved to getting the uninsured, last-known-piece-of-Ming-dynasty-China treatment."

He slipped a steadying hand around her waist as they scaled the steps. She felt she'd be secure if the whole country fell into the sea. Or he'd clasp her to his body and take off into the sky.

She leashed her desire to press into him. "Aha! I should have known you'd default on your declaration of my independence."

He grinned down at her as they reached the barbecue house. "Tales of your independence *have* been wildly exaggerated."

She made a face, ducked under the shade of the canvas canopy.

He gave her a smug look as he seated her, then went to the kitchen area and began preparing her "punishment."

She watched his every graceful move as putting out cooking utensils and food items and chopping and slicing were turned into a precision performance like his surgeries. When he ducked inside to get more articles, she exhaled at the interruption of her viewing pleasure, swept her gaze to the sparkling azure-emerald waters of the magnificent, channel-like part of the sea, the mile-long breathtaking sandy beach ensconced in a rocky hug.

The living, breathing tranquility imbued her. Most of the time she couldn't remember how she'd come to be here, or that she'd ever been anywhere else, that a world existed outside.

This place wasn't just a place. It was an...experience. A sense of completion, of arrival. A realm in time and space she'd never seen approximated, let alone replicated. An amalgam of nature's pristine grandeur and man's quest for the utmost in beauty and comfort. But all this would have been nothing without him.

It was being with him that made it embody heaven.

During the past weeks they'd made real fires, collected ripe fruits and vegetables, eaten their meals in the apartment-sized kitchen or in the cool barbecue house and held their after-dinner gatherings and entertainment in its lounge or in the huge pergola terrace.

She'd watched him play tennis on the floodlit court with the tireless Gustavo, swim endless laps in the half-Olympic-sized pool, drooled over his every move, longed to tear off her cast and shed her aches and throw herself into that pool after him....

"Ready for your punishment?"

She twinkled up at him. "Is it too heinous?"

He looked down at the salad bowls in his hands. "Atrocious."

"Gimme." She took her bowl, set it in front of her. And gaped. Then she crooked a challenging smile up at him. "It's colorful, I'll give you that. And...odorous." She tried not to wince as she picked up her fork. "*And* I didn't know these food items could go together."

He sat down across from her. "I didn't hear any objections as I tossed them into each other's company."

She chuckled. "I don't even know what said food items are."

His glance said her delaying tactics weren't working. "Eat."

She took a mouthful, trying not to inhale the stench, trying not to have what produced it hit her taste buds, to slide directly into her throat. Then it did hit, everywhere. And...wow.

She raised incredulous eyes to him. "You better get this patented. It's a-maaazing!"

He raised both eyebrows in disbelief. "You're just trying to prove nothing can gross you out, that I didn't and wouldn't succeed in punishing you, 'cause you can take anything."

"What am I, twelve?" She wolfed down another huge forkful.

He crooked his head to one side, considering. "So you like it."

"I love it," she exclaimed, mumbling around the food she'd stuffed into her mouth. "I *can* do without the smell, but it actually lessens as you eat, or your senses forgive it for being coupled with the delicious taste. At first I thought it was rotten fish."

"It *is* rotten fish."

She almost choked. "Now you're pulling my leg."

"Nope." The wattage of the wickedness in his eyes reached electrocuting levels. "But if you like it, does the label matter?"

She thought about that for a second, then said "Nah" and stuffed another forkful into her mouth.

He laughed as he began to eat his own serving. "It's actually only *semi*-rotten. It's called *feseekh*—sun dried then salted gray mullet. It's considered an acquired taste—which you must be the quickest to ever acquire—and a delicacy around here. It came to Catalonia with the Berbers, and they brought it all the way from Egypt. But I bet I'm the first one to mix it with a dozen unnamed leafy greens and the wild berries Gustavo grows and collects and gives to me to consume, assuring me they're the secret to my never needing any of our esteemed colleagues' services."

"So you can give me rotten and unidentified food to consume, but you balk at my walking faster than a turtle."

"The rotten ingredient has proved through centuries of folk experience to have potent antibacterial and digestive-regulating properties. It and the rest of the unidentified food have been repeatedly tested on yours truly, and I'm living proof to their efficacy. I haven't been sick a day in the last twenty years."

Her eyes rounded in alarm. "Okay, jinx much?"

He threw his head back on a guffaw. "You're superstitious? You think I'll get deathly sick now that I've dared tempt fate?"

"Who knows? Maybe fate doesn't like braggarts."

"Actually, I think fate doesn't like gamblers." Something dark flitted across his face. Before she analyzed it, he lowered his gaze, hid it. "Since I'm anything but, I'm a good candidate for staying on its good side. For as long as possible. That brings us back to your hare tactics. Maybe you don't have loose components inside your brain to be shaken and stirred, but running like one, if you stumble, you have only one hand to ward off a fall, and you might injure it, too, or end up reinjuring your arm. And though your first trimester has been the smoothest I've ever heard about, probably as a compensation for what you're already dealing with, you *are* pregnant."

She *did* forget sometimes that she was. Not that she wanted to forget. When she did remember, it was with a burst of joy, imagining that she had a life growing inside her, that she'd have a baby to love and cherish, who'd be her flesh and blood, the family she'd never had. If there had been one thing to thank Mel for, it was that he'd somehow talked her into conceiving that baby. But because she had no symptoms whatsoever, sometimes it *did* slip her mind.

"Okay, no hare tactics." Her smile widened as she repeated his term for her jog. "But since I have no loose components, you must tell Consuelo to stop chasing me around as if I'll scatter them."

He turned his head to both sides, looked behind him. Then he turned back to her, palm over chest with an expression of mock horror. "You're talking to *me?*"

Her lips twitched. "You're the one who sicced her on me."

"A man can start a nuclear reaction, but he surely has no way of stopping it once it becomes self-perpetuating."

"You gotta call her off. She'll brush my teeth for me next!"

"You really expect me to come between her and her hurt chick? I may be lord of all I survey back at the center, but here I'm just another in the line that marches to Consuelo's tune."

"Yeah, I noticed." She chuckled, loving how he could be so alpha and capable and overriding and yet be totally comfortable letting another, and a woman, have the upper hand where she was best suited to take it. She cocked her head at him. "Families are very matriarchal here, aren't they?"

He tossed her a piece of breath-freshening gum then piled their bowls in one hand and raised the other, ring and middle fingers folded by his thumb, fore and little fingers pointing up. "Women rule."

She spluttered at the sight of him, so virile and formidable and poised, making that goofy expression and pop culture gesture.

He headed into the barbecue house and she melted back in her chair, replete and blissful. She'd never laughed like that before him. Before being here with him in his paradise of a home.

He'd only left her side to fly to work—literally, via helicopter—and had cut down on his working hours, to be there for her. She'd insisted he shouldn't, that she was perfectly all right on her own or with Consuelo, Gustavo and their children.

But she'd stopped objecting, certain he wasn't neglecting his work, had everything under control. And she couldn't get enough of being with him. Against all resolutions, she reveled in his pampering, wished with all she had in her that she could repay him in kind. But he had everything. Needed nothing. Nothing but to heal emotionally.

So she contented herself with being there for him, hoping to see him heal. And he was healing. His moroseness had dissipated and his distance had vanished, had become a closeness like she'd never known, as they discovered each other, shared so many things she'd never thought she'd share with another.

She kept waiting for him to do something to annoy her, to disappoint her, as all human beings inevitably did. But the impossible man just wouldn't. Then he went further into the realm of impossibility, kept doing things that shocked her by how much they appealed to her, delighted her.

He was everything his foster parents had said they'd picked him for and far more. Everything she admired in a human being and a man, and the most effective power for good she'd ever had the fortune to meet. And that was what he was to the world.

To her, he was all that resonated with her preferences and peculiarities. They agreed on most everything, and what they disagreed on, they discussed, came out conceding a respect for the other's viewpoint and thrilled to have gained a new awareness.

And when she added up everything he'd done for her, had been to her—her savior, protector and support—he was, yes, just incredible.

Which was why every now and then the question popped into her head—where had this man been before the accident?

From the tatters she remembered, besides his reported promiscuity, he'd treated Mel with fed-up annoyance and everyone else with abrasive impatience. His treatment of her had been the worst. He'd barely spoken to her, had watched her with something almost vicious in his eyes, as if he'd thought her beneath his friend—his brother.

And every time there was one answer. The conclusion she'd made the first day she'd come here. Her memories had to be faulty.

This, *he,* must be the truth. The magnificent truth.

"Ready to go back to your keeper?"

Everything became more beautiful with his return. She surrendered to his effortless strength, let him draw her to feet that barely touched the ground because he existed, was near.

She ended up ensconced in his protective embrace. His face clenched with the intensity she now adored, his freshness and potency filling her lungs. And it was as necessary as her next breath that she show him what he was to her.

She moved against his solid heat and power, raised her face to him, the invocation that filled her with life and hope and the will to heal, to be, trembling on her lips. "Rodrigo…"

Chapter 8

Cybele's whisper skewered through Rodrigo, wrenching at all the emotions and responses he'd been repressing.

From every point where her body touched his, torrents of what felt like molten metal zapped through his nerves, converging to roar through his spine, jamming into his iron-hard erection.

Nothing was left in his raging depths but the need to crush her to his aching flesh, claim her, assimilate her into his being.

And he couldn't.

But how could he not—and remain sane?

Not that he was sane anymore. He hadn't been since the first time he'd laid eyes on her. And with every moment in her company, he'd been surrendering any desire to cling to sanity.

He'd plunged into the wonder of experiencing her, discovering her, sharing with her everything from his daily routines and professional pressures to his deepest beliefs and slightest whims.

And she was far more than anything he'd ever dreamed of. She was the best thing that had ever happened to him.

But whenever he was away from her, he kept dredging up the past, the suspicions and antipathies that had at once poisoned his existence and fueled his resistance. He'd *wanted* to hate and despise her, to believe the worst of her then. Because she'd been the only woman he'd ever truly wanted—and she'd been forever off-limits.

She was no longer off-limits. Not on account of Mel, nor on that of his objections to her character.

He'd moved from condemning her for tormenting Mel with her volatility to suspecting that the instability had been created in Mel's twisted psyche. Now that he was no longer jumping on anything to paint her as black as possible, and had seen all the evidence to the contrary, it made sense that a man in Mel's condition could have interpreted her acts of love—which he couldn't reciprocate in any healthy fashion—as emotional pressure and blackmail.

Later on, after their relationship had deteriorated further under the harsh realities of Mel's disability, it stood to reason that the money Mel had asked Rodrigo for to buy her things hadn't been things she'd hinted that she'd wanted. Mel had said he'd understood her demands, that she deserved some compensation to cheer her up in their endlessly trying situation.

But it could have been Mel who'd tried to satisfy any material desire of hers to placate her, to express his love in the only way he'd ever known how, and then to keep her from walking out on him in a fit of despair. And when that, too, had failed, he'd been down to the last thing he could do to prove to her that he didn't consider her his live-in nurse—give her a baby.

Rodrigo now thought her memory loss was probably her mind's way of protecting itself from being pulverized by grief if she remembered Mel and the desperate, traumatic love she'd felt for him.

After he'd reached that conviction, he'd fluctuated between thinking she was being so wonderful to *him* because she subconsciously saw him as all she had left of Mel, to thinking she treated him as she did *because* she didn't remember loving Mel, and that when she did she'd become cold and distant again. He'd thought her coolness had been a reaction to his own barely leashed antipathy. But maybe she'd really disliked him, for reasons that were now gone with her memory. Or maybe the injury *had* caused some radical changes in her personality.

Too many maybes, too many questions the answers to which only she knew and no longer remembered. And it was driving him mad.

What if her dislike came back in full force, and this persona he adored vanished when her mind and psyche did heal completely?

The temptation to claim her now, bind her to him, negate the possibility, was too much.

He looked down in her eyes. They were fathomless with need. He could reach out and take her, and she'd be his. Ecstatically. She seemed to want him as much as he wanted her.

But did she? Or did she only think she did, because

of some need to reassert her own life after surviving the accident that had claimed Mel's? Was he merely convenient, close? Or was she responding to him out of gratitude?

Whatever the reason, he didn't believe she was responsible for her desires, or capable of making a decision with so much missing from her memory.

And then there was *his* side of the story.

He had no doubt he wouldn't be betraying Mel's memory. Mel was dead, and even while he'd lived, his relationship with Cybele had been anything but healthy or happy. If *he* could be the one to offer her that relationship, he would do anything for that chance.

But how could he live with himself if he betrayed *her* trust? And she did trust him. Implicitly. With her life. Was now showing him that she trusted him with her body, maybe her heart and future.

Yet how could he resist? Need was gnawing him hollow. And feeling her answering yearning was sending him out of his mind.

He had to plan a distraction, an intervention.

He stopped himself from cupping her face, running his fingers down her elegant nose, her sculpted cheekbones, teasing those dainty lips open, plunging his thumb inside their moistness and dampening their rose-petal softness, bending to taste her then absorbing her gasps, thrusting inside her....

He staggered away from temptation, rasped, "I have to get back to work."

She gasped at the loss of his support, bit her lip, nodded.

Coward. Work was a few hours' excuse to stay away.

He *had* to do whatever would keep him away from

her until she healed and came to him with her full, un-clouded, unpressured choice.

He exerted what remained of his will. "And before I forget, I wanted to tell you that I'm inviting my family for a visit."

Cybele stared up at Rodrigo.

For a moment there, as he'd held her against him, she'd thought he felt what she did, wanted what she did. She'd thought he'd take her in his arms, and she'd never be homeless again.

But it had all been in her mind. He'd torn himself away, the fierceness and the bleakness that had evaporated during the past four weeks settling back over him. She'd read him all wrong.

But he'd read her all right. There was no way he hadn't seen her desire, understood her plea for him.

And he'd recoiled from her offer, from her need, as if they'd injured him, or worse, tainted him.

But though he was too kind to castigate her for testing the limits of their situation when he'd never encouraged her to, he'd still found a way to draw the line again and keep her behind it.

He was inviting his family over. Now that she'd been so stupid as to come on to him, to offer him what he hadn't asked for and didn't want, he was making sure she'd no longer have unsupervised access to him to repeat the mistake. He was inviting them as chaperones.

That had to be his reason for suddenly thinking of inviting them. Just yesterday, they'd been talking about their families and he hadn't brought up his intention. He'd even said it would be the first year that no one came to stay at his estate at all. And she'd gotten the distinct feeling he'd been…relieved about that fact. Probably because he'd had all the distractions he could afford in the form of Mel's death and her recuperation.

But her irresponsible behavior was forcing him to put up with even more distractions than she'd caused him, through his extensive family's presence, probably until he decreed she was well enough to be let back into the wild. Which could mean weeks, maybe months.

It felt like a wake-up slap. One she'd needed. Not only couldn't she let him swamp himself with family just to keep her at arm's length, she couldn't burden him with more responsibility toward her, this time over her emotions and desires—which in his terminal nobility he was probably taking full blame for inciting. She'd burdened him enough, when she had no right to burden him at all. She had to stop leaning on him, stop taking advantage of his kindness and support. And she had to do it now, before her emotions got any deeper.

Not that she thought they could. What she felt for him filled her, overflowed.

Only one bright side to this mess. Though she'd betrayed herself and imposed on him, she was now certain she hadn't done that when Mel had been in the picture. She'd repressed her feelings before, and they must have broken free after the accident.

All she could do now was fade from his life, let him continue it free from the liability of her. She had to pick up the pieces of her life, plan how to return to a demanding job with a baby on the way, without counting on the help of a mother she was now sure wouldn't come through for her as Cybele had remembered she'd promised.

Cybele didn't need her mother. She'd long ago learned

not to. And it wasn't Rodrigo's fault that she needed him emotionally. Any other kind of need had to end. Right now.

She had to leave immediately, so he wouldn't have to call his whole family to his rescue. She had to stop wasting his time, cutting into his focus and setting back his achievements.

The moment they reentered the house, she opened her mouth to say what she had to, but he talked over her.

"When I relocated here, it seemed to me that Catalans search for reasons to gather and celebrate. It was explained to me that because they've fought so fiercely to preserve their language and identity, they take extra pride in preparing and executing their celebrations. My family is thoroughly Catalan, and they're big on family unity and cultural traditions. And since I built this place over five years ago, it has replaced my grandparents' home as the place to gather. It would be a shame to interrupt the new tradition."

He was trying to make his sudden decision look as though it had nothing to do with her snuggling up against him like a cat in heat. She wanted to cry out for him to shut up and quit being so thoughtful. She had to say her piece and he was making it so much harder. Comparing those festivities and family gatherings with the barrenness of her own life was another knife that would twist in her heart once she was away from here.

She couldn't say anything. Her throat sealed over a molten pain that filled it as he escorted her like always to her quarters, continuing her education in Catalan traditions and his family's close-knit pursuits—all the things she'd never had and would never have. "Spring and summer are rife with *fiestas i carnaval*...that means—"

"Feasts and carnivals. I know," she mumbled. "But I—"

A smile invaded his eyes and lips again, cutting her off more effectively than if he'd shouted. "I sometimes forget how good your Spanish is, and I'm blown away by how colloquial your Catalan has become in this short period."

She nearly choked on the surge of emotion and pleasure his praise provoked, only for it to be followed by an even deeper dejection.

That deepened further when he swept his gaze ahead, animation draining from his voice, the newscaster-like delivery coming back. "The closest upcoming festival is *La Diada De Sant Jordi,* or St. George's Day, celebrating the patron saint of Catalonia, on the 23rd of April. There are many variations of the legend of St. George, but the Catalan version says there was a lake that was home to a dragon to which a maiden had to be sacrificed every day. One day, St. George killed the dragon and rescued that day's maiden. A red rose tree is supposed to have grown where the dragon's blood was spilled. Now on the day, the streets of Catalonia are filled with stands selling *rosas i libros*—roses and books. The rose is a symbol of love, while the book is a symbol of culture."

"I'm sure it would be a great time to be in Catalonia—"

He bulldozed over her attempt to interrupt him. "It certainly is. The celebrations are very lively and very participatory. Anyone walking down the streets anywhere in Catalonia is invited to join. Another similar celebration is Mother of God of Montserrat, on the 27th of April. In addition to these dates, each village and town has its own designated patron saint to pay homage to.

Those celebrations are much like the larger celebrations, with parades of giants made of papier-mâché, fireworks, music from live bands and more. My family may stay until the 23rd of June, which is the shortest day of the year and coincides with the summer solstice celebration and the festival honoring St. John. Here in Catalonia, we light bonfires when the sun is at its most northern point. Catalans believe this wards off disease, bad luck and assorted other demons."

She tried again. "Sounds like a fun time ahead for you and your family—"

"And for you, too. You'll love the energy and sheer fun of this time of year."

"I'm sure I would. But I won't be here for all that, so maybe another time?"

She felt his eyes turn to her then, felt their gaze as if it were his powerful arms hauling her back to him.

"What are you talking about?"

She kept walking, struggled not to give in to the need to look at him and catch his uncensored reaction to her announcement before the barrier of his surgical composure descended, obscured it. Stupid. Still wishing she mattered beyond being a duty.

"Based on your latest tests and diagnosis of my condition, and since you obviously won't do it, I'm giving myself a clean bill of health. Time to return to my life and job."

"And how do you propose to do that?" He stopped her midway in the huge sunlit corridor leading to her quarters. "You're left-handed and can barely move your fingers. It's going to be weeks before you can do a lot of basic things for yourself, months before you can go back to work."

"Countless people with more severe and permanent disabilities are forced to fend for themselves, and they manage—"

"But you won't only be fending for yourself now. You're having a baby. And you're *not* forced to do anything—you don't have to manage on your own. I won't allow you to, and I sure as hell am not allowing you to leave. And this is the last time we have this conversation, Cybele Wilkinson."

Her heart flapped faster with each adamant word until it felt blurred like the wings of a hummingbird.

She tried to tell herself it was moronic to feel that way. That even if she had to concede that he was correct, she should listen to the voice telling her to be indignant at his overruling tactics, to rebel against his cornering her at every turn into doing what he thought was right for her. That voice also insisted there was nothing to be so giddy about, that he wasn't doing it out of concern for *her*, but for his patient.

She couldn't listen. And if another voice said she was criminally weak to be forgetting her minutes-ago resolution and clinging to whatever time she could get with him, she could only admit it. She wasn't strong enough to throw away one second she could have in his company, extensive family and all.

As for walking away for his peace of mind, she believed his acute feelings of duty wouldn't leave him any if he let her go before he judged she could handle being on her own. She also had to believe *he* could handle her being here, or he would have been relieved at her offer to leave. And since he wasn't, she shouldn't feel bad about staying. She'd offered to go, and he'd said no. Such an incredibly alpha, protective and overriding *no*.

Still, some imp inside her, which she was certain had come to life during this past month, wouldn't let her grab at his lifeline without contention. Or without trying to do what it could to erase the damage her blunder had caused to their newfound ease and rapport.

"Okay, it's clear you believe you're right—"

"I *am* right."

She went on as if he hadn't growled over her challenging opening "—but that doesn't automatically mean I agree. I came here as an alternative to staying in your center as a teaching pincushion. *But,* if I'd been there, you would have discharged me long ago. No one stays in hospital until their fractures heal."

His eyebrows descended a fraction more. "Do you enjoy futility, Cybele? We've established that when I make a decision—"

"—saying no to you isn't an option," she finished for him, a smile trembling on her lips, inviting him to smile back at her, light up the world again, tell her that he'd look past her foolish moment of weakness. "But that was a decision based on a clinical picture from a month ago. Now that I'm diagnosed as having no rattling components, I should be left to fend for myself."

She waited for him to smile back at her, decimate her argument, embroil her in another verbal tournament that neither of them wanted to win, just to prolong the match and the enjoyment.

He did neither. No smile. No decimation. He brooded down at her, seemed to be struggling with something. A decision.

Then he voiced it. "*Muy bien,* Cybele. You win. If you insist on leaving, go ahead. Leave."

Her heart plummeted down a never-ending spiral.

And he was turning around, walking away.

He'd taken no for an answer.

But he never did. He'd told her so. She'd believed him. That was why she'd said what she had.

He *couldn't* take no for an answer. That meant she'd lose him now, not later. And she couldn't lose him now. She wasn't ready to be without him for the rest of her life.

She wanted to scream that she took it all back. That she'd only been trying to do what she thought she should, assert an independence she still couldn't handle, to relieve him of the burden of her.

She didn't make a sound. She couldn't. Because her heart had splintered. Because she had no right to ask for more from him, of him. He'd given her far more than she'd thought anyone could ever give. He'd given her back her life. And it was time to give him back his, after she'd inadvertently hijacked it.

She turned away, feeling as though ice had skewered from her gut to her heart, only the freezing felt now, the pain and damage still unregistered.

Her numb hand was on her doorknob when she heard him say, "By the way, Cybele, good luck getting past Consuelo."

She staggered around. He was looking at her over his shoulder from the end of the corridor, the light from the just-below-the-ceiling windows pouring over him like a spotlight. He looked like that archangel she'd thought him before. His lips were crooked.

He was teasing her!

He didn't want her to leave, hadn't accepted that she could.

Before she could do something colossally stupid, like

run and throw herself into his arms and sob her heart out, Consuelo, in a flaming red dress with a flaring skirt, swept by Rodrigo and down the corridor like a missile set on her coordinates.

She pounced on her. "You trying to undo all my work? *Seven* hours running around?" Consuelo turned and impaled Rodrigo with her displeasure. "And *you!* Letting your patient call the shots."

Rodrigo glared at her in mock-indignation before he gave Cybele a get-past-this wink. Then he turned and walked away, his bass chuckles resonating in the corridor, in her every cell.

Consuelo dragged her inside the room.

Feeling boneless with the reprieve, Cybele gave herself up to Consuelo's care, grinned as she lambasted her for her haggardness, ordered her on the scales and lamented her disappointing gains.

She'd missed out on having someone mother her. And for the time being, she'd enjoy Consuelo's mothering all she could. Along with Rodrigo's pampering and protection.

It would come to an end all too soon.

But not yet. *Not yet.*

Chapter 9

Rodrigo stood looking down at the approaching car procession.

His family was here.

He hadn't even thought of them since the accident. He hadn't for a while before that, either. He'd had nothing on his mind but Cybele and Mel and his turmoil over them both for over a year.

He'd remembered them only when he needed their presence to keep him away from Cybele. And he'd gotten what he deserved for neglecting them for so long. They'd all had other plans.

He'd ended up begging them to come. He'd evaded explaining the reason behind his desperation. They'd probably figure it out the moment they saw him with her.

In the end, he'd gotten them to come. And made them promise to stay. Long. He'd always wished they'd stay as long as possible.

This time he wondered if he'd survive it.

And here began his torment.

His grandparents stepped out of the limo he'd sent them, followed by three of his aunts. Out of the vans poured the aunts' adult children and their families plus a few cousins and their offspring.

Cybele stepped out of the French doors. He gritted his teeth against the violence of his response. He'd been wrestling with it for the past three days since that confrontation. He'd still almost ended up storming her bedroom every night. Her efforts to offer him sexually neutral friendliness were inflaming him far worse than if she'd been coming on to him hot and heavy.

Now she walked toward him with those energetic steps of hers, rod-straight, no wiggle anywhere, dressed in dark blue jeans and a crisp azure blouse that covered her from throat to elbows.

The way his hormones thundered, she could have been undulating toward him in stilettos, a push-up bra and a thong.

Dios. The…containment he now lived in had better be obscuring his condition.

He needed help. He needed the invasion of his family to keep him away from her door, from carrying her off to his bed.

Before she could say anything, since anything she said blinded him with an urge to plunder those mind-destroying lips, he said, "Come, let me introduce you to my tribe."

Tribe is right, Cybele thought.

She fell in step with Rodrigo as she counted thirty-eight men, women and children. More still poured from the vans. Four generations of Valderramas.

It was amazing what one marriage could end up producing.

Rodrigo had told her that his mother had been Esteban and Imelda's first child, had been only nineteen when she had him, that his grandparents had been in their early twenties when they got married. With him at thirty-eight, his grandparents must be in their late seventies or early eighties. They looked like a very good sixty. Must be the clean living Rodrigo had told her about.

She focused on his grandfather. It was uncanny, his resemblance to Rodrigo. This was what Rodrigo would look like in forty-something years' time. And it was amazingly good.

Her heart clenched on the foolish but burning wish to be around Rodrigo through all that time, to know him at that age.

She now watched as he met his family three-quarters of the way, smile and arms wide. Another wish seared her—to be the one he received with such pleasure, the one he missed that much. She envied each of those who had the right to rush to fill his arms, to be blessed by the knowledge of his vast and unconditional love. Her heart broke against the hopelessness of it all as his family took turns being clasped to his heart.

Then he turned to her, covered in kids from age two to midteens, his smile blazing as he beckoned to her to come be included in the boisterous affection of his family reunion.

She rushed to answer his invitation and found herself being received by his family with the same enthusiasm.

For the next eight hours, she talked and laughed non-stop, ate and drank more than she had in the last three days put together, put a name and a detailed history to each of the unpretentious, vital beings who swept her along the wave of their rowdy interaction and infectious joie de vivre.

All along she felt Rodrigo watching her even as he paid attention to every member of his family, clearly on the best possible terms with them all. She managed not to miss one of his actions either, even as she kept up her side of the conversations. Her pleasure mounted at seeing him at such ease, surrounded by all these people who loved him as he deserved to be loved. She kept smiling at him, showing him how happy she was for him, yet trying her best not to let her longing show.

She was deep in conversation with Consuelo and two of Rodrigo's aunts, Felicidad and Benita, when he stood up, exited her field of vision. She barely stopped herself from swinging around to follow his movement. Then she felt him. At her back. His approach was like a wave of electromagnetism, sending every hair on her body standing on end, crackling along her nerves. She hoped she didn't look the way she felt, a woman in the grip of emotional and physical tumult.

His hands descended on her shoulders. Somehow she didn't lurch. "Who's letting her patient call the shots, now?"

She looked up, caught his eyebrow wiggle at Consuelo. The urge to drag him down and devour that teasing smile right off his luscious lips drilled a hole in her midsection.

The three vociferous women launched into a repartee match with him. He volleyed each of their taunts with a witticism that was more funny and inventive than the last, until they were all howling with laughter. She laughed, too, if not as heartily. She was busy having mini-heart attacks as one of his hands kept smoothing her hair and sweeping it off her shoulders absently.

By the time he bent and said, "Bed," she almost begged, *Yes, please.*

He pulled her to her feet as everyone bid her a cheerful good-night. She insisted he didn't need to escort her to her room, that he remain with his family. She didn't think she had the strength tonight not to make a fool of herself. Again.

On *La Diada De Sant Jordi*, St. George's Day, Rodrigo's family had been there for four weeks. After the first four weeks with him, they were the second-best days of her life.

For the first time, she realized what a family was like, what being an accepted member of such a largely harmonious one could mean.

And they had more than accepted her. They'd reached out and assimilated her into their passionate-for-life, close-knit collective. The older members treated her with the same indulgence as Rodrigo, the younger ones with excitement and curiosity, loving to have someone new and interesting enter their lives. She almost couldn't remember her life before she'd met these people, before they'd made her one of their own. She didn't want to remember any time when Rodrigo hadn't filled her heart.

And he, being the magnificent human being that he was, had felt the melancholy that blunted her joy, had once again asked if her problems with her own family couldn't be healed, if he could intervene, as a neutral mediator, to bring about a reconciliation.

After she'd controlled her impulse to drown him in tears and kisses, she'd told him there hadn't exactly been a rift, no single, overwhelming episode or grievance that could be resolved. It was a lifetime of estrangement.

But the good news was—and that might be a side effect of her injuries—she was at last past the hurt of growing up the unwanted child. She'd finally come to terms with it, could finally see her mother's side of things. Though Cybele had been only six when her father had died, she'd been the difficult child of a disappointment of a husband, a constant reminder of her mother's worst years and biggest mistake. A daddy's girl who'd cried for him for years and told her mother she'd wished she'd been the one who'd died.

She could also see her stepfather's side, a man who'd found himself saddled with a dead man's hostile child as a price for having the woman he wanted, but who couldn't extend his support to tolerance or interest. They were only human, she'd finally admitted to herself, not just the grown-ups who'd neglected her. And that made it possible for her to put the past behind her.

As more good news, her mother had contacted her again, and though what she'd offered Cybele was no-where near the unreserved allegiance Rodrigo's family shared, she wanted to be on better terms.

The relationship would never be what she wished for, but she'd decided to do her share, meet her mother halfway, take what was on offer, what was possible with her family.

Rodrigo hadn't let the subject go until he'd pressed and persisted and made sure she was really at peace with that.

She now stood looking down the beach where the

children were flying kites and building sand castles. She pressed the sight between the pages of her mind, for when she was back to her monotone and animation-free life.

No. She'd never go back to that. Even when she exited Rodrigo's orbit, her baby would fill her life with—

"Do you have your book?"

She swung around to Imelda, her smile ready and wholehearted. She'd come to love the woman in that short time.

She admired Imelda's bottle-green outfit, which matched the eyes she'd passed on to Rodrigo, and was again struck by her beauty. She could barely imagine how Imelda might have looked in her prime.

Her eyes fell on the heavy volume in Imelda's hand. "What book?"

"*La Diada De Sant Jordi* is *rosas i libros* day."

"Oh, yes, Rodrigo told me."

"Men give women a red rose, and women give men a book."

Her heart skipped a beat. "Oh. I didn't know that."

"So now you know. Come on, *muchacha*, go pick a book. The men will be coming back any time now."

"Pick a book from where?"

"From Rodrigo's library, of course."

"I can't just take a book from his library."

"He'll be more than happy for you to. And then, it's what you choose that will have significance when you give it to him."

Okay. Why would Imelda suggest she give Rodrigo a book? Had she realized how Cybele felt about him and was trying to matchmake? Rodrigo hadn't been the one

to betray any special emotions. He'd been no more affectionate to her than he'd been to his cousins.

Better gloss over this. "So a woman picks any man
she knows, and gives him a book?"

"She can. But usually she picks the most important
man in her life."

Imelda knew what Rodrigo was to her. There was
certainty in her shrewd eyes, along with a don't-bother-
denying-it footnote.

Cybele couldn't corroborate her belief. It would be
imposing on Rodrigo. He probably knew how she felt,
but it was one thing to know, another to have it declared.
And then, *he* wouldn't give her a rose. Even if he did,
it would be because all the women had their husbands
with them for the fiesta, or because she was alone, or
any other reason. She wasn't the most important woman
in his life.

But after she walked back into the house with Imelda
and they parted ways, she found herself rushing to the
library.

She came out with the book of her choice, feeling agonizingly exposed each time one of the women passed
her and commented on her having a book like them.

Then the men came back from the next town, bearing
copious amounts of prepared and mouthwatering food.
And each man had a red rose for his woman. Rodrigo
didn't have one.

Her heart thudded with a force that almost made her
sick.

She had no right to be crushed by disappointment.
And no right to embarrass him. She'd give the book to
Esteban.

Then she moved, and her feet took her to Rodrigo.

Even if she had no claim on him, and there'd never be anything between them, he *was* the most important man in her life, and everyone knew it.

As she approached him, he watched her with that stillness and intensity that always made her almost howl with tension.

She stopped one step away, held out the book.

"Happy *La Diada De Sant Jordi*, Rodrigo."

He took the book, his eyes fixing on it, obscuring his reaction from her. She'd chosen a book about all the people who'd advanced modern medicine in the last century. He raised his eyes to her, clearly uncertain of the significance of her choice.

"Just a reminder," she whispered, "that in a collation of this century's medical giants, you'll be among them."

His eyes flared with such fierceness, it almost knocked her off her feet. Then he reached for her hand, pulled her to him. One hand clasped her back, the other traveled over her hair to cup her head. Then he enfolded her into him briefly, pressed a searing kiss on her forehead. *"Gracias mucho, querida.* It's enough for me to have your good opinion."

Next second, he let her go, turned to deliver a few festive words, starting the celebrations.

She didn't know how she functioned after that embrace. That kiss. Those words. That *querida*.

She evidently did function, even if she didn't remember anything she said or did during the next hours. Then Rodrigo was pulling her to her feet.

"Come. We're starting the Sardana, our national dance."

She flowed behind him, almost hovered as she smiled

up at him, her heart jiggling at seeing him at his most carefree.

The band consisted of eleven players. They'd already taken their place at an improvised stage in the terrace garden that had been cleared for the dancers, evidently all of Rodrigo's family.

"I had the nearest town's *cobla*, our Catalan music ensemble, come over to play for us. The Sardana is never the same without live music. It's always made of four Catalan shawm players…" He pointed toward four men holding double-reed woodwinds. "Two trumpets, two horns, one trombone and a double bass."

"And what's with that guy with the flutelike instrument and the small drum attached to his left arm?"

"He plays the *flabiol*, that three-holed flute, with his left hand and plays that *tamborí* with the right. He keeps the rhythm."

"Why not just have twelve players, instead of saddling one with this convoluted setup?"

He grinned. "It's a tradition some say goes back two thousand years. But wait till you see him play. He'll make it look like the easiest thing in the world."

She grimaced down at her casted arm. "One thing's for sure, I'm not a candidate for a *flabiol/tamborí* player right now."

He put a finger below her chin, raised her face to him. "You soon will be." Before she gave in and dragged his head down to her to take that kiss she was disintegrating for, he turned his head away. "Now watch closely. They're going to dance the first *tirada,* and we'll join in the second one. The steps are very simple."

Letting out a steaming exhalation, she forced her attention to the circle of dancers that was forming.

"It's usually one man, one woman and so on, but we have more women than men here, so excuse the nontraditional configuration."

She mimicked his earlier hand gesture, drawled, "Women rule."

He threw his head back on a peal of laughter at her reminder, kept chuckling as he watched his womenfolk herding and organizing their men and children. "They do indeed."

The dance began, heated, then Rodrigo tugged her to join the *rotllanes obertes,* the open circles. They danced the steps he'd rehearsed with her on the sidelines, laughed together until their sides hurt. Everything was like a dream. A dream where she felt more alert and alive than she ever had. A dream where she was one with Rodrigo, a part of him, and in tune with the music, his family and the whole world.

Then, like every dream, the festivities drew to an end.

After calling good-night to everyone, Rodrigo walked her as usual to her quarters, left her a few steps from her door.

Two steps into the room, she froze. Her mouth fell open. Her breath left her lungs under pressure, wouldn't be retrieved.

All around. On every surface. *Everywhere.*

Red roses.

Bunches and bunches and *bunches* of perfect, bloodred roses.

Oh. God. Oh…*God…*

She darted back outside, called out to him. But he'd gone.

She stood there vibrating with the need to rush after

him, find him wherever he was and smother him in kisses.

But…since he hadn't waited around for her reaction, maybe he hadn't anticipated it would be this fierce. Maybe he'd only meant to give her a nice surprise. Maybe he'd had every other woman's room filled with flowers, too. Which she wouldn't put past him. She'd never known anyone with his capacity for giving.

She staggered back into her room. The explosion of beauty and color and fragrance yanked her into its embrace again.

The need expanded, compressing her heart, her lungs.

It was no use. She had to do it. She had to go to him.

She grabbed a jacket, streaked outside.

His scent, his vibe led her to the roof.

He was standing at the waist-high stone balustrade overlooking a turbulent, after-midnight sea, a lone knight silvered by the moon, carved from the night.

She stopped a dozen steps away. He didn't turn, stood like a statue of a Titan, the only animate things his satin mane rioting around his leonine head and his clothes rustling around his steel-fleshed frame. There was no way he could have heard the staccato of her feet or the labor of her breathing over the wind's buffeting whistles. But she knew he felt her there. He was waiting for her to initiate this.

"Rodrigo." Her gasp trembled against the wind's dissipation. He turned then. Cool rays deposited glimmers in the emerald of his eyes, luster on the golden bronze of his ruggedness. She stepped closer, mesmerized by his magnificence. A step away, she reached for his hand. She wanted to take it to her lips. That hand that had saved her life, that changed the lives of countless others daily, giving them back their limbs and mobility and freeing them from pain and disability. She settled for squeezing it between both of her trembling ones. "Besides everything you've done for me, your roses are the best gift I've ever been given."

His stare roiled with his discomfort at receiving gratitude. Then he simply said, "Your book beats my roses any day."

A smile ached on her lips. "You have issues with hearing thanks, don't you?"

"Thanks are overrated."

"Nothing sincere can be rated highly enough."

"I do what I want to do, what pleases me. And I certainly never do anything expecting…anything in return."

Was he telling her that his gift wasn't hinting at any special involvement? Warning her about getting ideas?

It wouldn't change anything. She loved him with everything in her, would give him everything that she was if he'd only take it. But if he didn't want it, she *would* give him her unending appreciation. "And I thank you because I want to, because it pleases me. And I certainly don't expect you to do anything in return but accept. I accepted your thanks for the book, didn't I?"

His lips spread in one of those slow, scorching smiles of his, as if against his will. "I don't remember if I gave you a choice to accept it or not. I sort of overrode you."

"Hmm, you've got a point." Then, without warning, she tugged his hand. Surprise made him stumble the step that separated them, so that he ended up pressed against her from breast to calf. Her hand released his, went to his head, sifting through the silk of his mane, bringing it down to hers. How she wished she had the use of her other arm, so she could mimic his earlier embrace. She had to settle for pressing her longing against his fore-head with lips that shook on his name.

They slid down his nose…and a cell phone rang.

He sundered their communion in a jerk, stared down at her, his eyes echoing the sea's tumult. It was shuddering, disoriented moments before her brain rebooted after the shock of interruption, of separation from him. That was her cell phone's tone.

It was in her jacket. Rodrigo had given it her, and only he had called her on it so far. Who could be calling her?

"Are you expecting a call?" His rasp scraped her nerves.

"I didn't even know anyone had this number."

"It's probably a wrong number."

"Yeah, probably. Just a sec." She fumbled the phone out, hit Answer. A woman's tear-choked voice filled her head.

"Agnes? What's wrong?" Instant anxiety gripped Rodrigo, spilled into urgency that had his hand at the phone, demanding to bear bad news himself. She blurted out the question that she hoped would defuse his agitation, "Are you and Steven okay?"

"Yes, yes…it's not that."

Cybele covered the mouthpiece, rapped her urgent assurance to Rodrigo. "They're both fine. This is something else."

His alarm drained, but tension didn't. He eased a fraction away, let her take the call, watching for any sign that necessitated his intervention, his taking over the situation.

Agnes went on. "I hate to ask you this, Cybele, but if you've remembered your life with Mel, you might know how this happened."

Foreboding closed in on her. "How *what* happened?"

"M-many people have contacted us claiming that Mel owes them extensive amounts of money. And the hospital where you used to work together says the funding he offered in return for being the head of the new general surgery department was withdrawn and the projects that were under way have incurred overdrafts in the millions. Everyone is suing us—and you—as his next of kin and inheritors."

Chapter 10

"So you don't have any memory of those debts."

Cybele shook her head, feeling crushed by doubts and fears.

It didn't sound as if Rodrigo believed her. She had a feeling Agnes hadn't, either. Did they think Mel had incurred all those debts because of her? Worse, had he? If he had, how? Why?

Was that what Agnes had almost brought up during Mel's funeral? She'd thought Mel, in his inability to express his emotions for her any other way, had showered her with extravagant stuff? Not that she could think what could be *that* extravagant.

If that hadn't been the case, she could think of only one other way. She'd made demands of him, extensive, unreasonable ones, and he'd gone to insane lengths to meet them. But what could have forced him to do so?

Threats to leave him? If that were true, then she hadn't been only a heartless monster, but a manipulative, mercenary one, too.

She had to know. She couldn't take another breath if she didn't. "Do *you* know anything about them?"

Rodrigo's frown deepened as he shook his head slowly. But his eyes were thoughtful. With suspicions? Deductions? Realizations?

"You know something. Please, tell me. I have to know."

He looked down at her for a bone-shaking moment, moonlight coasting over his beauty, throwing its dominant slashes and hollows into a conflict of light and darkness, of confusion and certainty.

Then he shook his head again, as if he'd made up his mind. To her dismay, he ignored her plea. "What I want to know is what has taken those creditors so long to come forward."

"They actually did as soon as Mel's death was confirmed."

"Then what has taken Agnes and Steven so long to relate this, and why have they come to *you* with this, and not me?"

She gave him his foster mother's explanations. "They wanted to make sure of the claims first, and then they didn't want to bother you. They thought they could take care of it themselves. They called me in case I knew something only a wife would know, that would help them resolve this mess. And because I'm involved in the lawsuits."

"Well, they were wrong, on all counts." She almost cried out at the incensed edge that entered his voice and expression. The words to beg him not to take it up with them, that they had enough to deal with, had almost shot from her lips when he exhaled forcibly. "Not that they need to know that. They've been through enough, and they were as usual misguidedly trying not to impose on me. I think those two still don't believe me when I say they *are* my parents. But anyway, none of you have anything to worry about. I'll take care of everything."

She gaped at him. *Was* he real? Could she love him more?

All she could say was, "Thank you."

He squeezed his eyes on a grimace. "Don't."

"I will thank you, so live with it." He glowered at her. She went on, "And since I'm on a roll, throwing my problems in your lap, I need your opinion on another one. My arm."

His eyes narrowed. "What about it?"

"My fractures have healed, but the nerve damage isn't clearing. Eight weeks ago, you said I wouldn't be able to operate for months. Were you being overly optimistic? Will I ever regain the precision I used to have and need as a surgeon?"

"It's still early, Cybele."

"Please, Rodrigo, just give it to me straight. And before you say anything conciliatory, remember that I'll see through it."

"I would never condescend to you like that."

"Even to protect me from bad news?"

"Even then."

She believed him. He would never lie to her. He would never lie, period. So she pressed on. Needing the truth. About this, if she couldn't have it about anything else.

"Then tell me. I'm a left-handed surgeon who knows nothing else but to be one, and I need to know if in a few weeks I'll be looking to start a new career path. As you pointed out before, the arm attached to my hand had extensive nerve damage…."

"*And* I performed a meticulous peripheral nerve repair."

"Still, I have numbness and weakness, tremors—"

"It's *still* too early to predict a final prognosis. We'll start your active motion physiotherapy rehabilitation program the moment we have proof of perfect bone healing."

"We have that now."

"No, we don't. You're young and healthy and your bones *look* healed now, but I need them rock solid before I remove the cast. That won't be a day before twelve weeks after the surgery. Then we'll start your physiotherapy. We'll focus first on controlling the pain and swelling that accompanies splint removal and restoration of motion. Then we'll move to exercises to strengthen and stabilize the muscles around the wrist joint then to exercises to improve fine motor control and dexterity."

"What if none of it works? What if I regain enough motor control and dexterity to be self-sufficient but not a surgeon?"

"If that happens, you still have nothing to worry about. If worse comes to worst, I'll see to it that you change direction smoothly to whatever field of medicine will provide you with as much fulfillment. But I'm not giving up on your regaining full use of your arm and hand. I'm stopping at nothing until we get you back to normal. And don't even *think* about how long it will take, or what you'll do or where you'll be until it happens. You have all the time in the world to retrain your hand, to regain every last bit of power and control. You have a home here for as long as you wish and accept to stay. You have *me,* Cybele. *I'm* here for you, anytime, all the time, whatever happens."

And she couldn't hold back anymore.

She surged into him, tried to burrow inside him, her working arm shaking with the ferociousness of her hug. And she wept. She loved him so much, was so thankful he existed, it was agony.

He stilled, let her hug him and hold on to him and drench him in her tears. Then he wrapped her in his arms, caressed her from head to back, his lips by her ear, murmuring gentle and soothing words. Her heart expanded so quickly with a flood of love, it almost ruptured. Her tears gushed faster, her quakes nearly rattling flesh from bone.

He at last growled something as though agonized, snatched her from gravity's grasp into his, lifted her until she felt she'd float out to sea if he relinquished his hold.

He didn't, crushed her in his arms, squeezed her to his flesh until he forced every shudder and tear out of her.

Long after he'd dissipated her storm, he swayed with her, as if slow dancing the Sardana again, pressing her head into his shoulder, his other arm bearing her weight effortlessly as he raggedly swore to her in a loop of English and Catalan that he was there for her, that she'd never be without him. His movements morphed from soothing to inflaming to excruciating. But it was his promises that wrenched at the tethers of her heart.

For she knew he would honor every promise. He would remain in her life and that of her baby's. As the protector, the benefactor, the dutiful, doting uncle. And every time she saw him or heard from him it would pour fresh desperation on the desolation of loving him and never being able to have him.

She had to get away. Today. Now. Her mind was disintegrating, and she couldn't risk causing herself a deeper injury. Her baby needed her healthy and whole.

"Cybele…" He shifted his grip on her, and his hardness dug into her thigh.

She groped for air, arousal thundering through her. Voices inside her yelled that this was just a male reaction to having a female writhing in his arms, that it meant nothing.

She couldn't listen. It didn't matter. He was aroused. This could be her only chance to be with him. And she had to take it. She needed the memory, the knowledge that she'd shared her body with him to see her through the barrenness of a life without him.

She rubbed her face into his neck, opened her lips on his pulse. It bounded against her tongue, as if trying to drive deeper into her mouth, mate with her. Every steel muscle she was wrapped around expanded, bunched, buzzed. She whimpered at the feel of his flesh beneath her lips, the texture, the taste, at the sheer delight of breathing him in, absorbing his potency.

"Cybele, *querida*…" He began to put her down and she clung, captured his lips before he said any more, before he could tell her no.

She couldn't take no for an answer. Not this time. She had to have this time.

She caught his groans on her tongue, licked his lips of every breath, suckled his depths dry of every sound. She arched into his arousal, confessing hers without words. Then with them.

"Rodrigo—I *want* you." That came out a torn sob.

"If you want me, *please*—just take me. Don't hold back. Don't think. Don't worry. No consequences or considerations. No tomorrows."

Rodrigo surrendered to Cybele, let her take of him what she would, his response so vast it was like a hurricane building momentum before it unleashed its destruction.

But her tremulous words replayed in his mind as she rained petal softness and fragrant warmth all over his face, crooning and whimpering her pleas for his response, her offer of herself. He felt things burning inside him as he held back, the significance of her words expanding in his mind.

Carte blanche. That was what she was giving him. With her body, with herself. No strings. No promises. No expectations.

Because she didn't want any? Because her need was only sexual? Or because she couldn't handle more than that? But what if she couldn't handle *even* that? If he gave her what she thought she wanted and ended up damaging her more?

And though he was nearly mindless now, powerless against the force of her desire, he'd conditioned himself to protect her from his own. "Cybele, you're distraught—"

She sealed his lips again, stopping his objection, her tongue begging entry, her kisses growing fevered, singeing the last of his control. "With need for you. I sometimes feel it will shatter me. I know what I'm asking. Please, Rodrigo, please…just give me this time."

This time. She thought he could stop at once, that he could possess her then walk away? It wasn't carte blanche, just a one-time offer? Would all that need she talked about then be quenched? Did she not feel more for him because her emotions had been buried with Mel, even if she didn't remember?

That thought gave him the strength to put her down, step out of reach when she stumbled to embrace him again.

Her arms fell to her sides, her shoulders hunching as she suddenly looked fragile and lost.

Then her tears flowed again, so thick it seemed they shriveled up her face. "Oh, no—y-you already showed me that you don't want me, and I—I came on to you again…."

She choked up, stumbled around and disappeared from the roof.

He should let her go. Talk to her again when his body wasn't pummeling him in demand for hers. But even if he could survive his own disappointment, he couldn't survive hers. He couldn't let her think he didn't want her. He had to show her the truth, even if the price was having her only once. He would take anything he could have of her, give her anything she needed.

He tore after her, burst into her room, found her crumpled facedown on her bed, good arm thrown over one of the bouquets he'd flooded her room with. She lurched at his entry, half-twisted to watch his approach, her wet gaze wounded and wary.

He came down on his knees at the foot of the bed. Her smooth legs, which had tanned honey-colored under his agonized eyes these past weeks, were exposed as the long, traditionally Catalan red skirt he'd picked for her to wear today rode up above her knees.

He wanted to drag her to him, slam her into his flesh, overpower and invade her, brand her, devour her whole.

He wanted to cherish her, savor and pleasure her more.

She gasped as he slipped off her shoes, tried to turn to him fully. He stopped her with a gentle hand at the small of her back. She subsided with a whimpering exhalation, watched him with her lip caught in her teeth as he prowled on all fours, advancing over her, kissing and suckling his way from the soles of her feet, up her legs, her thighs, her buttocks and back, her nape. She lay beneath him, quaking and moaning at each touch until he traced the lines of her shuddering profile. The moment he reached her lips, she cried out, twisted onto her back, surged up to cling to his lips in a desperate, soul-wrenching kiss.

Without severing their meld, he scooped her up and stepped off the bed. She relinquished his lips on a gasp of surprise.

"I want you in my bed, *querida*."

She moaned, shook her head. "No, please." He jerked in alarm. She didn't want to be in his bed? He started to put her down when she buried her face and lips in his neck. "Here. Among the roses."

"Dios, si..."

He'd fantasized about having her in his bed from the day he'd first laid eyes on her. Even when she'd become a forbidden fantasy, her image, and the visualization of all the things he'd burned to do to her, with her, even when he'd hated her and himself and the whole world for it, had been what had fueled his self-pleasuring, providing the only relief he'd had.

He'd covered his bed with the royal blue of her eyes.

The rest of the room echoed the mahogany of her hair and the honey of her skin. He'd needed to sleep surrounded by her.

But this was far better than his fantasies. To have her here, among the blazing-red beauty of his blatant confession that she was his most important woman. His most important person.

He hadn't meant to confess it, but couldn't stop himself. He also hadn't dreamed it would lead to this. To beyond his dreams.

He laid her back on the bed, stood back taking her in. Unique, a ravishing human rose, her beauty eclipsing that of the flowers he'd filled her room with. She must have realized their significance, encouraging her to divulge her own need.

He felt his clothes dissolve off his body under the pressure of his own, under her wide-eyed awe, her breathless encouragement.

Then he was all over her again, caressing her elastic-waist skirt from her silky legs, kneading her jacket off, then the ensemble blouse over her head. Her bra and panties followed as he traced the tide of peach flooding her from toes to cheeks, tasting each tremor strumming her every fiber.

Then he was looking down on what no fantasy had conjured. Thankfully. Or he would have lost his mind for real long ago.

He remained above her, arms surrounding her head, thighs imprisoning hers, vibrating as the sight, the scent and sounds of her surrender pulverized his intentions to be infinitely slow and gentle. Blood thundered in his head, in his loins, tearing the last tatters of control from his grasp in a riptide.

Then she took it all out of his hands, her hand trembling over his back in entreaty, its power absolute.

He surrendered, moved between her shaking thighs, pressed her shuddering breasts beneath his aching chest. Then she conquered him, irrevocably.

Her lips trembled on his forehead, his name a litany of tremulous passion and longing as she enveloped him, clasped him to her body as if her life depended on his existence, his closeness, on knowing he was there, as if she couldn't believe he was.

Tenderness swamped him, choked him. He had to show her, prove to her, that he was there, was hers. He'd already given her all he had. All he had left to give her was his passion, his body.

He rose on his knees, cupped her head in one hand, her buttocks in the other, tilted one for his kiss, the other for his penetration. He bathed the head of his erection in her welcoming wetness, absorbed her cries of pleasure at the first contact of their intimate flesh, drank her pleas to take her, fill her.

He succumbed to the mercilessness of her need and his, drew back to watch her eyes as he started to drive into her, to join them. Her flesh fluttered around his advance, hot and tight almost beyond endurance, seeming to drag him inside and trying to push him out at once, begging for his invasion while resisting it.

He tried again and again, until she was writhing beneath him, eyes streaming, her whole body shaking and stained in the flush of uncontrollable arousal and unbearable frustration.

His mind filled with confusion and colliding diagnoses.

"Please, just do it, Rodrigo, hard, just take me."

The agony in her sobs was the last straw. He had to give her what she needed, couldn't draw his next breath if he didn't.

He thrust past her resistance, buried half of his shaft inside her rigid tightness.

It was only when her shriek tore through him that he understood what was that ripping sensation he'd felt as he'd driven into her. And he no longer understood anything.

It was impossible. Incomprehensible.

She was a *virgin?*

Chapter 11

Rodrigo froze on top of Cybele, half-buried in her depths, paralyzed. A virgin? *How?*

He raised himself on shaking arms. Her face contorted and a hot cry burst from her lips. He froze in midmotion, his gaze pinned on hers as he watched her eyes flood with the same confusion, the same shock along with tears.

"It shouldn't hurt that much, should it?" she quavered. "I couldn't have forgotten *that*."

Dios. He'd wanted to give her nothing but pleasure and more pleasure. And all he'd done was *hurt* her.

"No" was all he could choke out.

She digested that, reaching the same seemingly impossible explanation he had. "Then you have to be... my first."

Her first. The way she said that, with such shy wonder, made him want to thrust inside her and growl, *And your only.*

Something far outside his wrecked restraint—probably the debilitating cocktail of shock and shame at causing her pain—held him back from that mindless display of caveman possessiveness.

"I remember I wanted to wait until, y'know, I met… the one. I assumed that when I met Mel… But it—it seems I wanted to wait until we were married. But…"

He'd been trying to get himself to deflate, enough to slip out of her without causing her further pain. He expanded beyond anything he'd ever known instead. His mind's eye crowded with images of him devouring those lips that quivered out her earnest words, those breasts that swelled with her erratic breathing.

"But since there are ways for paraplegics to have sex, I still assumed we did one way or…" She choked with embarrassment. It was painfully endearing, when their bodies were joined in ultimate intimacy. "But it's clear we didn't, at least nothing invasive, and artificial insemination is essentially noninvasive…."

He shouldn't find her efforts at a logical, medically sound analysis that arousing as she lay beneath him, shaking, her impossible tightness throbbing around his shaft, her torn flesh singeing his own. But—curse him—it was arousing him to madness. He wanted to *give* her invasive.

He couldn't. He had to give her time, for the pain that gripped her body to subside. He started to withdraw. Her sob tore through him.

He froze, his own moan mingling with hers until she subsided. Then he tried to move again. But she clamped quaking legs around his hips, stopping him from exiting her body, pumping her own hips, impaling herself further on his erection.

"I'm hurting you." He barely recognized the butchered protest that cracked the panting-filled silence as his.

"Yes, oh, *yes*…" He heaved up in horror. She clung harder, her core clamping him like a fist of molten metal. "It's…*exquisite. You* are. I dreamed—but could have never dreamed how you'd feel inside me. You're burning me, filling me, making me feel—feel so—so—oh, Rodrigo, take me, do everything to me."

He roared with the spike of arousal her words lashed through him. Then, helpless to do anything but her bidding, he thrust back into her, shaking with the effort to be gentle, go slow. She thrashed her head against the sheets, splashing her satin tresses, bucking her hips beneath his, engulfing more of his near-bursting erection into her heat. "*Don't.* Give me…all of you, do it…hard."

He growled his capitulation as he rose, cupped her hips in his palms, tilted her and thrust himself to the hilt inside her.

At her feverish cry, he withdrew all the way, looked down at the awesome sight of his shaft sinking slowly inside her again.

He raised his eyes to hers, found her propped up on her elbows, watching too, lips crimson, swollen, open on frantic pants, eyes stunned, wet, stormy. He drew out, plunged again, and she collapsed back, crying out a gust of passion, opening wider for each thrust, a fusion of pain and pleasure slashing across her face, rippling through her body.

He kept his pace gentle, massaging her all over with his hands, his body, his mouth, bending to suckle her breasts, drain her lips, rain wonder all over her.

"Do you know what you are? *Usted es divina, mi belleza, divina.* Do you see what you do to me? What I'm doing to you?"

She writhed beneath him with every word, her hair rippling waves of copper-streaked gloss over the crisp white sheet, her breathing fevered, her whole body straining at him, around him, forcing him to pick up speed—though he managed not to give in to his body's uproar for more force.

"I *love* what you're doing to me—your flesh in mine—give it to me—give it all to me…."

He again obeyed, strengthened his thrusts until her depths started to ripple around him and she keened, bucked up, froze, then convulsion after convulsion squeezed soft shrieks out of her, squeezed her around his erection in wrenching spasms.

The force, the sight and sound and knowledge of her release smashed the last of his restraint. He roared, let go, his body all but detonating in ecstasy. His hips convulsed into hers and he felt his essence flow into her as he fed her pleasure to the last tremor, until her arm and legs fell off him in satiation.

He collapsed beside her, shaking with the aftershocks of his life's most violent and first profound orgasm, moved her over him with extreme care, careful to remain inside her.

She spread over him, limp, trembling and cooling. He'd never known physical intimacy could be like this, channeling into his spirit, his reason. It had been merciful he hadn't imagined how sublime making love to her would be. He *would* have long ago gone mad.

He encompassed her velvet firmness in caresses, letting the sensations replay in his mind and body, letting awe overtake him.

He was her first. And she'd needed him so much that even through her pain, she'd felt so much pleasure at their joining.

Not that it had mattered to him in any way when he'd thought she'd belonged to Mel, had probably been experienced before him.

But now he knew she'd been with no one else, he almost burst with pride and elation. She *was* meant to be his alone.

And he had to tell her that he was hers, too. He had to offer her. Everything. *Now.*

"Cybele, *mi corazón*," he murmured into her hair as he pressed her into his body, satiation, gratitude and love swamping him. *"Cásate conmigo, querida."*

Cybele lay draped over Rodrigo, shell-shocked by the transfiguring experience.

Every nerve crackled with Rodrigo-induced soreness and satiation and a profundity of bliss, amazement and disbelief.

She'd been a virgin. Wow.

And what he'd done to her. A few million wows.

The wows in fact rivaled the number of his billions since he'd given her all that pleasure when she'd simultaneously been writhing with the pain of his possession. But the very concept of having him inside her body, of being joined to him in such intimacy, at last, had swamped the pain, turned it into pleasure so excruciating she thought she *had* died in his arms for moments there.

Love welled inside her as she recalled him looking down at her in such adorable contrition and stupefaction.

The latter must have been because she'd babbled justifications for her virginal state with him buried inside her. Another breaker of heat crashed over her as she relived her mortification. Then the heat changed texture when she recalled every second of his domination.

What would he do to her when pain was no longer part of the equation? When he no longer feared hurting her? When he lost the last shred of inhibition and just plundered her?

She wondered if she'd survive such pleasure. And she couldn't wait to risk her life at the altar of his unbridled possession.

She was about to attempt to beg for more, needing to cram all she could into her one time in his arms. But she lost coherence as he caressed and crooned to her. Then his words registered.

Cásate conmigo, querida.

Marry me, darling.

Instinctive responses and emotions mushroomed, paralyzed her, muted her. Heart and mind ceased, time and existence froze.

Then everything rushed, streaked. Elation, disbelief, joy, shock, delight, doubt. The madly spinning roulette of emotions slowed down, and one flopped into the pocket. Distress.

She pushed away from the meld of their bodies, moaning at the burn of separation, rediscovering coordination from scratch. "I meant it when I said no tomorrows, Rodrigo. I don't expect anything."

He rose slowly to a sitting position, his masculinity taking on a harsher, more overwhelming edge among the dreamy softness of a background drenched in red roses. He looked like that wrathful god she'd seen in the beginning, decadent in beauty, uncaring of the effect his nakedness and the sight of his intact arousal had on flimsy mortals like her. "And you don't want it, either?"

"What I want isn't important."

He stopped her as she turned away, his grip on her arm gentleness itself, belying his intensity as he gritted, "It's *all*-important. And we've just established how much you want me."

"It still makes no difference. I—I can't marry you."

He went still. "Because of Mel? You feel guilty over him?"

She huffed a bitter laugh. "And you don't?"

"No, I don't," he shot back, adamant, final. "Mel is no longer here and this has nothing to do with him."

"Says the man whose every action for the last ten weeks had everything to do with Mel."

He rose to his knees, blocked her unsteady attempt to get off the bed. "Care to explain that?"

Air disappeared as his size dwarfed her, his heat bore down on her, as his erection burned into her waist. She wanted to throw herself down, beg him to forget about his honor-bound offer and just ride her to oblivion again.

She swallowed fire past her hoarse-with-shrieks-of-pleasure vocal cords. "I'm Mel's widow, and I'm carrying his unborn child. Need more clues?"

"You think all I did for you was out of duty for him?"

She shrugged dejectedly. "Duty, responsibility, dependability, heroism, nobility, honor. You're full of 'em."

And he did the last thing she'd expected in this tension.

He belted out one of those laughs that turned her to boiling goo. "You make it sound like I'm full of…it."

Words squeezed past the heart bobbing in her throat.

"I wish. You make it impossible to think the least negative thing of you."

He encroached on her as he again exposed her to that last thing she'd thought she'd ever see from him. Pure seduction, lazy and indulgent and annihilating. "And that's bad…why?"

Oh, *no*. She'd been in deep…it, when he'd been only lovely and friendly. Now, after he'd kick-started her sexuality software with such an explosive demonstration, had imprinted his code and password all over her cells, to all of a sudden see fit to turn on his sex appeal intentionally was cruel and unusual overkill.

She tried to put a breath between them. He wouldn't let her, backed her across the bed, a panther crowding his prey into a corner. She came up against the brass bars, grabbed them, tried to pull up from her swooning position.

"It's bad because it makes it impossible to say no to you."

His lips twitched as he prowled over her, imprisoning her in a cage of muscle and maleness. But instead of his previous solemn and tender intensity, that mind-messing predatory sexiness spiked to a whole new level. "That has always been my nefarious plan."

"Okay, Rodrigo, I'm confused here," she panted. "What's brought all…*this* about?"

His eyebrows shot up in mock surprise and affront. "You mean you don't remember? Seems I have to try much…harder—and longer—to make a more lasting impression."

She coughed in disbelief. "You're telling me you suddenly want to marry me because of the mind-blowing pleasure?"

He tightened his knees around her thighs, winding the pounding between them into a tighter rhythm, licking his lips as his gaze melted over her captive nakedness, making her feel as if he'd licked her all over again. "So it was mind-blowing for you?"

"Are you kidding? I'm surprised my head is still screwed on. But I can't believe it was for *you*. I'm not by any stretch hot stuff, not to mention I must have cramped your style, being your first pregnant virgin and all."

"I admit, I was and am still agonizingly cramped, as you can see. And feel." He pressed his erection into her belly. Feeling the marble smooth and hard column of hot flesh against hers, the awe that she'd accommodated all that inside her, the carnality of the sharply recalled sensations as he'd occupied her, stretched her into mindlessness made her gasp, arch up involuntarily into his hardness. He ground harder into her as he drove a knee between her thighs, coaxing their rigidity to melt apart for him. "And in case you want to know my style…" His other knee joined in splaying her thighs apart as he leaned over her, teasing her aching nipples with the silk-sprinkled power of his chest. "…it's a woman who has no idea she's inferno-level stuff who happens to be a pregnant virgin. Or who was one, until I put an end to that condition."

She couldn't wrap her head around this. "So if it isn't out of duty to Mel, it isn't something more moronically honorable as doing the 'right thing' since you took my 'innocence,' is it?"

He chuckled. "*Dios,* you say the funniest things. First, I don't equate virginity with innocence. Second, *your* innocence seems to be almost intact. But don't worry. I didn't even scratch the surface of all the ways I plan to rectify that." He nipped her nipple, had her coming off the bed with a sharp slam of pleasure. He withdrew on a sigh of satisfaction. "Any more far-fetched reasons you can come up with to explain why I'm proposing to you?"

"Why don't you tell me your not-so-far-fetched ones?" she gasped. "And don't say because I'm your one and only aphrodisiac. That wasn't the case up until a few hours ago."

"Up until a few hours ago, I didn't know you wanted me."

"That's as straight-faced a lie as I've ever heard," she scoffed. "I'm as transparent as the windows Consuelo keeps spotless. I showed you I wanted you weeks ago. Hell, I showed you I wanted you two minutes after I regained consciousness."

He tasted her nipples in soft pulls as if compelled. "That you did so soon, coupled with your loss of memory, made me wonder if your mind wasn't scrambled and you didn't know what you wanted, or why. I thought I might be what you clung to, to reaffirm your life after surviving such a catastrophe, or because I was the one closest to you, or the one you seemed to perceive as your savior."

She pushed his head away before her breasts—her whole body—exploded. "You *are* my savior, but that has nothing to do with my wanting you." She devoured his beauty as he loomed over her, felt her core clench with the memory, the knowledge of what he could do to it. "I remember you had hordes of women you didn't save panting for you. I think *not* wanting you is a feminine impossibility."

The intimacy and seduction on his face turned off like a light, plunging her world into darkness. "So it's only sexual for you? That's why you wanted it to be only once?"

"Which part of me lauding your responsibility, dependability, heroism, nobility and honor didn't you get?"

The mesmerizing heat flared back on like floodlights, making her squirm. "So you like me for my character not just my body?"

"I *love* you for your character." That made that smug, male assurance falter, crack. He stared at her, stunned, almost vulnerable. She groaned. "I didn't intend to say that, so don't go all noble pain-in-the-derriere on me and find it more reason to—"

He crashed his lips onto hers, silencing her, wrenching keens from her depths on scorching, devouring kisses. He came fully over her body, grinding into her belly, lifting her off the bed, one hand supporting her head for his ravaging, the other at her back holding her for his chest to torment her breasts into a frenzy.

She tore her lips away before she combusted and it was too late to vent her reservations. "Please, Rodrigo, don't feel you owe me anything. And I can't owe you any more than I already do."

He plastered her back to the bed, seemingly by the force of his conviction alone. "You owe me nothing, do you hear? It's been my privilege to see to your health, my joy to have you in my home, and yes, my mind-blowing pleasure to have you in my bed."

She started shaking again. It was too much. Loving him, needing to grab at him, to take him at his every magnificent word, blocking her mind to the fear that she'd be taking advantage of him, end up causing them both misery and heartache.

She trembled caresses over his beloved face. "I know

you're always right, but you're totally wrong here. I owe you far more than medical care and shelter. And mind-blowing pleasure. I owe you for restoring my faith in humanity, for showing me what a family could be like, and letting me be a part of yours for a while, for stabilizing my outlook so much that I feel I will at last have a relationship with my own family, not just cynical and bitter avoidance. I owe you memories and experiences that have made me a stronger, healthier person, that will be a part of me forever. And that was before what you offered me today."

He grabbed her hand, singed it in kisses, all lightness burned away as he, too, vibrated with emotion. "Mel's debts…"

She rushed to make one thing clear. "I don't know what hand I had in them, but if I had any, I'll pay my part, I swear."

"No, you won't. I said I'd take care of them."

"You'd do anything to protect your foster parents, and me, too, won't you? And *this* is what I'm indebted to you for. The—the…carte blanche support. And you're offering it forever now. And I can't accept. I can't burden you anymore with my problems. Any more support from you would burden *me*. Whatever your reasons are for offering to marry me, I have nothing to offer you in return."

His hands convulsed in her hair, pinned her for the full impact of his vehemence. "You have everything to offer me, *querida*. You've *already* offered me everything and I want it all for the rest of my life. I want your passion, your friendship, and now that I know I have it, I want your love. I *need* your love. And I want your baby as mine. I want us to be lovers, to be a family. And the only reason I want all this is because I love you."

She lurched so hard she nearly threw him off her. He pressed down harder, holding her head tighter to imprint her with every nuance of his confession. "I love you, *mi amor,* for your character and your body, for being such a responsible, dependable, heroic, noble and honorable pregnant has-been-virgin who had no idea you started a fire in me that can never be put out."

She broke into sobs. "How can you say that? I was going to leave, and if I hadn't almost attacked you, you would have never—"

"I would have *never* let you leave. Don't you get that yet? I was going to keep shooting down your reasons and demands to leave for months to come, and when I was out of arguments, I was going to make you offers you can't refuse so you'd have to stay. I would have confessed my feelings to you when I felt secure you could make such a life-changing decision and lifelong commitment, could handle my feelings and my passion. You only freed me from the agonizing wait. Thankfully. I was suffering serious damage holding back."

Her tears slowed down with each incredible word out of that mouth that sent her to heaven no matter what it did or said. Scary joy and certainty started to banish the agony of grief and doubt.

"You hid that perfectly," she hiccuped, her face trembling, with a smile of burgeoning belief in his reciprocated emotions.

His sincerity and intensity switched to bedevilment in a flash as his hands and lips started to roam her again. "I'm a neurosurgeon. Covert turmoil is one of my middle names."

"Another one?" She spluttered on mirth and emotion, finally felt she had the right to reciprocate his caresses, delighting in the silk of his polished, muscled back and swimmer's shoulders.

But she had to voice her concerns one last time. "This is a major step. Are you sure you considered all the ramifications?"

"The only thing that stopped me from snatching you up the first time you offered yourself was that I thought *you* were nowhere near aware of the ramifications, had no idea what you'd be letting yourself in for, weren't ready for a relationship so soon after such a loss and trauma. I, on the other hand, am positive of what I want. What I *have* to have. You, the baby. *Us*."

She cried out and dragged him down to her, surging up to meet his lips, devouring with her own. She was begging when he suddenly rose, swept her up in his arms and strode into her bathroom.

He put her down on the massage table and ran a bubble bath, came back to slide her off it, locking her thighs around his hips, gliding his erection along her core's molten lips before he leaned forward, pressed it to her belly, undulated against her, filled her gasping mouth with his tongue.

She arched, tried to bring him inside her. He held her down, wouldn't let her have what she felt she was imploding for.

"You haven't said yes."

"I've been saying 'yes…but' for a while now," she moaned.

"Didn't sound like that to me."

"Is that why you're punishing me now?"

"I would be punishing you if I gave you what you think you want again tonight. But don't worry, there

are so many other ways I'll go about erasing that innocence of yours."

"No, please...I want you again."

"Let me hear that *yes* without the *but* and you can
have me. For the rest of our lives."

"Yes."

And for the rest of the night, she lost count of how
many *yeses* she said.

Chapter 12

The Three months and a half to the day that Cybele opened her eyes in Rodrigo's world, she was trying not to run down the aisle to him.

She rushed down the path between their guests, his family and friends and colleagues, in one of the plateau gardens overlooking his vineyards on one side and the sea on the other, feeling like she was treading air, forging deeper into heaven.

He'd insisted on scheduling the wedding two weeks after he'd removed her cast, to give time for the physiotherapy to control any lingering discomforts. But he hadn't insisted on holding the wedding in Barcelona's biggest cathedral as he'd first planned, succumbing to her desire to hold it on his estate. The land that was now theirs. Their home. And their baby's home.

That was what completed her happiness. That it

wasn't only she who was being blessed by the best gift the world had to offer, but her baby, too. Only Rodrigo would love as his own the baby of the man he'd loved like a brother.

He stood there looking godlike in his tuxedo, his smile growing more intimate and delighted as she neared him. She only noticed Ramón standing beside him when she stumbled the last steps to grab Rodrigo's outstretched hand. She absently thought that they could be brothers. Not that Ramón, who was arguably as esthetically blessed as Rodrigo, was anywhere near as hard-hitting. Or perhaps it was she who had terminal one-man-one-woman syndrome.

Ramón winked at her as he kissed her and left them to the minister's ministrations. He'd come to her quarters an hour ago, where Rodrigo had insisted she remain until their wedding night, and performed the Catalan best man's duty of giving the bride her bouquet, which he'd picked for her, while reciting a poem he'd written. She'd almost had a heart attack laughing as he turned the poem that was supposed to extol her virtues and that of her groom into a hilariously wicked medical report.

Apart from that, and standing by Rodrigo's side until she reached him, Ramón's role had ended. In Catalonia there were no wedding rings for the best man to bear. Rodrigo would transfer the engagement ring from her right hand to her left one.

He was doing that now. She barely remembered the preceding ritual beyond repeating the vows, crying a river as Rodrigo made his own vows to her, lost in his eyes, singed by his love.

She watched their hands entwine as he slipped the ring onto her trembling finger, the ten-carat blue diamond part of the set she was wearing that totaled a breath-depleting fifty carats. He'd said he'd picked them for being a lighter version of her eyes.

Then he kissed her. As if they were now one. Forever.

From then on, everything blurred even more as their guests carried them away to another extensive session of Sardana dances and many other wedding customs and festivities.

At one point she thought she'd had a brief exchange with Mel's parents. She had the impression that they were doing much better and seemed genuinely happy for her and Rodrigo. Her family was here, too, flown in by Rodrigo. His magic had encompassed them, as well, had infused them with a warmth they'd never exhibited before.

Then the dreamlike wedding was over and he carried her to his quarters. Theirs now. At last.

She'd almost lost her mind with craving these past weeks, as she hadn't slept curved into his body, or taken him inside of hers.

She was in a serious state by now. She'd die if he took her slowly and gently like he'd done that first night.

She was about to beg him not to when he set her down, pressed her against the door and crashed his lips onto hers.

She cried out her welcome and relief at his fierceness, surrendered to his surging tongue. His hands were all over her as he plundered her mouth, removing the *peineta* and pins that held her cutwork lace veil in place, shaking her hair out of the imprisonment of her Spanish chignon, undoing the string lacing of her traditional wedding gown's front.

He pushed it off her shoulders, spilling her breasts

into his palms, weighing and kneading them until she felt they would burst if he didn't devour them. He was looking down at them as if he really would. Then he crushed them beneath his chest, her lips beneath his, rubbing, thrusting, maddening.

"Do you have any idea how much I've hungered for you?" he groaned against her lips. "What these past weeks were like?"

"If it's half as much as I hungered for you, and they were half as excruciating as mine, then…serves you right."

He grunted a sound so carnal and predatory yet amused, sowed a chain of nips from her lips to her nipples in chastisement as he dragged her dress down. It snagged on her hips.

He reversed his efforts, tried to get it over her head, and she hissed, "Rip it."

His eyes widened. Then with a growl, he ripped the white satin in two. She lurched and moaned, relishing his ferocity, fueling it.

He swept her underwear down her legs, then stood to fling away his jacket, cummerbund and tie then gave her a violent strip-show shredding of his shirt. Candlelight cast a hypnotic glow to accompany his performance. Passion rose from her depths at the savage poetry of his every straining muscle. To her disappointment, he kept his pants on.

Before she could beg him to complete his show, he came down before her, buried his face in her flesh, in her core, muttered love and lust. When she was begging for him, he rose with her wrapped around him, took her to bed, laid her on her back on its edge, kneeled between her thighs, probed her with deft fingers.

He growled his satisfaction as her slick flesh gripped them. "Do you know what it does to me—to feel you like this, to have this privilege, this freedom? Do you know what it means to me, that you let me, that you want me, that you're mine?"

Sensation rocketed, more at the emotion and passion fueling his words than at his expert pleasuring. She keened, opened herself fully to him, now willing to accept pleasure any way he gave it, knowing he craved her surrender, her pleasure. She'd always give him all he wanted.

He came over her, thrust his tongue inside her mouth to the rhythm of his invading fingers, his thumb grinding her bud in escalating circles. He swallowed every whimper, every tremulous word, every tear, until she shuddered apart in his arms.

She collapsed, nerveless and sated. For about two minutes.

Then she was all over him, kissing, licking, nipping and kneading him through his pants. He rasped, "Release me."

She lowered the zipper with shaking hands. Her mouth watered as he sprang heavy and hard into her palms. He groaned in a bass voice that spilled magma from her core, "Play with me, *mi amor*. Own me. I'm yours."

"And do you know what hearing you say this means to me?" she groaned back.

He growled as her hands traveled up and down his shaft, pumping his potency in delight. She slithered down his body, tasted him down to his hot, smooth crown. His scent, taste and texture made her shudder with need for all of him. She spread her lips over him, took all she could of him inside. He grunted his ecstasy, thrust his mighty hips to her suckling rhythm.

His hand in her hair stopped her. "I need to be inside you."

She clambered over him, kissing her way to his lips, "And I need you inside me. Don't you dare go slow or gentle...*please*..."

With that last plea, she found herself on her back beneath him, impaled, filled beyond capacity, complete, the pleasure of his occupation insupportable.

"Cybele, *mi amor, mi vida,*" he breathed into her mouth, as he gave her what she'd been disintegrating for, with the exact force and pace that had her thrashing in pleasure, driving deeper and deeper into her, until he nudged her womb.

Her world imploded into a pinpoint of shearing sensation, then exploded in one detonation after another of bone-rattling pleasure. He fed her convulsions, slamming into her, pumping her to the last abrading twitches of fulfillment.

Then he surrendered to his own climax, and the sight and sound of him reaching completion inside her, the feel of his body shuddering over hers with the force of the pleasure he'd found inside her, his seed jetting into her core, filling her to overflowing, had her in the throes of another orgasm until she was weeping, the world receding as pleasure overloaded her.

She came to, to Rodrigo kissing her, worry roughening his voice. "Cybele, *mi alma, por favor,* open your eyes."

Her lids weighed tons, but she opened them to allay his anxiety. "I thought you knocked me senseless the first time because it *was* the first time. Seems it's going to be the norm. Not that you'll hear anything but cries for an encore from this end."

She felt the tension drain from his body, pour into the erection still buried inside her. His gaze probed her tear-drenched face, proprietary satisfaction replacing the agitation in eyes that gleamed with that Catalan imperiousness. "In that case, prepare to spend half of our married life knocked senseless."

She giggled as he wrapped her nerveless body around him and prowled to the bathroom. He took her into the tub, already filled, laid her between his thighs, her back to his front, supporting her as she half floated. He moved water over her satiated body, massaging her with it as he did with his legs and lips. She hummed with the bliss reverberating in her bones.

She would have taken once with him, would have lived on the memory forever. But this *was* forever. It was so unbelievable that sometimes she woke up feeling as if she were suffocating, believing that it had all been a delusion.

She had serious security issues. This perfection was making her more scared something would happen to shatter it all.

He sighed in contentment. *"Mi amor milagrosa."*

She turned her face into his chest, was about to whisper back that it was he who was the miracle lover when a ring sounded from the bedroom. The center calling.

He exhaled a rough breath. "They've *got* to be kidding."

She turned in his arms. "It has to be something major, if they're calling you on your wedding night. You have to answer."

He harrumphed as he rose, dried himself haphazardly

and went to answer. He came back frowning. "Pile up, serious injuries. Son and wife of an old friend among them." He drove his fingers in his hair. "*¡Maldita sea!* I only started making love to you."

"Hey. Surgeon here, too, remember? Nature of the beast." She left the tub, dried quickly, hugged him with both arms—an incredible sensation. "And you don't have to leave me behind. Let me come. I hear from my previous employers that I was a damn good surgeon. I can be of use to you and the casualties."

His frown dissolved, until his smile blinded her with his delight. "This isn't how I visualized spending our wedding night, *mi corazon*. But having you across a table in my OR is second on my list only to having you wrapped all around me in my bed."

After the emergency, during which their intervention was thankfully lifesaving, they had two weeks of total seclusion on his estate.

The three weeks after that, Cybele ticked off the two top items on Rodrigo's list, over and over. Daily, in fact.

They worked together during the days, discovering yet another area in which they were attuned. It became a constant joy and stimulation, to keep realizing how fully they could share their lives and careers.

Then came the nights. And if their first time and their semi-aborted wedding night had been world-shaking, she'd had no idea how true intimacy would escalate the pleasure and creativity of their encounters. Even those momentous occasions paled by comparison.

It was their five-week anniversary today.

She was in her twenty-second week of pregnancy and she'd never felt healthier or happier. Not that that convinced Rodrigo to change her prenatal checkups from weekly to biweekly.

"Ready, *mi amor?*"

She sprang to her feet, dissolved into his embrace. He kissed her until she was wrapped around him, begging him to postpone her checkup. She had an emergency only he could handle.

He bit her lip gently, put her away. "It'll take all of fifteen minutes. Then I'm all yours. As always."

She hooked her arm through his, inhaled his hormone-stimulating scent. "Do you want to find out the gender of the baby?"

He looked at her intently, as if wanting to make sure of her wish before he voiced his opinion. Seemed he didn't want to risk volunteering one that opposed hers. "Do you?"

She decided to let the delicious man off the hook. "I do."

His smile dawned. He *did* want to know, but considered it up to her to decide. Surely she couldn't love him more, could she?

"Then we find out."

"So what do you hope it is?"

He didn't hesitate, nuzzled her neck, whispered, "A girl. A tiny replica of her unique mother."

She surrendered to his cosseting, delight swirling inside her. "Would you be disappointed if it's a boy?"

His smile answered unequivocally. "I'm just being greedy. And then, you know how seriously cool it is to be female around here."

She made the goofy gesture and expression that had become their catchphrase. "Women rule."

* * *

Four hours later, they were back in their bedroom.

They'd made love for two of those, only stopped because they had a dinner date with Ramón and other colleagues in Barcelona.

She was leaning into him, gazing in wonder at his reflection in the mirror as he towered behind her, kissing her neck, caressing her zipper up her humming body, taking extra care of her rounding belly. She sighed her bliss. "Think Steven and Agnes will be happy it's a boy?"

His indulgent smile didn't waver. But she was so attuned to his every nuance of expression now, she could tell the question disturbed him. Since it indirectly brought up Mel.

And the mention of Mel had been the only thing to make him tense since they'd gotten married, to make him even testy and irritated. He'd once even snapped at her. She'd been shocked that day. And for a moment, black thoughts had swamped her.

She'd wondered if this fierceness was different from his early moroseness concerning Mel, if now that he was her husband, Mel was no longer simply his dead foster brother, but her dead first husband and he hated her mentioning Mel, out of jealousy.

The implications of that were so insupportable, she'd nearly choked on them. But only for a moment. Then he'd apologized so incredibly and she'd remembered what he was, what Mel had been to him.

She'd come to the conclusion that the memory of Mel was still a gaping wound inside him. One that hurt more as time passed, as the loss solidified. With him busy being the tower of strength everyone clung to, he hadn't dealt with his own grief. He hadn't attained the closure he'd made possible for everyone else to have. She hoped their baby would heal the wound, provide that closure.

His hands resumed caressing her belly. "I think they'll be happy as long as the baby is healthy."

And she had to get something else out of the way. "I called Agnes this morning and she sounded happier than I've ever heard her. She said those who filed the lawsuits weren't creditors but investors who gave Mel money to invest in the hospital, and that the money was found in an account they didn't know about."

His hands stopped their caresses. "That's right."

"But why didn't they ask for their money instead of resorting to legal action, adding insult to injury to bereaved parents? A simple request would have sent Agnes and Steven looking through Mel's documents and talking to his lawyer and accountant."

"Maybe they feared Agnes and Steven wouldn't give back the money without a strong incentive."

"Apart from finding this an incredibly irrational fear since Mel and his parents are upstanding people, there must have been legal provisos in place to assure everyone's rights."

"I don't know why they acted as they did. What's important is that the situation's over, and no harm's done to anyone."

And she saw it in his eyes. The lie.

She grabbed his hands. "You're not telling me the truth." He tried to pull his hand away. She clung. "Please, tell me."

That bleak look, which she'd almost forgotten had ever marred his beauty, was back like a swirl of ink muddying clear water.

But it was worse. He pushed away from her, glared at her in the mirror like a tiger enraged at someone pulling on a half ripped-out claw.

"You want the truth? Or do you just want me to confirm that those people acted irrationally, that Mel was an upstanding man? If so, you should do like Agnes and Steven, grab at my explanation for this mess, turn a blind eye and cling to your illusions."

She swung around to face him. "You made up this story to comfort them. The debts were real. And you must have done more than settle them to make Mel's creditors change their story."

"What do you care about the sordid details?"

Sordid? Oh, God. "Did…did I have something to do with this? Are you still protecting me, too?"

"*No.* You had nothing to do with any of it. It was just more lies Mel fed me, poisoned me with. I lived my life cleaning up after him, covering up for him. And now he's reaching back from the grave and forcing me to keep on doing it. And you know what? I'm *sick* of it. I've been getting sicker by the day, of embellishing his image and memory to you, to Agnes and Steven, of gritting my teeth on the need to tell you what I figured out he'd done to me. To *us.*"

She staggered backward under the impact of his exasperated aggression. "What did he do? And what do you mean, to 'us'?"

"How can I tell you? It would be my word against a man who can't defend himself. It would make me a monster in your eyes."

"No." She threw herself in his path. "Nothing would make you anything but the man I love with every fiber of my being."

He held her at arm's length. "Just forget it, Cybele. I shouldn't have said anything... *Dios,* I wish I could take it back."

But the damage had been done. Rodrigo's feelings about Mel seemed to be worse than she'd ever feared. And she had to know. The rest. Everything. Now. "Please, Rodrigo, I have to know."

"How can I begin to explain, when you don't even remember how *we* first met?"

She stared at him, the ferocity of his frustration pummeling her, bloodying her. She gasped, the wish to remember so violent, it smashed at the insides of her skull like giant hammers.

Suddenly, the last barricade shattered. Memories burst out of the last dark chasm in her mind, snowballing into an avalanche.

She remembered.

Chapter 13

She swung away, a frantic beast needing a way out.

The world tilted, the ground rushed at her at a crazy angle.

"Cybele."

Her name thundered over her, then lightning hit her, intercepted her fall, live wires snaring her in cabled strength before she reinjured her arm beneath her plummeting weight.

Memories flooded through her like water through a drowning woman's lungs. In brutal sequence.

She'd first seen Rodrigo at a fund-raiser for her hospital. Across the ballroom, towering above everyone, canceling out their existence. She'd felt hit by lightning then, too.

She'd stood there, unable to tear her eyes off him as people kept swamping him in relentless waves, moths to his irresistible fire. All through, he'd somehow never taken his eyes off her. She'd been sure she'd seen the same response in his eyes, the same inability to believe its power, to resist it.

Then Ramón had joined him, turned to look at her, too, and she knew Rodrigo was telling him about her. He left Ramón's side, charted a course for her. She stood there, shaking, knowing her life would change the moment he reached her.

Then a man next to her had collapsed. Even disoriented by Rodrigo's hypnotic effect, her doctor auto-function took over, and she'd rushed to the man's rescue.

She'd kept up her resuscitation efforts until paramedics came, and then she'd swayed up to look frantically for Rodrigo. But he'd vanished.

Disappointment crushed her even when she kept telling herself she'd imagined it all, her own response, too, that if she'd talked to him she would have found out he was nothing like the man she'd created in her mind.

Within days, she'd met Mel. He came with a huge donation to her hospital and became the head of the new surgery department. He offered her a position and started pursuing her almost at once. Flattered by his attention, she'd accepted a couple of dates. Then he proposed. By then, she had suspected he was a risk-taking jerk, and turned him down. But he'd said he used that persona at work to keep everyone on their toes, and showed himself to be diametrically different, everything she'd hoped for in a man, until she accepted.

Then Mel had introduced Rodrigo as his best friend.

She was shocked—and distraught that she hadn't imagined his effect on her. But she'd certainly imagined her effect on him. He seemed to find her abhorrent.

Mel, unaware of the tension between the two people he
said meant the most to him, insisted on having Rodrigo
with them all the time. And though Mel's bragging ac-
counts of his friend's mile-high bedpost notches had her
despising Rodrigo right back, she'd realized she couldn't
marry Mel while she felt that unstoppable attraction to
his best friend. So she broke off the engagement. And
it was then that Mel drove off in a violent huff and had
the accident that had crippled him.

Feeling devastated by guilt when Mel accused her of
being the reason he'd been crippled, Cybele took back
her ring. They got married in a ceremony attended by
only his parents a month after he was discharged from
hospital. Rodrigo had left for Spain after he'd made sure
there was nothing more he could do for his friend at that
time, and to Cybele's relief, he didn't attend.

But the best of intentions didn't help her cope with
the reality of living with a bitter, volatile man. They'd
discussed with a specialist the ways to have a sex life,
but his difficulties had agonized him even though Cybele assured him it didn't matter. She didn't feel the loss
of what she'd never had, was relieved when Mel gave
up trying, and poured her energy into helping him return to the OR while struggling to catch up with her job.

Then Rodrigo came back, and Mel's erratic behavior
spiked. She'd confronted him, and he said he felt insecure around any able-bodied man, especially Rodrigo,
but needed him more than ever. He was the world's leading miracle worker in spinal injuries, and he was working on putting Mel back on his feet.

But there was one thing Mel needed even more now.
He was making progress with the sex therapy specialists,
but until he could be a full husband to her, he wanted

something to bind them, beyond her sense of duty and honor and a shared house. A baby.

Cybele had known he was testing her commitment. But was feeling guiltier now that she'd lived with his affliction reason enough to take such a major step at such an inappropriate time? Would a baby make him feel more of a man? Was it wise to introduce a baby into the instability of their relationship?

Guilt won, and with her mother promising she'd help out with the baby, she had the artificial insemination.

Within a week, her conception was confirmed. The news only made Mel unbearably volatile, until she'd said she was done tiptoeing around him since it only made him worse. He apologized, said he couldn't take the pressure, needed time off. And again Cybele succumbed, suspended her residency even knowing she'd lose her position, to help him and to work out their problems. Then he dropped another bombshell on her. He wanted them to spend that time off on Rodrigo's estate.

When she'd resisted, he said it would be a double benefit, as Rodrigo wanted Mel there for tests for the surgeries that would give Mel back the use of his legs. And she'd had to agree.

When they'd arrived in Barcelona, Rodrigo had sent them a limo. Mel had it drive them to the airfield where his plane was kept. When she objected, he said he didn't need legs to fly, that flying would make him feel like he was whole again.

But during the flight, in answer to some innocuous comments, he got nasty then abusive. She held her tongue and temper, knowing it wasn't the place to escalate their arguments, but she decided that once they landed, she'd face him, as she'd faced herself, and say that their relationship wasn't working, and it wasn't because of his turmoil, but because of who he was. A man of a dual nature, one side she'd loved but could no longer find, and the other she couldn't bear and seemed was all that remained.

But they hadn't landed.

Now she heaved as the collage of the crash detonated in image after shearing image, accompanied by a hurricane of deafening cacophony and suffocating terror.

Then the maelstrom exchanged its churning motion for a linear trajectory as all trivial memories of every day of the year before the accident burst like flashes of sickening light, obliterating the blessed darkness of the past months.

Everything decelerated, came to a lurching stop.

Her face was being wiped in coolness, her whole self bathed in Rodrigo's concern. She raised sore eyes to his reddened ones.

His lips feathered over them with trembling kisses. "You remember."

"My end of things," she rasped. "Tell me yours."

The heart beneath her ear felt as if it would ram out of his chest.

Then he spoke. "When I saw you at that fund-raiser, it was like seeing my destiny. I told Ramón that, and he said that if anyone else had said that, he would have laughed. But coming from me, I, who always know what's right for me, he believed it, and to go get you. But as I moved to do that, all hell broke loose. You rushed to that man's aid and I was called to deal with multiple neuro-trauma cases back here. I asked Ramón to find out all he could about you, so I could seek you out the moment I came back.

"I tried for the last almost eighteen months not to reconstruct what I instinctively knew and didn't want to—*couldn't* face. But the more I knew you, the more inconsistencies I discovered since the accident, the more I couldn't pretend not to know how it all happened anymore. Mel was there, too, that initial day. He was right behind me as I turned away from Ramón. He must have overheard my intentions. And he decided to beat me to you."

She couldn't even gasp. Shock fizzled inside her like a spark in a depleted battery.

"And he did. Using money I gave him to gain his new position, he put himself where he'd have access to you. For the six weeks I stayed away performing one surgery after another, all the time burning for the moment I could come back and search you out, he was pursuing you. The moment you accepted his proposal, he called me to tell me that he was engaged. He left your name out.

"The day I rushed back to the States to find you, he insisted I go see him first, meet his fiancée. I can never describe my horror when I found out it was you.

"I kept telling myself it couldn't have been intentional, that he wouldn't be so cruel, that he couldn't be shoving down my throat the fact that he was the one who'd gotten you. But I remember his glee as he recounted how it had been love at first sight, that you couldn't get enough of him, and realized he was having a huge laugh at my expense, wallowing in his triumph over me, all the while dangling you in front of me until I was crazed with pain."

"Was that why…?" She choked off. It was too much.

"Why I behaved as if I hated you? *Sí.* I hated everything at the time. Mel, myself, you, the world, the very

life I woke up to every morning in which you could
never be mine."

"B-but you had so many other lovers."

"I had *nobody*. Since I laid eyes on you. Those women
were smoke screens so that I wouldn't sit through our
outings like a third-wheel fool, something to distract me
so I wouldn't lose my mind wanting you more with each
passing day. But nothing worked. Not my efforts to despise you, not your answering antipathy. So I left, and
would have never come back. But he forced me back.
He crippled himself, as I and his parents always warned
him he one day would."

A shudder rattled her at the memory. "He said I made
him lose his mind, drove him to it...."

He looked beyond horrified. "*No. Dios,* Cybele...it
had *nothing* to do with you, do you hear? Mel never took
responsibility for any problem he created for himself.
He always found someone else to accuse, usually me or
his parents. *Dios*—that he turned on you, too, accused
you of this!" His face turned a burnt bronze, his lips
worked, thinning with the effort to contain his aggression. She had the feeling that if Mel were alive and here,
Rodrigo would have dragged him out of his wheelchair
and taken him apart.

At last he rasped, "It had to do with his own gam-
bler's behavior. He always took insane risks, in driving,
in sports, in surgeries. One of those insane risks was
the gambling that landed him in so much debt. I gave
him the money to gamble, too. He told me it was to buy
you the things you wanted. But I investigated. He never
bought you anything."

So this was it. The explanation he'd withheld.

"As for the stunt that cost him his life and could have

cost yours, it wasn't his first plane crash but his third. He walked away from so many disasters he caused without a scratch that even the one that cut him in half didn't convince him that his luck had run out and the next time would probably be fatal. As it was."

For a long moment, all she heard was her choppy breath, the blood swooshing in her ears, his harsh breathing.

Then he added, "Or maybe he wanted to die."

"Why would he?" she rasped. "He believed you'd put him back on his feet. He said you were very optimistic."

He looked as if he'd explode. "Then he lied to you. Again. There was nothing I could do for him. I made it absolutely clear."

She squeezed her eyes shut. "So he was really desperate."

"I think he was worse than that." His hiss felt as if it would scrape her flesh from her bone. "I think he'd gone over the edge, wanted to take you with him. So I would never have you."

She lurched as if under a flesh-gouging lash.

Rodrigo went on, bitterness pouring out of him. "Mel always had a sickness. Me. Since the first day I set foot in the Braddocks' house, he idolized me and seethed with jealousy of me, alternated between emulating me to the point of impersonation, to doing everything to be my opposite, between loving and hating me."

It all made so much sense it was horrifying. How she'd found Mel so different at first, how he'd switched to the seamless act of emulating Rodrigo. So it *had* been Rodrigo she'd fallen in love with all along. It was unbelievable. Yet it was the truth.

And it dictated her next action. The only thing she could do.

She pushed out of his arms, rose to unsteady feet, looked down at him, the man she loved beyond life itself.

And she cut her heart out. "I want a divorce."

Cybele's demand fell on Rodrigo like a scythe.

Rage, at himself, hacked him much more viciously.

He'd been so *stupid.* He'd railed at a dead man, not just the man he'd considered his younger brother, but the man Cybele still loved, evidently more than she could ever love him.

He shot to his feet, desperation the one thing powering him. "Cybele, *no. Lo siento, mi amor.* I didn't mean…"

She shut her eyes in rejection, stopping his apology and explanation. "You meant every word. And you had every right. Because you *are* right. You at last explained my disappointment in Mel, my resentment toward him. You rid me of any guilt I ever felt toward him."

Rodrigo reeled. "You—you didn't love Mel?"

She shook her head. Then in a dead monotone, she told him her side of the story.

"Seems I always sensed his manipulations, even if I would have never guessed their reason or extent. My subconscious must have considered it a violation, so it wiped out the traumatic time until I was strong enough. I still woke up with overpowering gut feelings. But without context, they weren't enough to stop me from tormenting myself when I felt nothing but relief at his death and anger toward him, when I wanted you from the moment I woke up. Now I know. I always wanted you."

Elation and confusion tore him in two. "You did? *Dios*—then why are you asking for a divorce?"

"Because I don't matter. Only my baby does. I would never have married you if I'd realized you would be the worst father for him. Instead of loving his father, you hate Mel with a lifelong passion. And though you have every right to feel that way, I can never subject my child to the life I had. Worse than the life I had. My stepfather didn't know my father, and he also didn't consider me the bane of his life. He just cared nothing for me. But it was my mother's love for him, her love for the children she had with him, that alienated her from me. And she doesn't love him a fraction of how much I love you."

He should have realized all that. He knew her scars in detail, knew she was barely coping now, as an adult, with her alienated childhood and current bland family situation. But he got it now. The sheer magnitude of his blunder. It could cost him his life. *Her.*

"I never hated Mel," he pleaded. "It was Mel who considered me the usurper of his parents' respect and affection. I loved him, like brothers love their imperfect siblings. Mel did have a lot to him that I appreciated, and I always hoped he'd believe that, be happy playing on his own strengths and stop competing with me in mine. But I could never convince him, and it ate at him until he lashed out, injured you while trying to get to me, the source of his discontent. It was foolish, tragic, and I *do* hate his taking you away from me, but I don't hate *him.* You have to believe that."

She clearly didn't. And she had every reason to distrust his words after that moronic display of bitterness and anger.

She confirmed his worst fears, her voice as inanimate as her face. "I can't take the chance with my baby's life."

Agony bled out of him. "Do you think so little of me, Cybele? You claim to love me, and you still think I'd be so petty, so cruel, as to take whatever I felt for Mel out on an innocent child?"

She stumbled two steps back to escape his pleading hands. "You might not be able to help it. He did injure you, repeatedly, throughout his life. That he's now dead doesn't mean that you can forget. Or forgive. I wouldn't blame you if you could do neither."

"But that baby is *yours,* Cybele. He could be yours from the very devil and I'd still love and cherish him because he's yours. Because I love you. I would die for you."

The stone that seemed to be encasing her cracked, and she came apart, a mass of tremors and tears. "And I would d-die for you. I feel I *will* die without you. And that only makes me more scared, of what I'd do to please you, to keep your love, if I weaken now, and it turns out, with your best intentions, you'd never be able to love my baby as he deserves to be loved. And I—I can't risk that. Please, I beg you, don't make it impossible to leave you. *Please*…let me go."

He lunged for her, as if to grab her before she vanished. "I *can't,* Cybele."

She wrenched away, tears splashing over his hands. His arms fell to his sides, empty, pain impaling his heart, despair wrecking his sanity.

Suddenly, realization hit him like a vicious uppercut.

He couldn't *believe* it. *Dios*, he was far worse than a moron.

He *did* have the solution to everything.

He blocked her path. "*Querida*, forgive me, I'm such an idiot. I conditioned myself so hard to never let the truth slip, that even after you told me your real feelings for Mel, it took seeing you almost walking out on me to make me realize I don't have to hide it anymore. It is true I would have loved any baby of yours as mine, no matter what. But I love *this* baby, I want him and I would die for him, too. Because he *is* mine. Literally."

Chapter 14

"I *am* the baby's father."

Cybele stared at Rodrigo, comprehension suspended.

"If you don't believe me, a DNA test will prove it."

And it ripped through her like a knife in her gut.

One thing was left in her mind, in the world. A question.

She croaked it. "How?"

He looked as if he'd rather she asked him to step in front of a raging bull. Then he exhaled. "A few years back, Mel had a paternity suit. During the tests to prove that he didn't father the child, he found out that he was infertile. Then he told me that you were demanding proof of his commitment to your marriage, the emotional security of a baby. He said he couldn't bear to reveal another shortcoming to you, that he couldn't lose you, that you were what kept him alive. He asked me to donate the sperm. Just imagining you blossoming with my baby, nurturing it, while I could never claim it or you, almost killed *me*.

"But I believed him when he said he'd die if you left him. And even suspecting how he'd stolen you from me, I would have done anything to save him. And I knew if I said no, he would have gotten any sperm donor sample and passed it as his. I couldn't have you bear some stranger's baby. So I agreed.

"But believing you were suffering from psychogenic amnesia so that your mind wouldn't buckle under the trauma of losing him, I couldn't let you know you'd lost what you thought remained of him. I wouldn't cause you further psychological damage. I would have settled for being my baby's father by adoption when he was mine for real."

So that was why. His change toward her after the accident, treating her like she was the most precious thing in the world, binding himself to her forever. This explained everything much more convincingly than his claim that he'd loved her all along.

It had all been for his baby.

"Te quiero tanto, Cybele, *más que la vida. Usted es mi corazón, mi alma."*

Hearing him say he loved her, more than life, that she was his heart, his soul now that she knew the truth was…unbearable.

Feeling her life had come to an end, she pushed out of his arms and ran.

Rodrigo restrained himself from charging after her and hauling her back and never letting her go ever again with an exertion of will that left him panting.

He had to let her go. She had to have time alone to

come to terms with the shocks, to realize that although
they'd taken a rough course to reach this point, both Mel
and fate had ended up giving them their future and perfect happiness together.

He lasted an hour. Then he went after her. He found
her gone.

Consuelo told him Cybele had asked Gustavo to drive
her to the city, where he'd dropped her off at a hotel near
the center.

He felt as if the world had vanished from around him.

She'd left him. But…why? She'd said she loved him,
too.

When his head was almost bursting with confusion
and dread, he found a note on their bed.

The lines swam as if under a lens of trembling liquid.

Rodrigo,
You should have told me that my baby was yours
from the start. I would have accepted your care for
its real reason—a man safeguarding the woman
who is carrying his baby. Knowing you and your
devotion to family, your need to have your flesh
and blood surrounding you, I know you want this
baby fiercely, want to give him the most stable
family you can, the one neither of us had. Had you
told me, I would have done anything to cooperate
with you so the baby would have parents who dote
on him and who treat each other with utmost af-
fection and respect. I don't have to be your wife to
do that. You can divorce me if you wish, and I'll
still remain your friend and colleague, will live in
Spain as long as you do, so you'll have constant
access to your son.
Cybele.

Rodrigo read the note until he felt the words begin to burn a brand into his retinas, his brain.

After all the lies and manipulations she'd been victim to, she had every right to distrust his emotions and motives toward her. From her standpoint, he could be saying and doing whatever it took to get his son.

But he'd prove his sincerity if it was the last thing he did.

If he lost her, it just might be.

Twenty-four hours later, he stood outside her hotel room door, feeling he'd aged twenty-four years.

She opened the door, looking as miserable as he felt.

All he wanted was to take her in his arms, kiss her until she was incoherent with desire, but he knew that might only prove to her that he was manipulating her even worse than Mel had.

He never gambled. But he'd never known true desperation, either. Now a gamble, with potentially catastrophic results, was the last resort he had left.

Without a word, he handed her the divorce papers.

Cybele's heart stopped, felt it would never beat again.

She'd made a desperate gamble. And lost. She'd owed him the choice, the freedom to have his baby without remaining her husband. She'd prayed he'd choose to be with her anyway.

He hadn't. He was giving her proof, now that she'd assured him he'd always have his son, that he'd rather be free of her.

Then her eyes fell on the heading of one of the papers.

Before the dread fully formed inside her mind, it spilled from her lips. "You won't take the baby away, will you? Any court in the world would give you custody, I know, but please don't—"

He grimaced as if she'd stabbed him. "Cybele, *querida, por favor, le pido.* I beg you…stop. Do you distrust me that much?"

Mortification swallowed her whole. "No…no—oh, God. But I—I don't *know.* Anything. It's like you're three people in my mind. The one who seemed to hate me, the one who saved me, took such infinite care of me, who seemed to want me as much as I want you, and the one who always had an agenda, who's handing me divorce papers. I don't know who you are, or what to believe anymore."

"Let me explain." His hands descended on her shoulders.

"No." She staggered around before his grip could tighten. She couldn't hear that he cared, but not enough to remain married to her. She fumbled for a pen by the hotel's writing pad. The papers slid from her hands, scattered across the desk. Fat tears splashed over the blurring lines that mimicked the chaos inside her. "After I sign these papers, I want a couple of days. I'll call you when I'm thinking straight again and we can discuss how we handle things from now on."

His hands clamped the top of her arms, hauled her back against the living rock of his body. She struggled to escape, couldn't bear the agony his feel, his touch, had coursing in hers.

He pressed her harder to his length. She felt his hardness digging into her buttocks, couldn't understand.

He still wanted her? But if he was divorcing her, then all the hunger she'd thought only she could arouse in him had just been the insatiable sexual appetite of the hot-blooded male that he was. And now…what? Her struggles were arousing him?

All thought evaporated as his lips latched onto her neck, drew on her flesh, wrenching her desire, her very life force with openmouthed kisses and suckles. She tried to twist away, but he lifted her off the ground, carried her to the wall, spread her against it and pinned her there with his bulk, his knee driven between her thighs, his erection grinding against her belly.

He caught her lower lip in a growling bite, sucked and pulled on it until she cried out, opened wide for him. Then he plunged, took, gave, tongue and teeth and voracity. Wave after wave of readiness flooded her core. She squirmed against him, everything disintegrating with her need to crawl under his skin, take him into hers. His fingers found her under her panties, probed her to a screeching climax. Then she begged for him.

In a few moments and moves, he gave her more than she could take, all of him, driving inside her drenched, clenching tightness. Pleasure detonated from every inch of flesh that yielded to the invasion of the red-hot satin of his thickness and length. He powered into her, poured driven words in an inextricable mix of English and Catalan, of love and lust and unbearable pleasure into her gasping mouth as his thrusting tongue ravaged her with possession and mindlessness.

Pleasure reverberated inside her with each thrust, each word, each melding kiss, like the rushing and receding of a tide gone mad. It all gathered, towered, held at its zenith like a tidal wave before the devastating crash. Then the blows of release hit like those of a giant hammer, striking her core again and again, expanding shock waves that razed her, wrung her around his girth in contractions so violent they fractured breath and heartbeats. She clung to him in the frenzy, inside and out as if she'd assimilate him, dissolve around him. Then she felt him roar his release as he jammed his erection to her womb, jetting his pleasure to fill it, causing another wave to crash over her, shattering her with the power of the sensations, of wishing that they'd make a baby this way in the future. When they didn't have one…

She came back to awareness to find him beneath her on the bed, still hard and pulsating inside her, setting off mini quakes that kept her in a state of continuous orgasm.

A question wavered from her in a scratchy rasp. "So was that goodbye sex?"

He jerked beneath her. "You go out of your way to pick the exact words that will cut me deepest, don't you?"

And she wailed, "What else could it be?"

"It was you-turn-me-into-a-raging-beast-in-perpetual-mating-frenzy sex. It was I-can't-have-enough-of-your-pleasure-and-your-intimacy lovemaking." Every word flowed over her like a balm on a wound, drowning the doubt demons who whispered he was just over-endowed and would enjoy any sexually voracious female. "Not that that excuses what I did. I didn't come here intending to take you like that. I was resolved not to confuse issues. But I saw you about to sign those papers and almost burst an artery."

Her lips twitched in spite of her confusion. "Glad the pressure found another outlet." She relived the moments when it had, splashing against her inner walls, filling her with his scalding essence, mixing with her pleasure… But…wait a sec! "But you *want* me to sign the papers."

He rose onto his elbow, looked at her with the last trace of heavy-lidded male possession vanishing, that bleakness taking over his eyes. "I want a bullet between the eyes more." She gasped, the thought of anything happening to him paralyzing her with terror. "But since I can't prove that to you by words or lovemaking, and you have every right not to accept either as proof, after all the lies that almost cost you your mind and your very life, I'm down to action. And the proof of time."

He extricated himself from her, rose off the bed, walked to gather the papers and came back to lay them beside her.

Before she could say she didn't want any proof, just wanted to be his, if he really wanted her, he turned and gathered his clothes.

She sat up shakily as he started dressing, his movements stiff, his face clenched with that intensity she now believed betrayed his turmoil. And finally, she understood. Just as she'd given him the freedom to divorce her, the divorce papers were his proof that she was equally free. Even if he'd rather end his life than lose her, he was letting her go, if it meant her peace of mind. Oh, God…

She'd caused him so much pain, even if inadvertently. Then, when he'd told her how long and how much he'd been hurting, she'd added indelible insult to injury when she'd imposed her distrust of those who'd blighted her life with letdowns, who'd made her doubt that she was deserving of love, as pretext to condemn his motivations.

But a man who wanted only his child wouldn't have done one thousandth of the things he'd done for her. He would never have said he loved her, would rather die than lose her. And even if any other man might have lied to that extent to achieve what he considered a highest cause, the stability of his child's family life, Rodrigo wouldn't. He was too honorable.

Even when he'd kept the truth about their baby's paternity from her, he'd done it only to protect her, had been willing to never proclaim his baby as his own flesh and blood, to preserve the illusion he'd thought essential to her well-being.

She made a grab for the papers, sprang off the bed and ran to him, grabbed one of his hands as he started buttoning up his shirt, tears of humility and contrition and heart-piercing adoration pouring from her very soul to scorch down her cheeks. "Those papers are your I'm-free-to-come-back-to-you-of-my-own-free-will gesture, right?"

He seemed to struggle to stop himself. He lost the fight, reached out with his other hand, wiped away her tears, cupped her cheek, his face the embodiment of tenderness. "They're not a gesture. You *are* free. And you must not consider me in your decision. You're not responsible for how I feel." Exactly the opposite of what Mel and her family had done to her. They'd made her feel responsible for their feelings toward her, guilty of inciting Mel's pathological possessiveness or their equally unnatural negligence. "In time, if you become satisfied that I am what you need, what will make you happy, come back to me. If you don't, then sign those papers and send them back to me instead. The other documents should prove you are in no way pressured to make the best of it for anybody else's sake but yours."

And she revealed her last and biggest fear. "W-what if in time *you* decide I'm not what you need?"

He huffed a harsh laugh, as if she were asking if he might one day fly under his own power. Certainty solidified in her every cell as she grinned up at him with sudden unbridled ecstasy. Then the rest of his words registered. "The other documents…"

She looked through the papers, found those with the heading that had triggered her crazy doubt that he'd take the baby.

Custody papers. Giving away his parental rights. To her. Unconditionally. She'd choose if he was part of his baby's life.

She stared at the words, their meaning too huge to take in.

Her eyes flew dazedly up to his solemn ones. "Why?"

"Because without you, nothing is worth having, not even my child. Because I trust you not to deprive him of my love even if you decide to end our marriage. Because I want you to be totally free to make that decision if you need to, without fearing you'll lose your baby, or become embroiled in a custody case. Because I need to know that if you come back to me, you do it not out of need or gratitude or for our baby's best interests, but because it's in *your* best interests. Because you want me."

Then he turned away, looking like a man who had nothing to look forward to but waiting for an uncertain verdict.

She flew after him, joy and distress tearing at her. She wrenched him around, jumped on him, climbed him, wrapped herself around him and squeezed him as if she'd merge them. His shuddering groan quaked through her as he hugged her back, crushed her to him, his arms trembling his relief.

She covered his face and neck and anything she could reach of him in tear-drenched kisses and wept. "I don't just *want* you! I worship you, I crave and adore and love

you far more than life. And it's not out of need or gratitude. Not the way you fear. I don't need you to survive,
but I need you to be alive. I'm grateful you exist, and a
few light years beyond that that you love me, too. I don't
deserve you or that you should feel the same for me. I—I
hurt you and mistrusted you and it doesn't matter that
I was reeling from the shock of the regained memories
and the revelations—"

His lips crushed the rest of her outburst in savage
kisses. Then she was on the bed again, on her back,
filled with him as he drove into her, growled to her
again and again that he believed her and in her, and she
screamed and sobbed her relief and gratitude and love
and pleasure.

It was hours before that storm abated and she lay
over him, free of doubt or worry, of gravity and physical limitations.

She told him, "You make me feel—limitless, just like
what I feel for you. But you are too much, give too much.
It would have been criminal to have all this without paying in advance with some serious misery and heartache.
I love the fates that tossed me around only to land me in
your lap, and by some miracle make you love me, too.
I just adore every bit of misfortune and unhappiness I
had that now make me savor every second of what we
share all the more."

Rodrigo swept Cybele with caresses, agreed to every
word she said. They were the exact ones that filled his
being. He did believe they wouldn't have come to share
this purity and intensity without surviving so many tests
and…

He shot up, his nerves going haywire.

Under his palm. He'd felt it.

"The baby…" he choked. "He moved." And for the first time since he'd shed tears over his mother's death, his tears flowed. With too much love, pride and gratitude.

She pushed him onto his back, rained frantic kisses all over his face. "No, please—I can't bear seeing your tears, even ones of joy." That only made the tears flow thicker. After moments of panting consternation, wickedness replaced the stricken look on her face and she attacked him with tickling.

He guffawed and flopped her onto her back, imprisoning what he swore were electricity-and magic-wielding hands over her head with one of his, his other returning the sensual torment.

She squirmed under his hand, nuzzled his chest. "I can't wait to have our baby. And I can't wait to have another one. One we'll make as we lose ourselves in love and pleasure, flesh in flesh."

"This one *was* made of our love…well, my love, at least."

She nipped him. "Yeah, I have to make up for my initial lack of participation in the love department. But from now on, I'm sharing everything with you. And not only about our baby. I want to be involved in everything you do, your research, your surgeries…." The radiant animation on her face faltered. "Uh—that came out as if I'll hound your every step…."

He squeezed her, cutting short her mortification, laughter booming out of his depths. "Oh, please, do. Gives me an excuse to hound yours." Then he grew serious. "But I know exactly how you meant it. I want you involved in everything I do, too. I've never felt more stimulated, more empowered, more satisfied with my work than when you were there with me. And then there's every other instance when I see or feel or think anything, and it isn't right, isn't complete until I share it with you, knowing you're the only one who'll understand, appreciate."

She attacked him with another giggling, weeping kiss that almost extracted his soul. Then she raised a radiant face, gestured for him to stay where he was.

He watched her bounce out of bed to rummage in her suitcase. He hardened to steel again, licking at the lingering taste of her on his lips as she walked back, ripe and tousled and a little awkward, all the effects of his love and loving, short- and long-term ones. She was holding something behind her back, impishness turning her beauty from breathtaking to heartbreaking.

"Close your eyes." He chuckled, obeyed at once. He couldn't wait to "see" what she had in store for him.

Her weight dipped the mattress. Then he almost came off it.

She was licking him. All over his chest and abdomen.

He growled, tried to hold her head closer, thrusting at her, offering all of him for her delicate devouring.

"Keep those lethal weapons of yours closed."

He did, his heart almost rattling the whole bed in anticipation. Then he felt a sting on his chest.

The tail end of the sensation was a lance of pleasure that corkscrewed to his erection. It slammed against his abdomen. Air left his lungs on a bellow of stimulation.

Another sting followed. Then another and another, on a path of fiery pain and pleasure down his body. He'd never felt anything like this sourceless manipulation of his sensations. He could swear she wasn't touching him, was pricking each individual nerve cluster mentally.

He thrust at her, incoherent with arousal, his growls becoming those of a beast in a frenzy. He at last thrust his hands into her hair, tugged until she moaned with enjoyment.

"Tell me to open my eyes," he panted the order, the plea.

Another skewer of delight. "Uh-uh."

"I don't need them open to take you until you weep with pleasure," he threatened, almost weeping himself again with the sharpness of the sensations she'd buried him under.

"Which you routinely do." Another sting. He roared. She purred, "Okay, just because you threatened so nicely. Open 'em."

He did. And couldn't credit their evidence for moments.

Then he rasped between gasps as she continued her meticulous sensual torture, "This is—hands down—the most innovative use of a micro-grasping forceps I've ever seen."

She was tugging at his hairs using the most delicate forceps used in micro-neurosurgery. And sending him stark raving mad.

"It's also the most hands-on method I could think of to say thanks." Her eyes glittered up at him, flooding him with love.

"Not that I'm not deliriously thankful for whatever made you invent this new…procedure, but thanks for what, *mi vida?*"

"Thanks for all the patience and perseverance you

put into getting my hand back to this level of fine co-ordination."

He dropped his gaze to her hand. It was true. There was no sign of clumsiness, weakness or pain as her precious hand performed her pioneering form of carnal torment.

He groaned, glided her over his aching body, grasped her hand gently and took it to his lips, thanked the fates for her, for letting him be the instrument of her happiness and well-being.

"Thank *you*, for existing, for letting me be forever yours."

Cybele cupped his face as he continued his homage, wondering how one being could contain all the love she felt for him.

She caressed his hewn cheek, traced the planes of his chiseled lips. "If you're satisfied with my precision, can I apprentice at your hands in neurosurgery?"

He enfolded her and she felt as if his heart gave her the answer. To everything. "Just wish for it and it's done, *mi alma*. Anything you want, the whole world is yours for the asking."

She took his lips with a whimper, then she whispered into his mouth, "I already have the whole world. You, our baby and our love."

* * * * *

COMING NEXT MONTH FROM

HARLEQUIN®

Desire

Available February 3, 2015

#2353 HER FORBIDDEN COWBOY
Moonlight Beach Bachelors • by Charlene Sands
When his late wife's younger sister needs a place to heal after being jilted at the altar, country-and-western star Zane Williams offers comfort at his beachfront mansion. But when he takes her in his arms, they enter forbidden territory...

#2354 HIS LOST AND FOUND FAMILY
Texas Cattleman's Club: After the Storm
by Sarah M. Anderson
Tracking down his estranged wife to their hometown hospital, entrepreneur Jake Holt discovers she's lost her memory—and had his baby. Will their renewed love stand the test when she remembers what drove them apart?

#2355 THE BLACKSTONE HEIR
Billionaires and Babies • by Dani Wade
Mill owner Jacob Blackstone is all business; bartender KC Gatlin goes with the flow. But her baby secret is about to shake things up as these two very different people come together for their child's future...and their own.

#2356 THIRTY DAYS TO WIN HIS WIFE
Brides and Belles • by Andrea Laurence
Thinking twice after a reckless Vegas elopement, two best friends find their divorce plans derailed by a surprise pregnancy. Will a relationship trial run prove they might be perfect partners, after all?

#2357 THE TEXAN'S ROYAL M.D.
Duchess Diaries • by Merline Lovelace
When a sexy doctor from a royal bloodline saves the nephew of a Texas billionaire, she loses her heart in the process. But secrets from her past may keep her from the man she loves...

#2358 TERMS OF A TEXAS MARRIAGE
by Lauren Canan
The fine print of a hundred-year-old land lease will dictate Shea Hardin's fate: she must marry a bully or lose it all. But what happens when she falls for her fake husband...hard?

HDCNM0115

Here's a sneak peek at the next
TEXAS CATTLEMAN'S CLUB:
AFTER THE STORM *installment,*
HIS LOST AND FOUND FAMILY
by **Sarah M. Anderson**

*Separated and on the verge of divorce, Jake Holt is
determined to confront his wife. But when he arrives
in Royal, Texas, he finds that Skye has been keeping
secrets...*

Jake had spent the past four years pointedly not caring
about what his family was doing. They'd wanted him to
put the family above his wife. Nothing had been more
important to him than Skye.

He was not staying in Royal long. Just enough to get
Skye back on her feet and figure out where they stood.

Just then, the baby made a little hiccup-sigh noise that
pulled at his heartstrings.

Jake's brother picked the baby up so smoothly that
Jake was jealous.

"Grace, honey—this is your daddy," Keaton said as he
rubbed her back. Then, to Jake, he added, "You ready?"

Not really—but Jake wasn't going to admit that to
Keaton. He tried to cradle his arms in the right way. Then
Keaton laid the baby in them.

The world seemed to tilt off its axis as Jake looked
down into his daughter's eyes. They were a pale blue—

just like her mother's. Up close now, he could see that Grace had wispy hairs on her head that were so white and fine they were almost see-through.

She didn't start bawling, which he took as a good sign. Instead, she waved her tiny hands around, so of course he had to offer her one of his fingers. When she latched on to it, he felt lost and yet *not* lost at the same time.

He was responsible for this little girl from this moment until the day he drew his last breath. The weight of it hit him so hard that if he hadn't already been sitting, his knees would have buckled.

This was his daughter. He and Skye had created this little person.

God, he wished Skye was here with him. That things between them had been different. That he'd been different.

But he couldn't change the past, not when his present—and his future—was gripping his little finger with surprising strength.

Don't miss what happens next in
HIS LOST AND FOUND FAMILY
by Sarah M. Anderson!

Available February 2015,
wherever Harlequin® Desire books and ebooks are sold.

JUST CAN'T GET ENOUGH?

Join our social communities
and talk to us online.

You will have access to the latest
news on upcoming titles and special
promotions, but most importantly,
you can talk to other fans about your
favorite Harlequin reads.

Harlequin.com/Community

Facebook.com/HarlequinBooks

Twitter.com/HarlequinBooks

Pinterest.com/HarlequinBooks